Sacrificial Princess and the King of Beasts

4

Yu Tomofuji

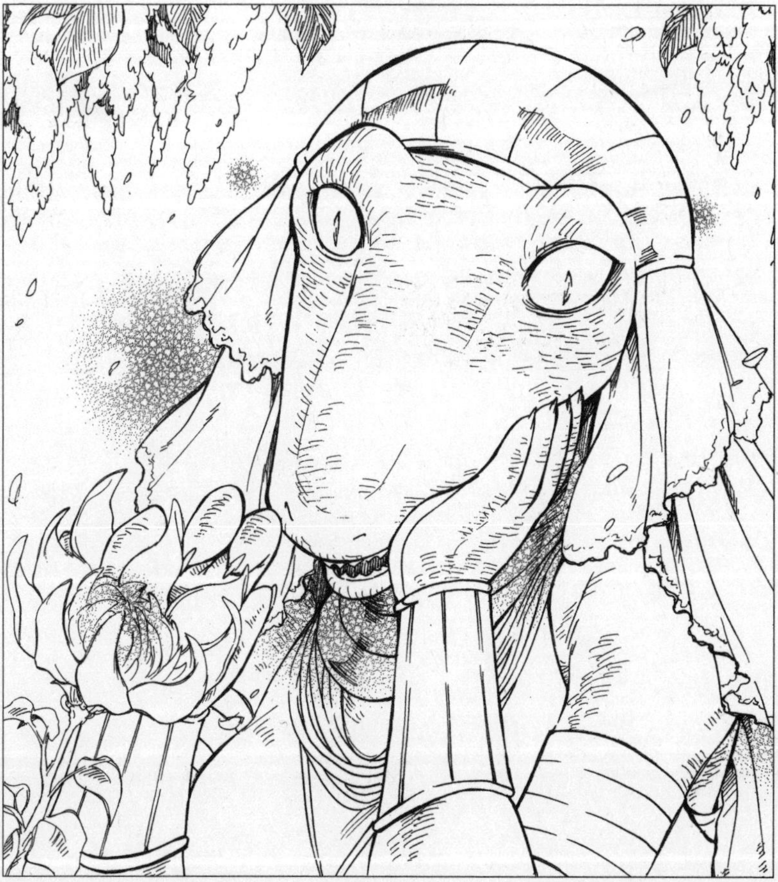

SACRIFICIAL PRINCESS AND THE King of Beasts

4

contents

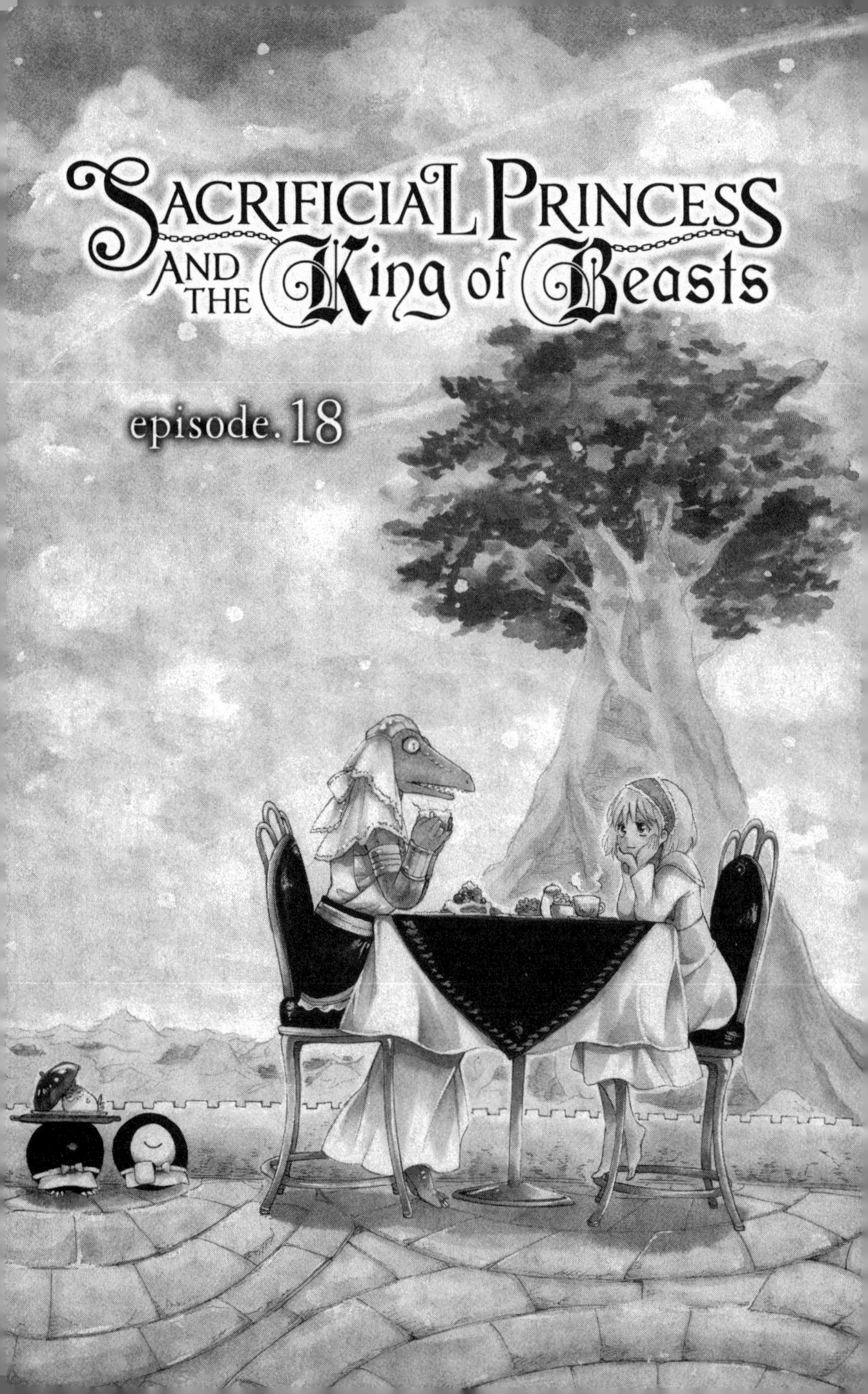
SACRIFICIAL PRINCESS AND THE King of Beasts
episode. 18

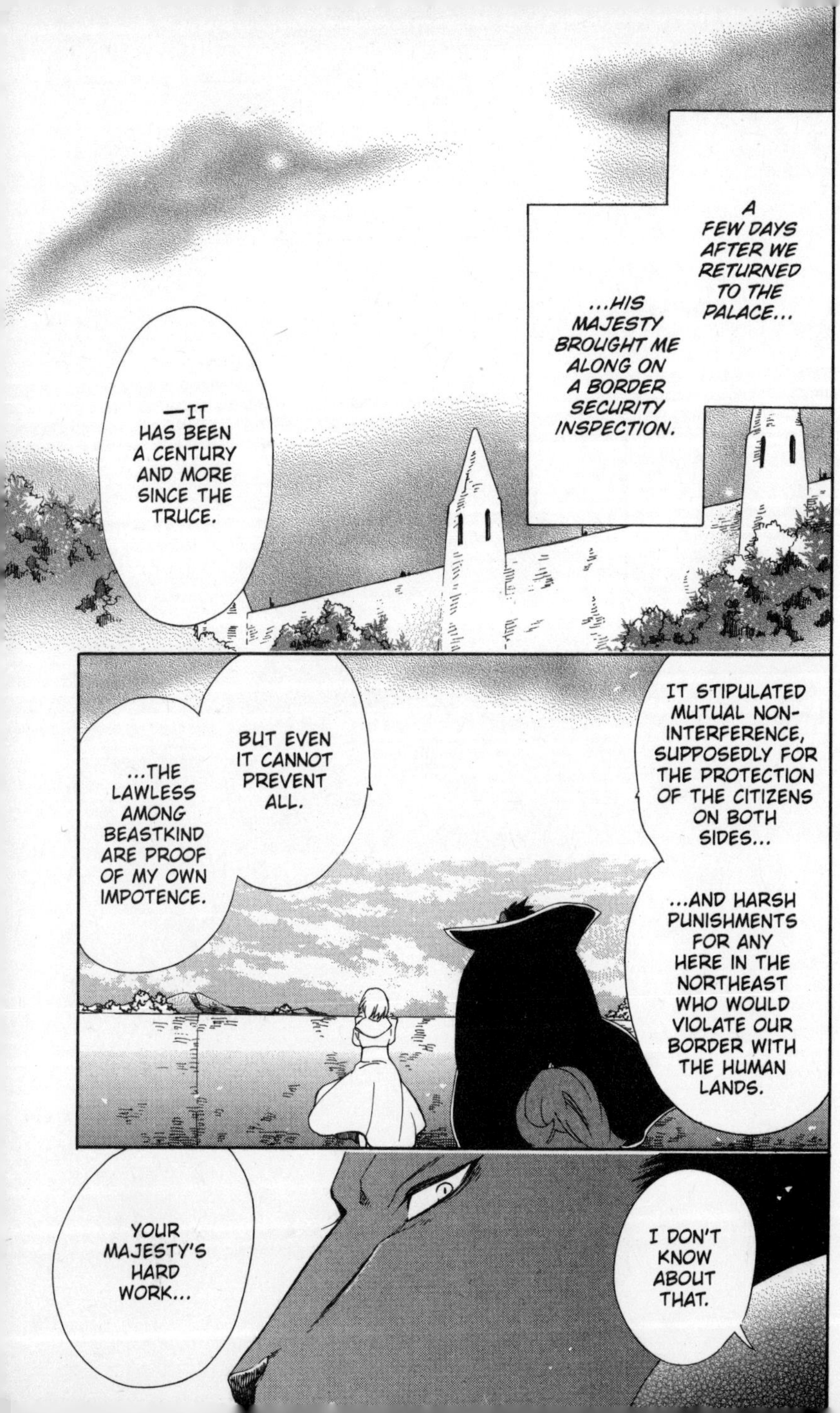
A FEW DAYS AFTER WE RETURNED TO THE PALACE...
...HIS MAJESTY BROUGHT ME ALONG ON A BORDER SECURITY INSPECTION.
—IT HAS BEEN A CENTURY AND MORE SINCE THE TRUCE.
IT STIPULATED MUTUAL NON-INTERFERENCE, SUPPOSEDLY FOR THE PROTECTION OF THE CITIZENS ON BOTH SIDES...
...AND HARSH PUNISHMENTS FOR ANY HERE IN THE NORTHEAST WHO WOULD VIOLATE OUR BORDER WITH THE HUMAN LANDS.
BUT EVEN IT CANNOT PREVENT ALL.
...THE LAWLESS AMONG BEASTKIND ARE PROOF OF MY OWN IMPOTENCE.
I DON'T KNOW ABOUT THAT.
YOUR MAJESTY'S HARD WORK...

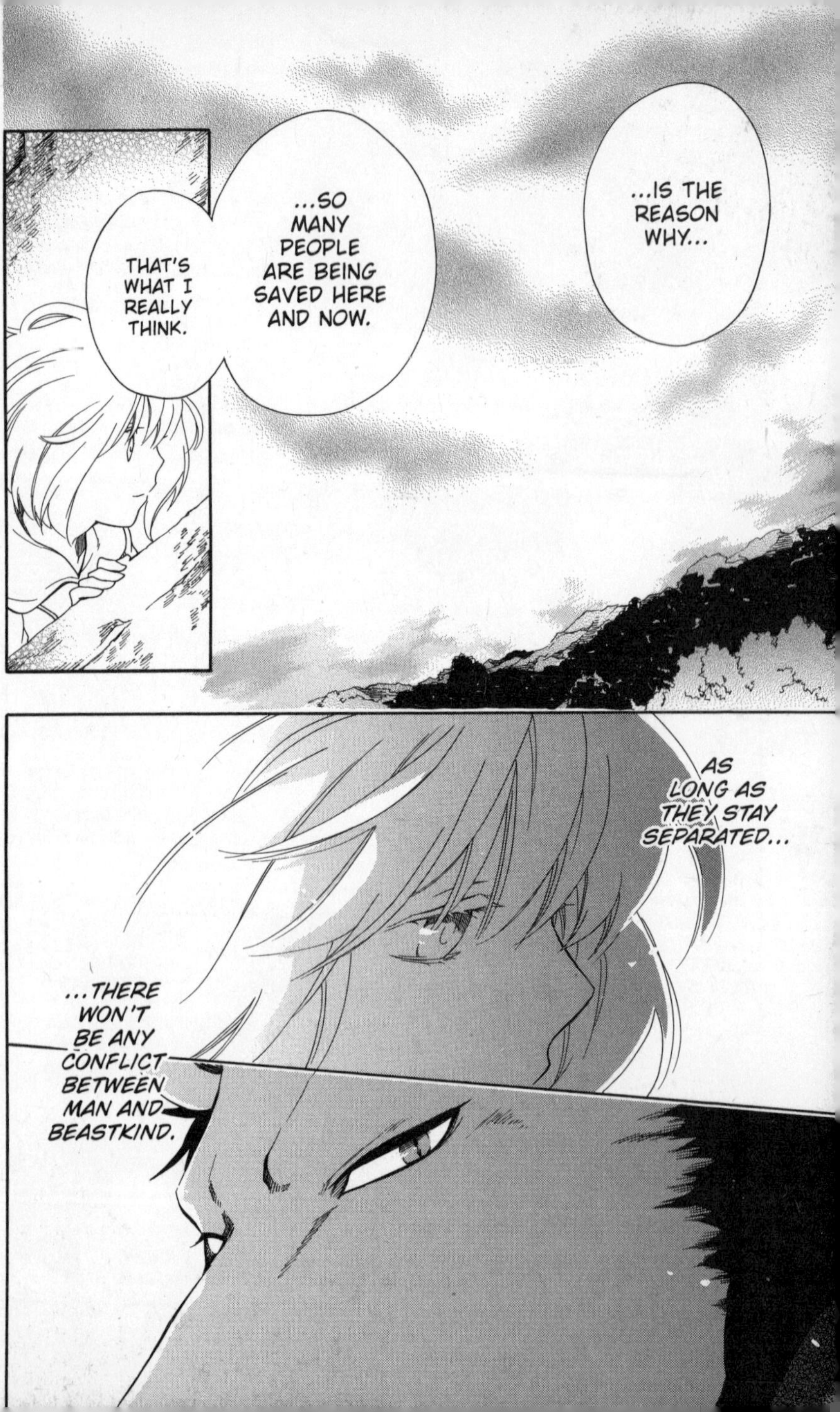
...IS THE REASON WHY...
...SO MANY PEOPLE ARE BEING SAVED HERE AND NOW.
THAT'S WHAT I REALLY THINK.
AS LONG AS THEY STAY SEPARATED...
...THERE WON'T BE ANY CONFLICT BETWEEN MAN AND BEASTKIND.

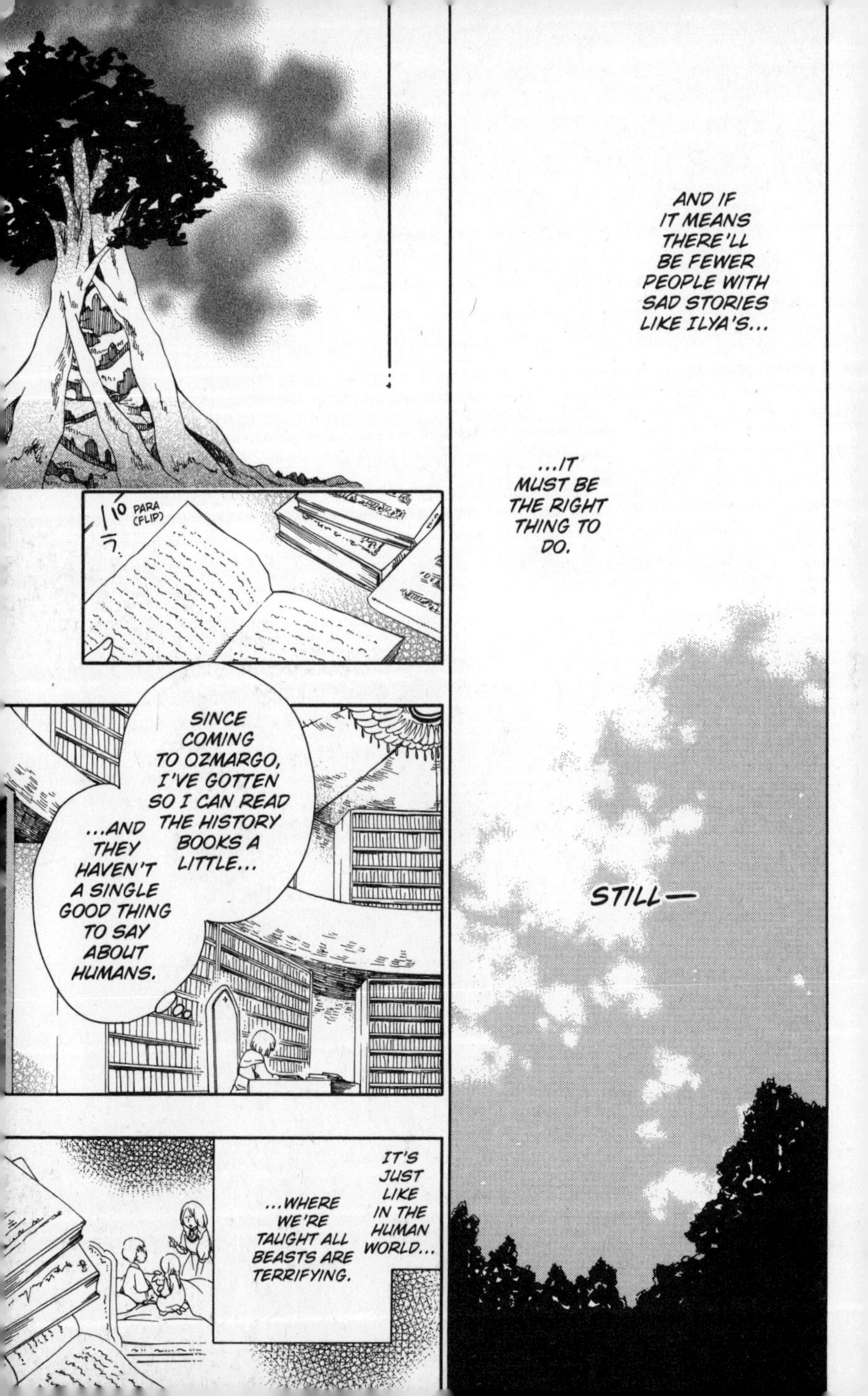
AND IF IT MEANS THERE'LL BE FEWER PEOPLE WITH SAD STORIES LIKE ILYA'S...
...IT MUST BE THE RIGHT THING TO DO.
STILL—
PARA (FLIP)
SINCE COMING TO OZMARGO, I'VE GOTTEN SO I CAN READ THE HISTORY BOOKS A LITTLE...
...AND THEY HAVEN'T A SINGLE GOOD THING TO SAY ABOUT HUMANS.
IT'S JUST LIKE IN THE HUMAN WORLD...
...WHERE WE'RE TAUGHT ALL BEASTS ARE TERRIFYING.

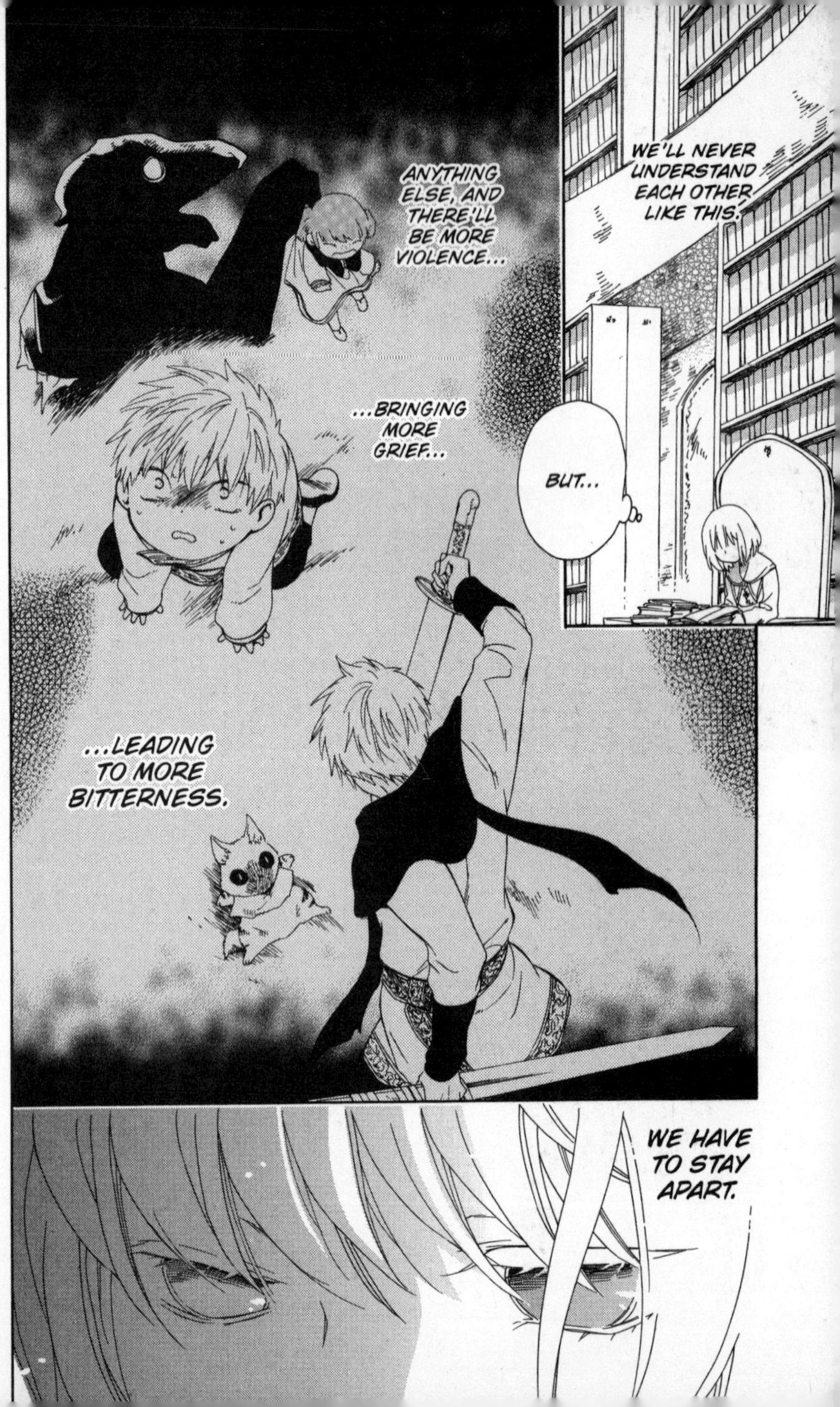
WE'LL NEVER UNDERSTAND EACH OTHER LIKE THIS.
BUT...
ANYTHING ELSE, AND THERE'LL BE MORE VIOLENCE...
...BRINGING MORE GRIEF...
...LEADING TO MORE BITTERNESS.
WE HAVE TO STAY APART.

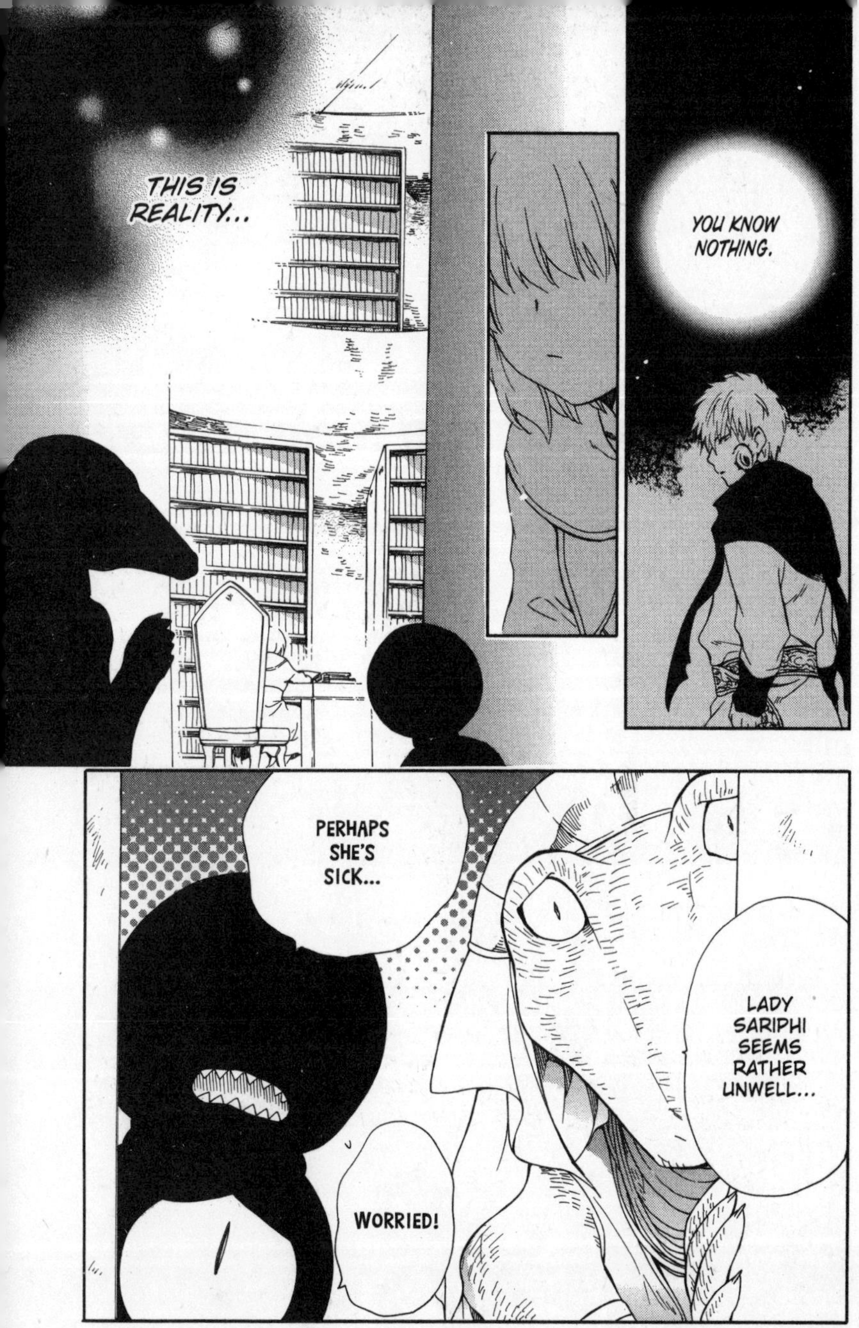
YOU KNOW NOTHING.
THIS IS REALITY...
LADY SARIPHI SEEMS RATHER UNWELL...
PERHAPS SHE'S SICK...
WORRIED!

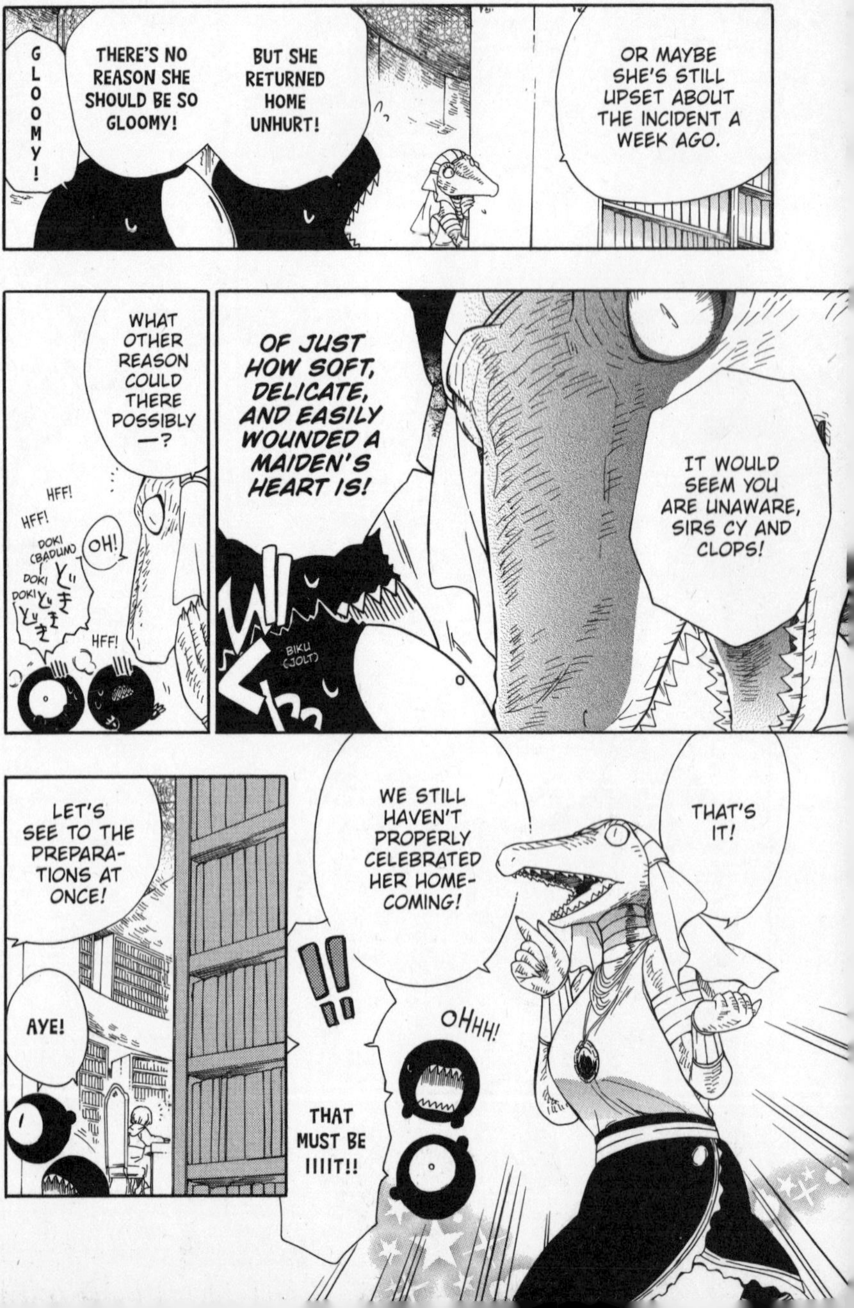
OR MAYBE SHE'S STILL UPSET ABOUT THE INCIDENT A WEEK AGO.
BUT SHE RETURNED HOME UNHURT!
THERE'S NO REASON SHE SHOULD BE SO GLOOMY!
GLOOMY!
IT WOULD SEEM YOU ARE UNAWARE, SIRS CY AND CLOPS!
OF JUST HOW SOFT, DELICATE, AND EASILY WOUNDED A MAIDEN'S HEART IS!
BIKU (JOLT)
WHAT OTHER REASON COULD THERE POSSIBLY—?
HFF!
HFF!
OH!
DOKI (BADUMP) DOKI DOKI
HFF!
THAT'S IT!
WE STILL HAVEN'T PROPERLY CELEBRATED HER HOME-COMING!
!!
OHHH!
THAT MUST BE IIIIT!!
LET'S SEE TO THE PREPARA-TIONS AT ONCE!
AYE!

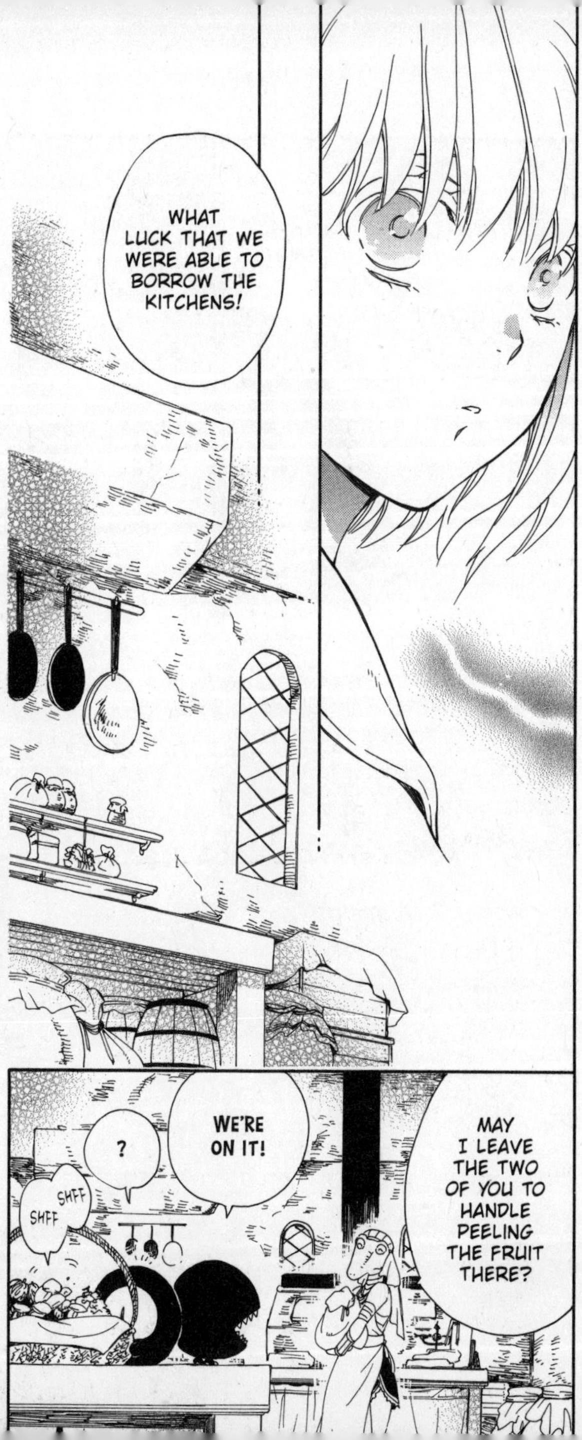
WHAT LUCK THAT WE WERE ABLE TO BORROW THE KITCHENS!
MAY I LEAVE THE TWO OF YOU TO HANDLE PEELING THE FRUIT THERE?
WE'RE ON IT!
?
SHFF
SHFF
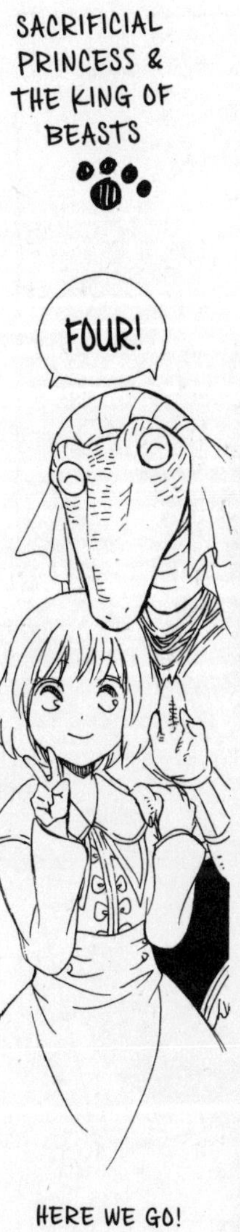
SACRIFICIAL PRINCESS & THE KING OF BEASTS
FOUR!
HERE WE GO!

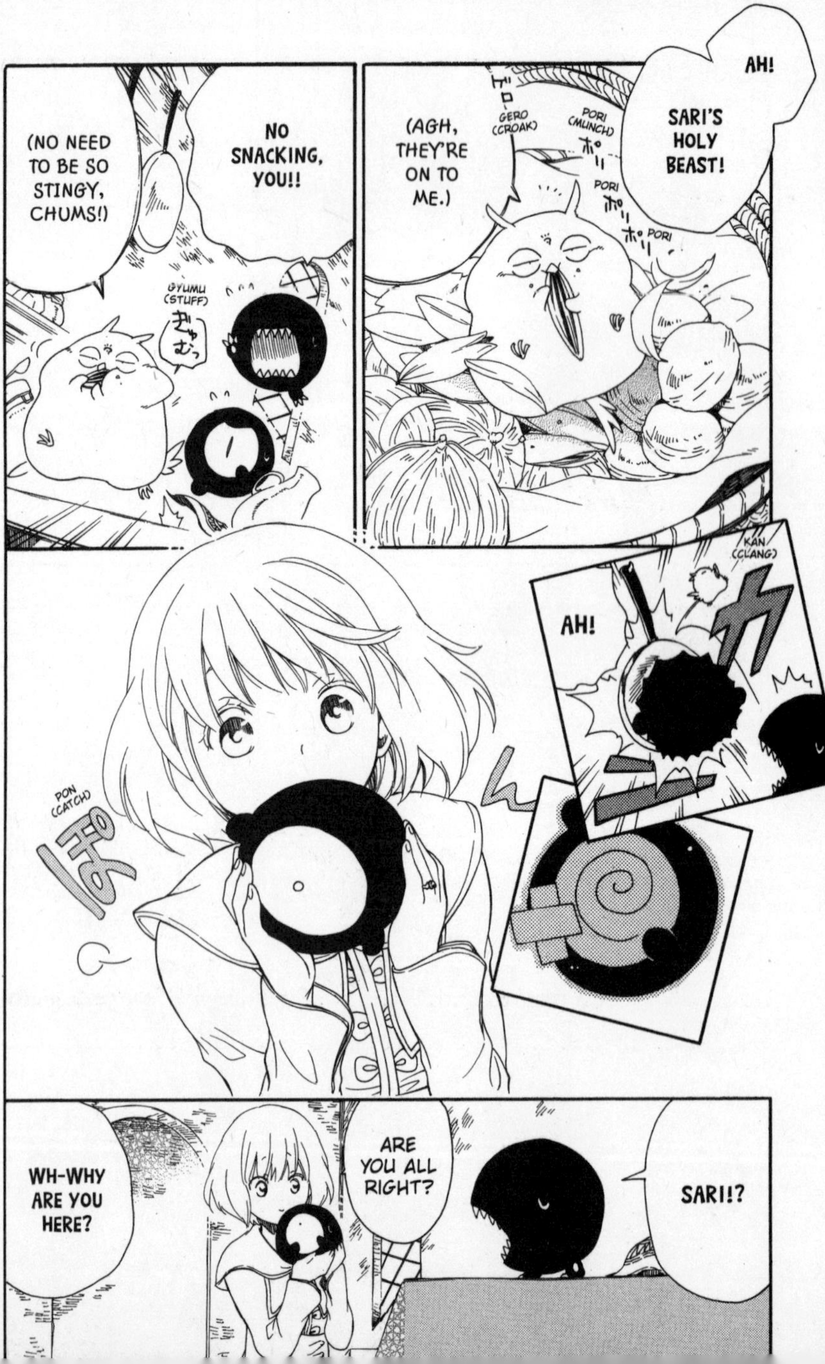

AH! SARI'S HOLY BEAST!
PORI (MUNCH)
PORI
PORI
GERO (CROAK)
(AGH, THEY'RE ON TO ME.)
NO SNACKING, YOU!!
(NO NEED TO BE SO STINGY, CHUMS!)
GYUMU (STUFF)
KAN (CLANG)
AH!
PON (CATCH)
SARI!?
ARE YOU ALL RIGHT?
WH-WHY ARE YOU HERE?

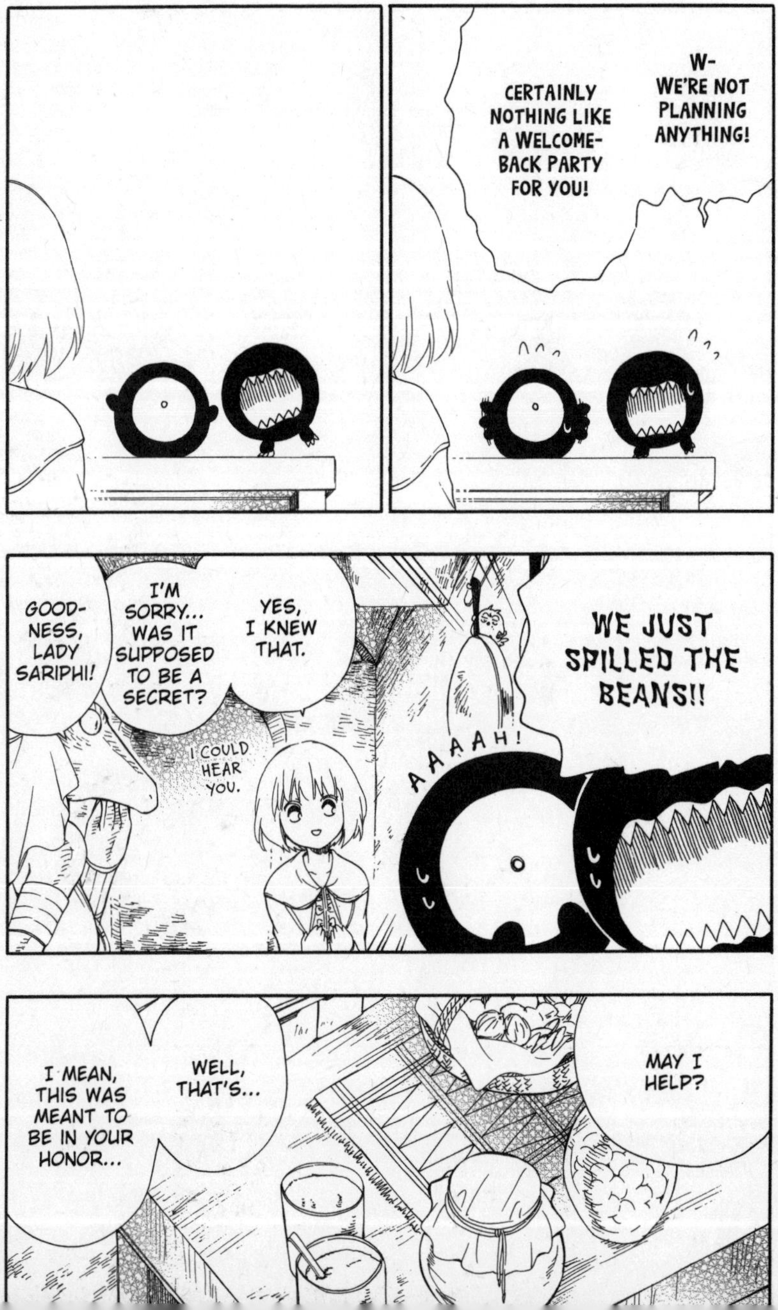
W-
WE'RE NOT PLANNING ANYTHING!
CERTAINLY NOTHING LIKE A WELCOME-BACK PARTY FOR YOU!
WE JUST SPILLED THE BEANS!!
AAAAH!
YES, I KNEW THAT.
I'M SORRY... WAS IT SUPPOSED TO BE A SECRET?
I COULD HEAR YOU.
GOODNESS, LADY SARIPHI!
MAY I HELP?
WELL, THAT'S...
I MEAN, THIS WAS MEANT TO BE IN YOUR HONOR...

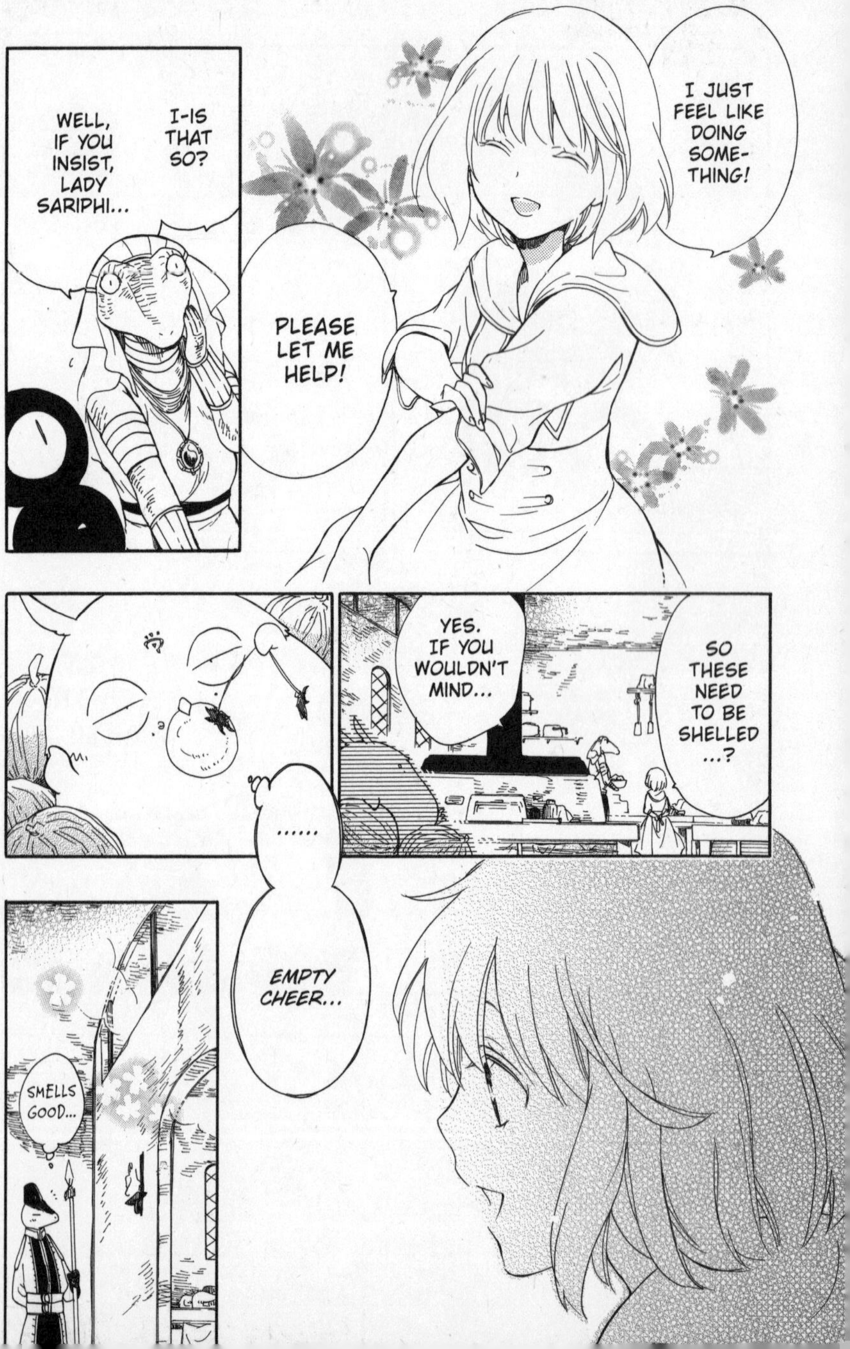
I JUST FEEL LIKE DOING SOME-THING!
PLEASE LET ME HELP!
I-IS THAT SO?
WELL, IF YOU INSIST, LADY SARIPHI...
SO THESE NEED TO BE SHELLED ...?
YES. IF YOU WOULDN'T MIND...
......
EMPTY CHEER...
SMELLS GOOD...

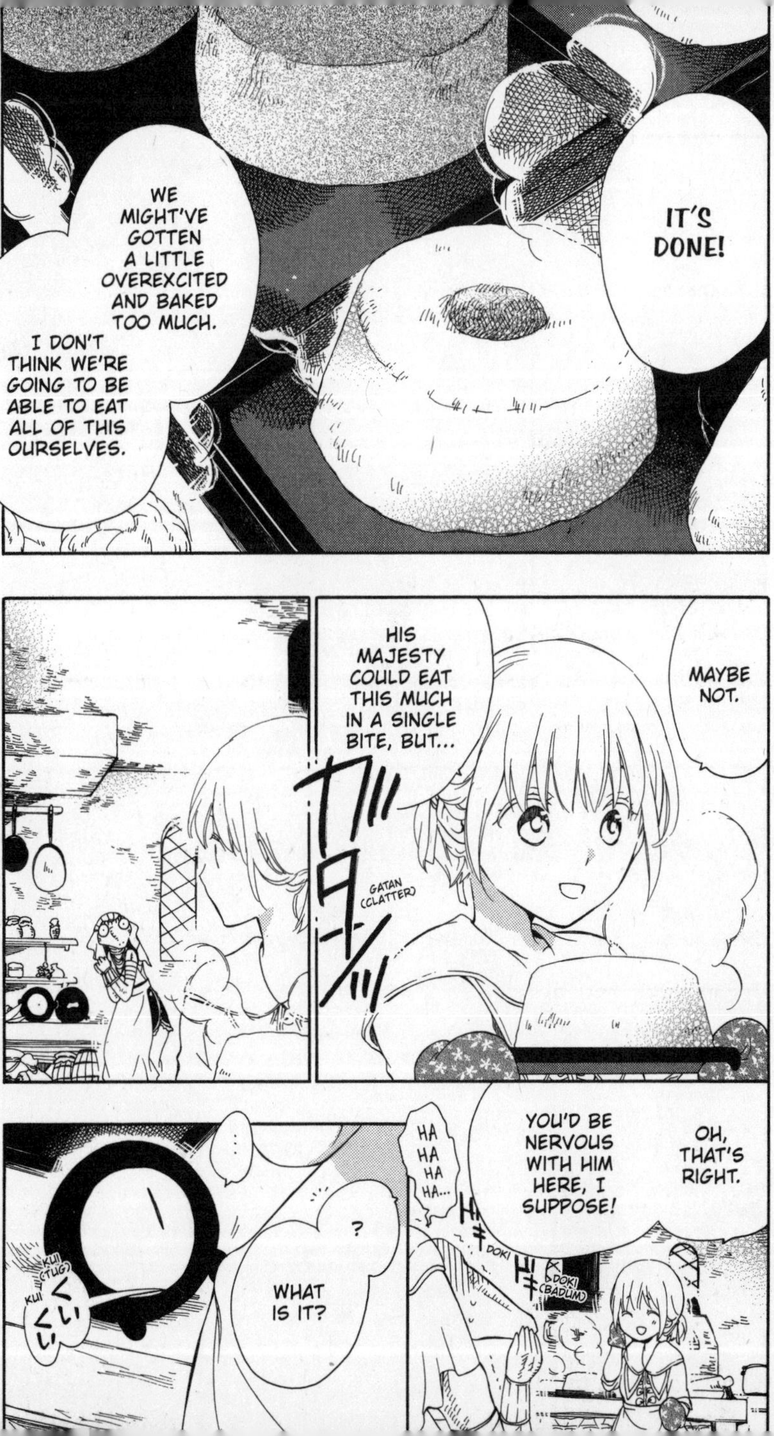
IT'S DONE!
WE MIGHT'VE GOTTEN A LITTLE OVEREXCITED AND BAKED TOO MUCH.
I DON'T THINK WE'RE GOING TO BE ABLE TO EAT ALL OF THIS OURSELVES.
HIS MAJESTY COULD EAT THIS MUCH IN A SINGLE BITE, BUT...
MAYBE NOT.
ガタン
GATAN (CLATTER)
OH, THAT'S RIGHT.
YOU'D BE NERVOUS WITH HIM HERE, I SUPPOSE!
HA HA HA HA...
ドキ
DOKI
ドキ
DOKI (BADUM)
...
?
WHAT IS IT?
くい くい
KUI (TUG)
KUI

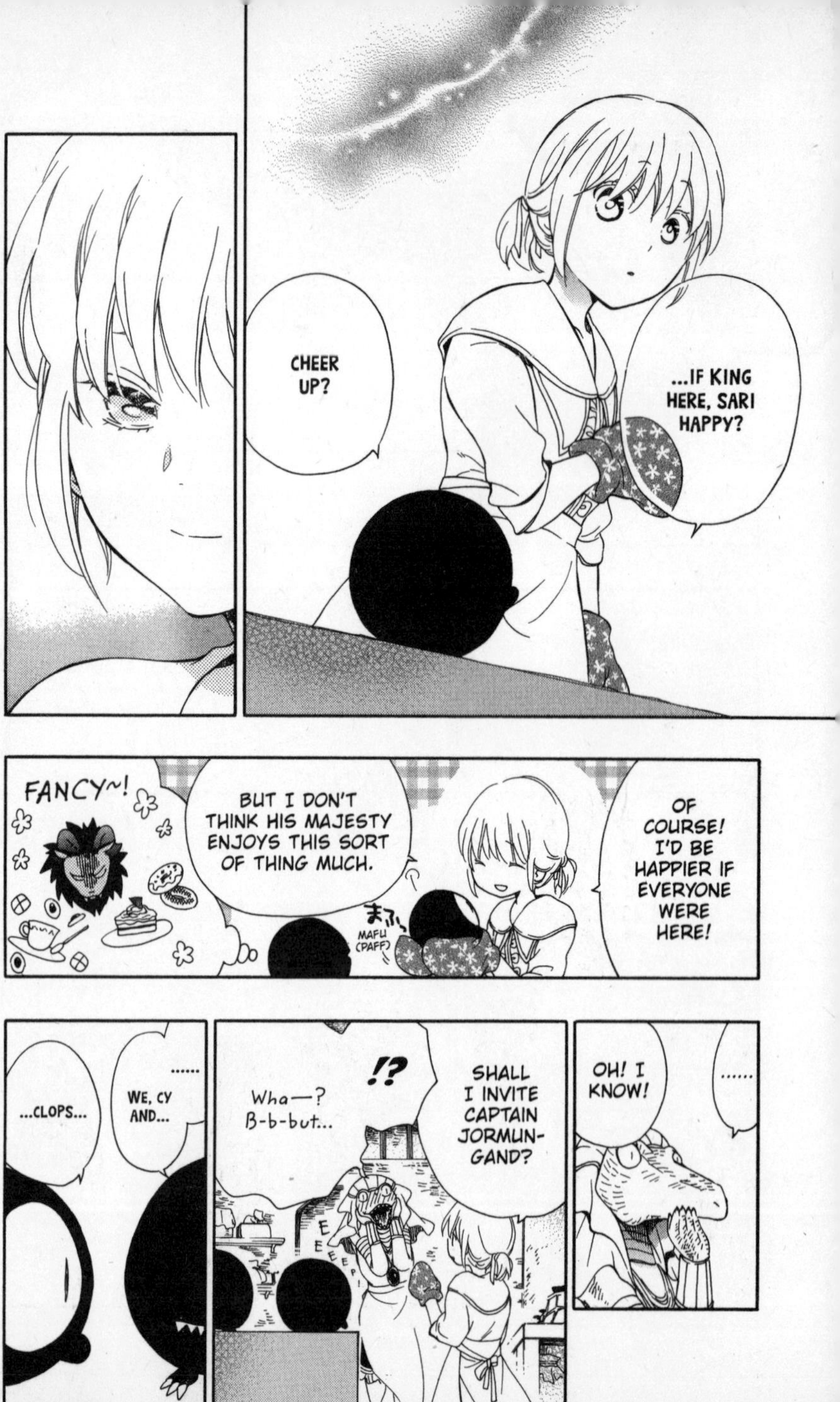
...IF KING HERE, SARI HAPPY?
CHEER UP?
OF COURSE! I'D BE HAPPIER IF EVERYONE WERE HERE!
BUT I DON'T THINK HIS MAJESTY ENJOYS THIS SORT OF THING MUCH.
まふっ
MAFU (PAFF)
FANCY~!
......
OH! I KNOW!
SHALL I INVITE CAPTAIN JORMUN-GAND?
!?
Wha—? B-b-but...
EEEEP!
......
WE, CY AND...
...CLOPS...

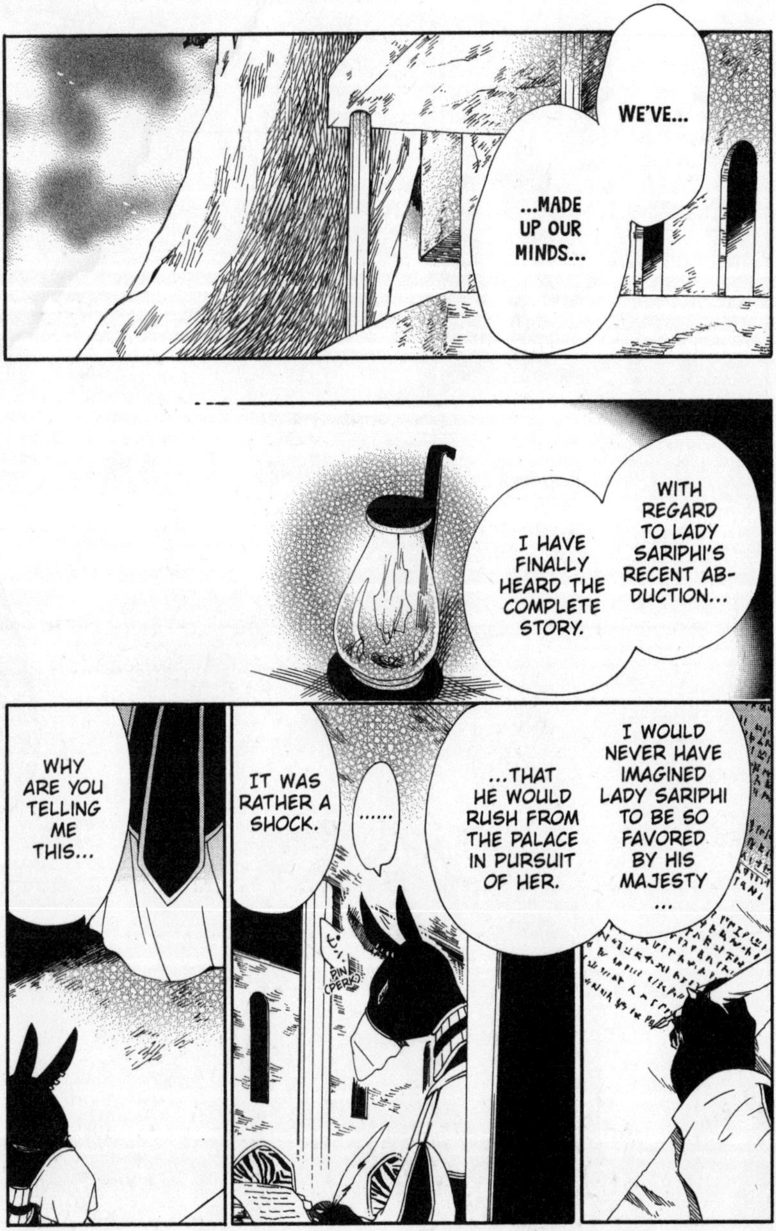
WE'VE...
...MADE UP OUR MINDS...
WITH REGARD TO LADY SARIPHI'S RECENT AB-DUCTION...
I HAVE FINALLY HEARD THE COMPLETE STORY.
I WOULD NEVER HAVE IMAGINED LADY SARIPHI TO BE SO FAVORED BY HIS MAJESTY ...
...THAT HE WOULD RUSH FROM THE PALACE IN PURSUIT OF HER.
......
IT WAS RATHER A SHOCK.
PIN (PERK)
WHY ARE YOU TELLING ME THIS...

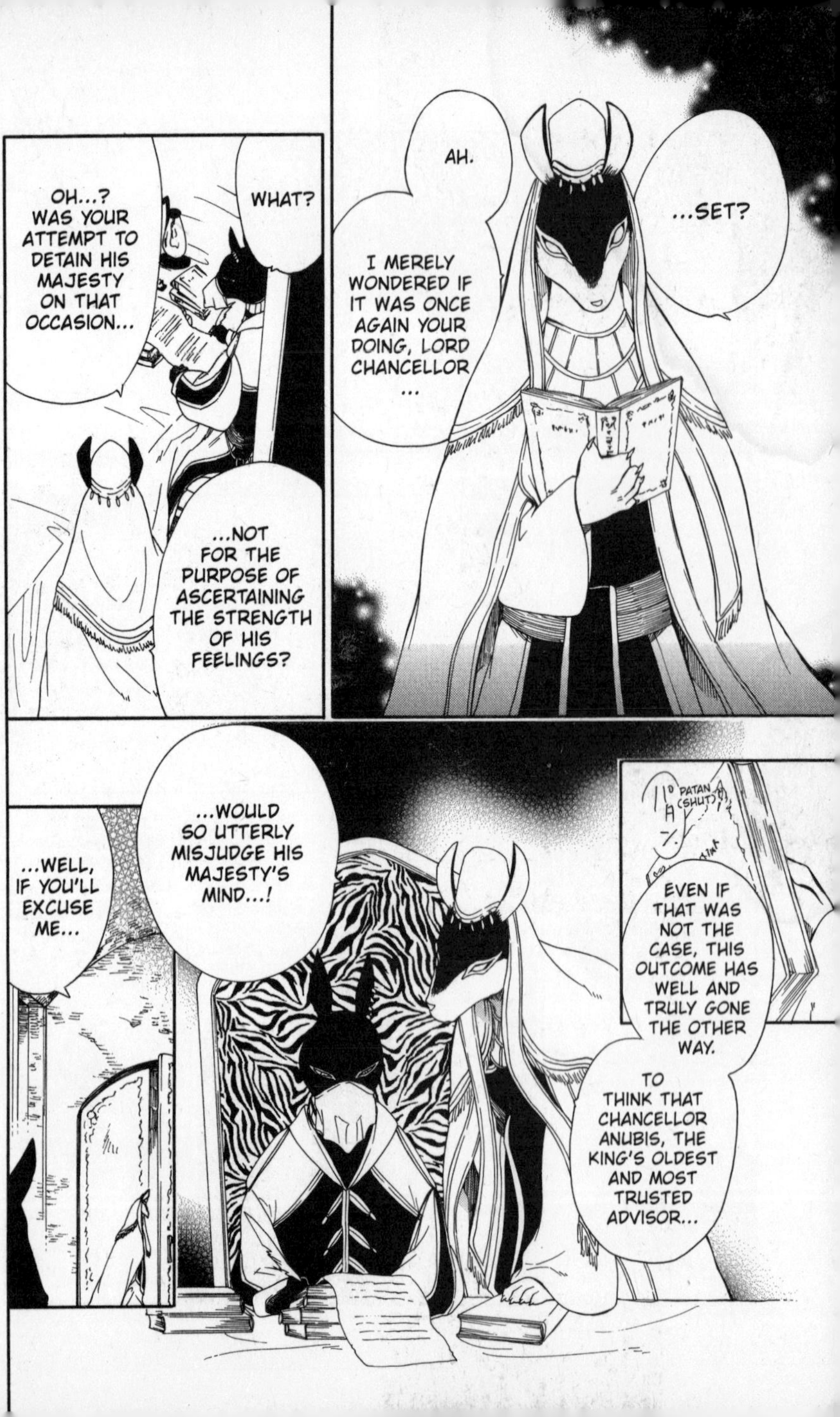
AH.
...SET?
I MERELY WONDERED IF IT WAS ONCE AGAIN YOUR DOING, LORD CHANCELLOR...
WHAT?
OH...? WAS YOUR ATTEMPT TO DETAIN HIS MAJESTY ON THAT OCCASION...
...NOT FOR THE PURPOSE OF ASCERTAINING THE STRENGTH OF HIS FEELINGS?
PATAN (SHUT)
EVEN IF THAT WAS NOT THE CASE, THIS OUTCOME HAS WELL AND TRULY GONE THE OTHER WAY.
TO THINK THAT CHANCELLOR ANUBIS, THE KING'S OLDEST AND MOST TRUSTED ADVISOR...
...WOULD SO UTTERLY MISJUDGE HIS MAJESTY'S MIND...!
...WELL, IF YOU'LL EXCUSE ME...

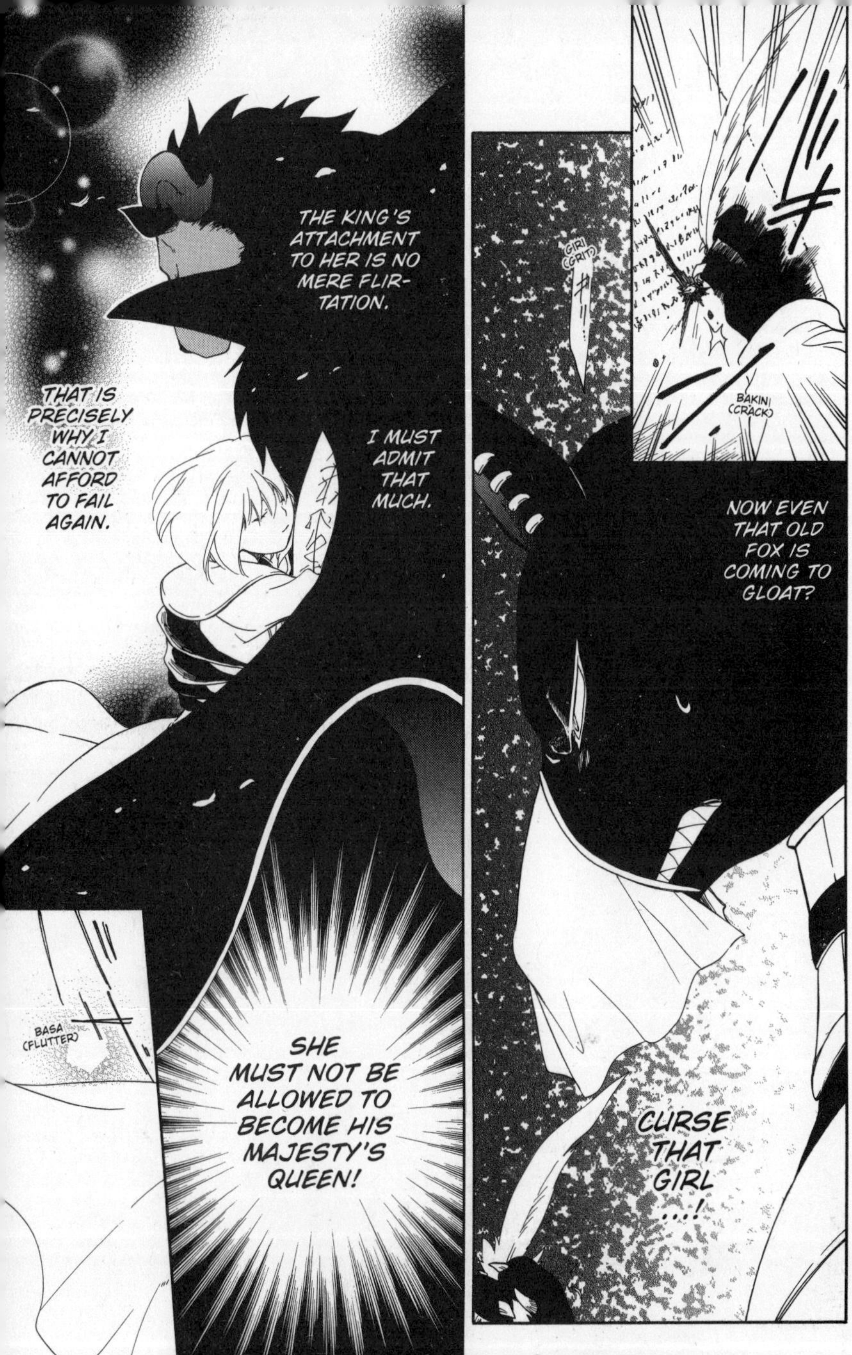
BAKIN! (CRACK)
GIRI (GRIT)
NOW EVEN THAT OLD FOX IS COMING TO GLOAT?
CURSE THAT GIRL ...!
THE KING'S ATTACHMENT TO HER IS NO MERE FLIRTATION.
I MUST ADMIT THAT MUCH.
THAT IS PRECISELY WHY I CANNOT AFFORD TO FAIL AGAIN.
BASA (FLUTTER)
SHE MUST NOT BE ALLOWED TO BECOME HIS MAJESTY'S QUEEN!

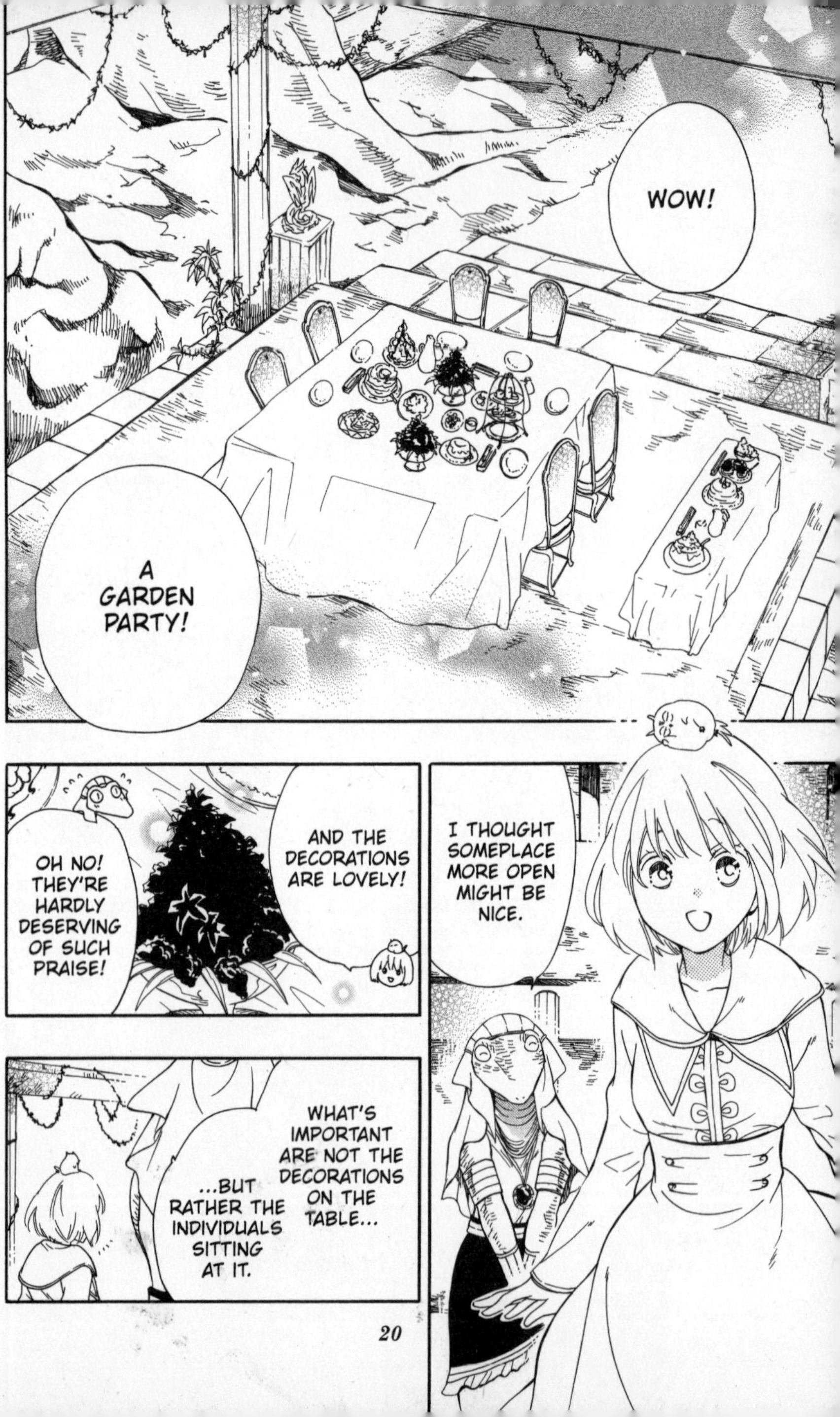
WOW!
A GARDEN PARTY!
I THOUGHT SOMEPLACE MORE OPEN MIGHT BE NICE.
AND THE DECORATIONS ARE LOVELY!
OH NO! THEY'RE HARDLY DESERVING OF SUCH PRAISE!
WHAT'S IMPORTANT ARE NOT THE DECORATIONS ON THE TABLE...
...BUT RATHER THE INDIVIDUALS SITTING AT IT.

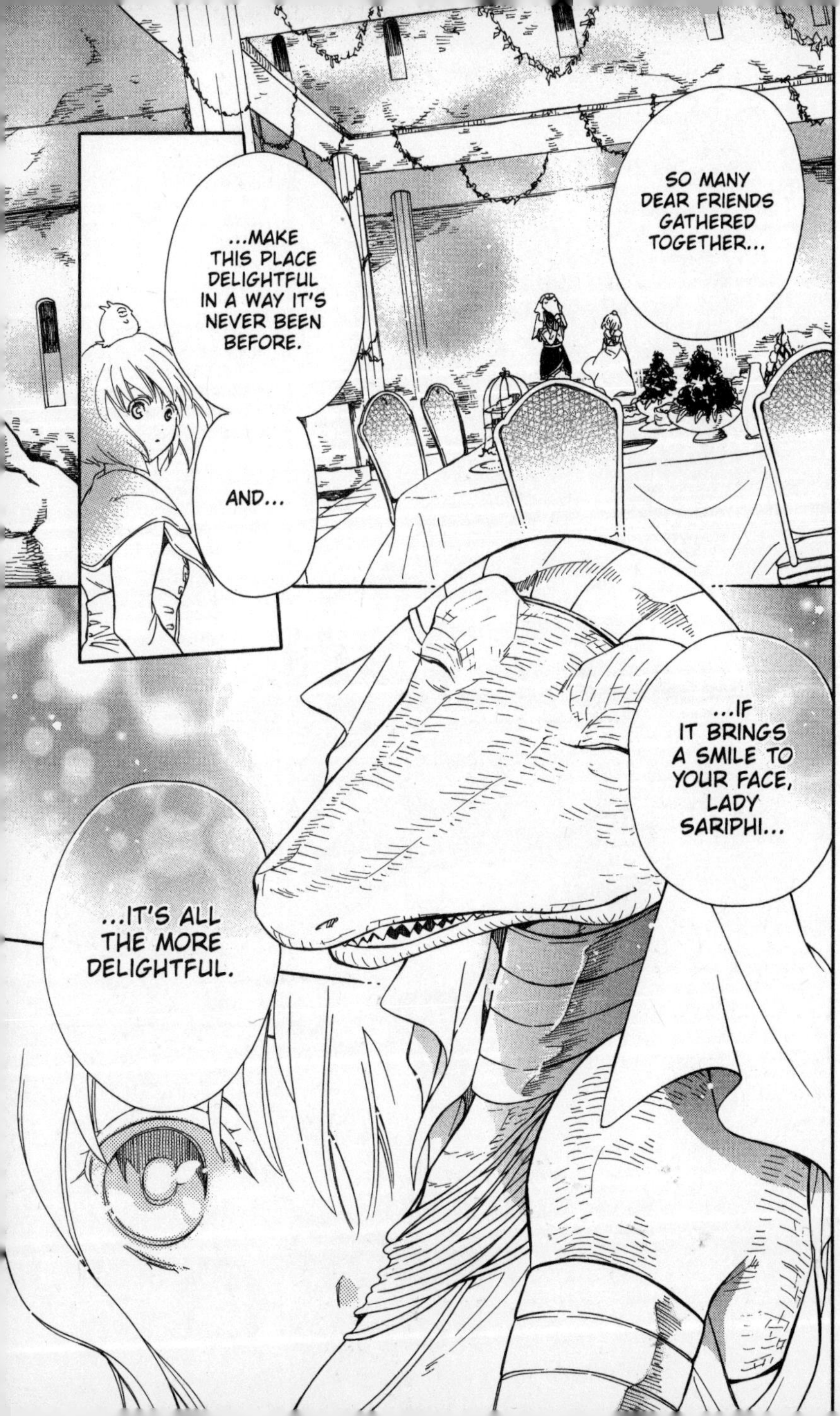
SO MANY DEAR FRIENDS GATHERED TOGETHER...
...MAKE THIS PLACE DELIGHTFUL IN A WAY IT'S NEVER BEEN BEFORE.
AND...
...IF IT BRINGS A SMILE TO YOUR FACE, LADY SARIPHI...
...IT'S ALL THE MORE DELIGHTFUL.

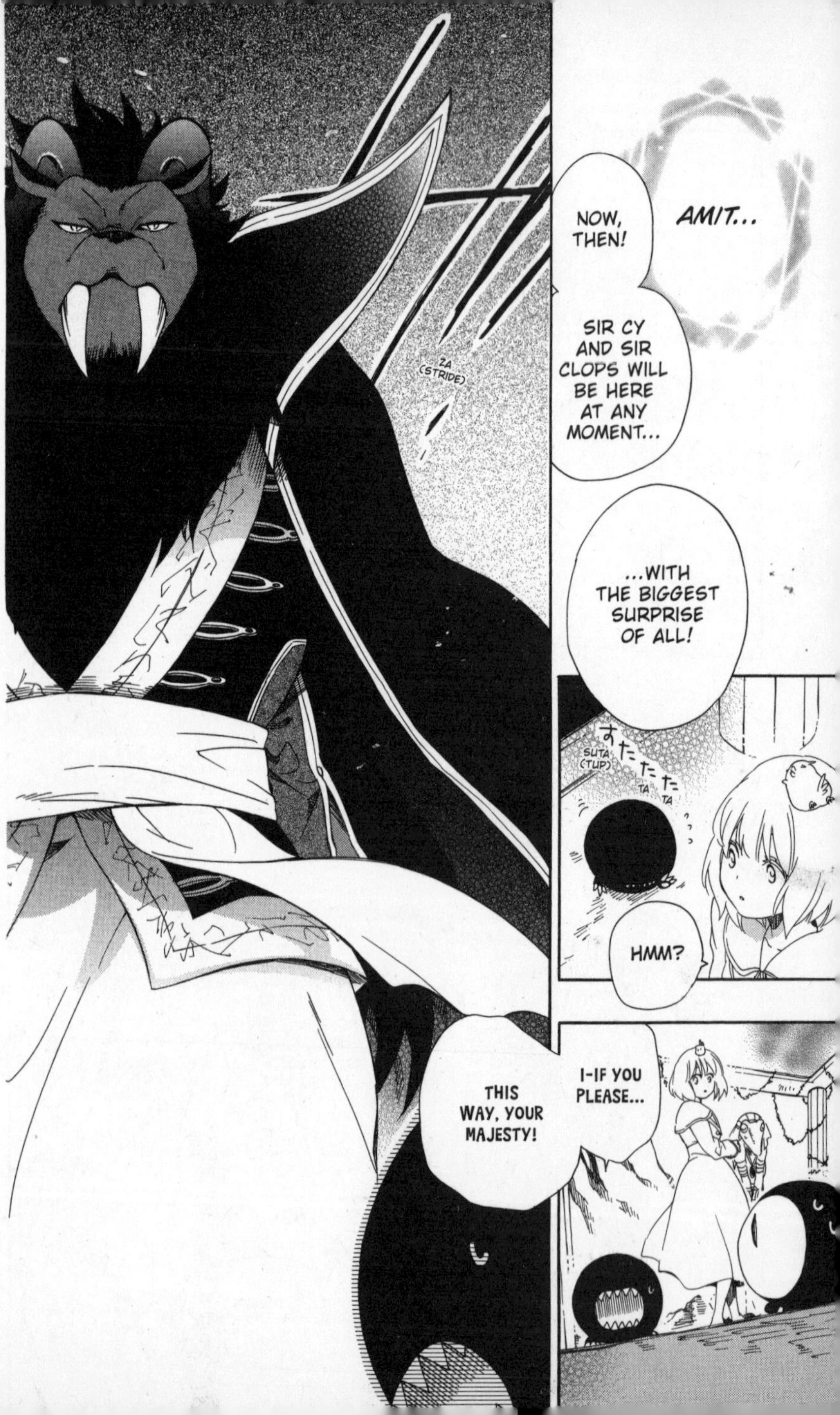
AMIT...
NOW, THEN!
SIR CY AND SIR CLOPS WILL BE HERE AT ANY MOMENT...
...WITH THE BIGGEST SURPRISE OF ALL!
すたたた
SUTA (TUP)
TA
TA
HMM?
I-IF YOU PLEASE...
THIS WAY, YOUR MAJESTY!
ZA (STRIDE)

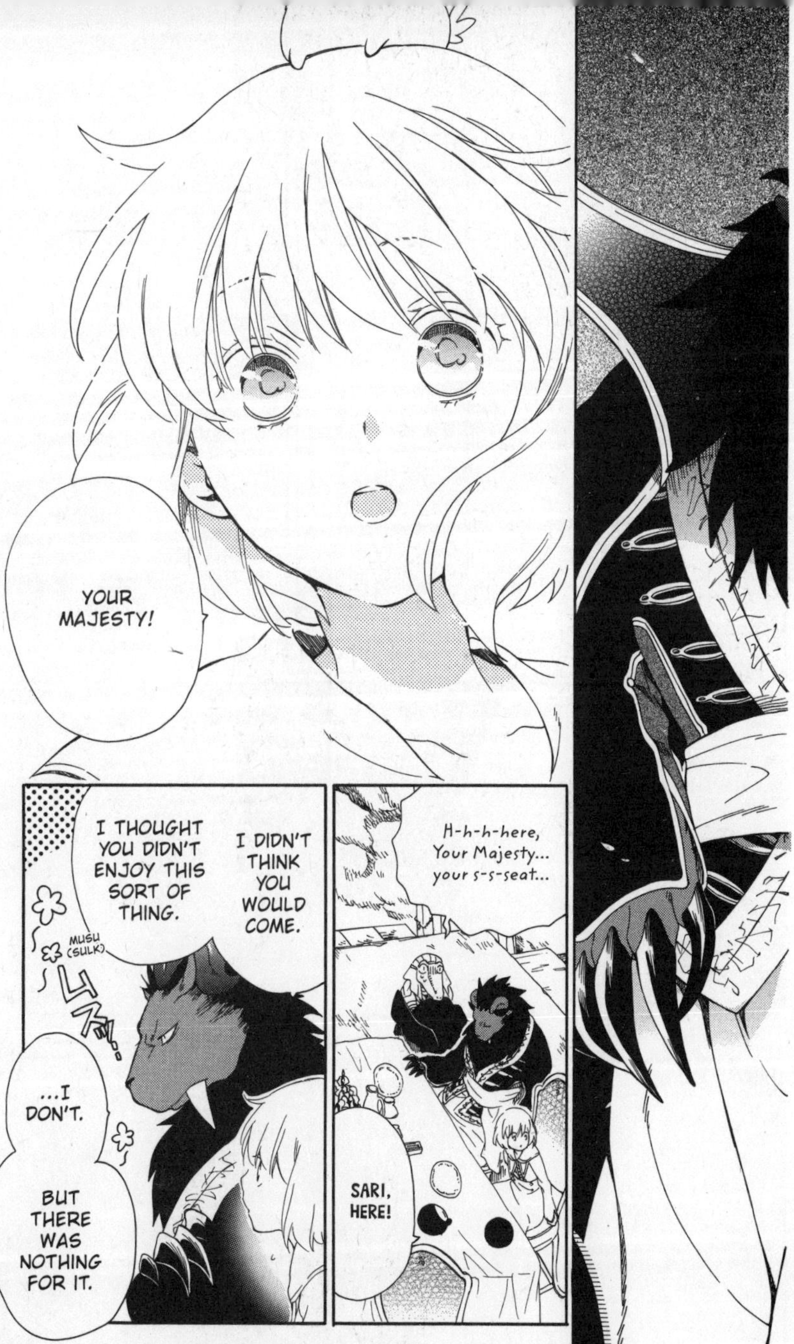
YOUR MAJESTY!
H-h-h-here, Your Majesty... your s-s-seat...
SARI, HERE!
I DIDN'T THINK YOU WOULD COME.
I THOUGHT YOU DIDN'T ENJOY THIS SORT OF THING.
MUSU (SULK)
...I DON'T.
BUT THERE WAS NOTHING FOR IT.

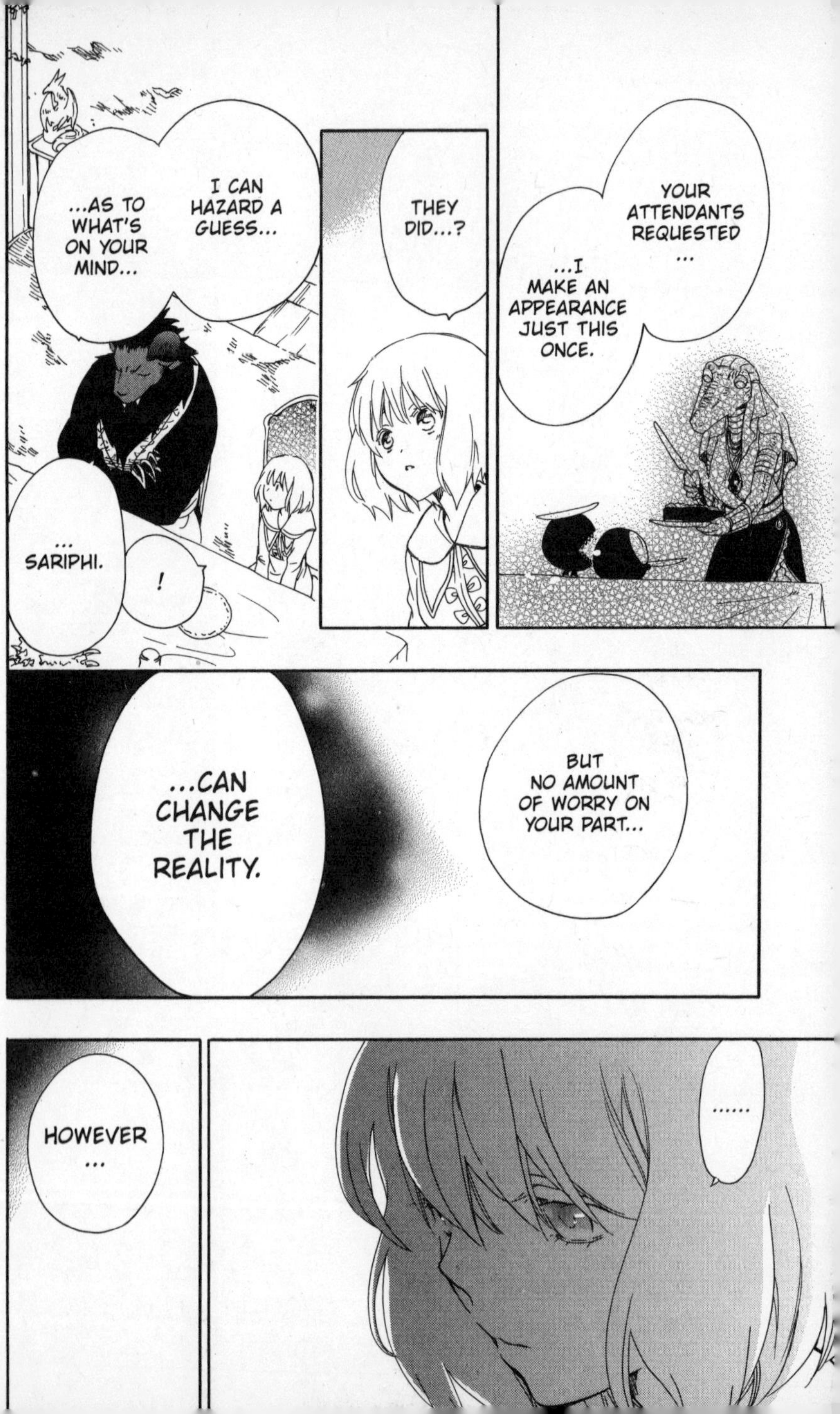
YOUR ATTENDANTS REQUESTED ...
...I MAKE AN APPEARANCE JUST THIS ONCE.
THEY DID...?
I CAN HAZARD A GUESS...
...AS TO WHAT'S ON YOUR MIND...
... SARIPHI.
!
BUT NO AMOUNT OF WORRY ON YOUR PART...
...CAN CHANGE THE REALITY.
......
HOWEVER ...

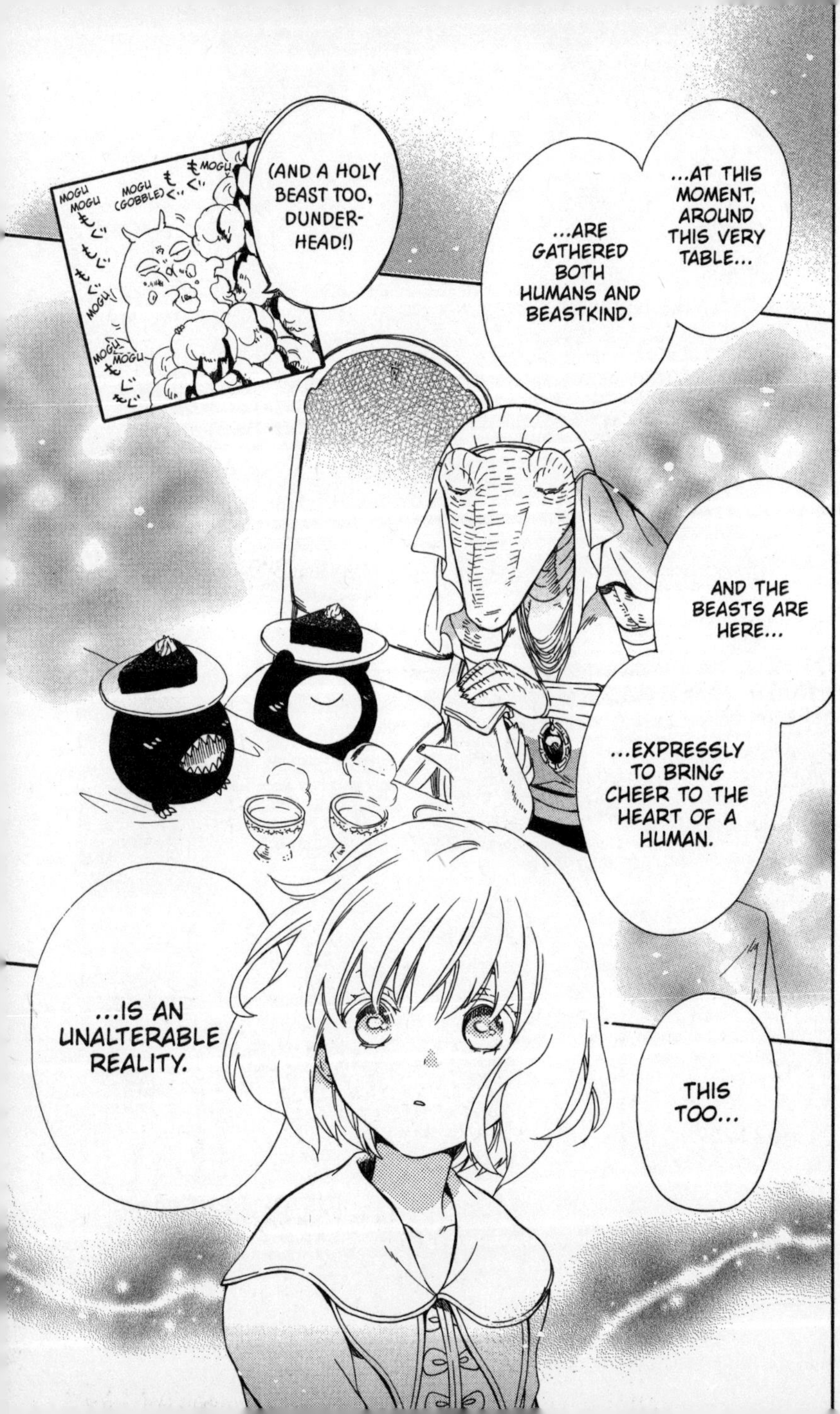
...AT THIS MOMENT, AROUND THIS VERY TABLE...
...ARE GATHERED BOTH HUMANS AND BEASTKIND.
(AND A HOLY BEAST TOO, DUNDER-HEAD!)
MOGU
MOGU (GOBBLE)
MOGU MOGU
MOGU!
MOGU MOGU
AND THE BEASTS ARE HERE...
...EXPRESSLY TO BRING CHEER TO THE HEART OF A HUMAN.
THIS TOO...
...IS AN UNALTERABLE REALITY.

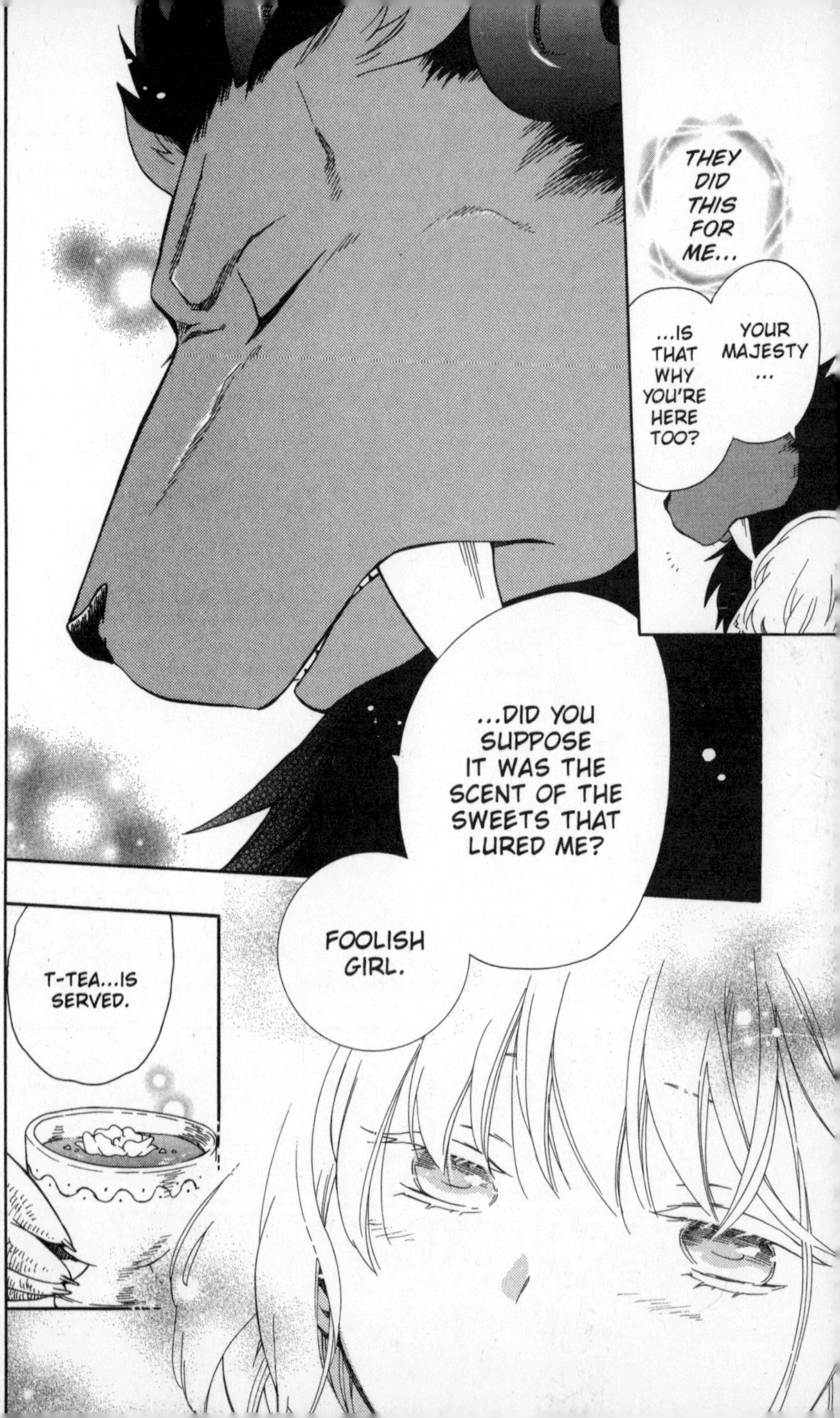
THEY DID THIS FOR ME...
YOUR MAJESTY...
...IS THAT WHY YOU'RE HERE TOO?
...DID YOU SUPPOSE IT WAS THE SCENT OF THE SWEETS THAT LURED ME?
FOOLISH GIRL.
T-TEA...IS SERVED.

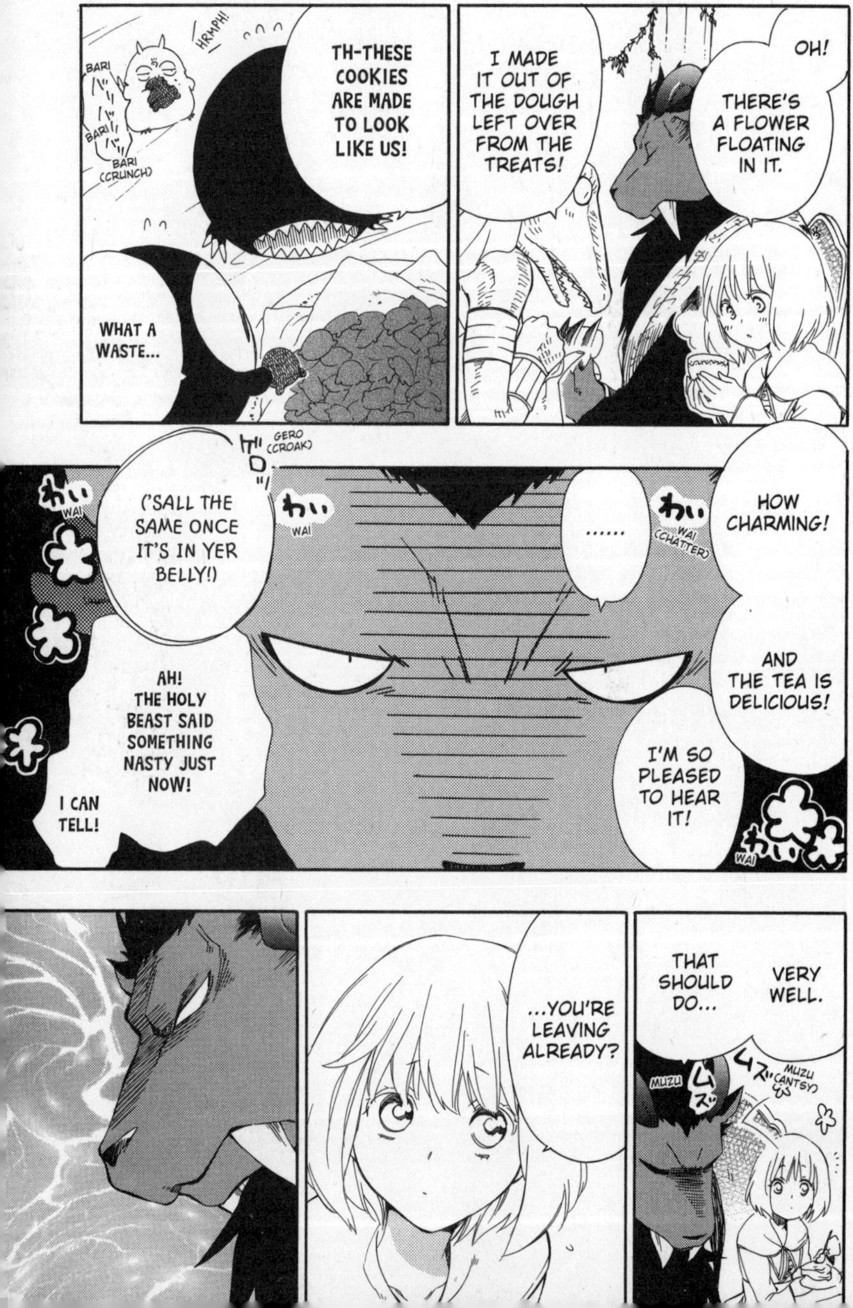
OH!
THERE'S A FLOWER FLOATING IN IT.
I MADE IT OUT OF THE DOUGH LEFT OVER FROM THE TREATS!
TH-THESE COOKIES ARE MADE TO LOOK LIKE US!
HRMPH!
BARI
BARI
BARI (CRUNCH)
WHAT A WASTE...
HOW CHARMING!
AND THE TEA IS DELICIOUS!
I'M SO PLEASED TO HEAR IT!
WAI
WAI (CHATTER)
......
WAI
GERO (CROAK)
('SALL THE SAME ONCE IT'S IN YER BELLY!)
WAI
AH! THE HOLY BEAST SAID SOMETHING NASTY JUST NOW!
I CAN TELL!
VERY WELL.
THAT SHOULD DO...
MUZU (ANTSY)
MUZU
...YOU'RE LEAVING ALREADY?

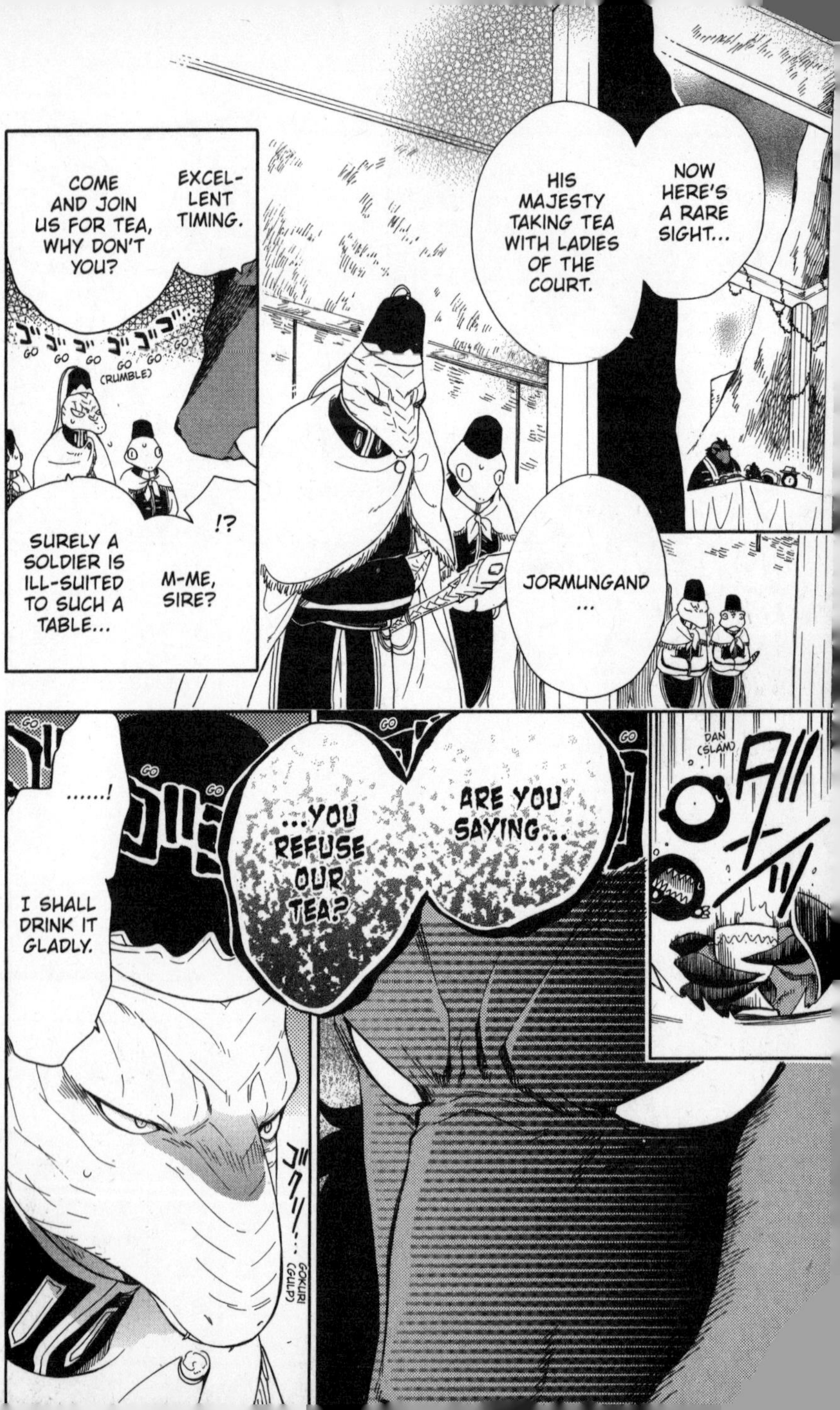
NOW HERE'S A RARE SIGHT...
HIS MAJESTY TAKING TEA WITH LADIES OF THE COURT.
JORMUNGAND ...
EXCEL-LENT TIMING.
COME AND JOIN US FOR TEA, WHY DON'T YOU?
GO GO GO GO GO GO (RUMBLE)
!?
M-ME, SIRE?
SURELY A SOLDIER IS ILL-SUITED TO SUCH A TABLE...
DAN (SLAM)
ARE YOU SAYING...
...YOU REFUSE OUR TEA?
GO GO GO GO
......!
I SHALL DRINK IT GLADLY.
GOKURI (GULP)

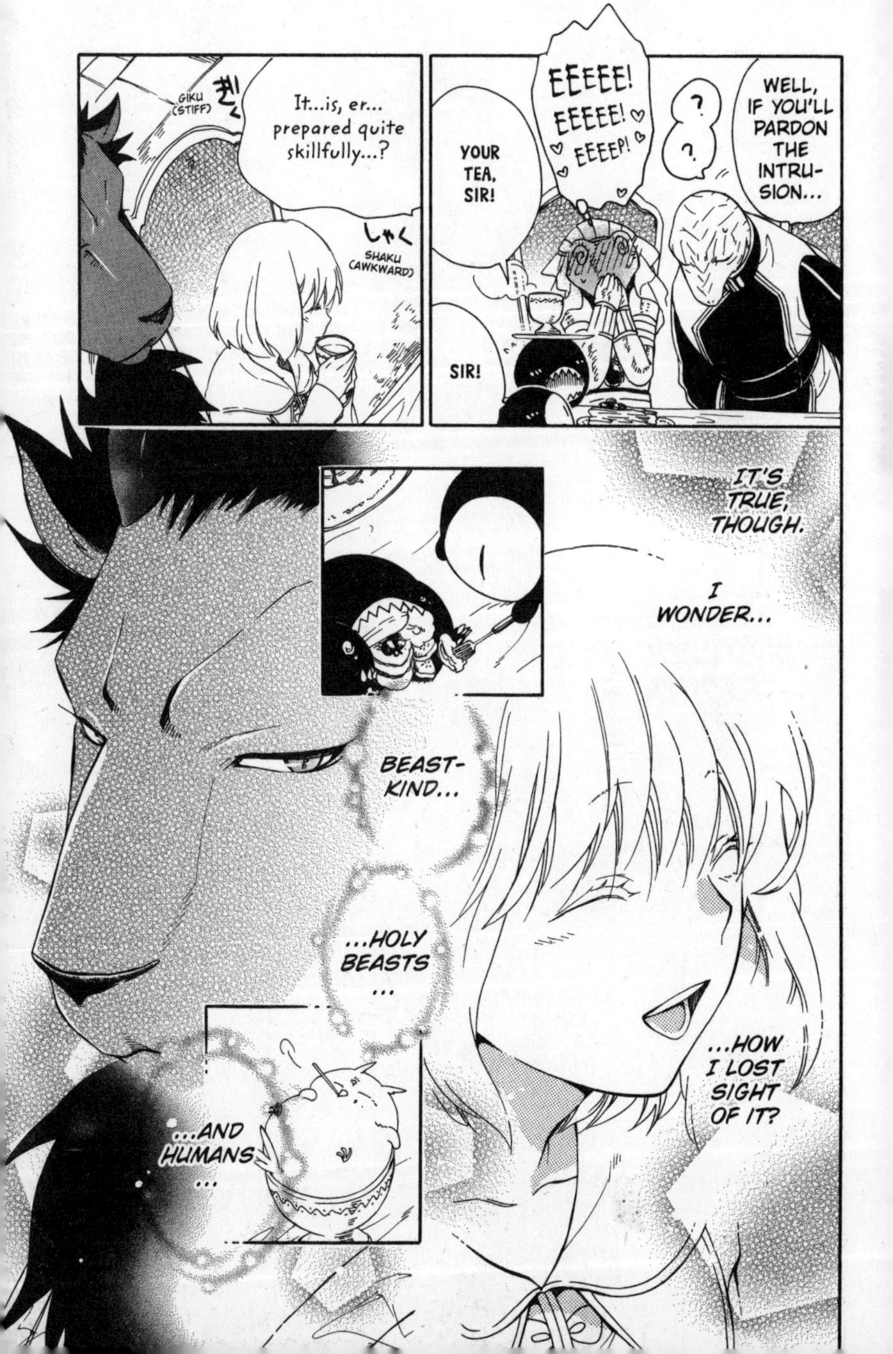
WELL, IF YOU'LL PARDON THE INTRUSION...
?
?
EEEEE! EEEEE! EEEEP!
YOUR TEA, SIR!
SIR!
It...is, er... prepared quite skillfully...?
GIKU (STIFF)
しゃく
SHAKU (AWKWARD)
IT'S TRUE, THOUGH.
I WONDER...
BEAST-KIND...
...HOLY BEASTS...
...AND HUMANS...
...HOW I LOST SIGHT OF IT?

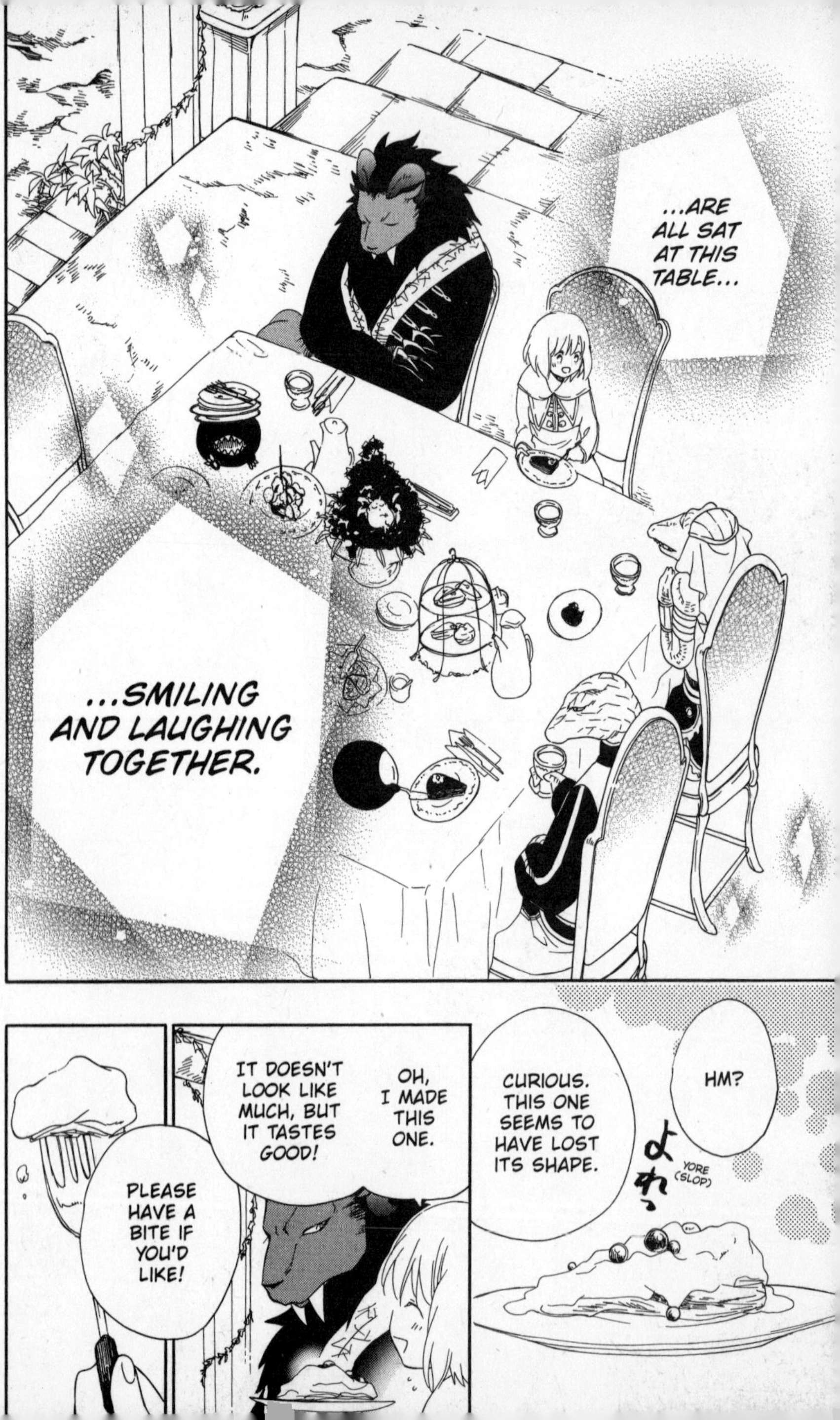
...ARE ALL SAT AT THIS TABLE...
...SMILING AND LAUGHING TOGETHER.
HM?
CURIOUS. THIS ONE SEEMS TO HAVE LOST ITS SHAPE.
よれっ
YORE (SLOP)
OH, I MADE THIS ONE.
IT DOESN'T LOOK LIKE MUCH, BUT IT TASTES GOOD!
PLEASE HAVE A BITE IF YOU'D LIKE!

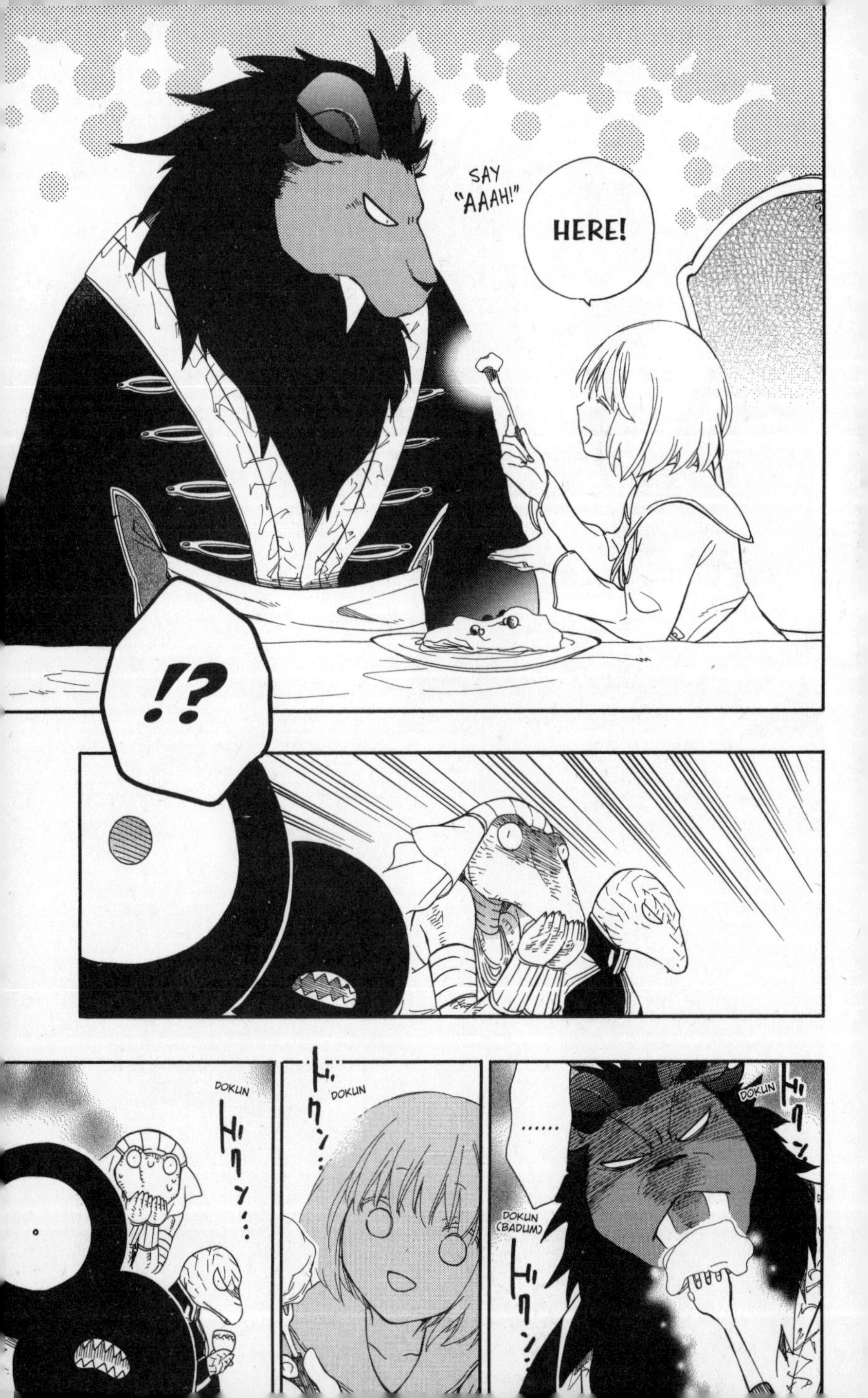
HERE!
SAY "AAAH!"
!?
DOKUN
......
DOKUN (BADUM)
DOKUN
DOKUN

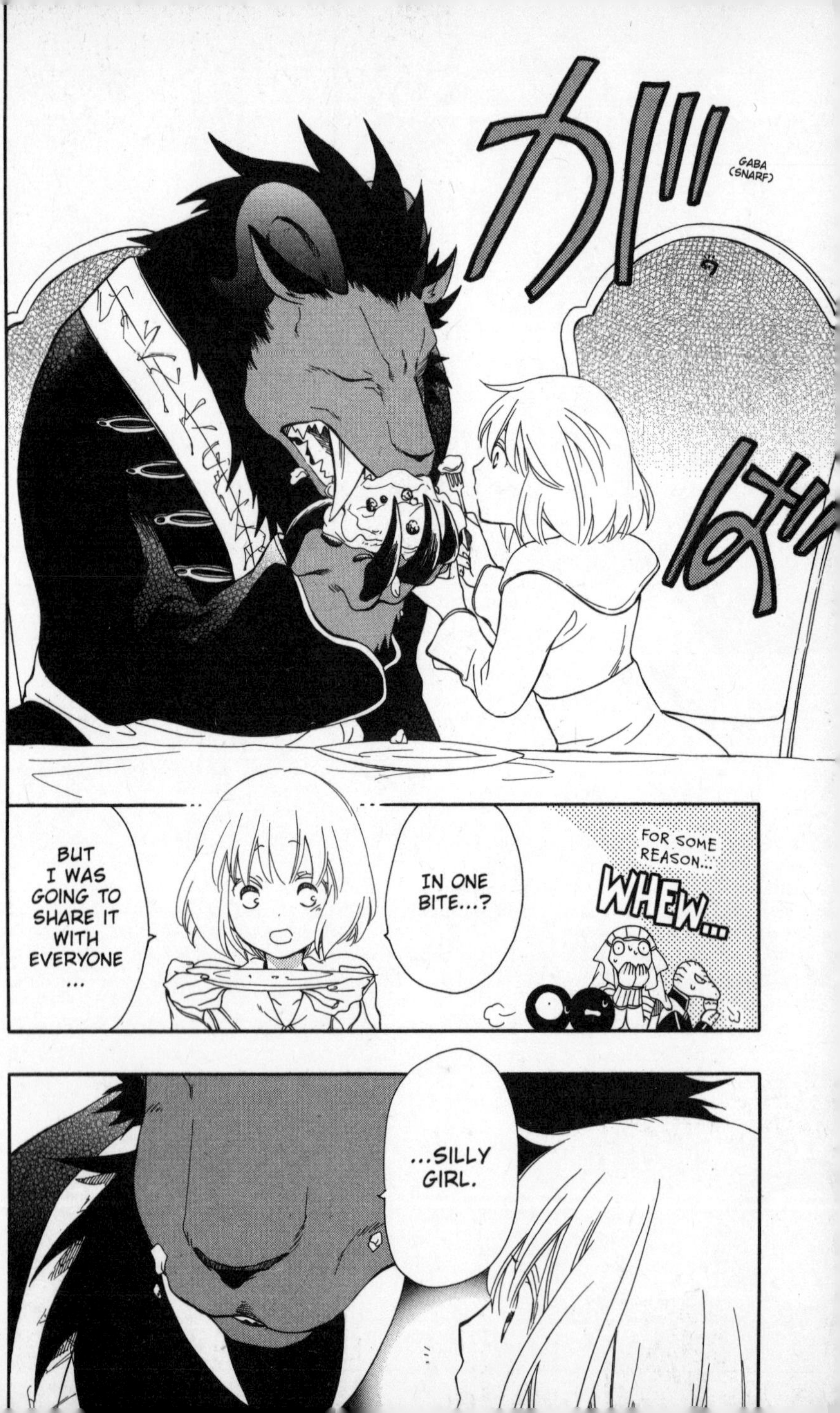
GABA (SNARF)
FOR SOME REASON...
WHEW...
IN ONE BITE...?
BUT I WAS GOING TO SHARE IT WITH EVERYONE ...
...SILLY GIRL.

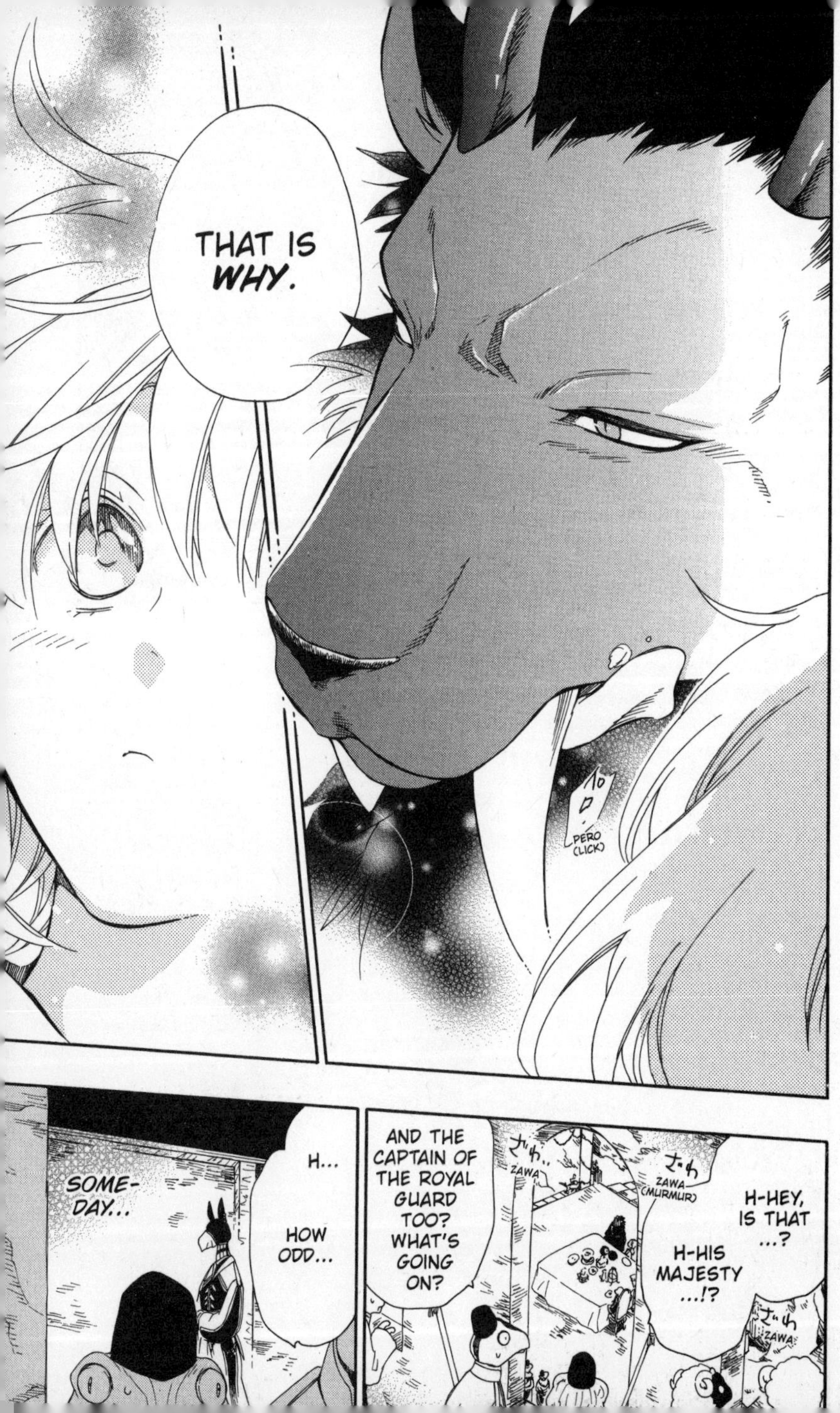
THAT IS WHY.
ペロ
PERO (LICK)
ざわ
ZAWA (MURMUR)
H-HEY, IS THAT ...?
ざわ
ZAWA
AND THE CAPTAIN OF THE ROYAL GUARD TOO? WHAT'S GOING ON?
H-HIS MAJESTY ...!?
ざわ
ZAWA
H...
HOW ODD...
SOME-DAY...

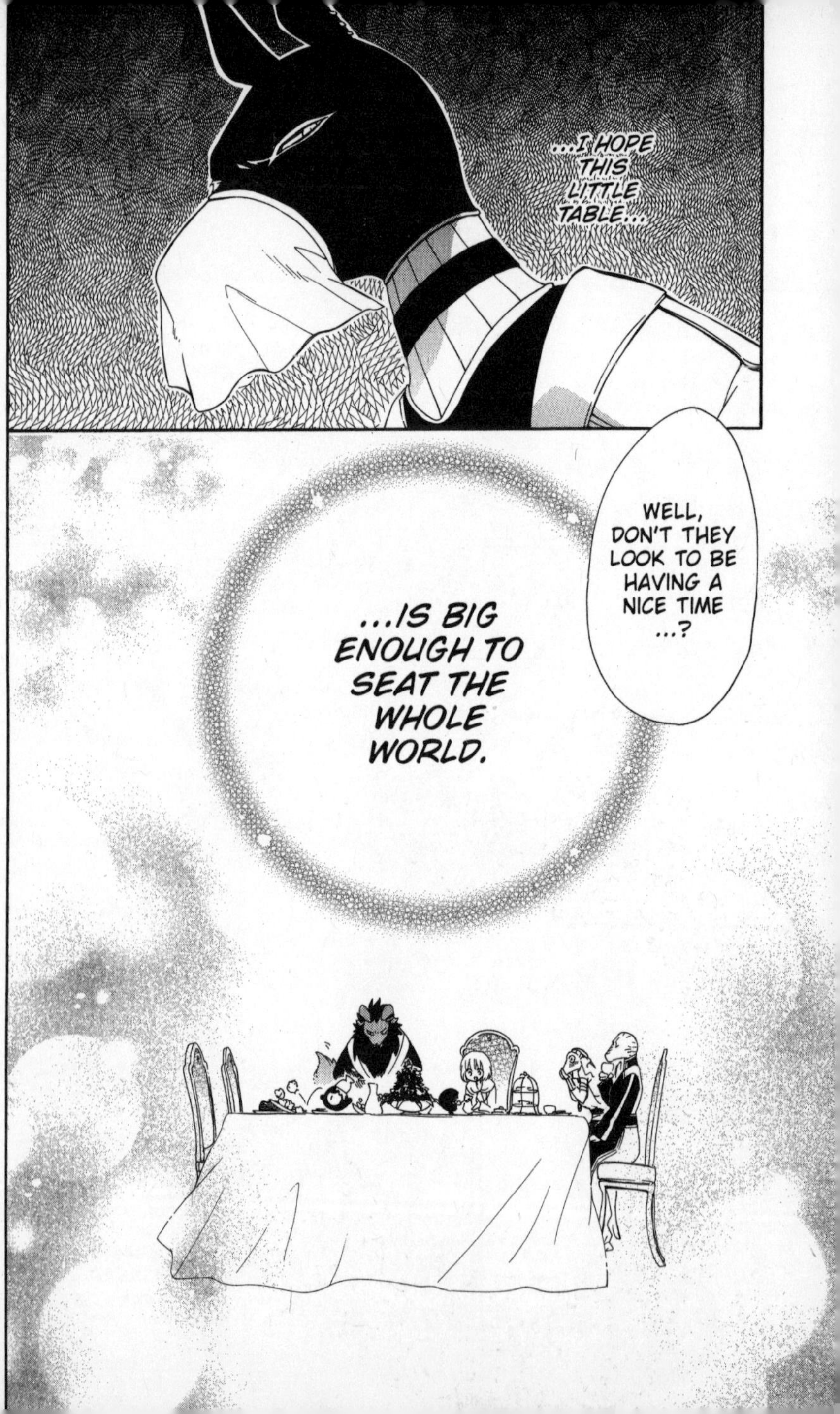
...I HOPE THIS LITTLE TABLE...
WELL, DON'T THEY LOOK TO BE HAVING A NICE TIME ...?
...IS BIG ENOUGH TO SEAT THE WHOLE WORLD.

episode. 19

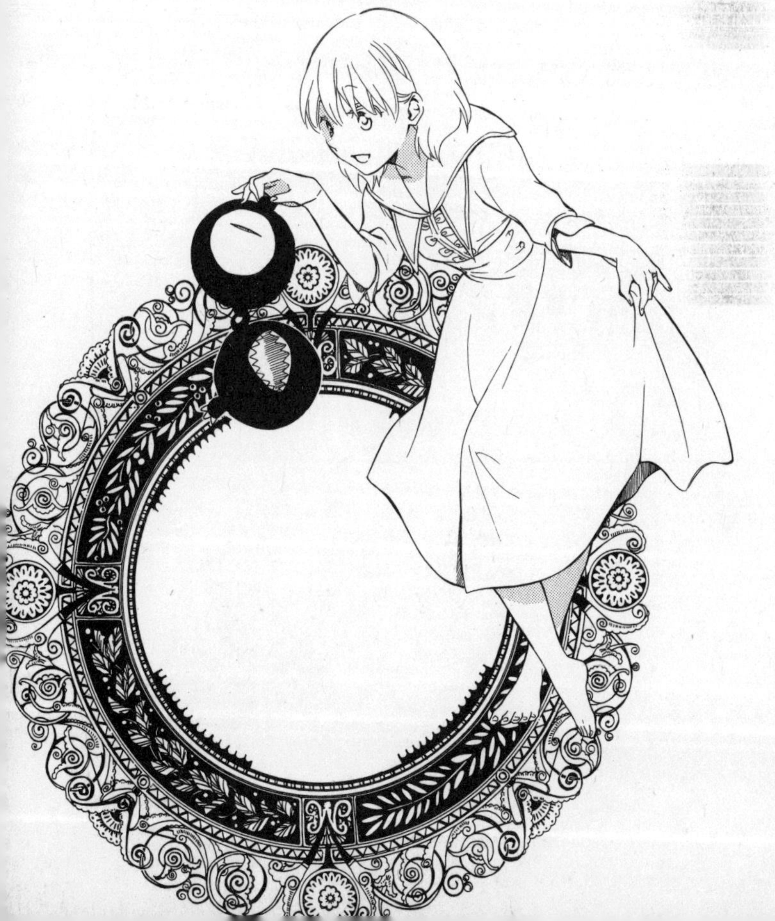

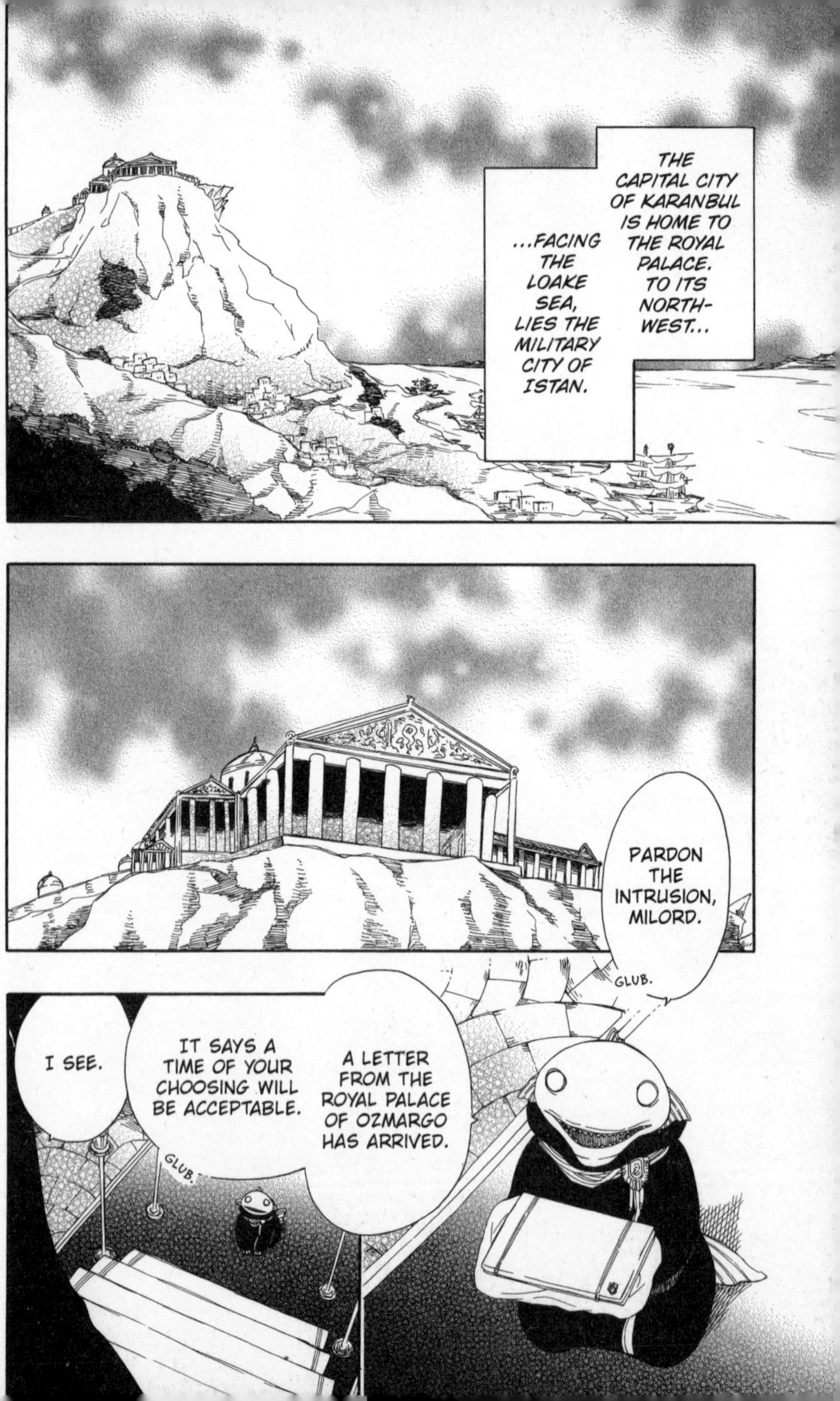
THE CAPITAL CITY OF KARANBUL IS HOME TO THE ROYAL PALACE. TO ITS NORTH-WEST...
...FACING THE LOAKE SEA, LIES THE MILITARY CITY OF ISTAN.
PARDON THE INTRUSION, MILORD.
GLUB.
A LETTER FROM THE ROYAL PALACE OF OZMARGO HAS ARRIVED.
IT SAYS A TIME OF YOUR CHOOSING WILL BE ACCEPTABLE.
GLUB.
I SEE.

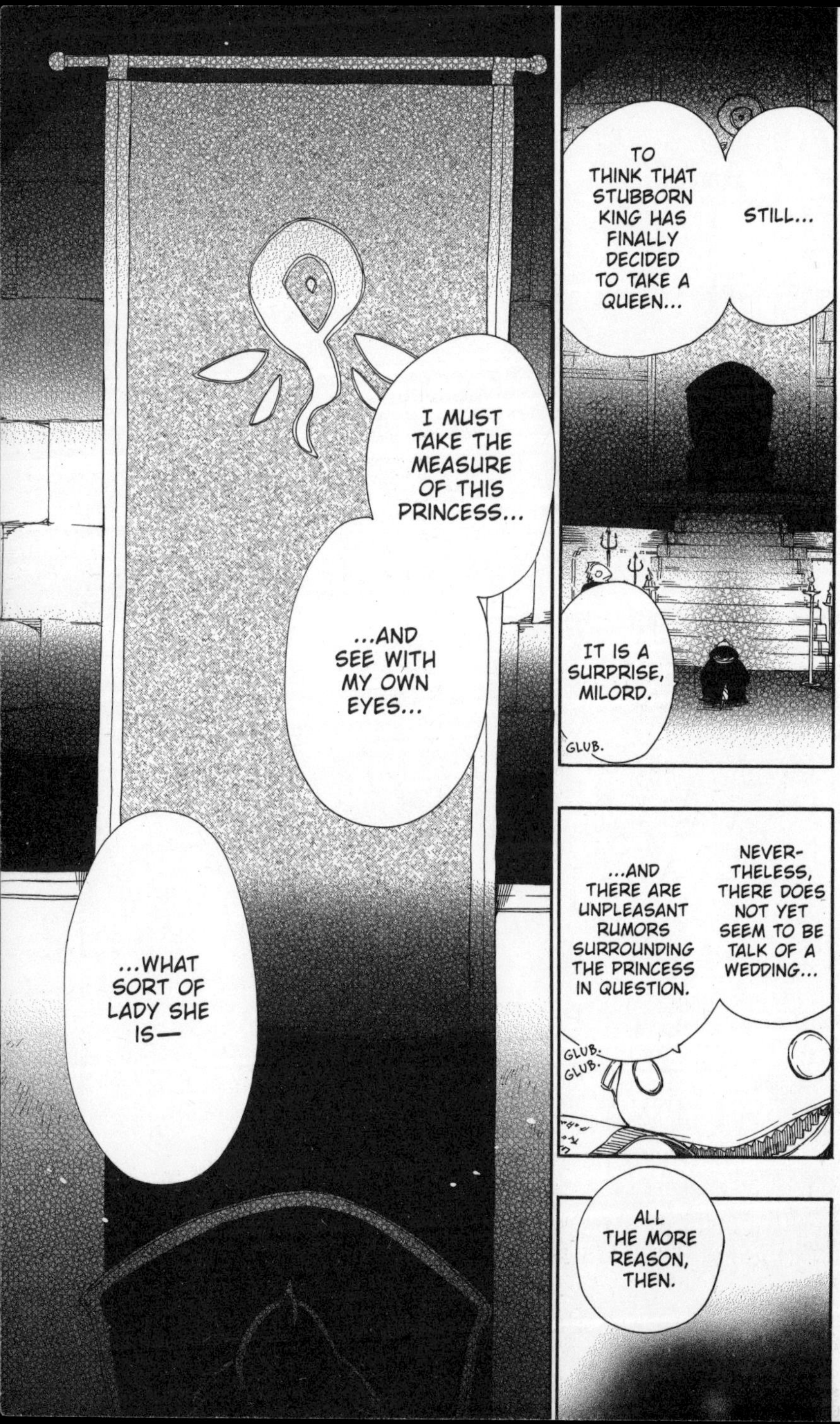
STILL...
TO THINK THAT STUBBORN KING HAS FINALLY DECIDED TO TAKE A QUEEN...
IT IS A SURPRISE, MILORD.
GLUB.
NEVER-THELESS, THERE DOES NOT YET SEEM TO BE TALK OF A WEDDING...
...AND THERE ARE UNPLEASANT RUMORS SURROUNDING THE PRINCESS IN QUESTION.
GLUB. GLUB.
ALL THE MORE REASON, THEN.
I MUST TAKE THE MEASURE OF THIS PRINCESS...
...AND SEE WITH MY OWN EYES...
...WHAT SORT OF LADY SHE IS—

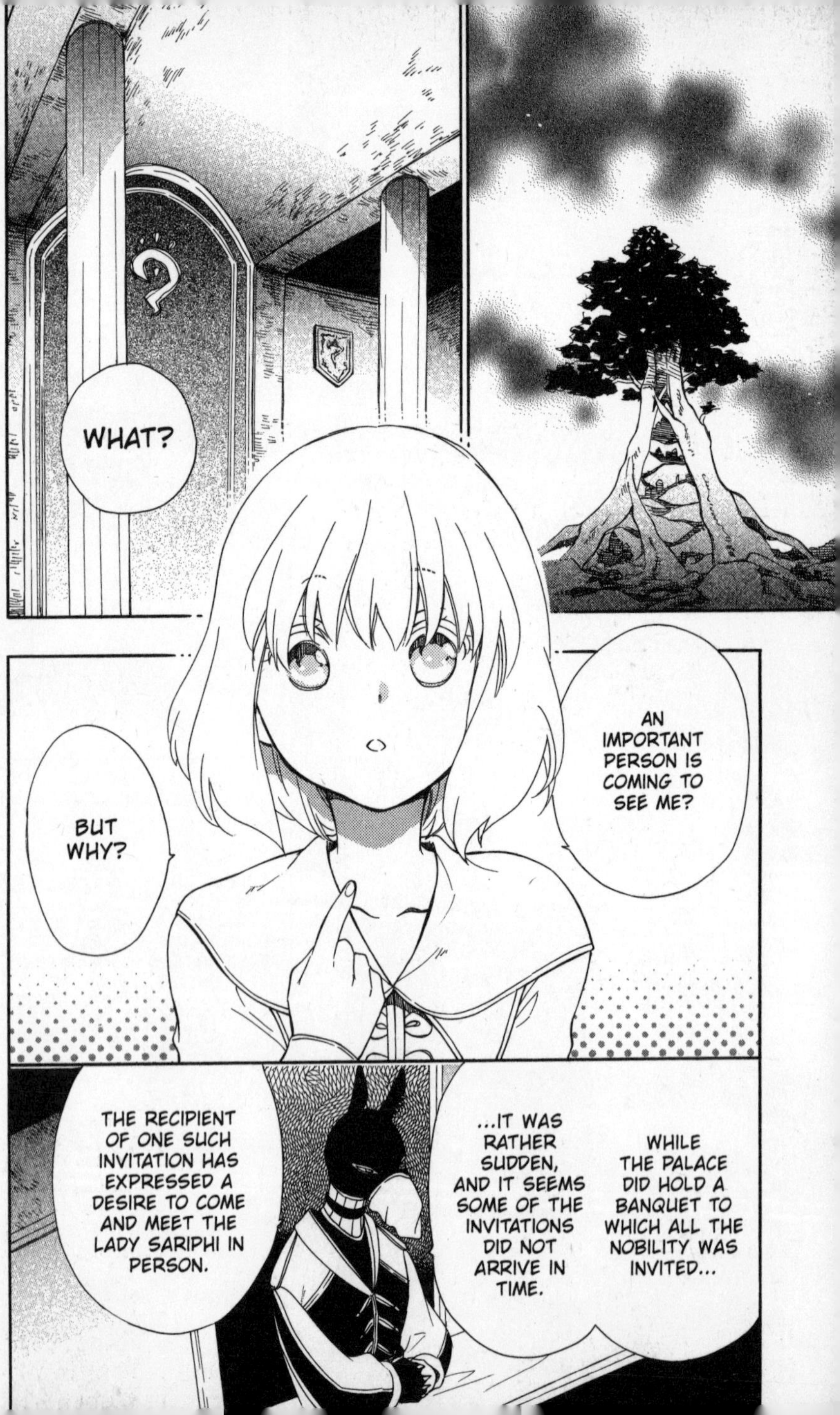
WHAT?
AN IMPORTANT PERSON IS COMING TO SEE ME?
BUT WHY?
WHILE THE PALACE DID HOLD A BANQUET TO WHICH ALL THE NOBILITY WAS INVITED...
...IT WAS RATHER SUDDEN, AND IT SEEMS SOME OF THE INVITATIONS DID NOT ARRIVE IN TIME.
THE RECIPIENT OF ONE SUCH INVITATION HAS EXPRESSED A DESIRE TO COME AND MEET THE LADY SARIPHI IN PERSON.

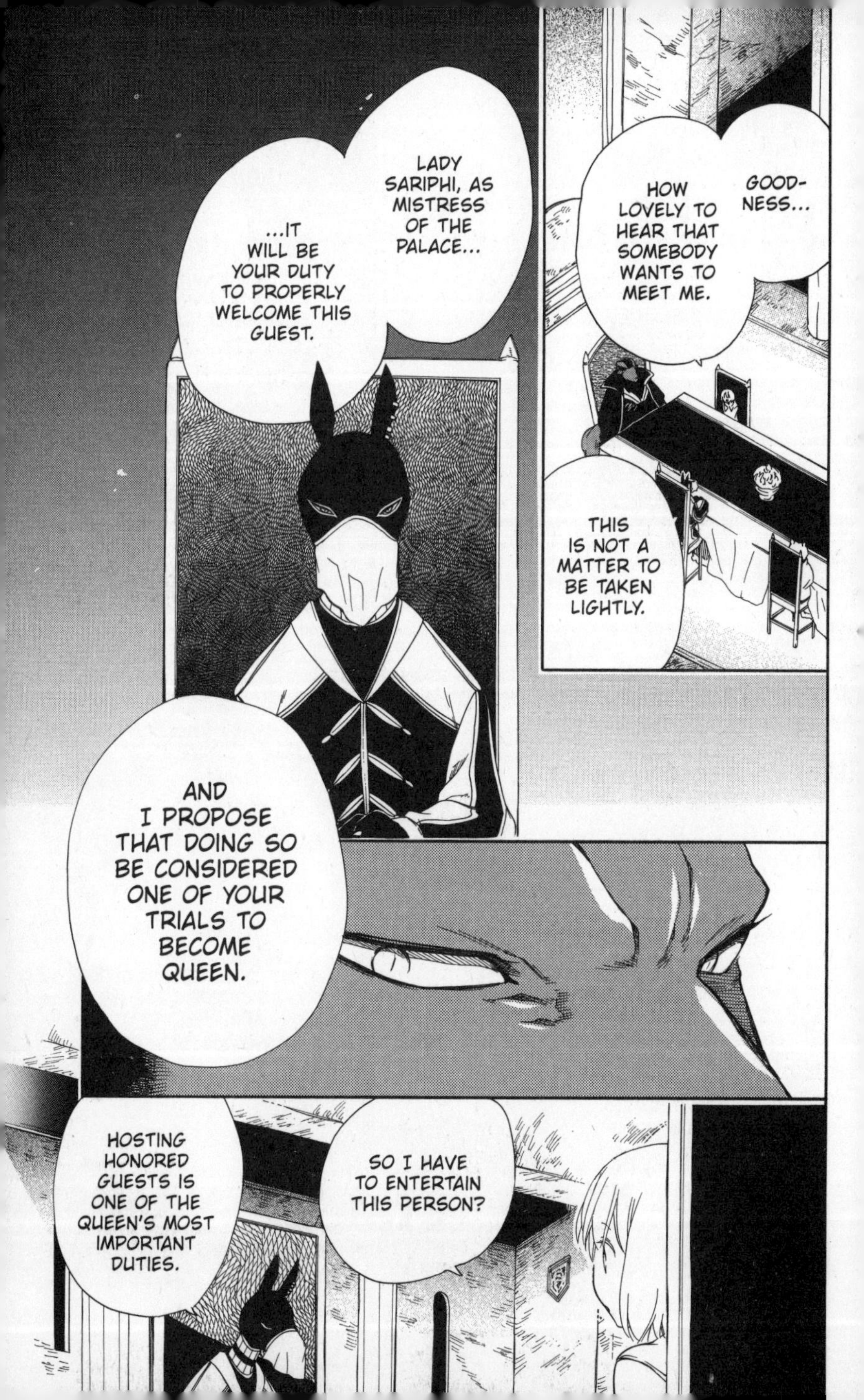
GOOD-NESS...
HOW LOVELY TO HEAR THAT SOMEBODY WANTS TO MEET ME.
THIS IS NOT A MATTER TO BE TAKEN LIGHTLY.
LADY SARIPHI, AS MISTRESS OF THE PALACE...
...IT WILL BE YOUR DUTY TO PROPERLY WELCOME THIS GUEST.
AND I PROPOSE THAT DOING SO BE CONSIDERED ONE OF YOUR TRIALS TO BECOME QUEEN.
SO I HAVE TO ENTERTAIN THIS PERSON?
HOSTING HONORED GUESTS IS ONE OF THE QUEEN'S MOST IMPORTANT DUTIES.

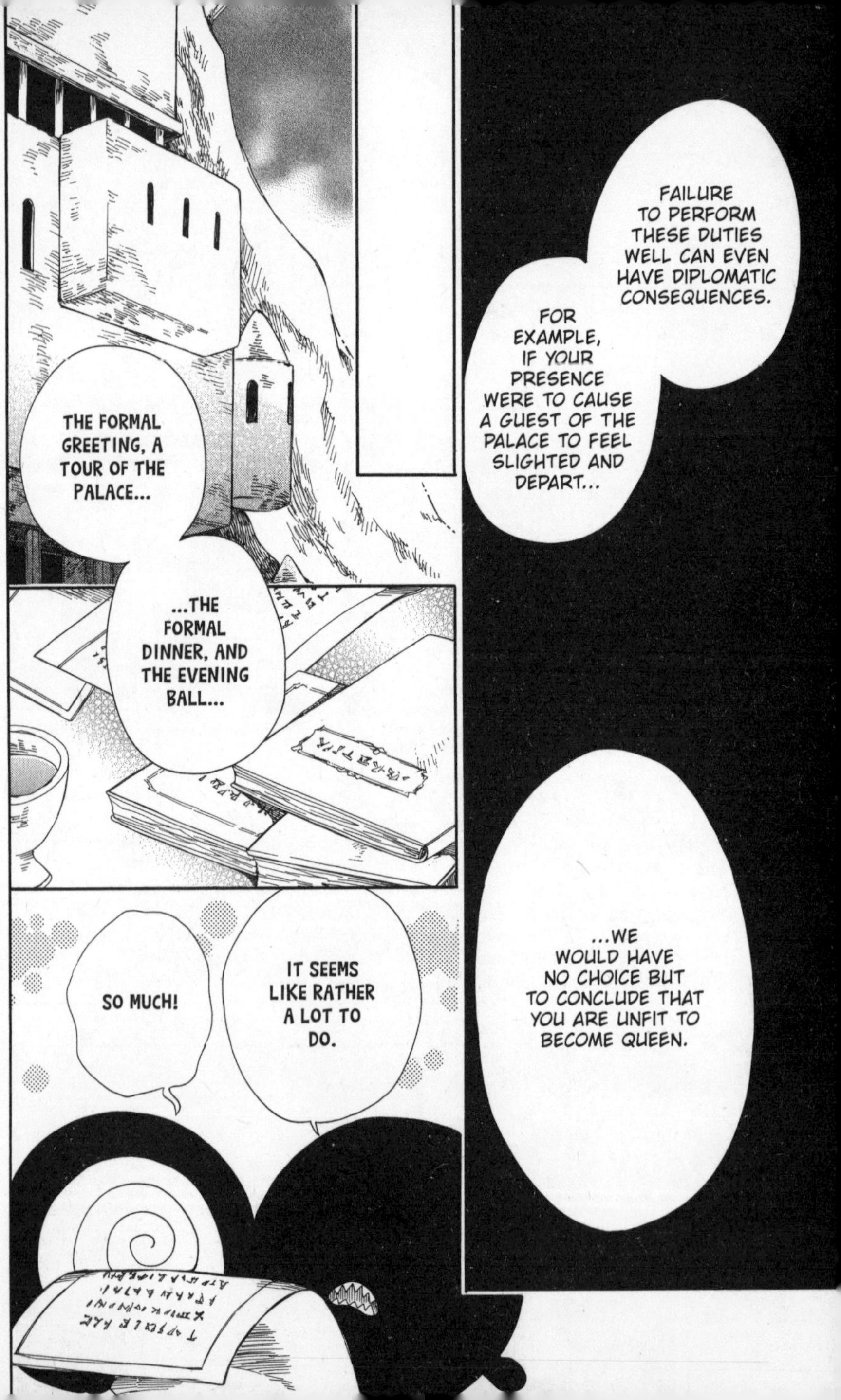
FAILURE TO PERFORM THESE DUTIES WELL CAN EVEN HAVE DIPLOMATIC CONSEQUENCES.
FOR EXAMPLE, IF YOUR PRESENCE WERE TO CAUSE A GUEST OF THE PALACE TO FEEL SLIGHTED AND DEPART...
...WE WOULD HAVE NO CHOICE BUT TO CONCLUDE THAT YOU ARE UNFIT TO BECOME QUEEN.
THE FORMAL GREETING, A TOUR OF THE PALACE...
...THE FORMAL DINNER, AND THE EVENING BALL...
IT SEEMS LIKE RATHER A LOT TO DO.
SO MUCH!

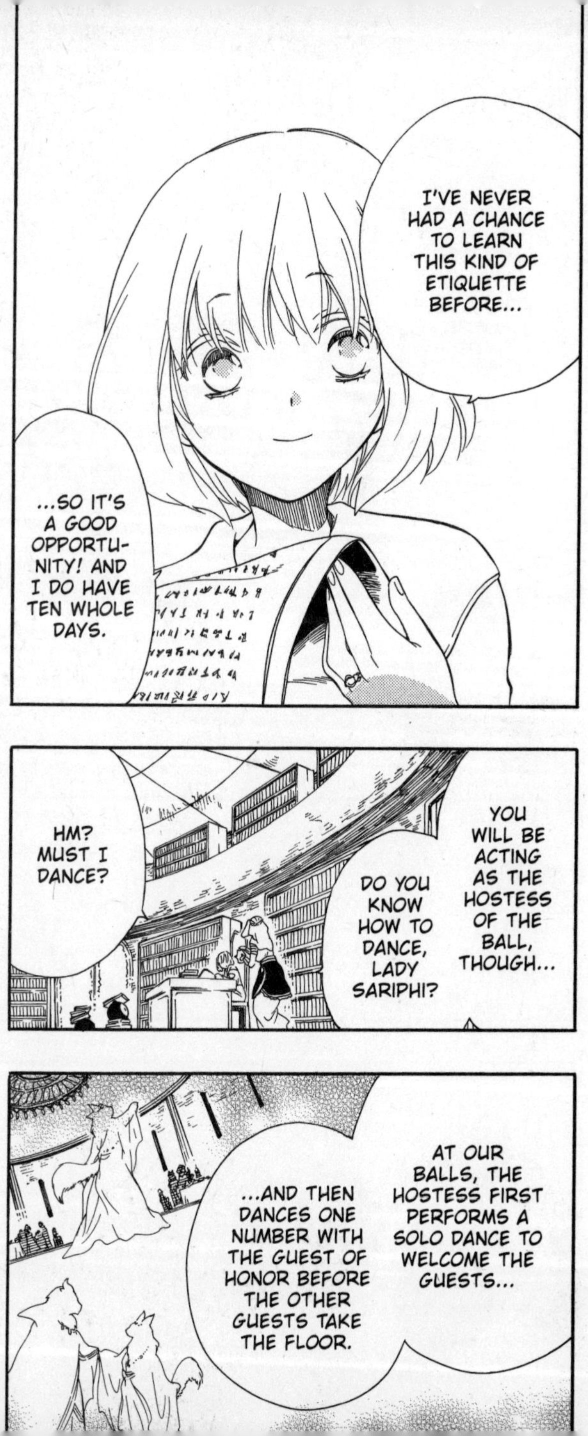
I'VE NEVER HAD A CHANCE TO LEARN THIS KIND OF ETIQUETTE BEFORE...
...SO IT'S A GOOD OPPORTU-NITY! AND I DO HAVE TEN WHOLE DAYS.
YOU WILL BE ACTING AS THE HOSTESS OF THE BALL, THOUGH...
DO YOU KNOW HOW TO DANCE, LADY SARIPHI?
HM? MUST I DANCE?
AT OUR BALLS, THE HOSTESS FIRST PERFORMS A SOLO DANCE TO WELCOME THE GUESTS...
...AND THEN DANCES ONE NUMBER WITH THE GUEST OF HONOR BEFORE THE OTHER GUESTS TAKE THE FLOOR.

QUICK & DIRTY DETAILS

SARIPHI

- ~FIFTEEN YEARS OLD
- ~153cm TALL (5')

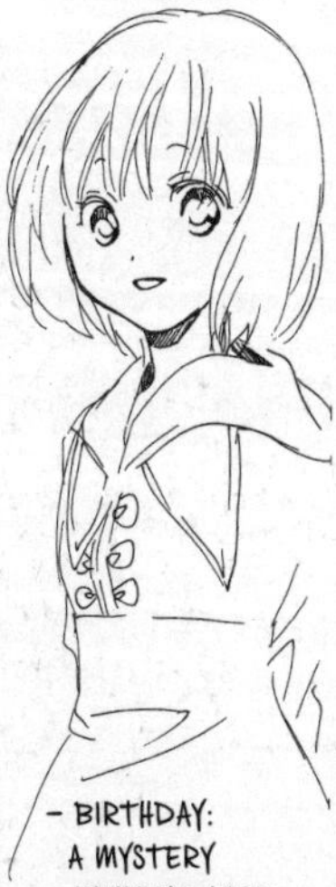

- BIRTHDAY: A MYSTERY
- FAVORITE FOOD: ANYTHING AS LONG AS IT'S TASTY

CY & CLOPS

- ABOUT 20cm IN DIAMETER (8")

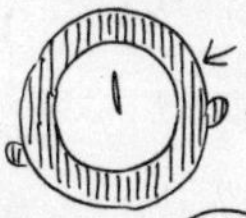

VISUAL ACUITY: 20/20

BILINGUAL IN BEASTKIND AND HUMAN TONGUES

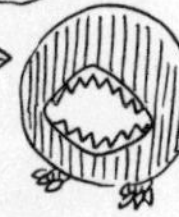

- LIKES: KINDESS
- DISLIKES: MEANNESS

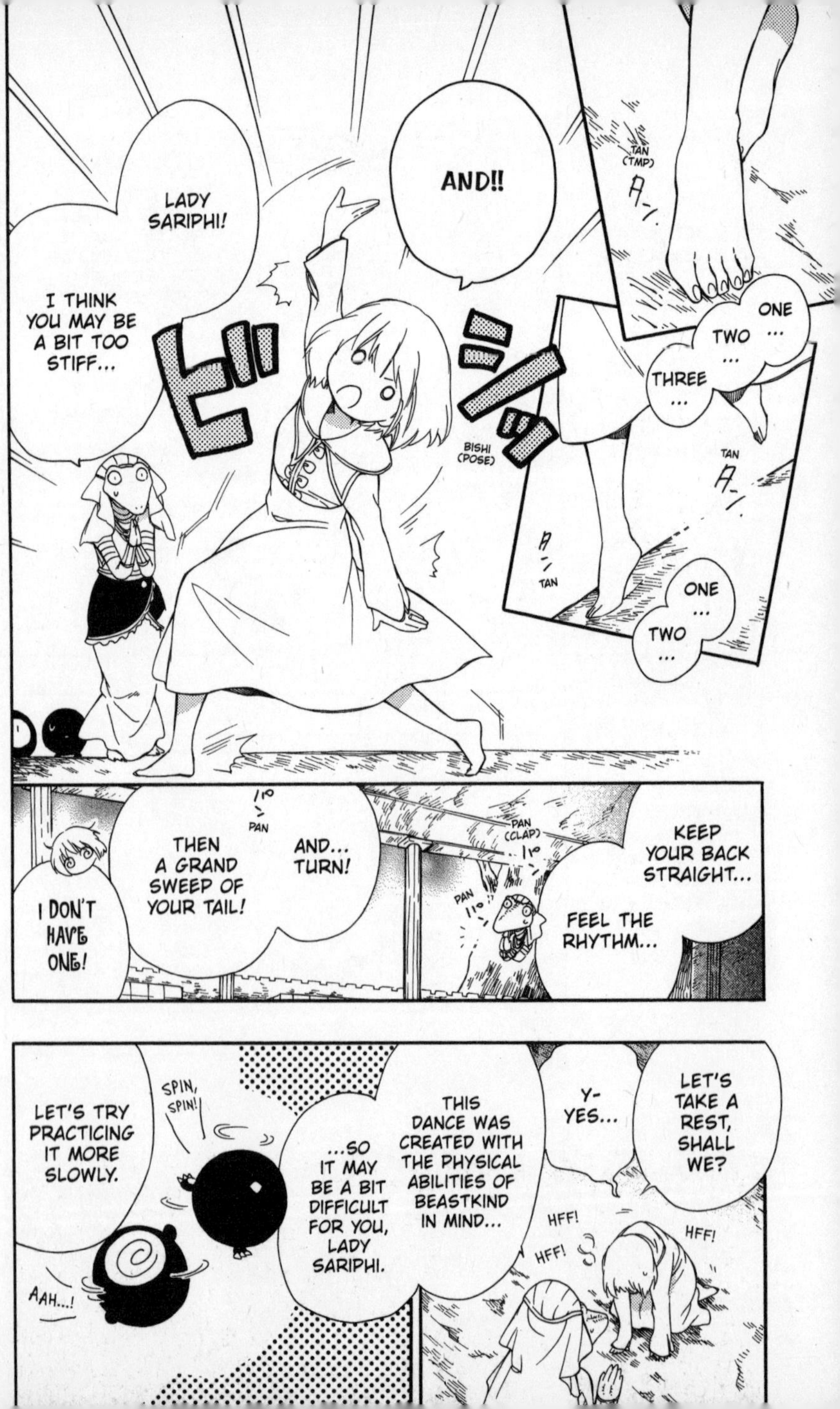
TAN (TMP)
ONE… TWO… THREE…
TAN
TAN
ONE… TWO…
AND!!
BISHI (POSE)
LADY SARIPHI!
I THINK YOU MAY BE A BIT TOO STIFF…
KEEP YOUR BACK STRAIGHT…
FEEL THE RHYTHM…
PAN (CLAP)
PAN
PAN
AND… TURN!
THEN A GRAND SWEEP OF YOUR TAIL!
I DON'T HAVE ONE!
LET'S TAKE A REST, SHALL WE?
Y-YES…
HFF!
HFF!
HFF!
THIS DANCE WAS CREATED WITH THE PHYSICAL ABILITIES OF BEASTKIND IN MIND…
…SO IT MAY BE A BIT DIFFICULT FOR YOU, LADY SARIPHI.
SPIN, SPIN!
LET'S TRY PRACTICING IT MORE SLOWLY.
AAH…!

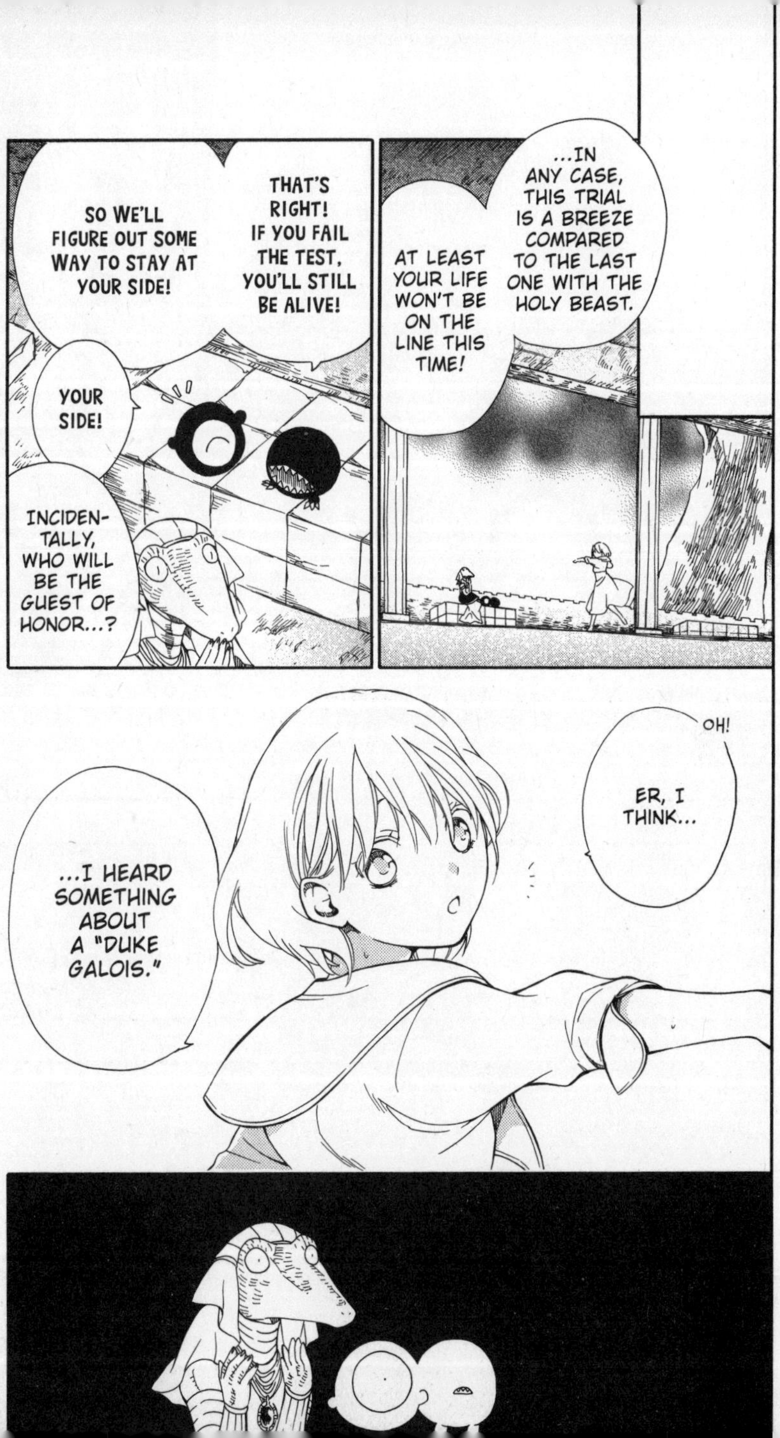
...IN ANY CASE, THIS TRIAL IS A BREEZE COMPARED TO THE LAST ONE WITH THE HOLY BEAST.
AT LEAST YOUR LIFE WON'T BE ON THE LINE THIS TIME!
THAT'S RIGHT! IF YOU FAIL THE TEST, YOU'LL STILL BE ALIVE!
SO WE'LL FIGURE OUT SOME WAY TO STAY AT YOUR SIDE!
YOUR SIDE!
INCIDEN-TALLY, WHO WILL BE THE GUEST OF HONOR...?
OH!
ER, I THINK...
...I HEARD SOMETHING ABOUT A "DUKE GALOIS."

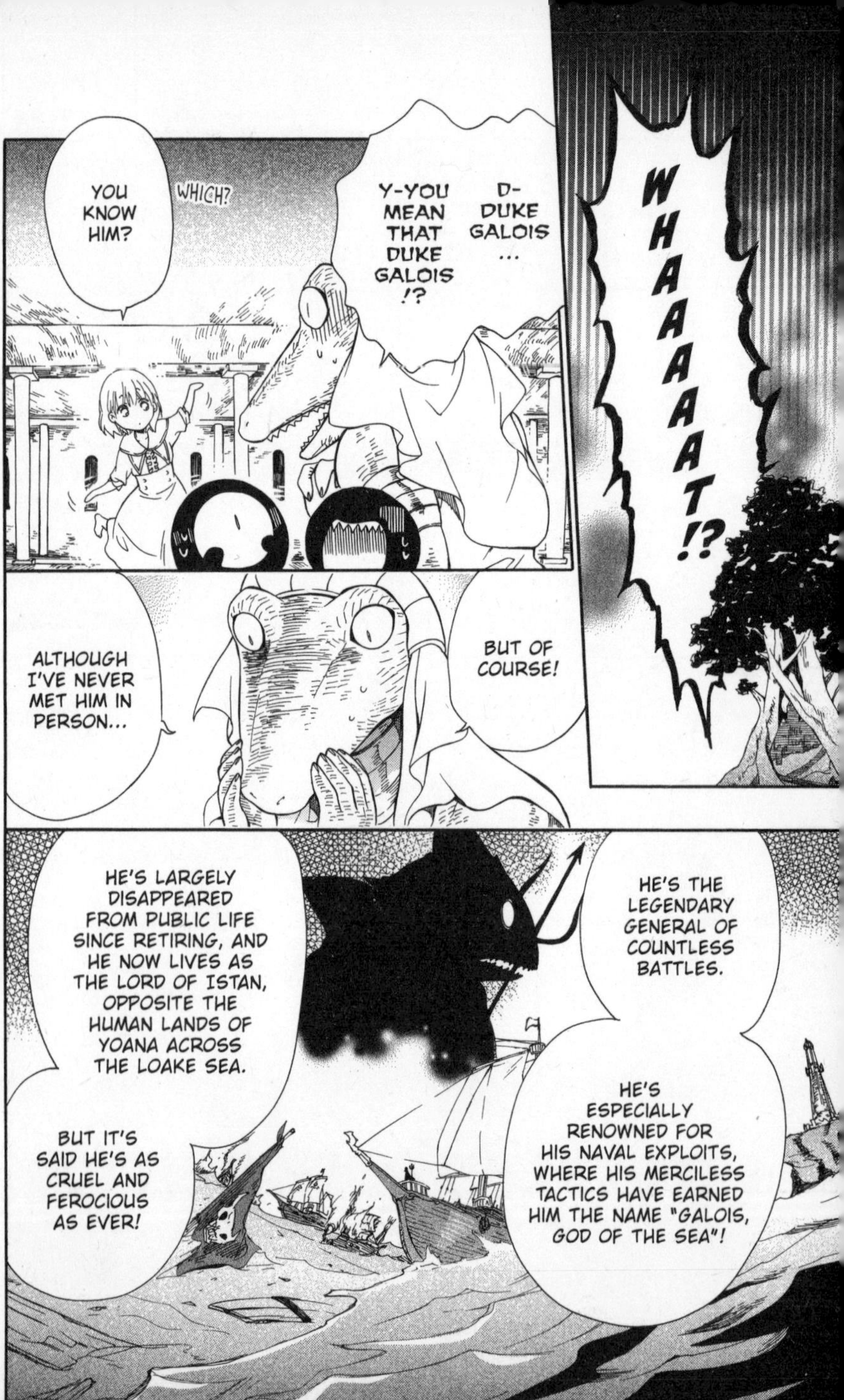
WHAAAAAAT!?
D-DUKE GALOIS ...
Y-YOU MEAN THAT DUKE GALOIS !?
WHICH?
YOU KNOW HIM?
BUT OF COURSE!
ALTHOUGH I'VE NEVER MET HIM IN PERSON...
HE'S THE LEGENDARY GENERAL OF COUNTLESS BATTLES.
HE'S LARGELY DISAPPEARED FROM PUBLIC LIFE SINCE RETIRING, AND HE NOW LIVES AS THE LORD OF ISTAN, OPPOSITE THE HUMAN LANDS OF YOANA ACROSS THE LOAKE SEA.
HE'S ESPECIALLY RENOWNED FOR HIS NAVAL EXPLOITS, WHERE HIS MERCILESS TACTICS HAVE EARNED HIM THE NAME "GALOIS, GOD OF THE SEA"!
BUT IT'S SAID HE'S AS CRUEL AND FEROCIOUS AS EVER!

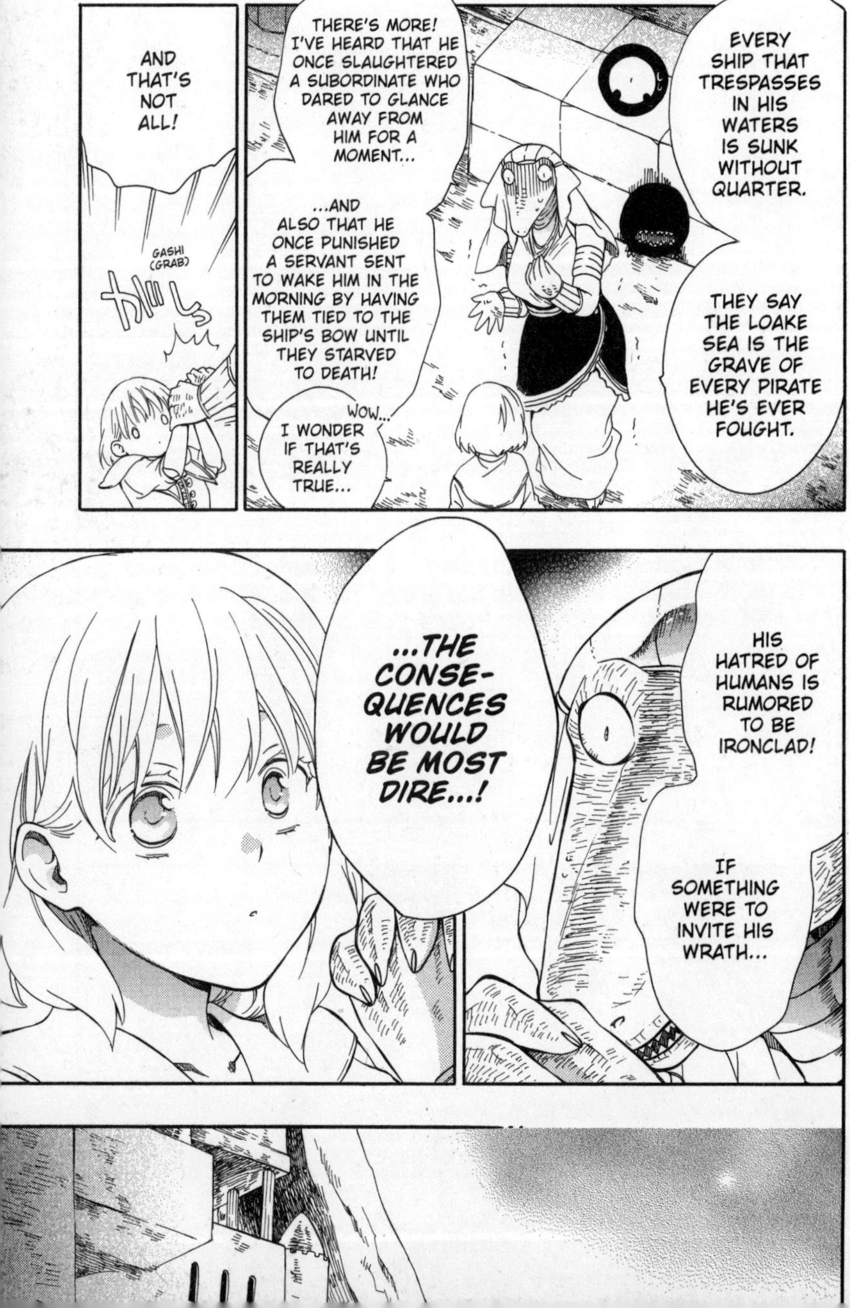
EVERY SHIP THAT TRESPASSES IN HIS WATERS IS SUNK WITHOUT QUARTER.
THEY SAY THE LOAKE SEA IS THE GRAVE OF EVERY PIRATE HE'S EVER FOUGHT.
THERE'S MORE! I'VE HEARD THAT HE ONCE SLAUGHTERED A SUBORDINATE WHO DARED TO GLANCE AWAY FROM HIM FOR A MOMENT...
...AND ALSO THAT HE ONCE PUNISHED A SERVANT SENT TO WAKE HIM IN THE MORNING BY HAVING THEM TIED TO THE SHIP'S BOW UNTIL THEY STARVED TO DEATH!
WOW... I WONDER IF THAT'S REALLY TRUE...
AND THAT'S NOT ALL!
がしっ
GASHI (GRAB)
HIS HATRED OF HUMANS IS RUMORED TO BE IRONCLAD!
IF SOMETHING WERE TO INVITE HIS WRATH...
...THE CONSEQUENCES WOULD BE MOST DIRE...!

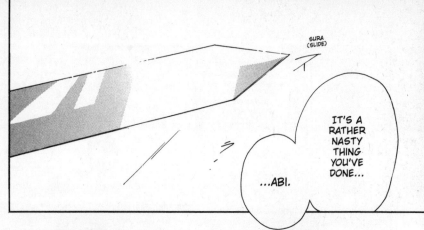

SURA (SLIDE)
IT'S A RATHER NASTY THING YOU'VE DONE...
...ABI.
COAXING THE NOTORIOUSLY PRICKLY DUKE GALOIS HERE...
...TO USE IN YOUR TRIALS FOR THE WOULD-BE QUEEN...
IT WAS DUKE GALOIS WHO REQUESTED A VISIT TO THE PALACE.
I HAD NO HAND IN THIS.
BUT YOU DO REALIZE YOU'RE ESSENTIALLY ASKING THE HUMAN PRINCESS TO COMMIT A BLUNDER...
...AT A FORMAL BALL THAT MUST BE THROWN WITH THE UTMOST OF CARE TO PROPERLY WELCOME SUCH A GUEST?

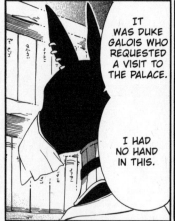

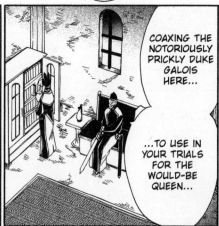

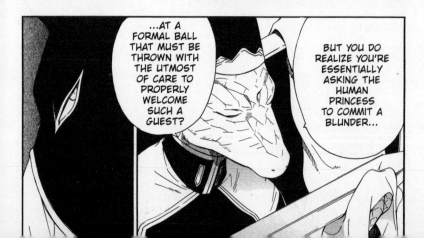

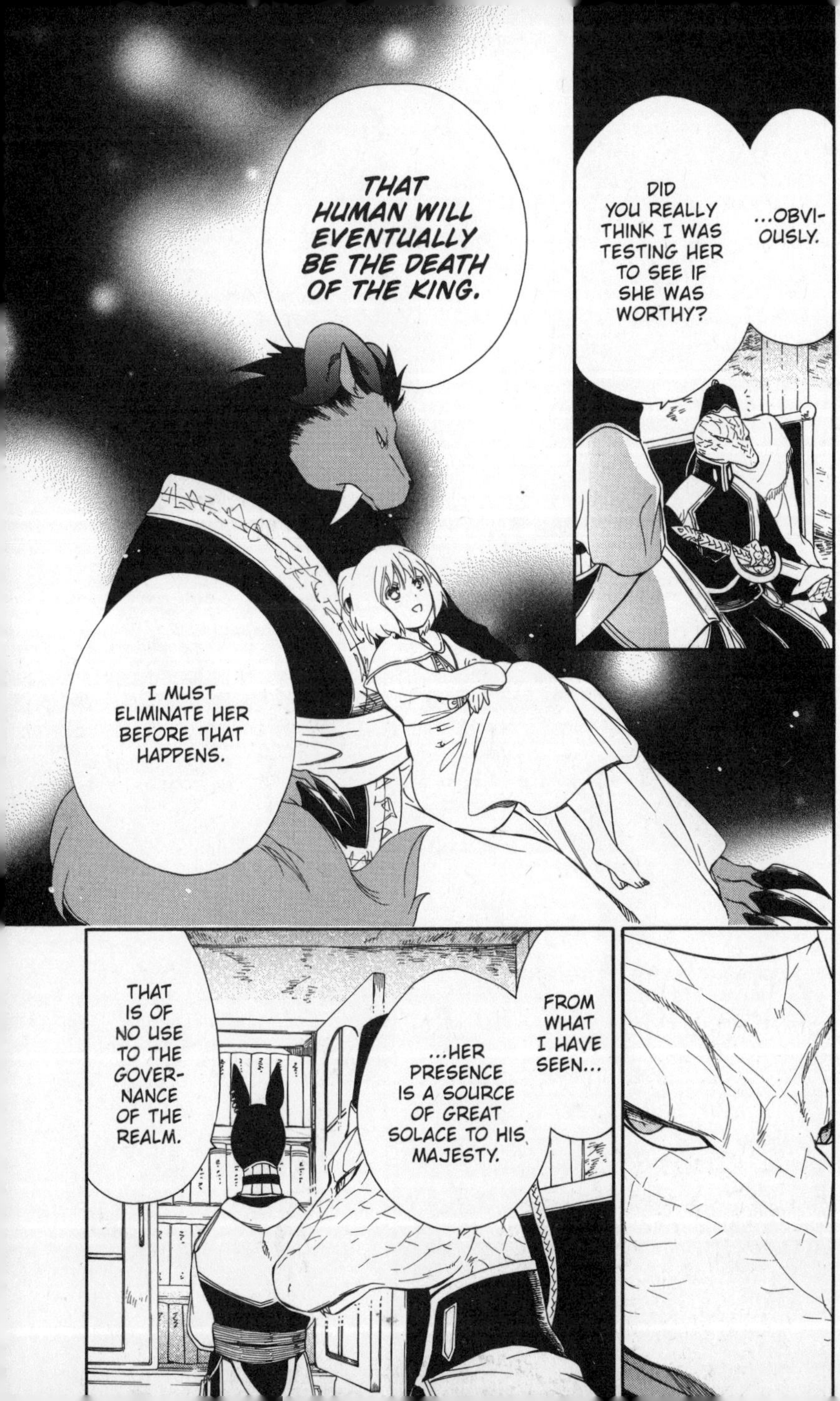
...OBVI-OUSLY.
DID YOU REALLY THINK I WAS TESTING HER TO SEE IF SHE WAS WORTHY?
THAT HUMAN WILL EVENTUALLY BE THE DEATH OF THE KING.
I MUST ELIMINATE HER BEFORE THAT HAPPENS.
FROM WHAT I HAVE SEEN...
...HER PRESENCE IS A SOURCE OF GREAT SOLACE TO HIS MAJESTY.
THAT IS OF NO USE TO THE GOVER-NANCE OF THE REALM.

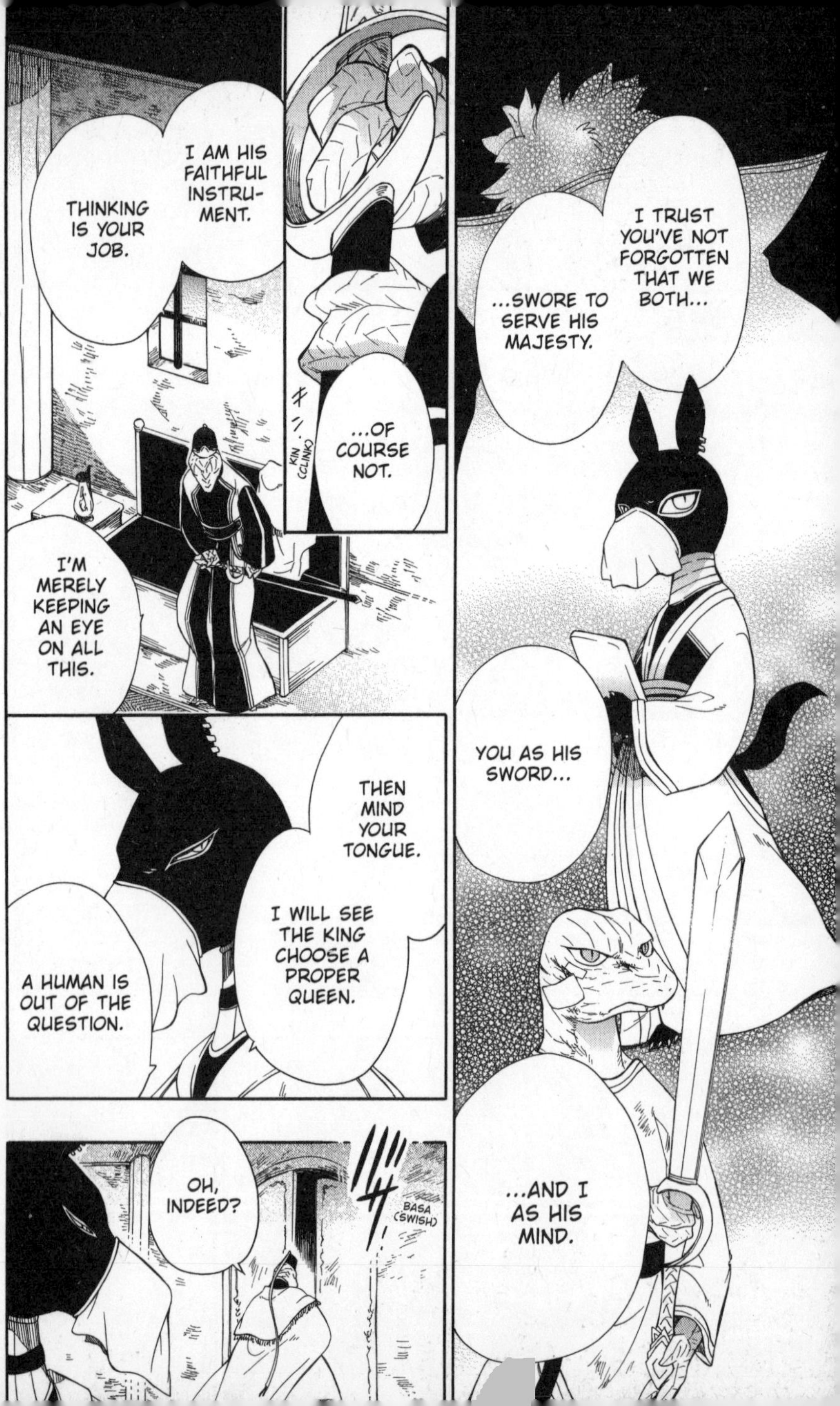
I TRUST YOU'VE NOT FORGOTTEN THAT WE BOTH...
...SWORE TO SERVE HIS MAJESTY.
YOU AS HIS SWORD...
...AND I AS HIS MIND.
KIN (CLINK)
...OF COURSE NOT.
I AM HIS FAITHFUL INSTRU-MENT.
THINKING IS YOUR JOB.
I'M MERELY KEEPING AN EYE ON ALL THIS.
THEN MIND YOUR TONGUE.
I WILL SEE THE KING CHOOSE A PROPER QUEEN.
A HUMAN IS OUT OF THE QUESTION.
BASA (SWISH)
OH, INDEED?

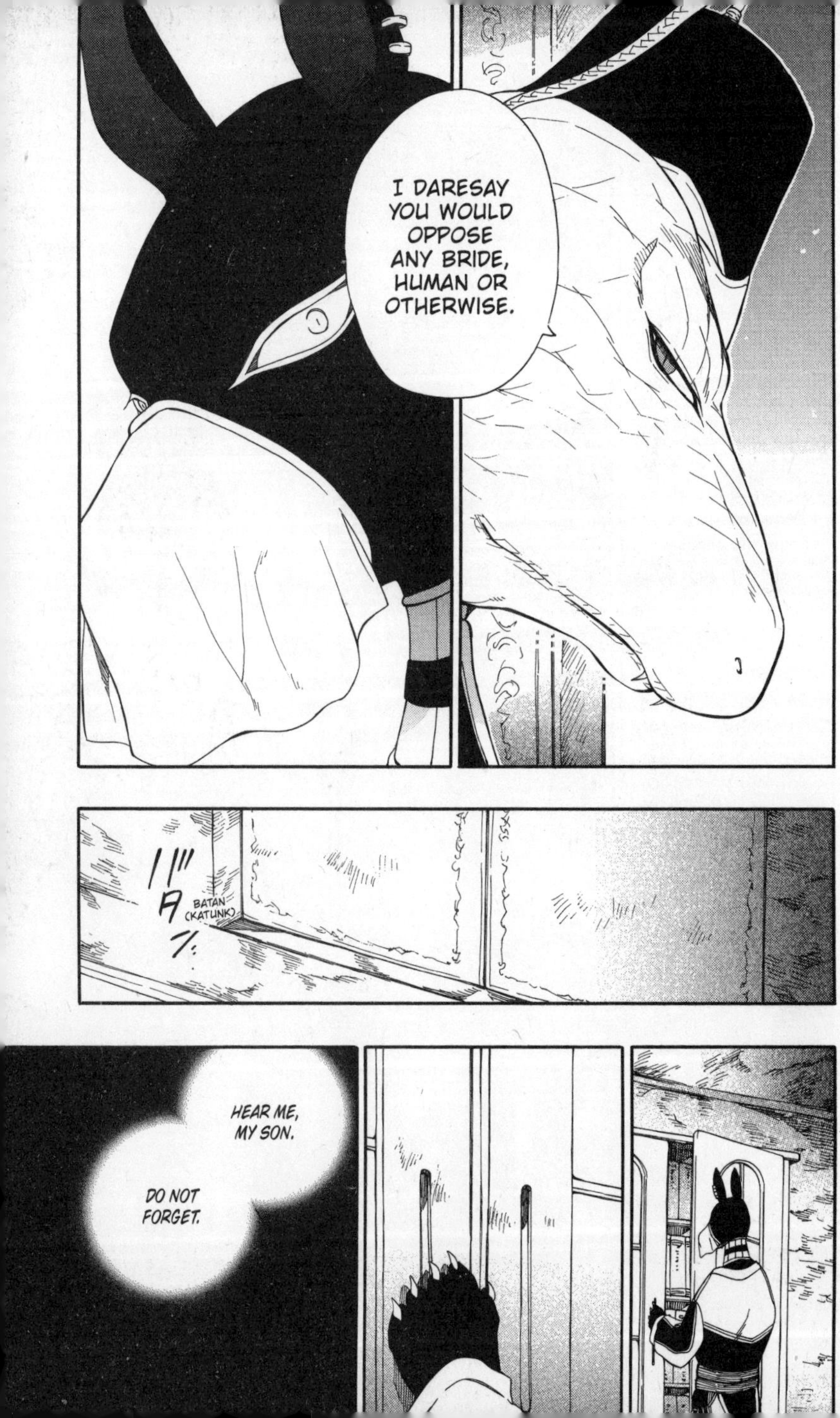
I DARESAY YOU WOULD OPPOSE ANY BRIDE, HUMAN OR OTHERWISE.
BATAN (KATUNK)
HEAR ME, MY SON.
DO NOT FORGET.

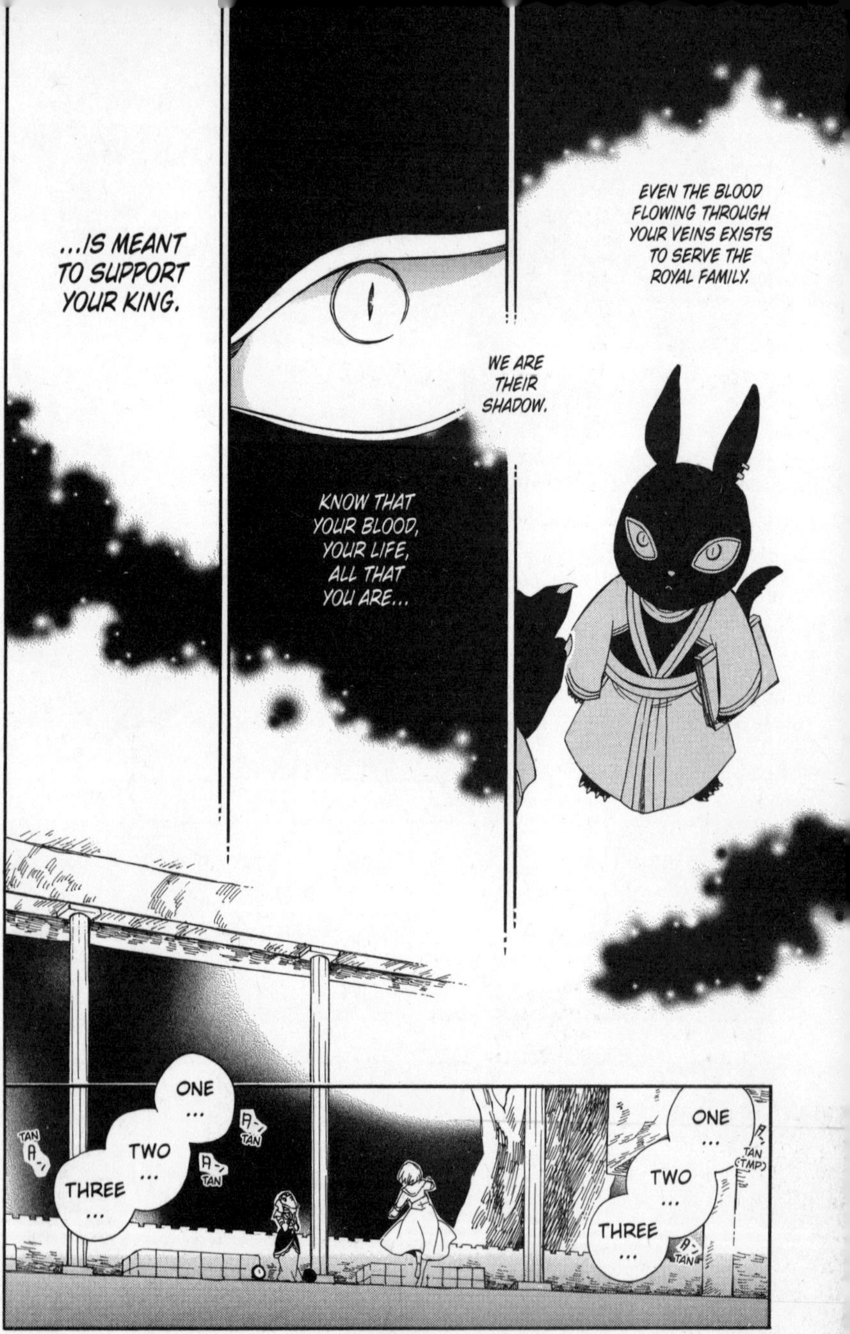
EVEN THE BLOOD FLOWING THROUGH YOUR VEINS EXISTS TO SERVE THE ROYAL FAMILY.
WE ARE THEIR SHADOW.
KNOW THAT YOUR BLOOD, YOUR LIFE, ALL THAT YOU ARE...
...IS MEANT TO SUPPORT YOUR KING.
ONE ...
TAN (TMP)
TWO ...
THREE ...
TAN
ONE ...
TAN
TWO ...
TAN
THREE ...
TAN

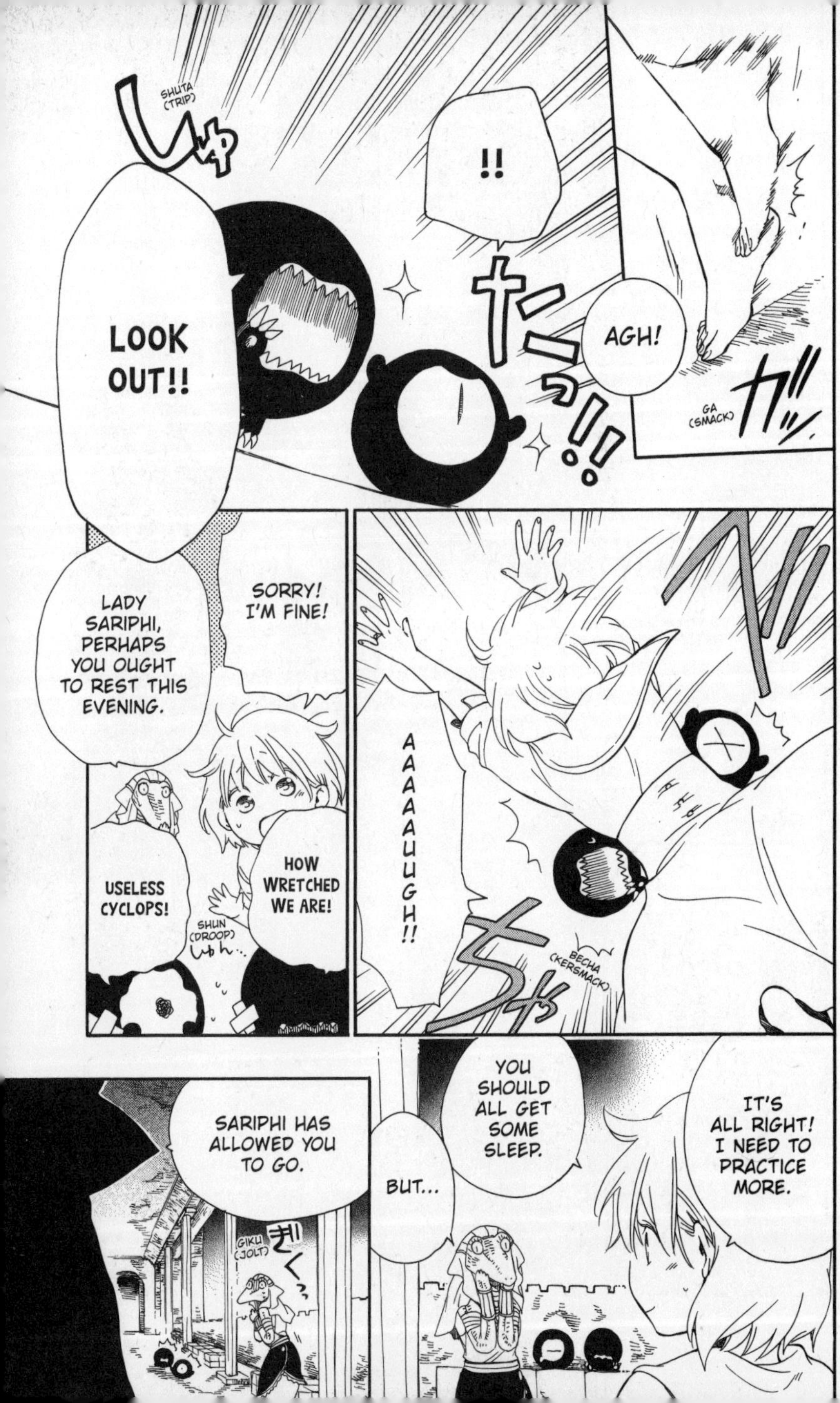

GA (SMACK)
AGH!
!!
SHUTA (TRIP)
LOOK OUT!!
AAAAAUGH!!
BECHA (KERSMACK)
SORRY! I'M FINE!
LADY SARIPHI, PERHAPS YOU OUGHT TO REST THIS EVENING.
HOW WRETCHED WE ARE!
USELESS CYCLOPS!
SHUN (DROOP)
IT'S ALL RIGHT! I NEED TO PRACTICE MORE.
YOU SHOULD ALL GET SOME SLEEP.
BUT...
SARIPHI HAS ALLOWED YOU TO GO.
GIKU (JOLT)

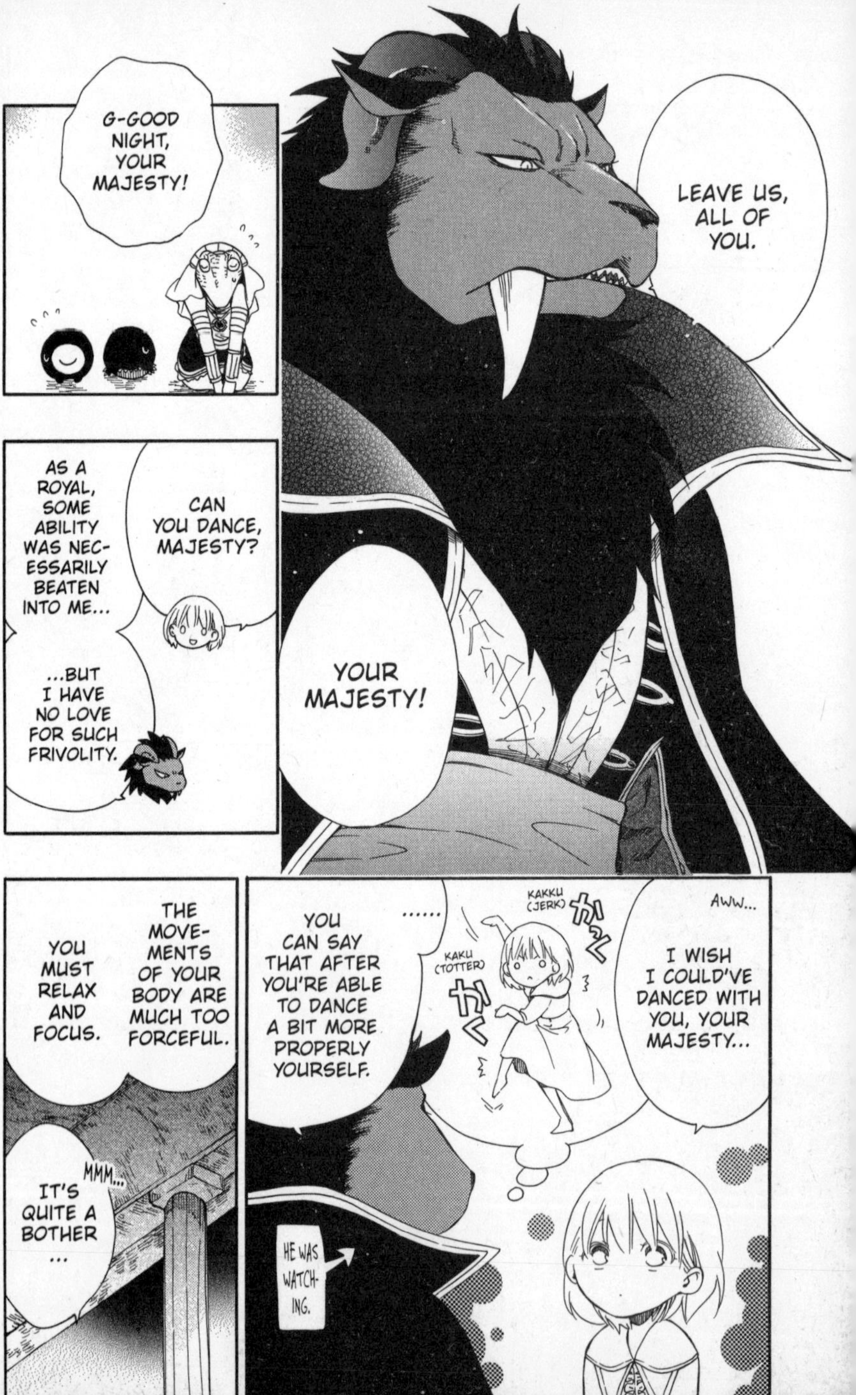
LEAVE US, ALL OF YOU.
YOUR MAJESTY!
G-GOOD NIGHT, YOUR MAJESTY!
CAN YOU DANCE, MAJESTY?
AS A ROYAL, SOME ABILITY WAS NECESSARILY BEATEN INTO ME...
...BUT I HAVE NO LOVE FOR SUCH FRIVOLITY.
AWW...
I WISH I COULD'VE DANCED WITH YOU, YOUR MAJESTY...
かっく
KAKKU (JERK)
かく
KAKU (TOTTER)
......
YOU CAN SAY THAT AFTER YOU'RE ABLE TO DANCE A BIT MORE PROPERLY YOURSELF.
HE WAS WATCHING.
THE MOVEMENTS OF YOUR BODY ARE MUCH TOO FORCEFUL.
YOU MUST RELAX AND FOCUS.
MMM...
IT'S QUITE A BOTHER ...

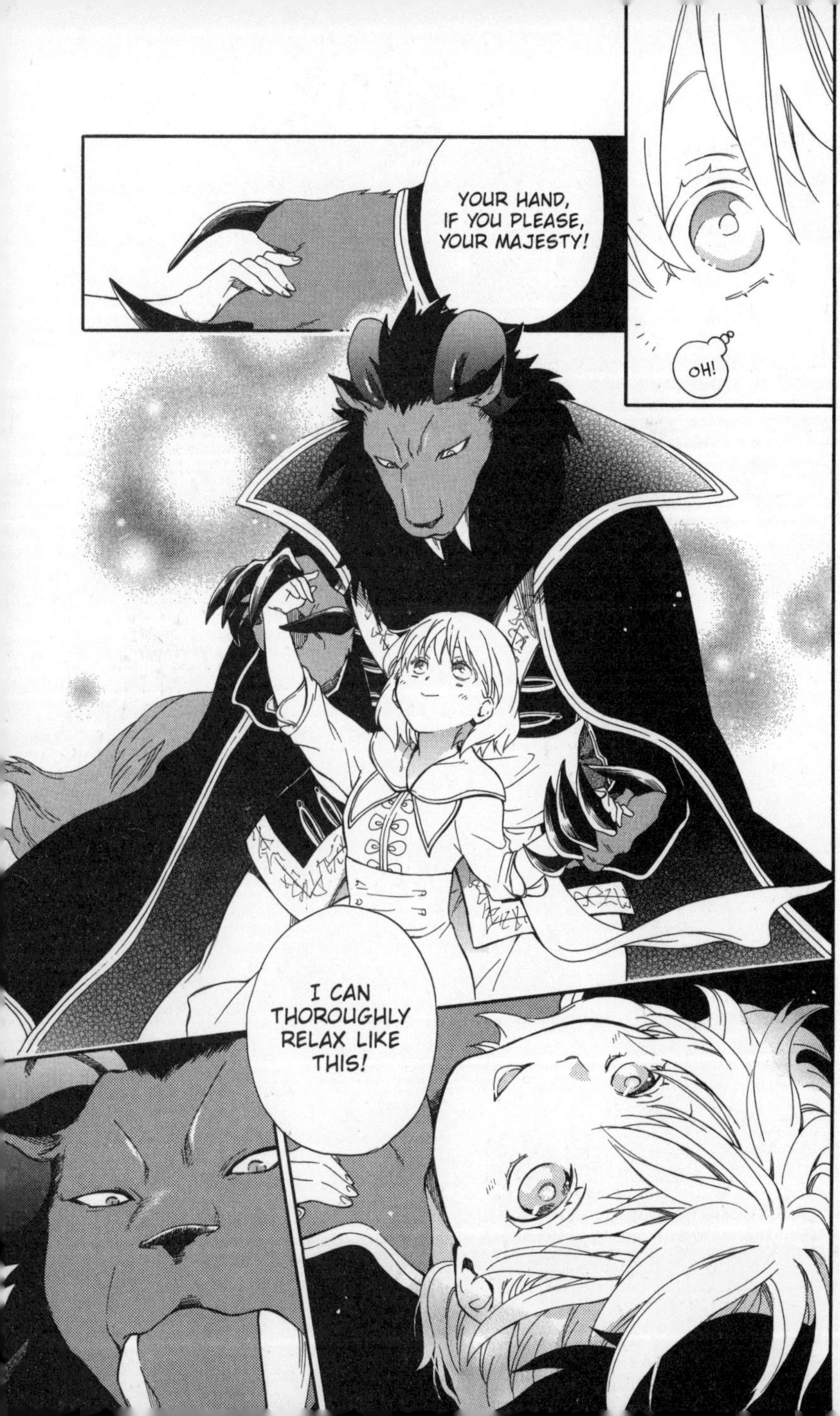
OH!
YOUR HAND, IF YOU PLEASE, YOUR MAJESTY!
I CAN THOROUGHLY RELAX LIKE THIS!

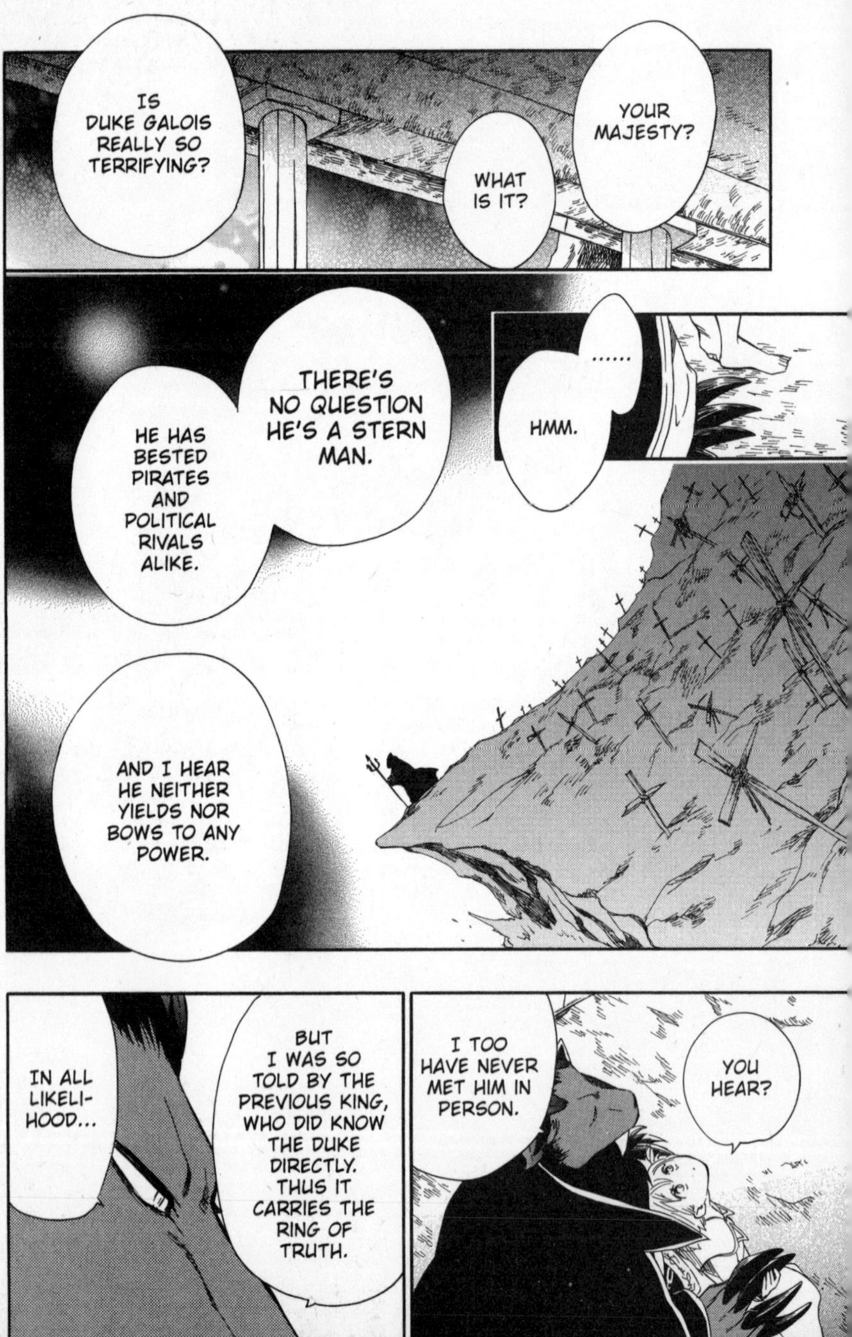
YOUR MAJESTY?
WHAT IS IT?
IS DUKE GALOIS REALLY SO TERRIFYING?
......
HMM.
THERE'S NO QUESTION HE'S A STERN MAN.
HE HAS BESTED PIRATES AND POLITICAL RIVALS ALIKE.
AND I HEAR HE NEITHER YIELDS NOR BOWS TO ANY POWER.
YOU HEAR?
I TOO HAVE NEVER MET HIM IN PERSON.
BUT I WAS SO TOLD BY THE PREVIOUS KING, WHO DID KNOW THE DUKE DIRECTLY. THUS IT CARRIES THE RING OF TRUTH.
IN ALL LIKELI-HOOD...

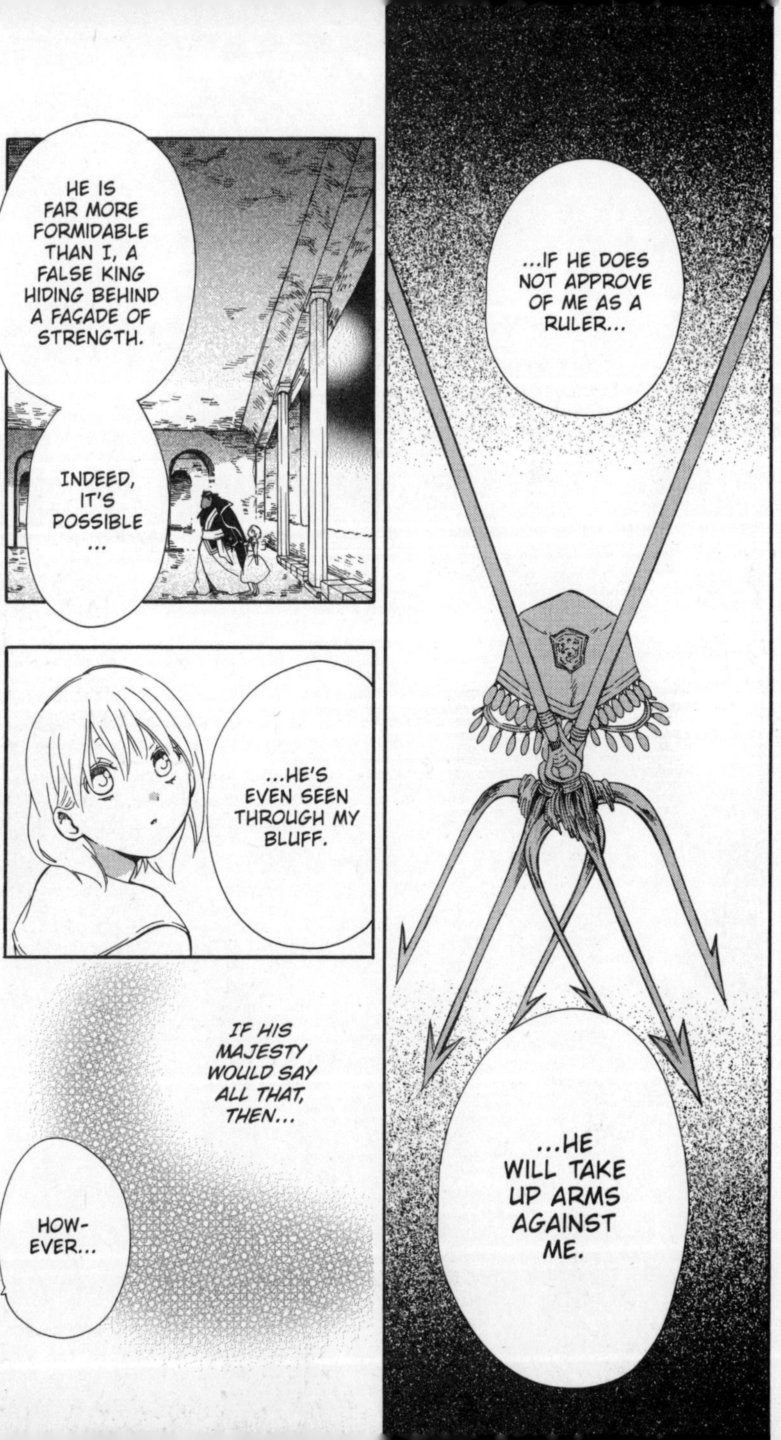

...IF HE DOES NOT APPROVE OF ME AS A RULER...
...HE WILL TAKE UP ARMS AGAINST ME.
HE IS FAR MORE FORMIDABLE THAN I, A FALSE KING HIDING BEHIND A FAÇADE OF STRENGTH.
INDEED, IT'S POSSIBLE...
...HE'S EVEN SEEN THROUGH MY BLUFF.
IF HIS MAJESTY WOULD SAY ALL THAT, THEN...
HOW-EVER...

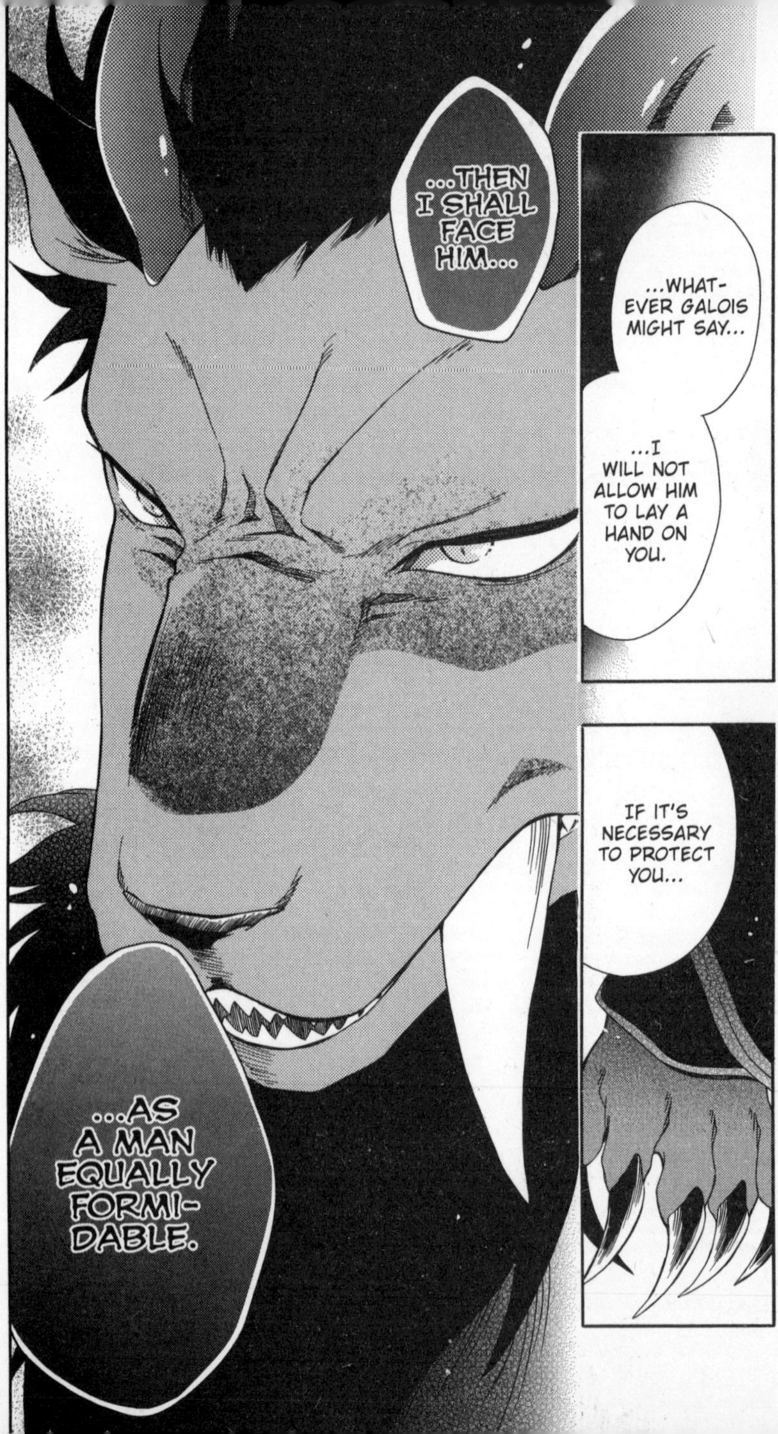
...WHAT-EVER GALOIS MIGHT SAY...
...I WILL NOT ALLOW HIM TO LAY A HAND ON YOU.
IF IT'S NECESSARY TO PROTECT YOU...
...THEN I SHALL FACE HIM...
...AS A MAN EQUALLY FORMI-DABLE.

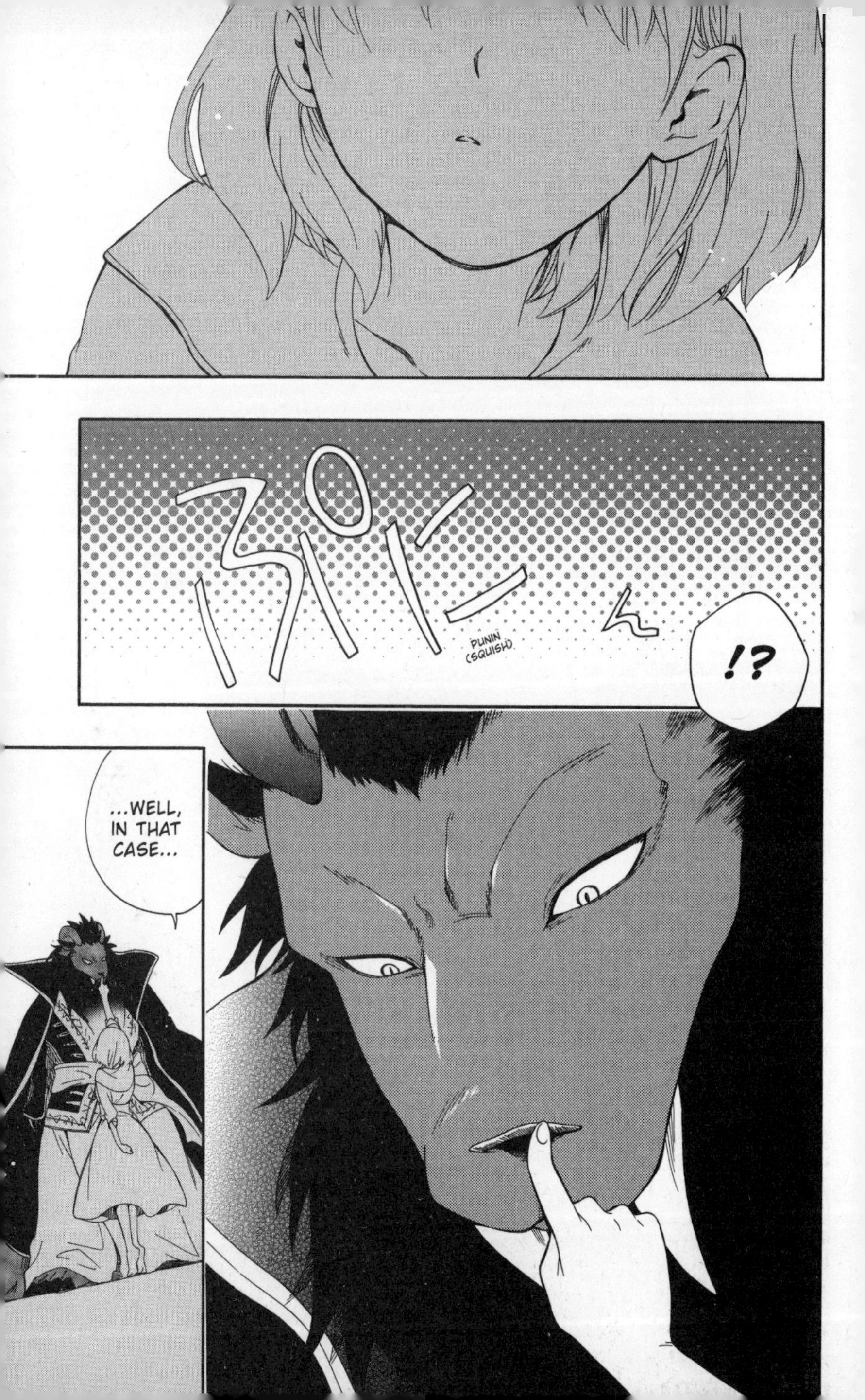
ぷにーん
PUNIN (SQUISH)
!?
...WELL, IN THAT CASE...

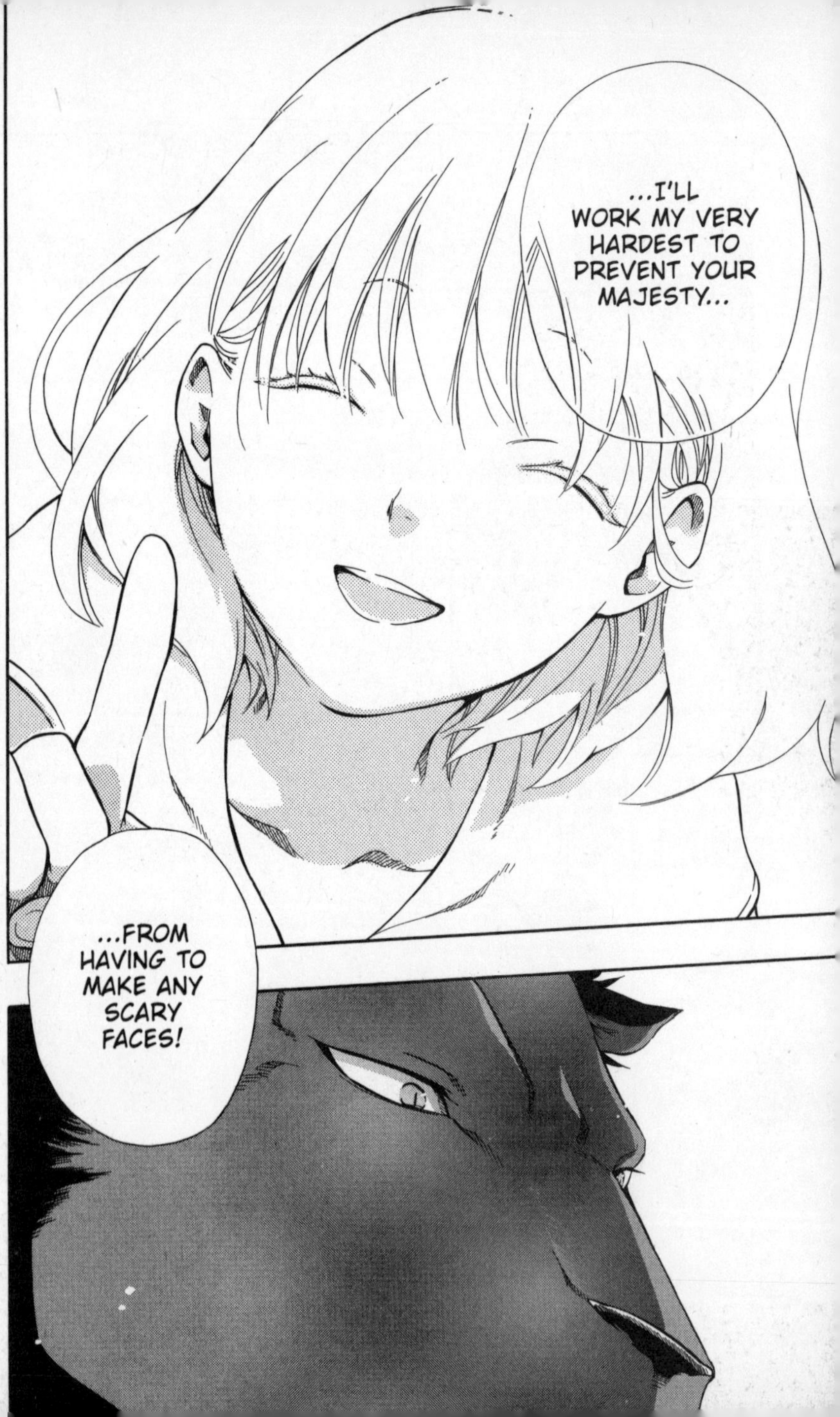
...I'LL WORK MY VERY HARDEST TO PREVENT YOUR MAJESTY...
...FROM HAVING TO MAKE ANY SCARY FACES!

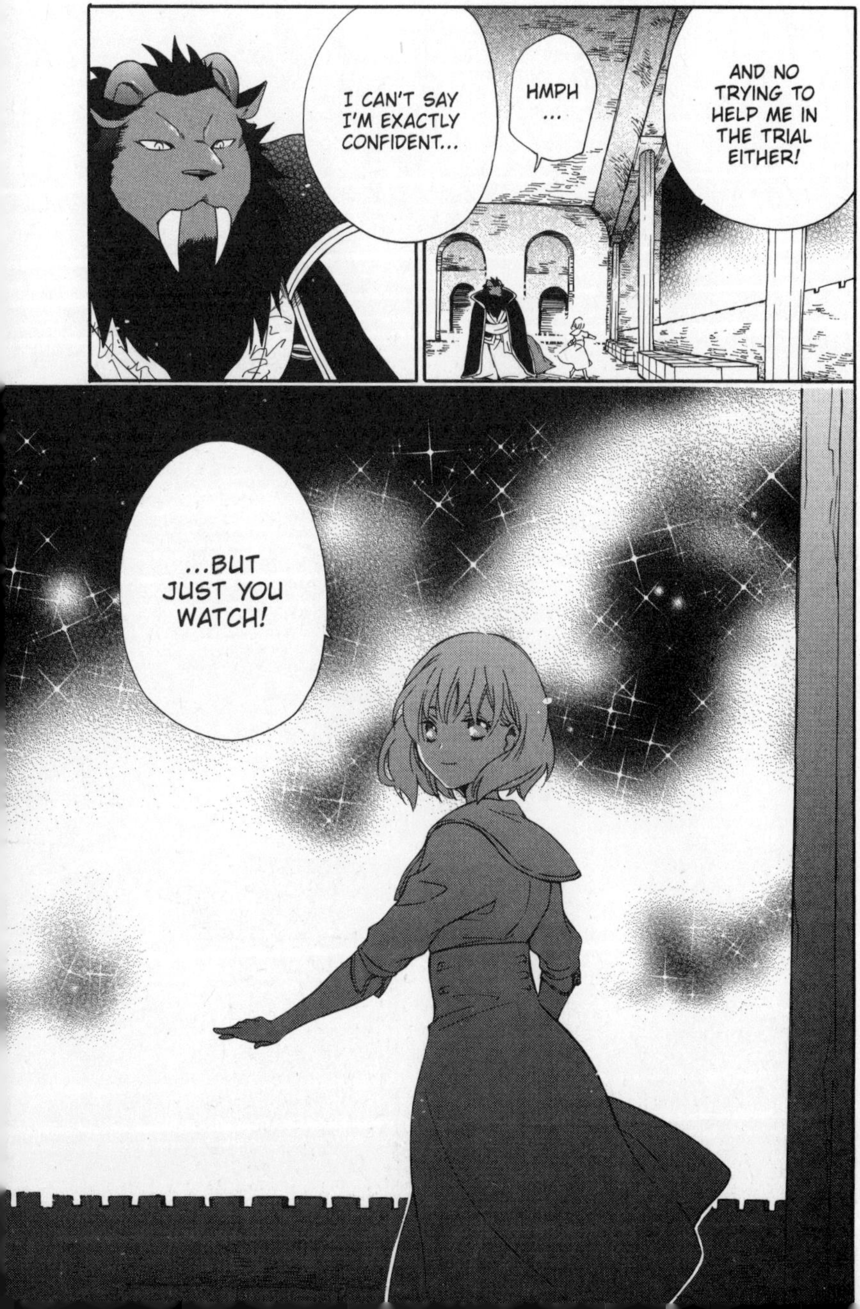
AND NO TRYING TO HELP ME IN THE TRIAL EITHER!
HMPH ...
I CAN'T SAY I'M EXACTLY CONFIDENT...
...BUT JUST YOU WATCH!

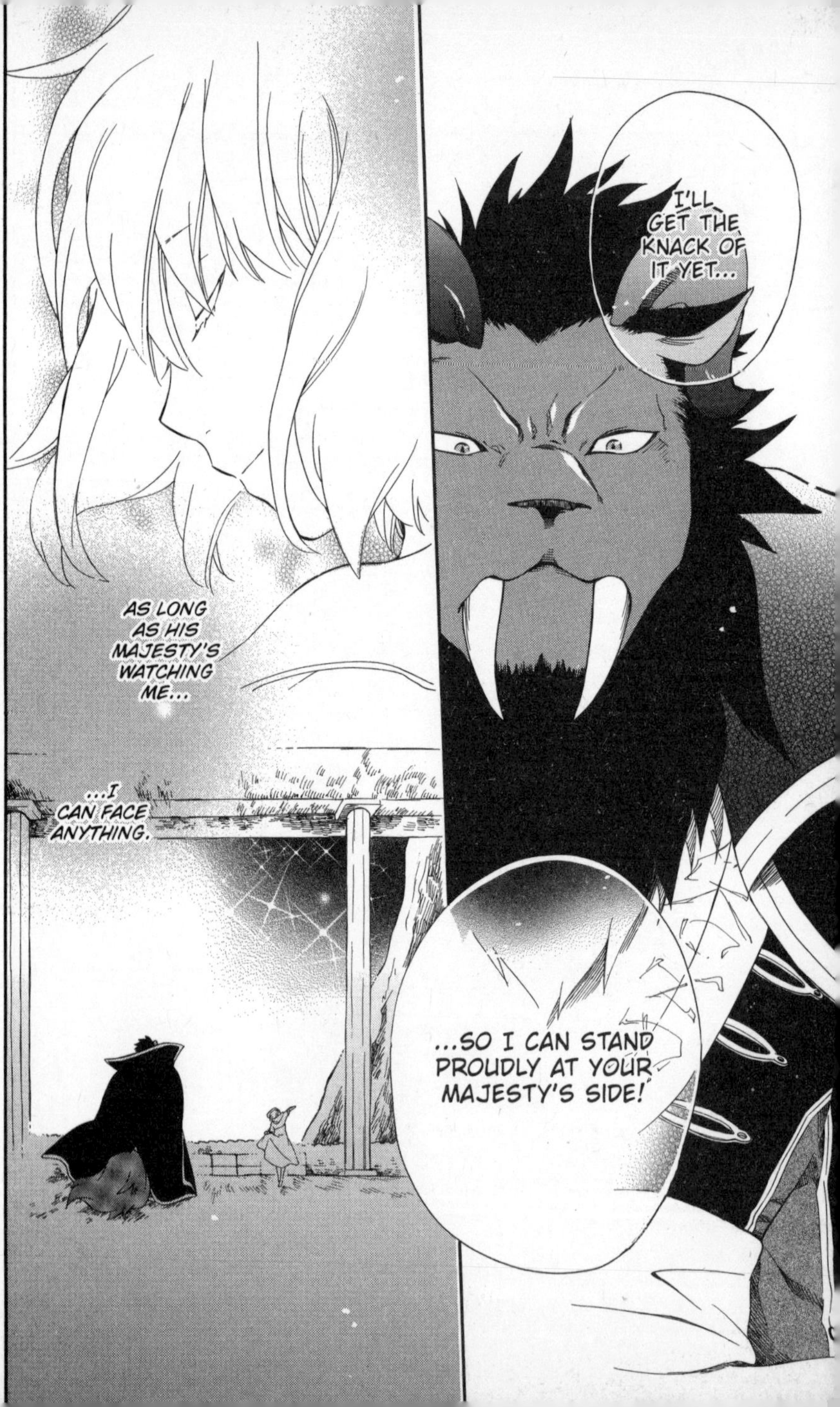
I'LL GET THE KNACK OF IT YET...
...SO I CAN STAND PROUDLY AT YOUR MAJESTY'S SIDE!
AS LONG AS HIS MAJESTY'S WATCHING ME...
...I CAN FACE ANYTHING.

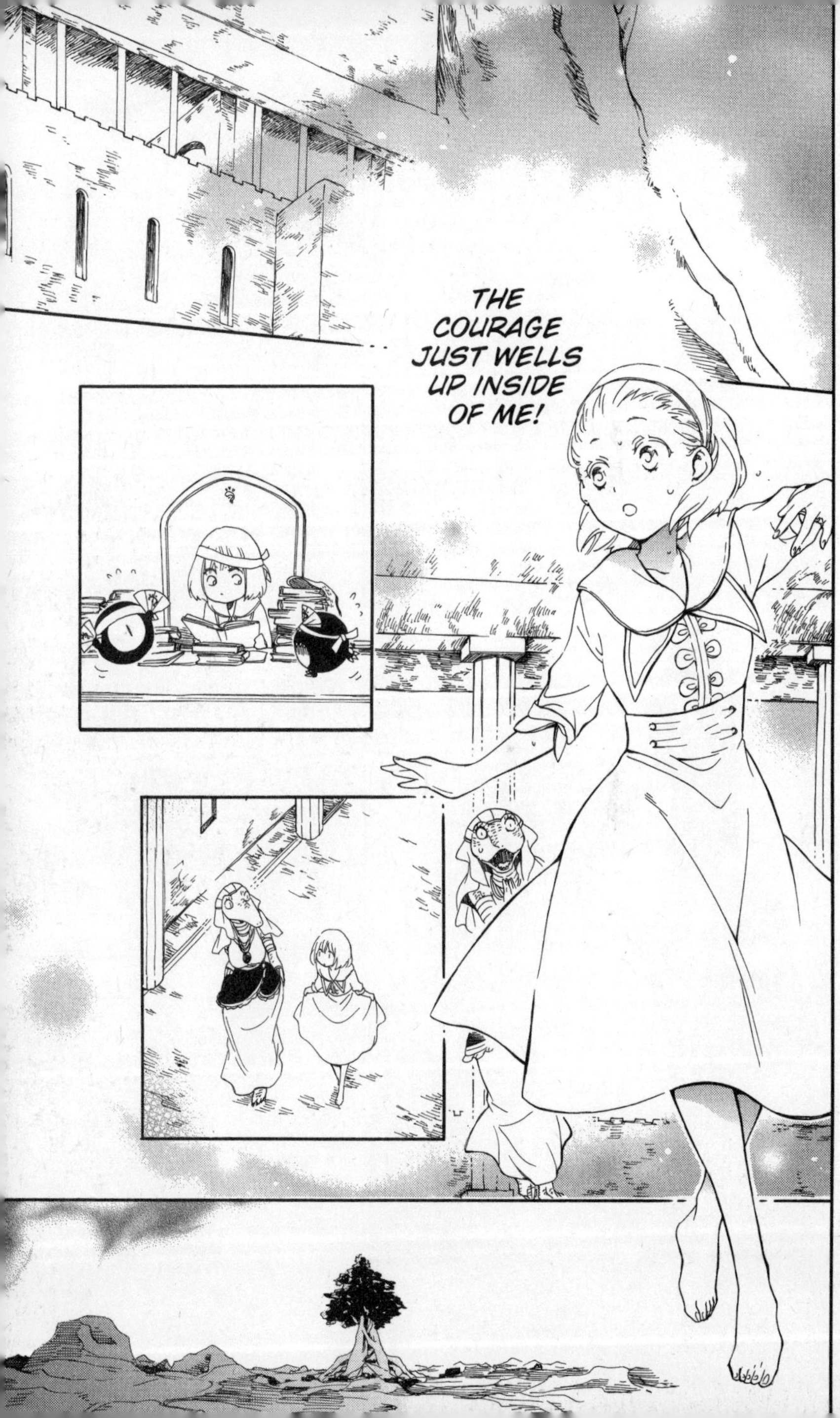
THE COURAGE JUST WELLS UP INSIDE OF ME!

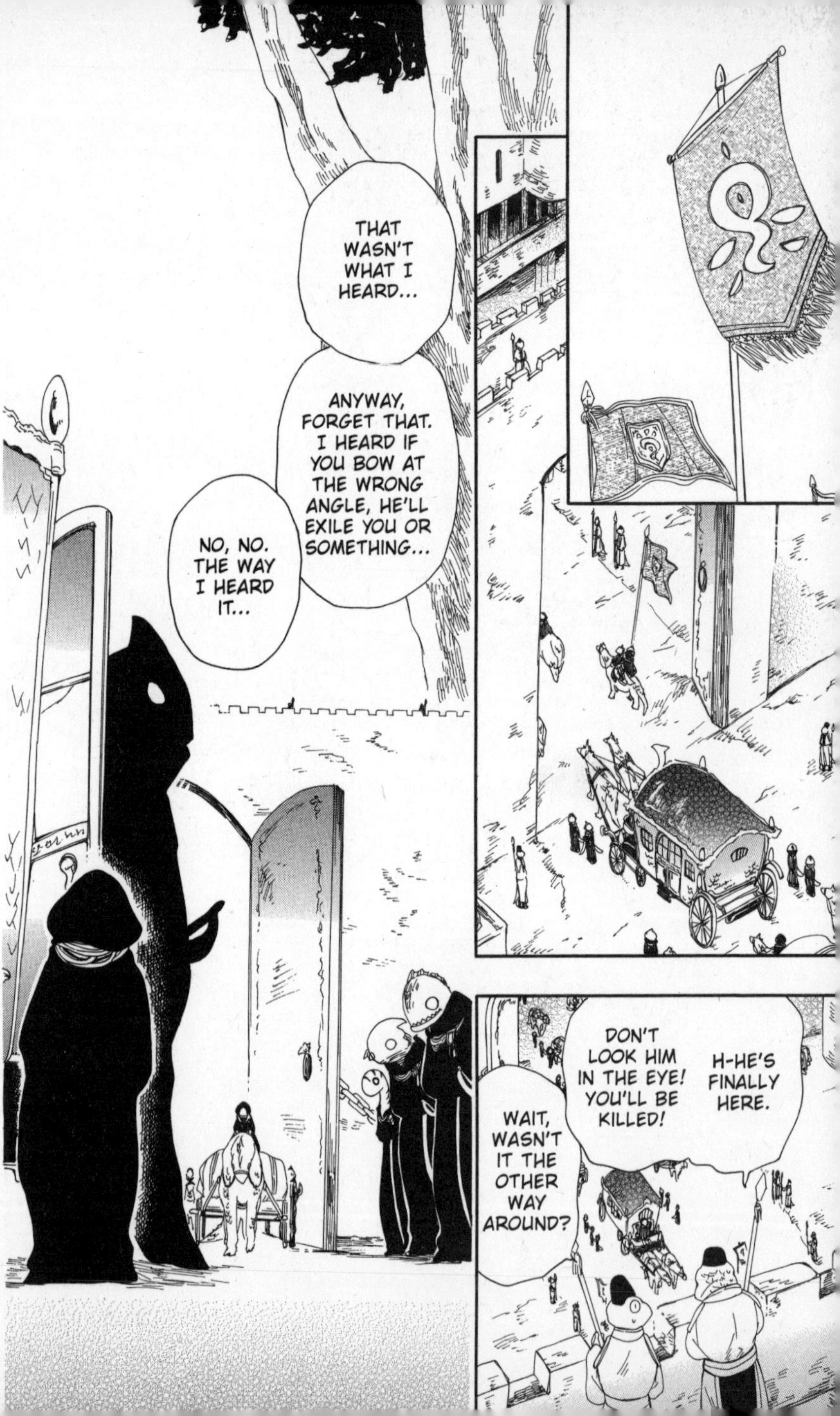
H-HE'S FINALLY HERE.
DON'T LOOK HIM IN THE EYE! YOU'LL BE KILLED!
WAIT, WASN'T IT THE OTHER WAY AROUND?
THAT WASN'T WHAT I HEARD...
ANYWAY, FORGET THAT. I HEARD IF YOU BOW AT THE WRONG ANGLE, HE'LL EXILE YOU OR SOMETHING...
NO, NO. THE WAY I HEARD IT...

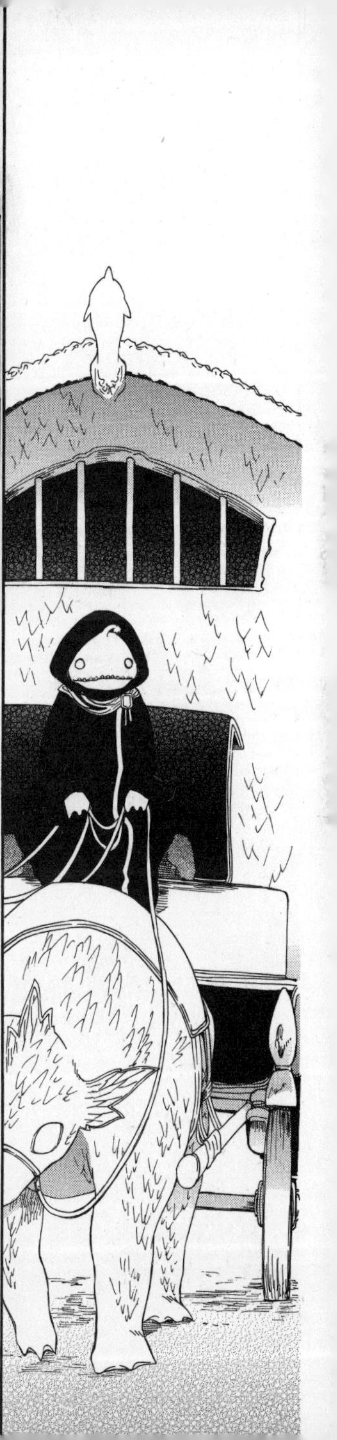

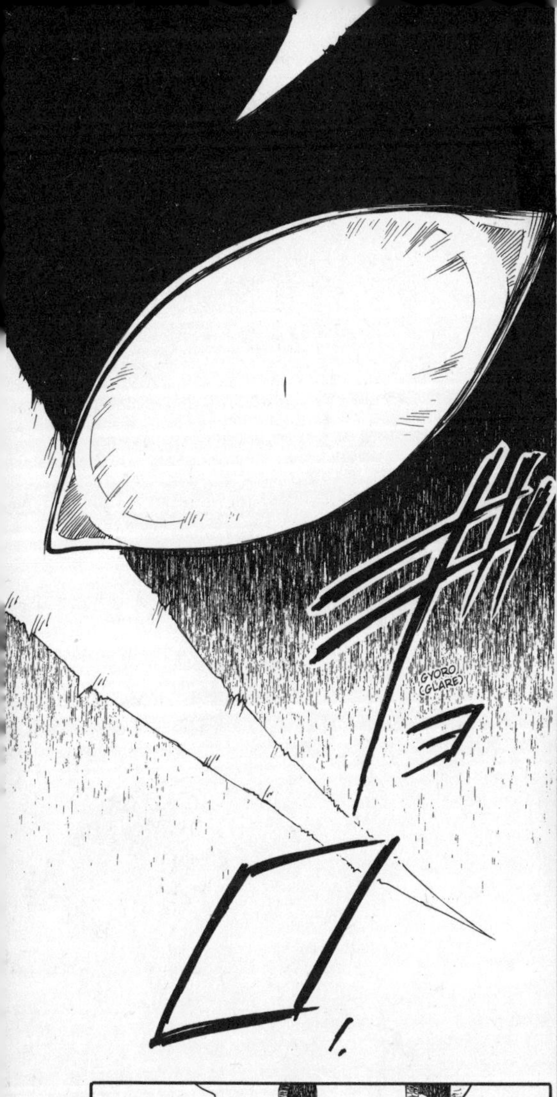
GYORO (GLARE)
THAT'S THE GOD OF THE SEA...
!!

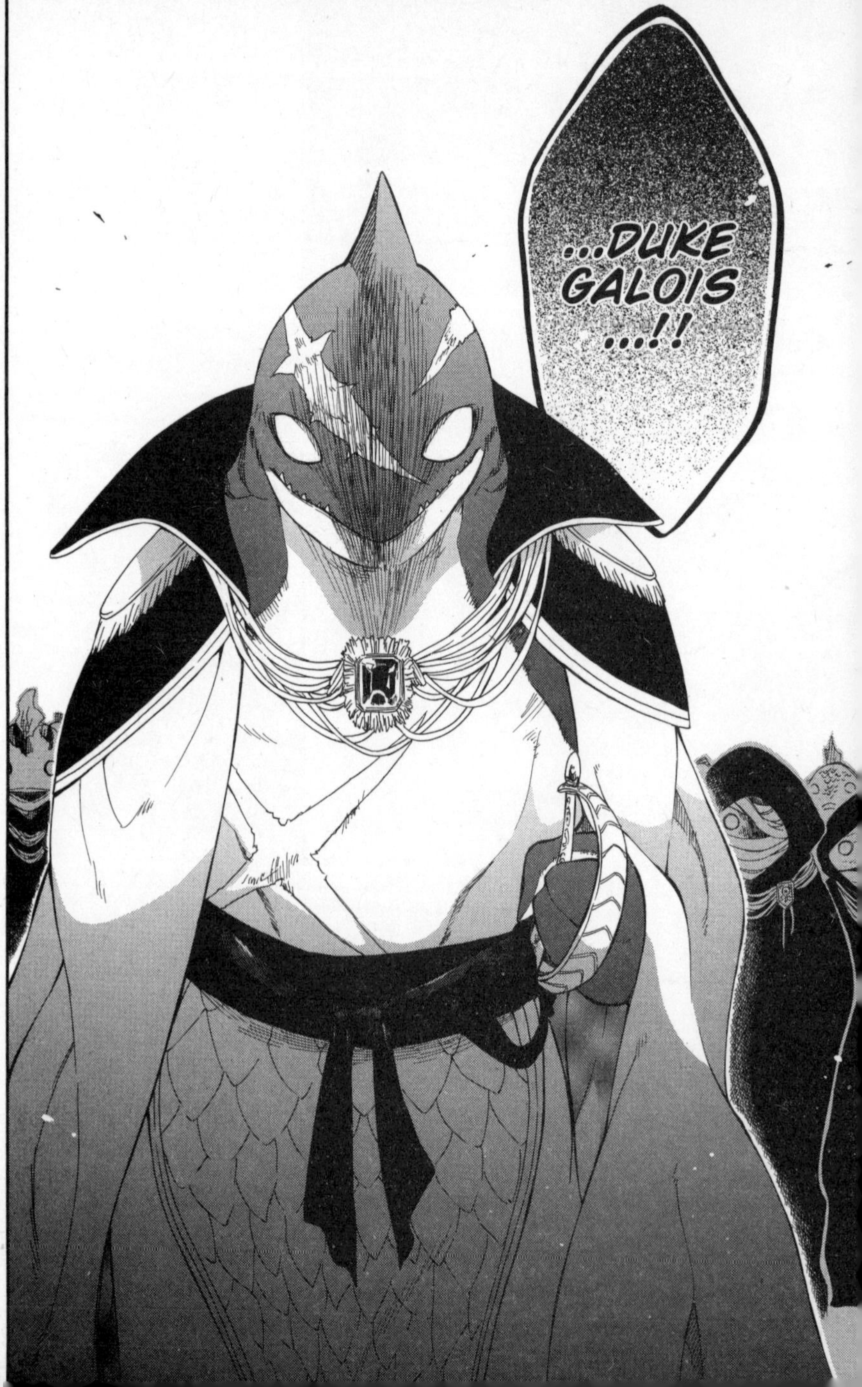
...DUKE GALOIS ...!!

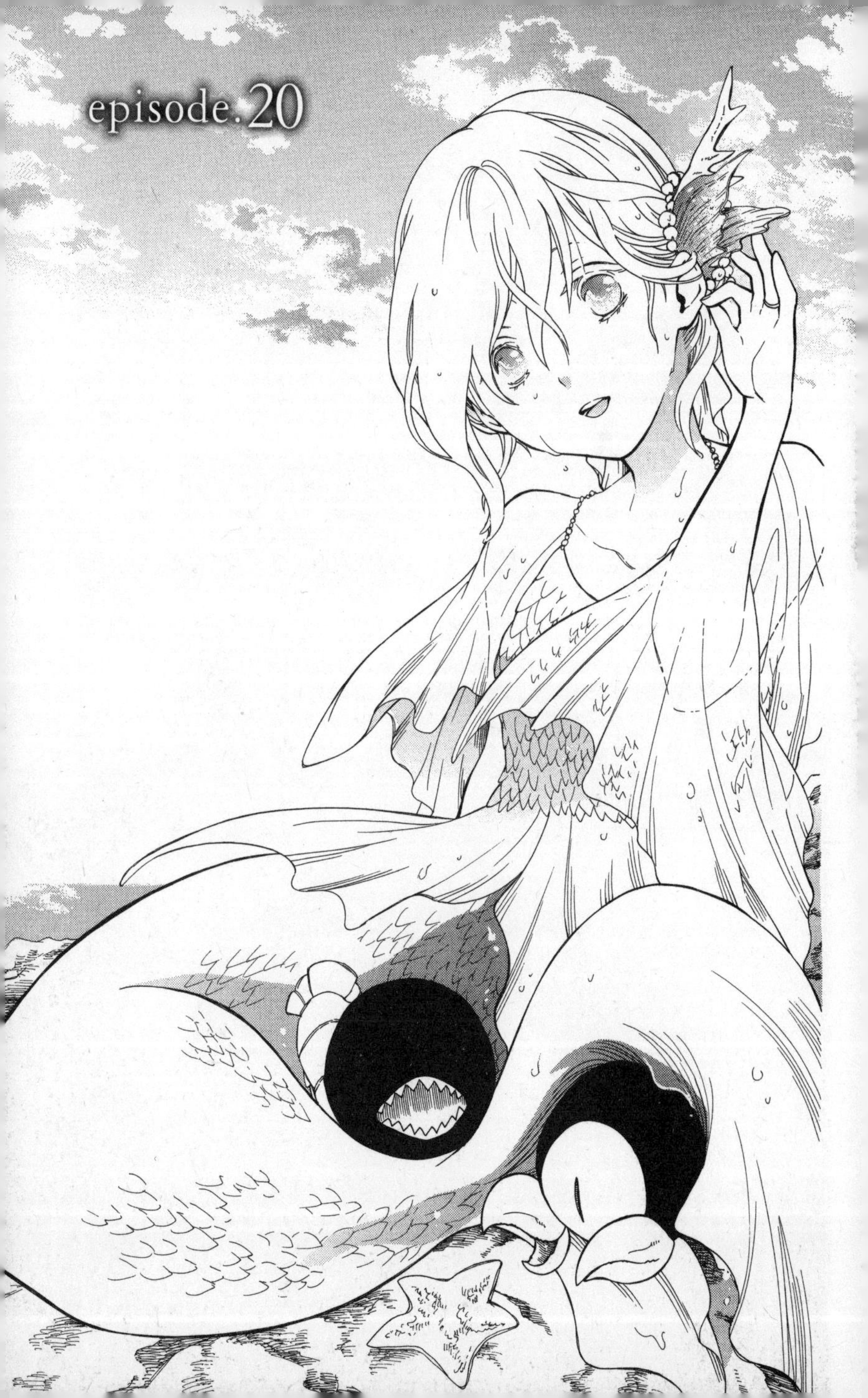
episode. 20

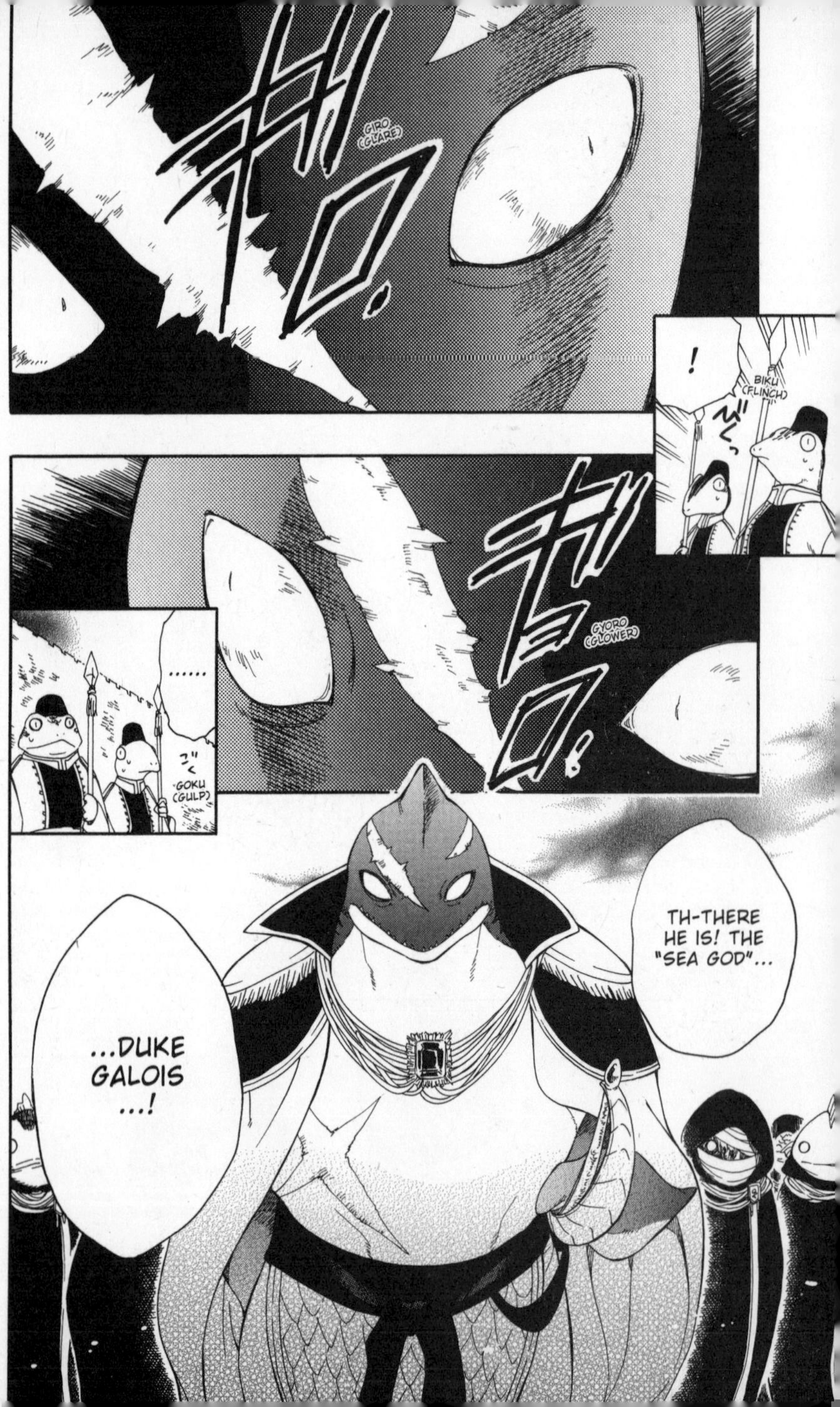
GIRO (GLARE)
!
BIKU (FLINCH)
GYORO (GLOWER)
......
GOKU (GULP)
TH-THERE HE IS! THE "SEA GOD"...
...DUKE GALOIS ...!

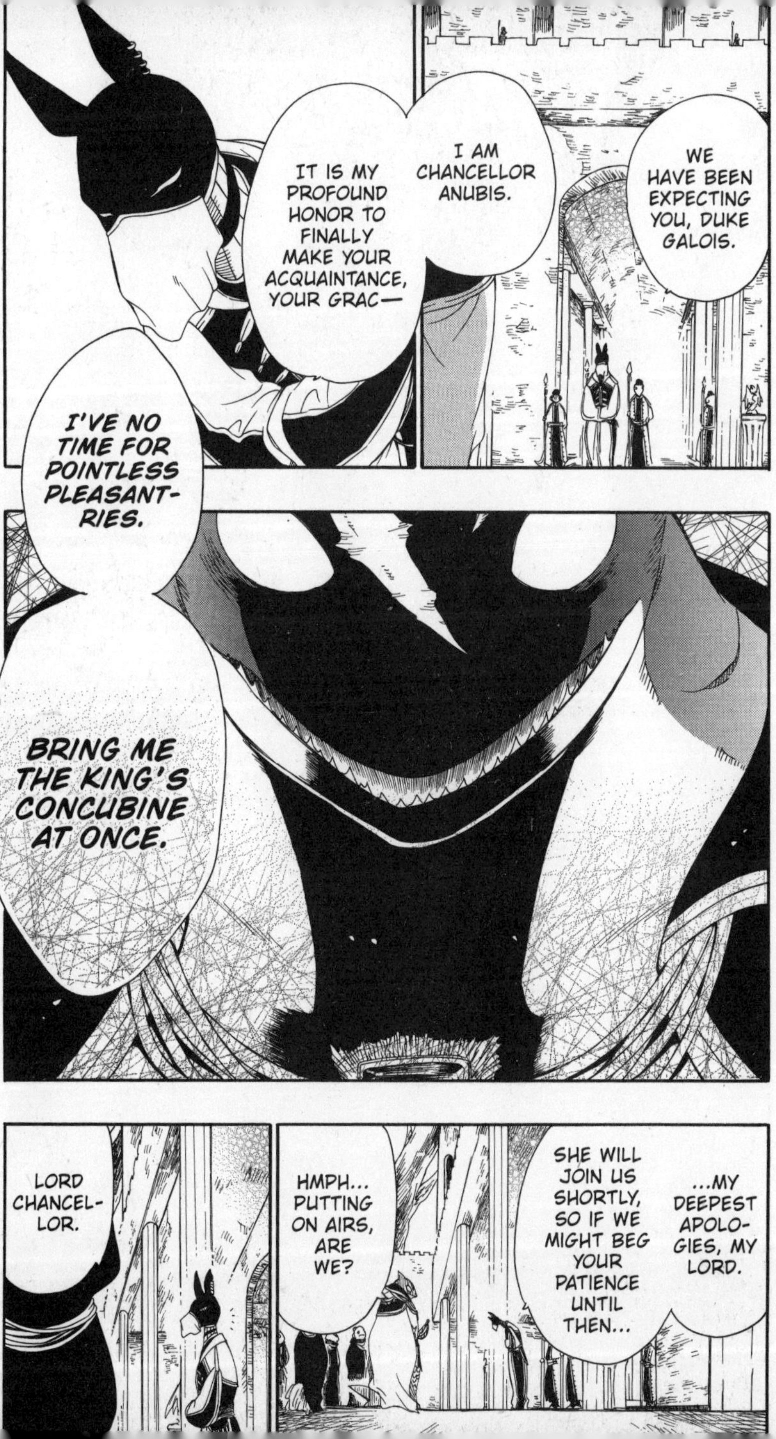
WE HAVE BEEN EXPECTING YOU, DUKE GALOIS.
I AM CHANCELLOR ANUBIS.
IT IS MY PROFOUND HONOR TO FINALLY MAKE YOUR ACQUAINTANCE, YOUR GRAC—
I'VE NO TIME FOR POINTLESS PLEASANT-RIES.
BRING ME THE KING'S CONCUBINE AT ONCE.
...MY DEEPEST APOLO-GIES, MY LORD.
SHE WILL JOIN US SHORTLY, SO IF WE MIGHT BEG YOUR PATIENCE UNTIL THEN...
HMPH... PUTTING ON AIRS, ARE WE?
LORD CHANCEL-LOR.

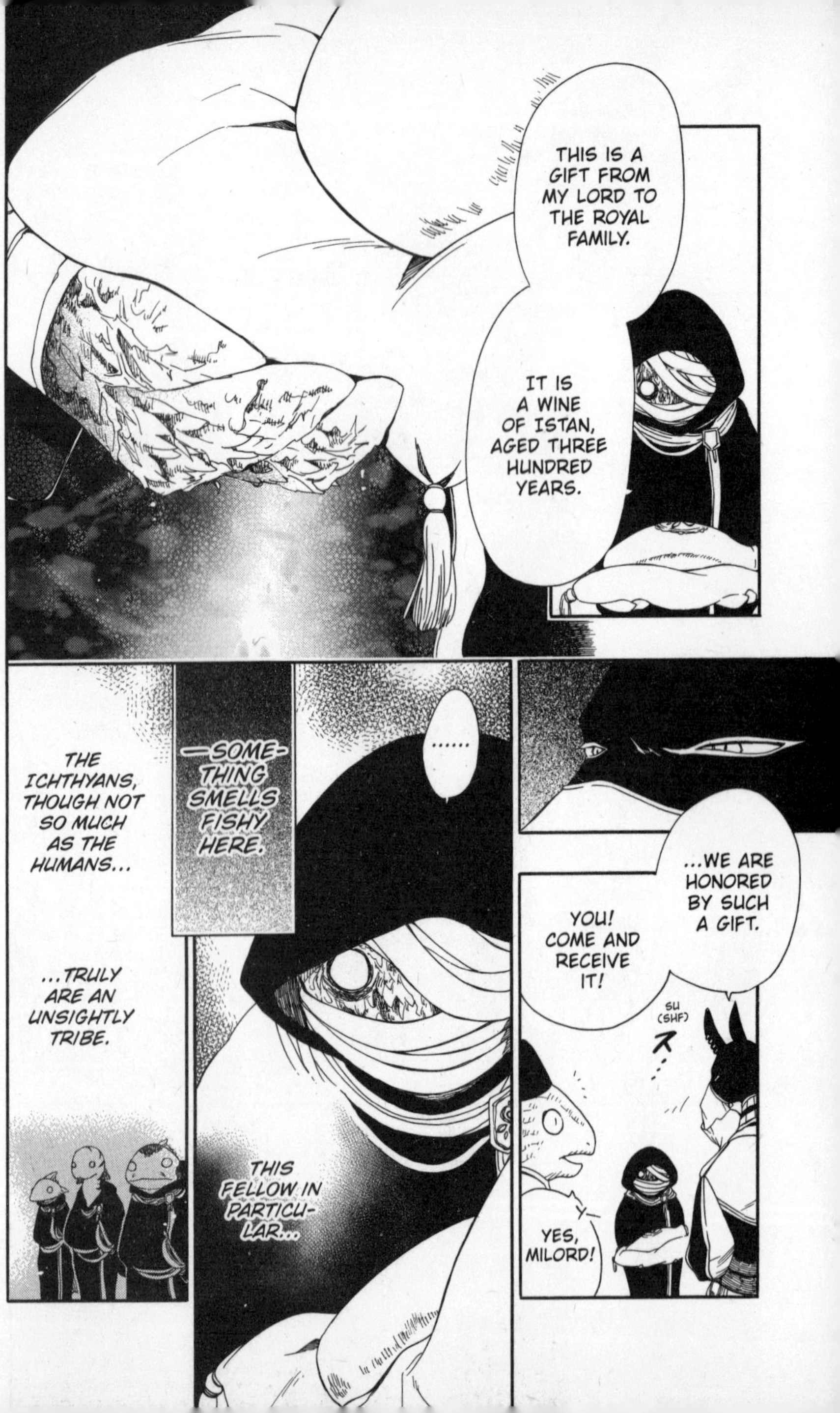
THIS IS A GIFT FROM MY LORD TO THE ROYAL FAMILY.
IT IS A WINE OF ISTAN, AGED THREE HUNDRED YEARS.
...WE ARE HONORED BY SUCH A GIFT.
YOU! COME AND RECEIVE IT!
SU (SHF)
YES, MILORD!
......
—SOME-THING SMELLS FISHY HERE.
THIS FELLOW IN PARTICU-LAR...
THE ICHTHYANS, THOUGH NOT SO MUCH AS THE HUMANS...
...TRULY ARE AN UNSIGHTLY TRIBE.

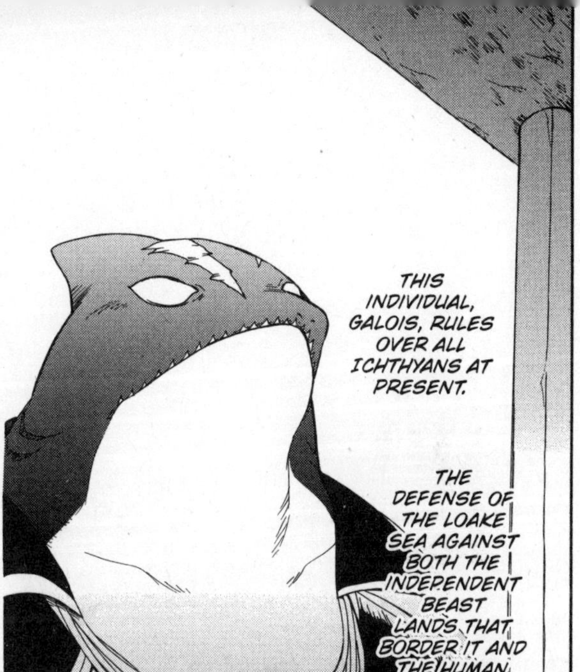
THIS INDIVIDUAL, GALOIS, RULES OVER ALL ICHTHYANS AT PRESENT.
THE DEFENSE OF THE LOAKE SEA AGAINST BOTH THE INDEPENDENT BEAST LANDS THAT BORDER IT AND THE HUMAN NATION OF YOANA...
...IS POSSIBLE ALMOST ENTIRELY THANKS TO HIM.

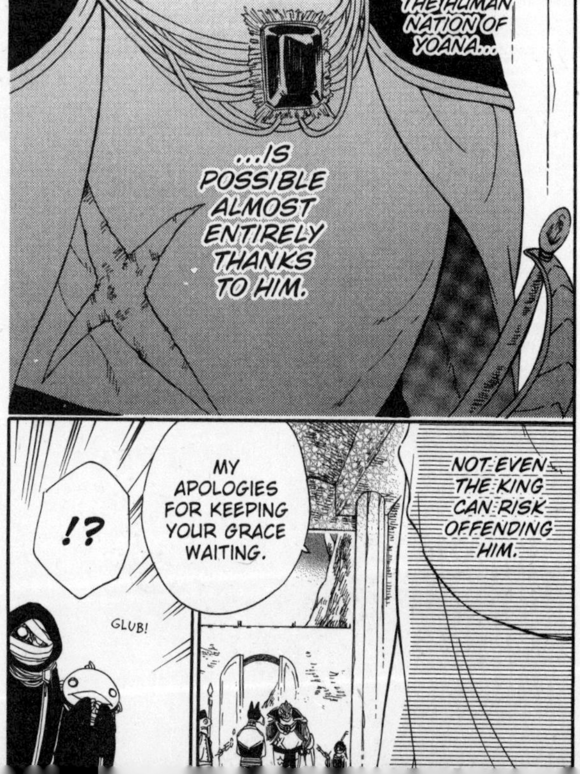
NOT EVEN THE KING CAN RISK OFFENDING HIM.
MY APOLOGIES FOR KEEPING YOUR GRACE WAITING.
!?
GLUB!

QUICK & DIRTY DETAILS

HIS MAJESTY (BEAST)

- IN HIS MID-TWENTIES IN HUMAN YEARS
- OVER TWO METERS (6'6") TALL

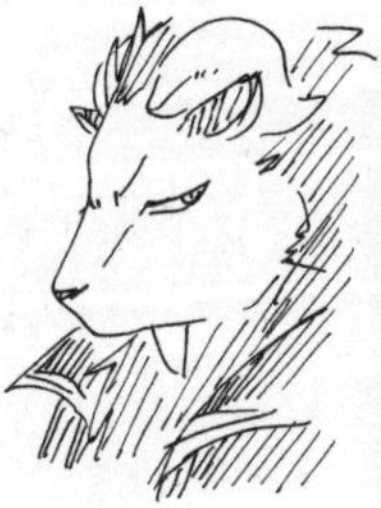

- LIKES: FOOD WITH GOOD, TOUGH TEXTURE
- DISLIKES: HIMSELF IN HUMAN FORM

HIS MAJESTY (HUMAN)

- 180cm (5'10") TALL

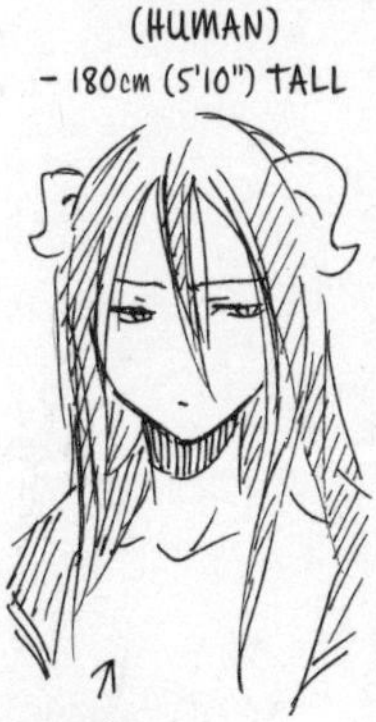

PHYSICAL ABILITIES ARE ALL ESSENTIALLY HUMAN

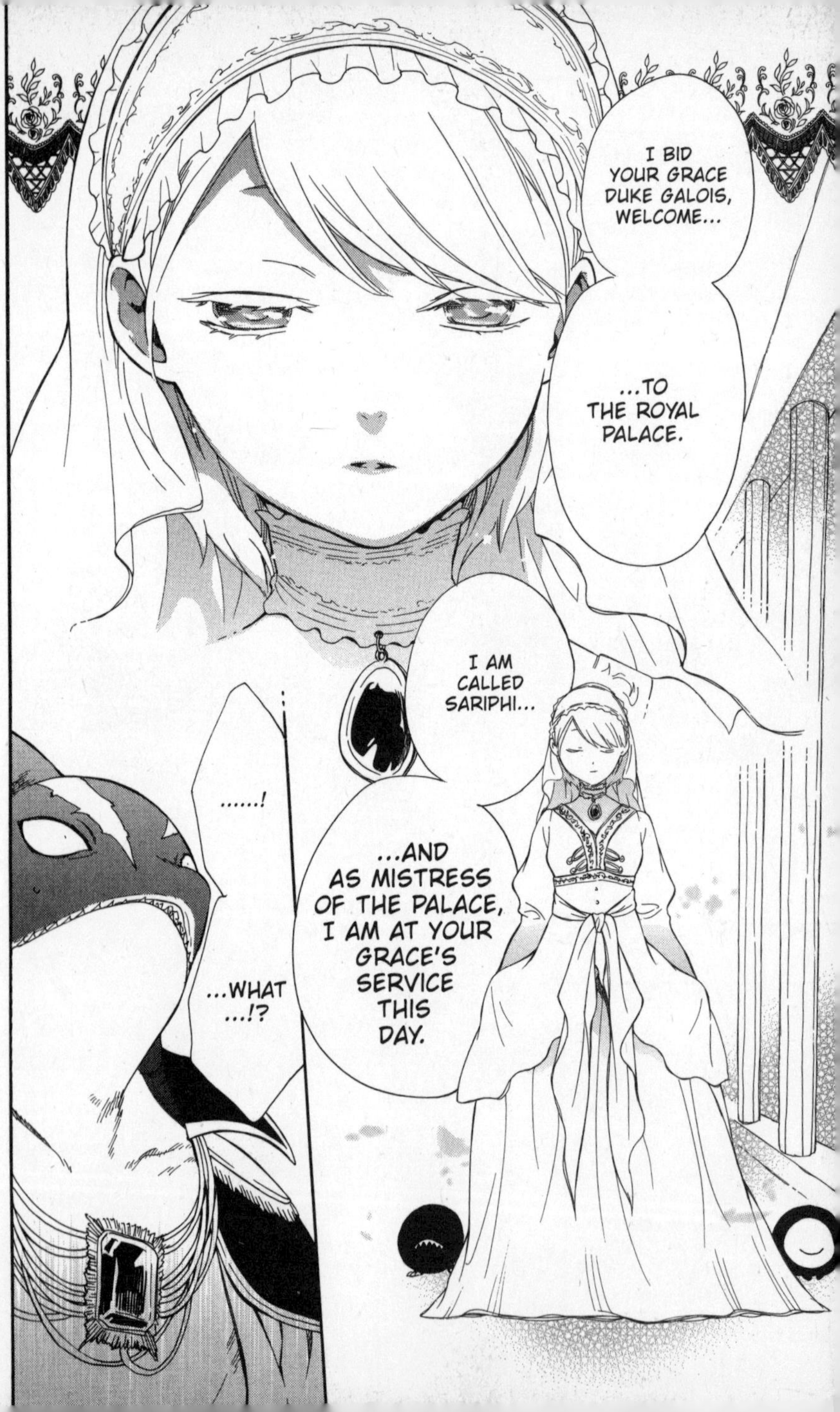
I BID YOUR GRACE DUKE GALOIS, WELCOME...
...TO THE ROYAL PALACE.
I AM CALLED SARIPHI...
...AND AS MISTRESS OF THE PALACE, I AM AT YOUR GRACE'S SERVICE THIS DAY.
......!
...WHAT ...!?

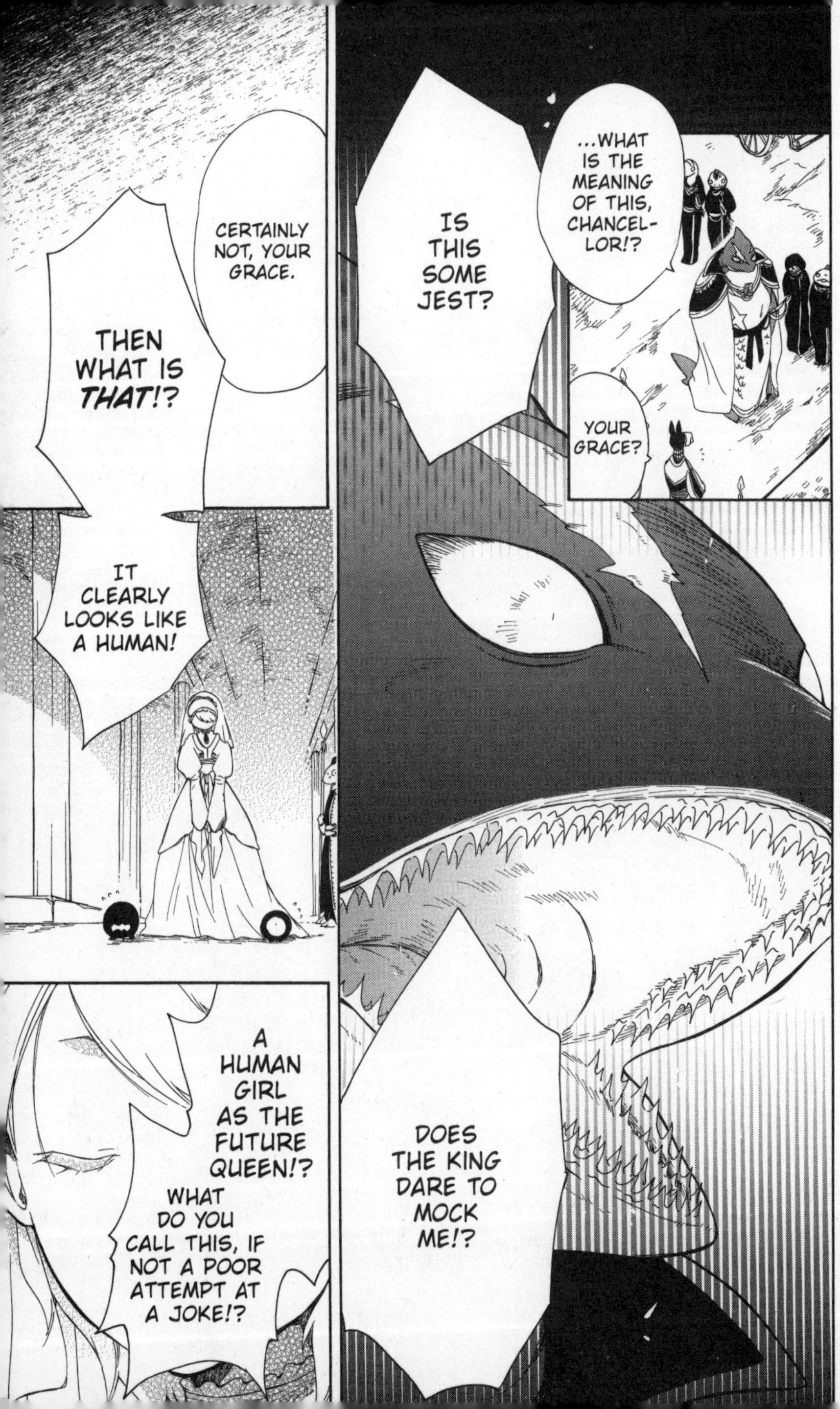

...WHAT IS THE MEANING OF THIS, CHANCELLOR!?
YOUR GRACE?
IS THIS SOME JEST?
DOES THE KING DARE TO MOCK ME!?
CERTAINLY NOT, YOUR GRACE.
THEN WHAT IS *THAT*!?
IT CLEARLY LOOKS LIKE A HUMAN!
A HUMAN GIRL AS THE FUTURE QUEEN!?
WHAT DO YOU CALL THIS, IF NOT A POOR ATTEMPT AT A JOKE!?

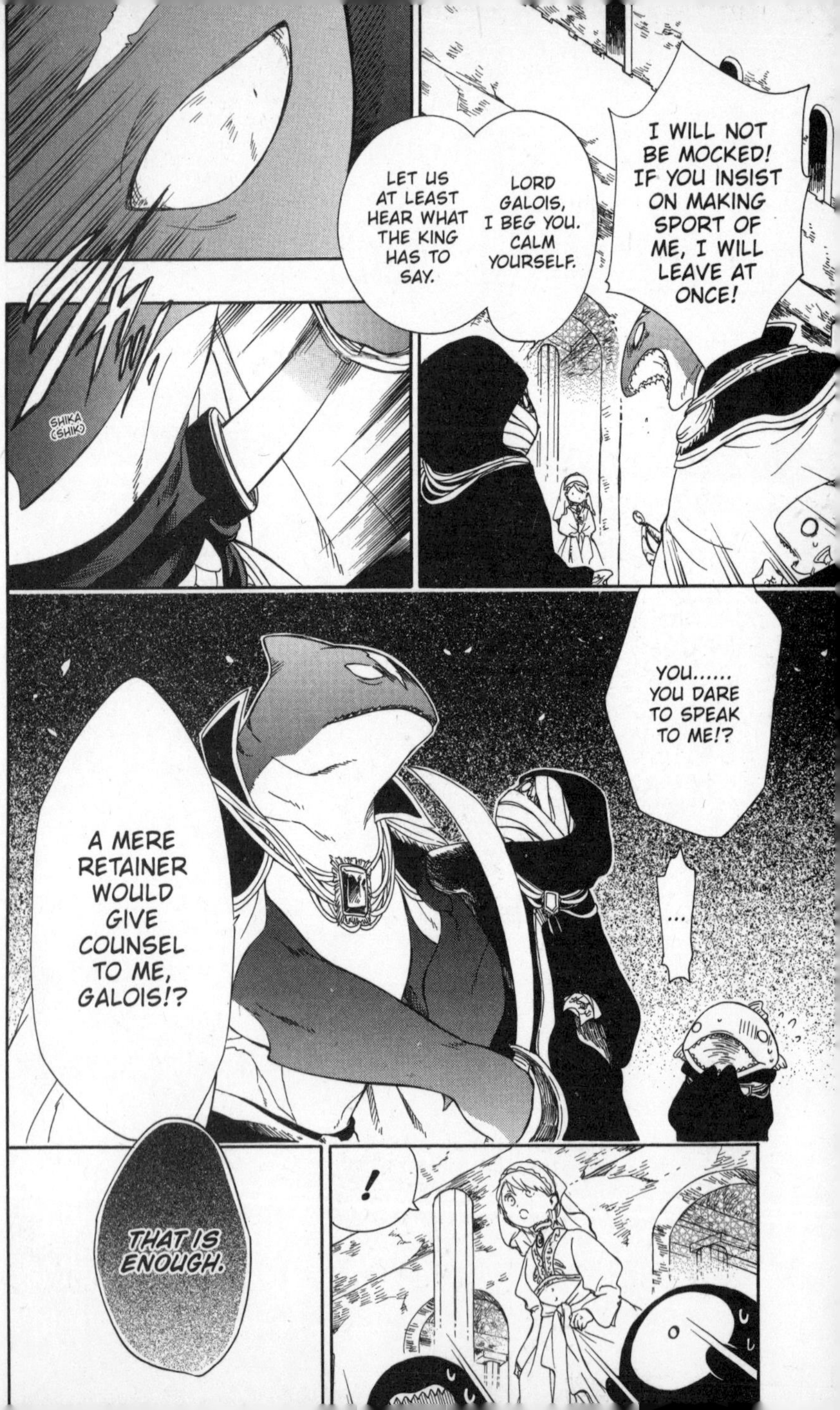
I WILL NOT BE MOCKED! IF YOU INSIST ON MAKING SPORT OF ME, I WILL LEAVE AT ONCE!
LORD GALOIS, I BEG YOU. CALM YOURSELF.
LET US AT LEAST HEAR WHAT THE KING HAS TO SAY.
SHIKA (SHIK)
YOU...... YOU DARE TO SPEAK TO ME!?
...
A MERE RETAINER WOULD GIVE COUNSEL TO ME, GALOIS!?
!
THAT IS ENOUGH.

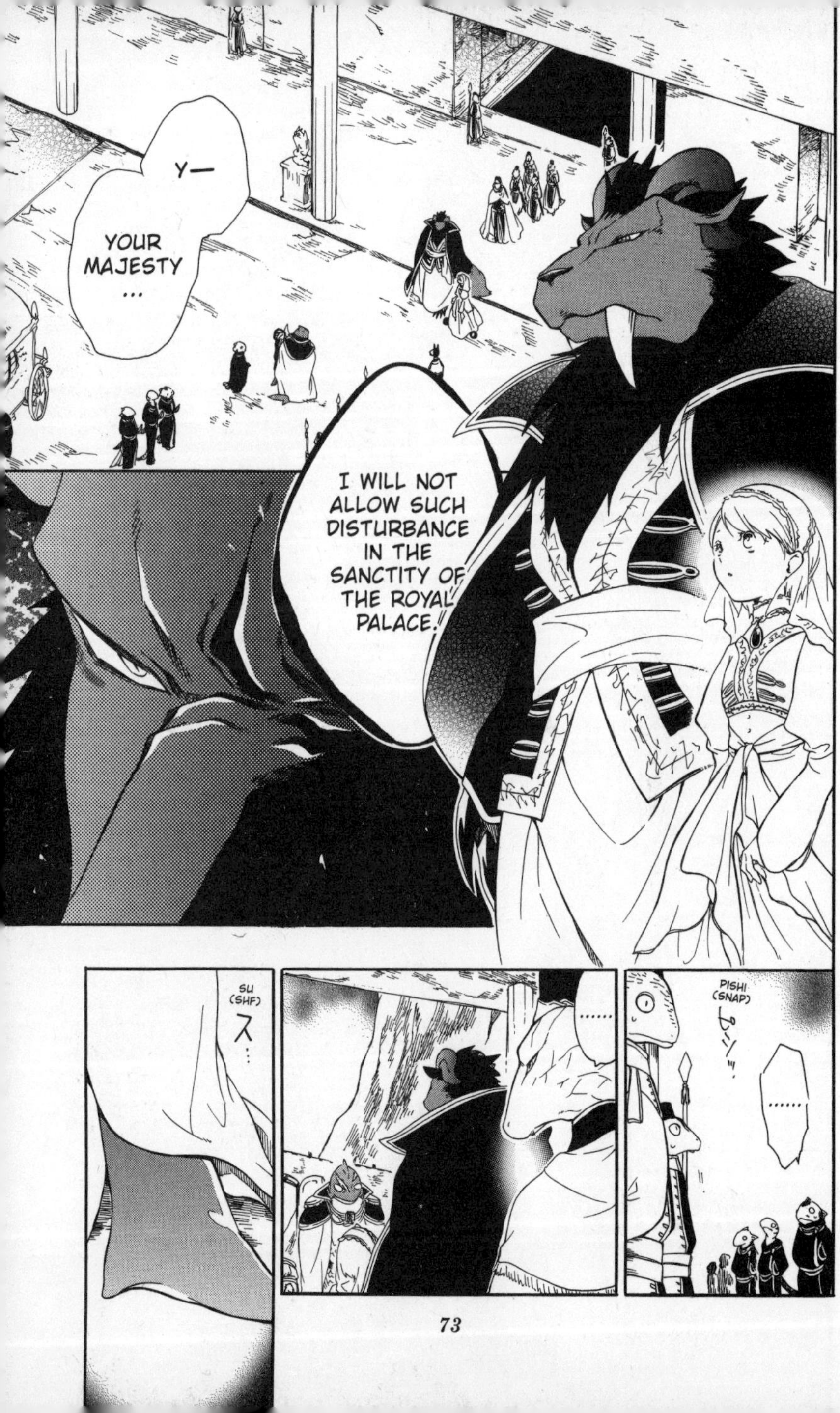
I WILL NOT ALLOW SUCH DISTURBANCE IN THE SANCTITY OF THE ROYAL PALACE.
Y—
YOUR MAJESTY ...
PISHI (SNAP)
ピシッ
......
......
SU (SHF)
ス...

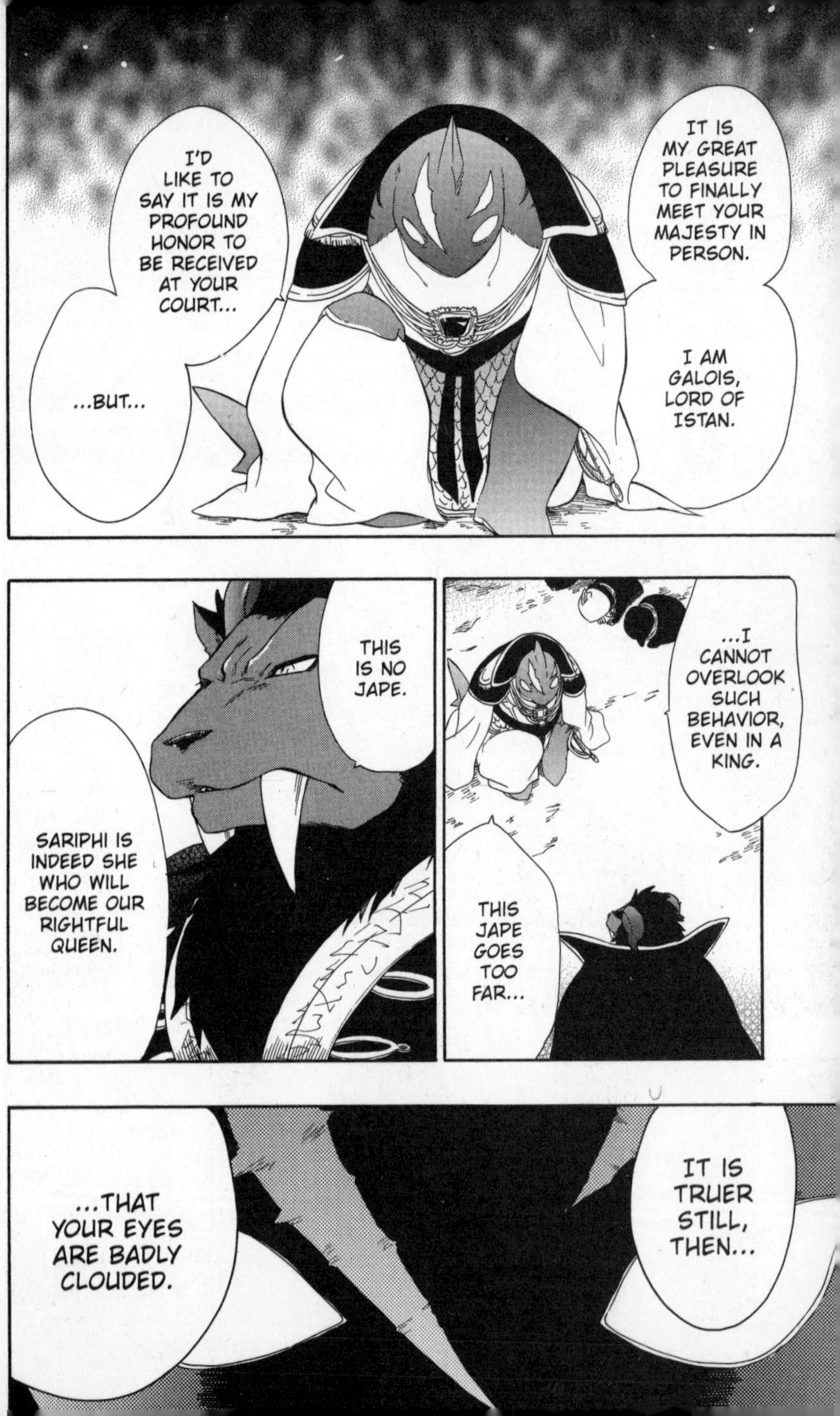
IT IS MY GREAT PLEASURE TO FINALLY MEET YOUR MAJESTY IN PERSON.
I AM GALOIS, LORD OF ISTAN.
I'D LIKE TO SAY IT IS MY PROFOUND HONOR TO BE RECEIVED AT YOUR COURT...
...BUT...
...I CANNOT OVERLOOK SUCH BEHAVIOR, EVEN IN A KING.
THIS JAPE GOES TOO FAR...
THIS IS NO JAPE.
SARIPHI IS INDEED SHE WHO WILL BECOME OUR RIGHTFUL QUEEN.
IT IS TRUER STILL, THEN...
...THAT YOUR EYES ARE BADLY CLOUDED.

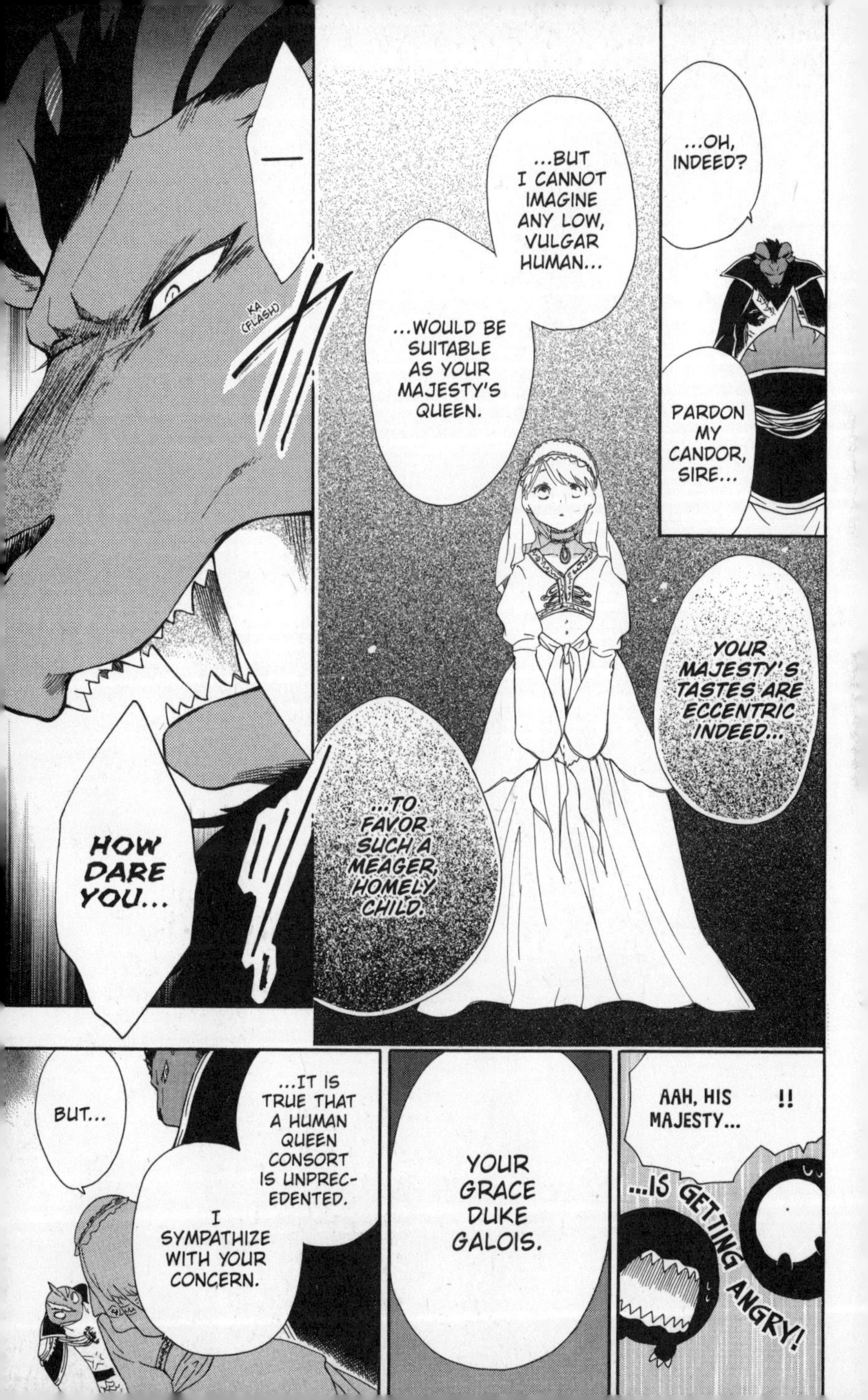
...OH, INDEED?
PARDON MY CANDOR, SIRE...
...BUT I CANNOT IMAGINE ANY LOW, VULGAR HUMAN...
...WOULD BE SUITABLE AS YOUR MAJESTY'S QUEEN.
YOUR MAJESTY'S TASTES ARE ECCENTRIC INDEED...
...TO FAVOR SUCH A MEAGER, HOMELY CHILD.
—
KA (FLASH)
HOW DARE YOU...
AAH, HIS MAJESTY...
!!
...IS GETTING ANGRY!
YOUR GRACE DUKE GALOIS.
...IT IS TRUE THAT A HUMAN QUEEN CONSORT IS UNPREC-EDENTED.
I SYMPATHIZE WITH YOUR CONCERN.
BUT...

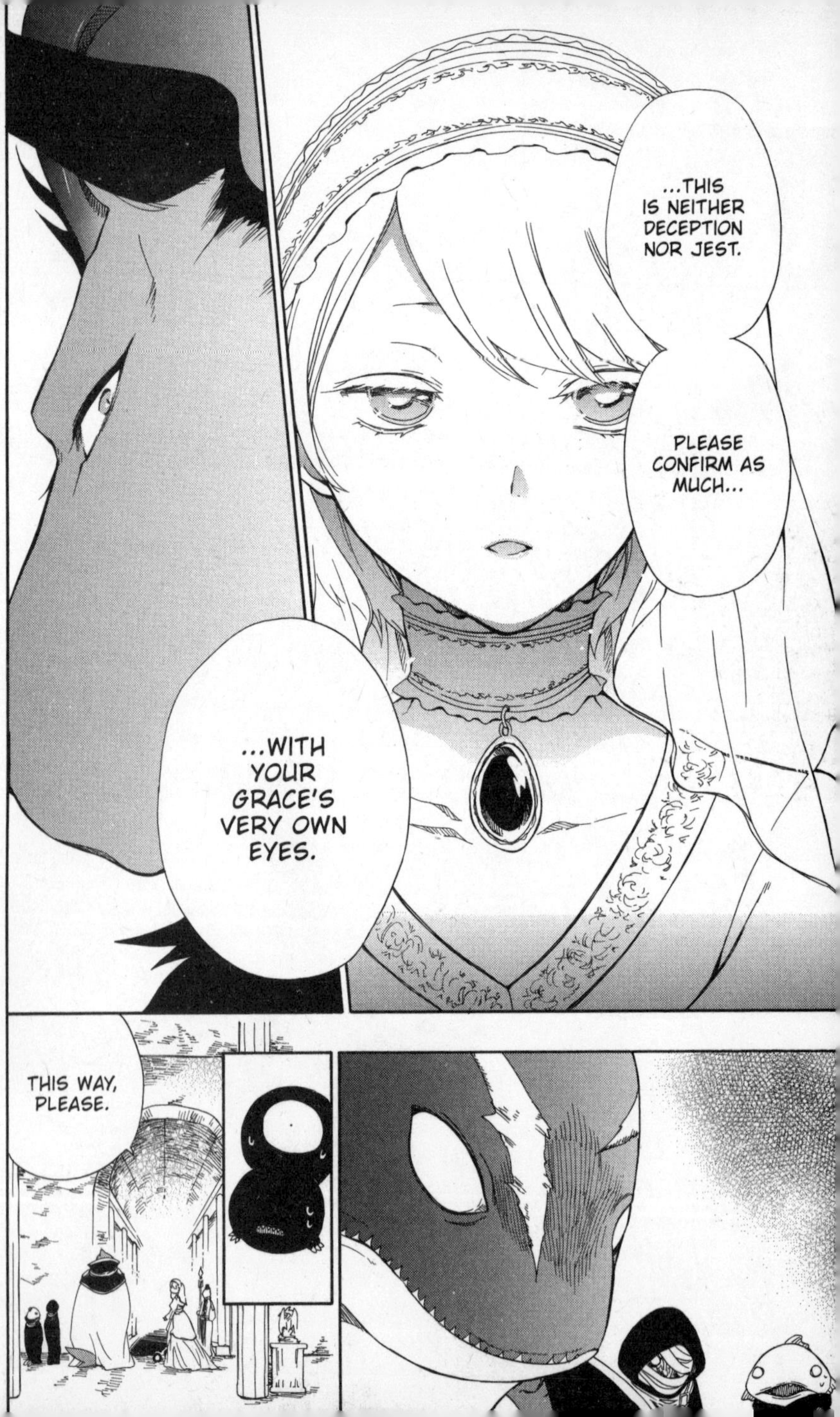
...THIS IS NEITHER DECEPTION NOR JEST.
PLEASE CONFIRM AS MUCH...
...WITH YOUR GRACE'S VERY OWN EYES.
THIS WAY, PLEASE.

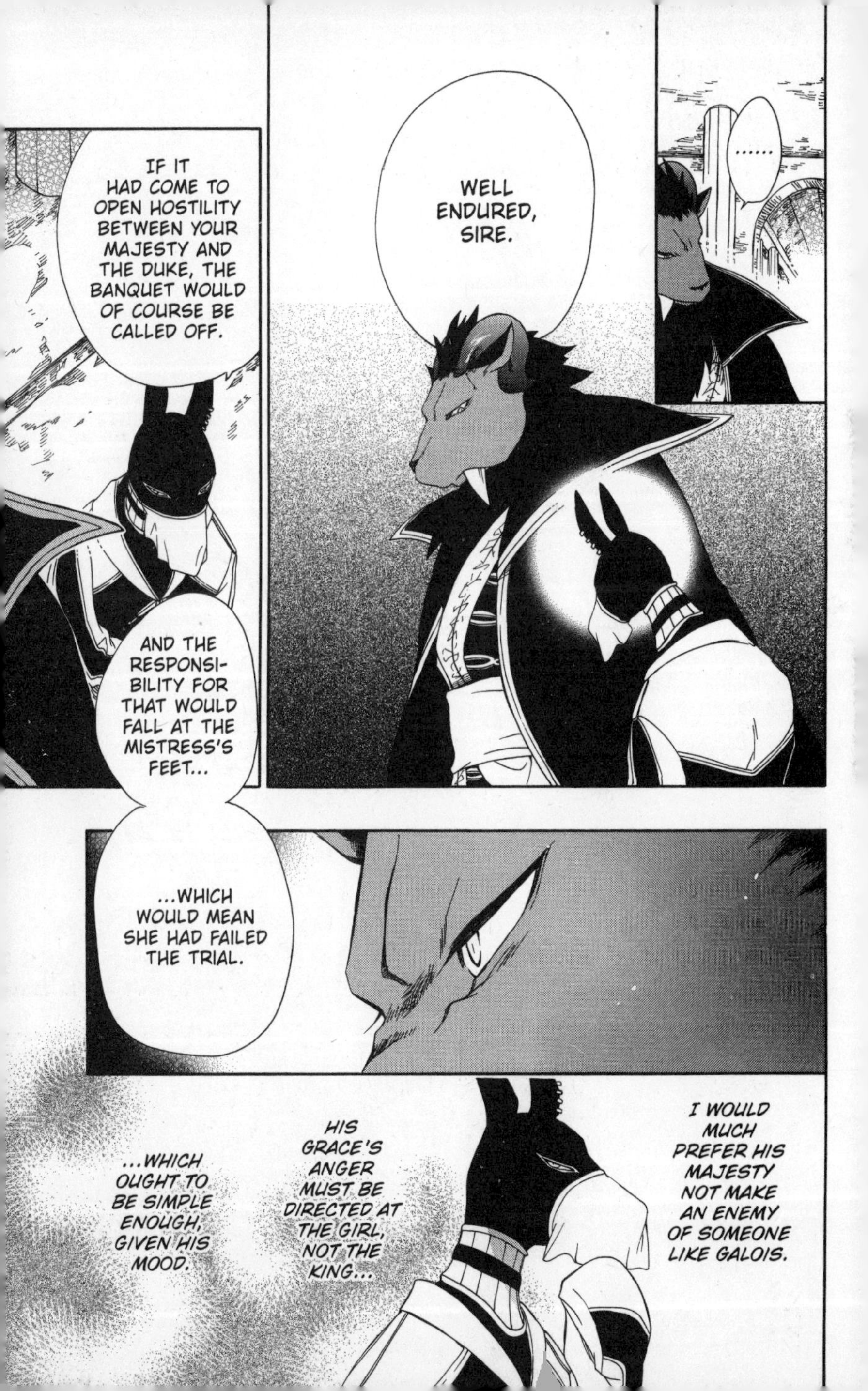
......
WELL ENDURED, SIRE.
IF IT HAD COME TO OPEN HOSTILITY BETWEEN YOUR MAJESTY AND THE DUKE, THE BANQUET WOULD OF COURSE BE CALLED OFF.
AND THE RESPONSI-BILITY FOR THAT WOULD FALL AT THE MISTRESS'S FEET...
...WHICH WOULD MEAN SHE HAD FAILED THE TRIAL.
I WOULD MUCH PREFER HIS MAJESTY NOT MAKE AN ENEMY OF SOMEONE LIKE GALOIS.
HIS GRACE'S ANGER MUST BE DIRECTED AT THE GIRL, NOT THE KING...
...WHICH OUGHT TO BE SIMPLE ENOUGH, GIVEN HIS MOOD.

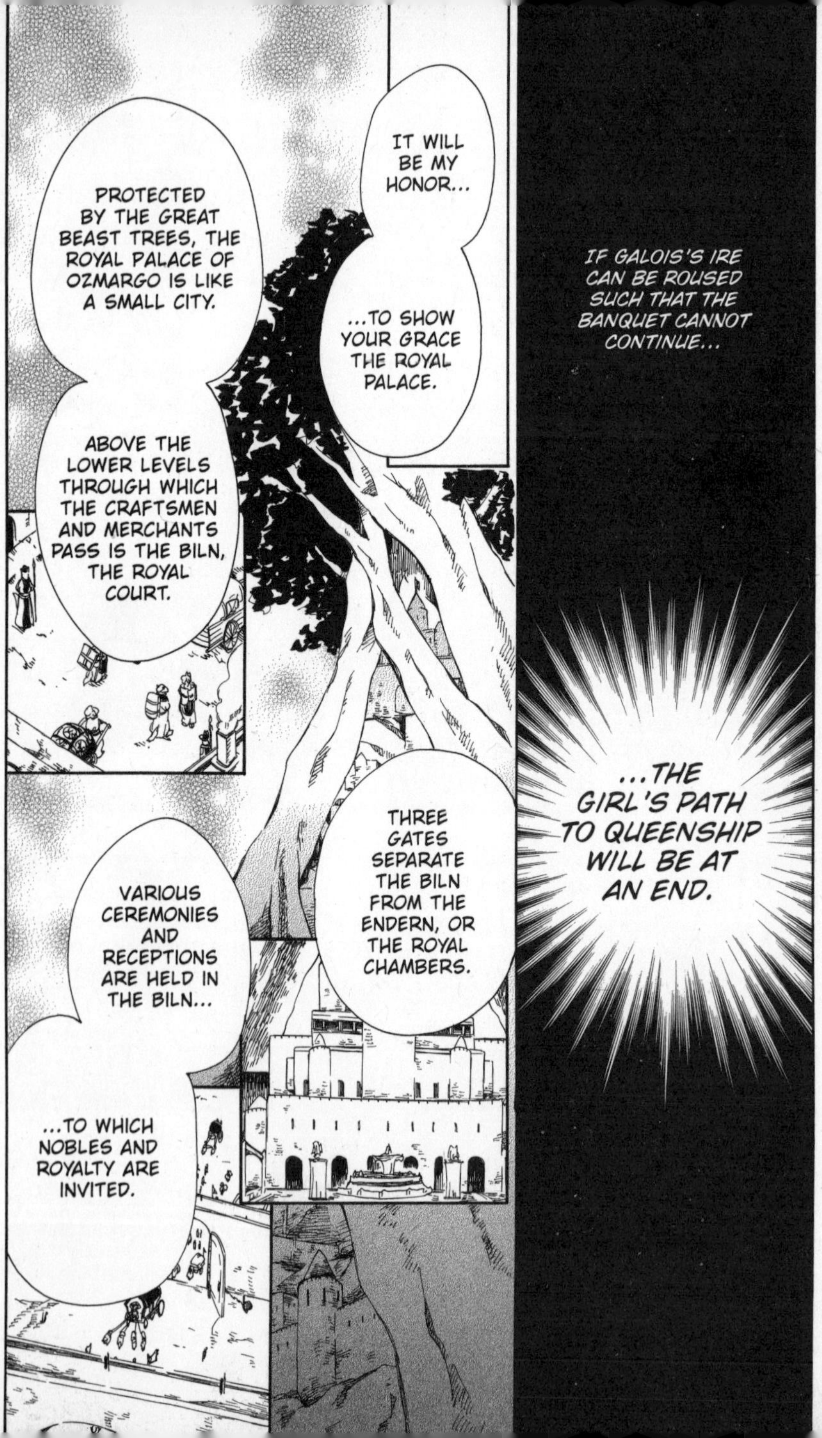
IF GALOIS'S IRE CAN BE ROUSED SUCH THAT THE BANQUET CANNOT CONTINUE...
...THE GIRL'S PATH TO QUEENSHIP WILL BE AT AN END.
IT WILL BE MY HONOR...
...TO SHOW YOUR GRACE THE ROYAL PALACE.
PROTECTED BY THE GREAT BEAST TREES, THE ROYAL PALACE OF OZMARGO IS LIKE A SMALL CITY.
ABOVE THE LOWER LEVELS THROUGH WHICH THE CRAFTSMEN AND MERCHANTS PASS IS THE BILN, THE ROYAL COURT.
THREE GATES SEPARATE THE BILN FROM THE ENDERN, OR THE ROYAL CHAMBERS.
VARIOUS CEREMONIES AND RECEPTIONS ARE HELD IN THE BILN...
...TO WHICH NOBLES AND ROYALTY ARE INVITED.

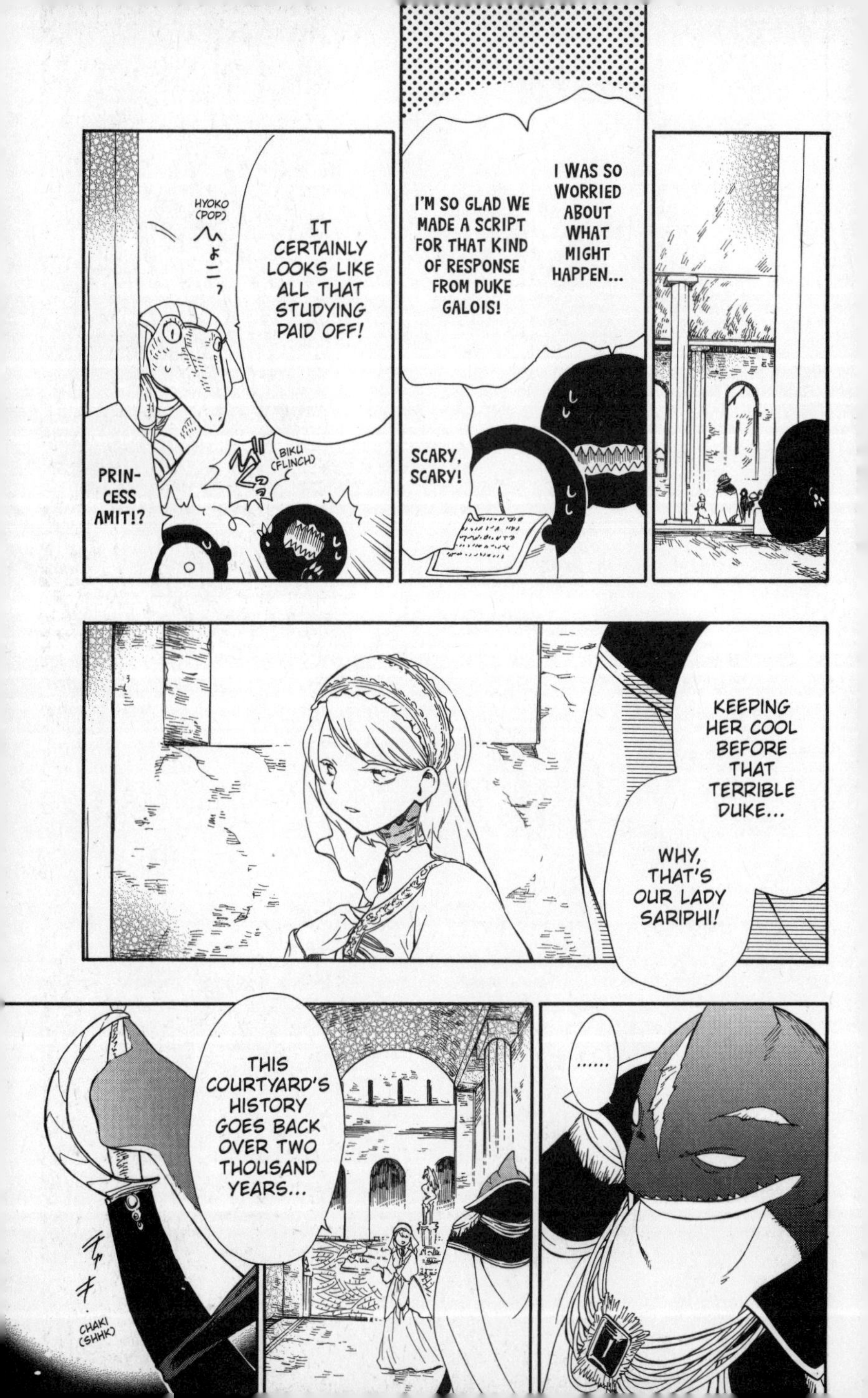
I WAS SO WORRIED ABOUT WHAT MIGHT HAPPEN...
I'M SO GLAD WE MADE A SCRIPT FOR THAT KIND OF RESPONSE FROM DUKE GALOIS!
SCARY, SCARY!
IT CERTAINLY LOOKS LIKE ALL THAT STUDYING PAID OFF!
HYOKO (POP)
BIKU (FLINCH)
PRIN-CESS AMIT!?
KEEPING HER COOL BEFORE THAT TERRIBLE DUKE...
WHY, THAT'S OUR LADY SARIPHI!
......
THIS COURTYARD'S HISTORY GOES BACK OVER TWO THOUSAND YEARS...
CHAKI (SHHK)

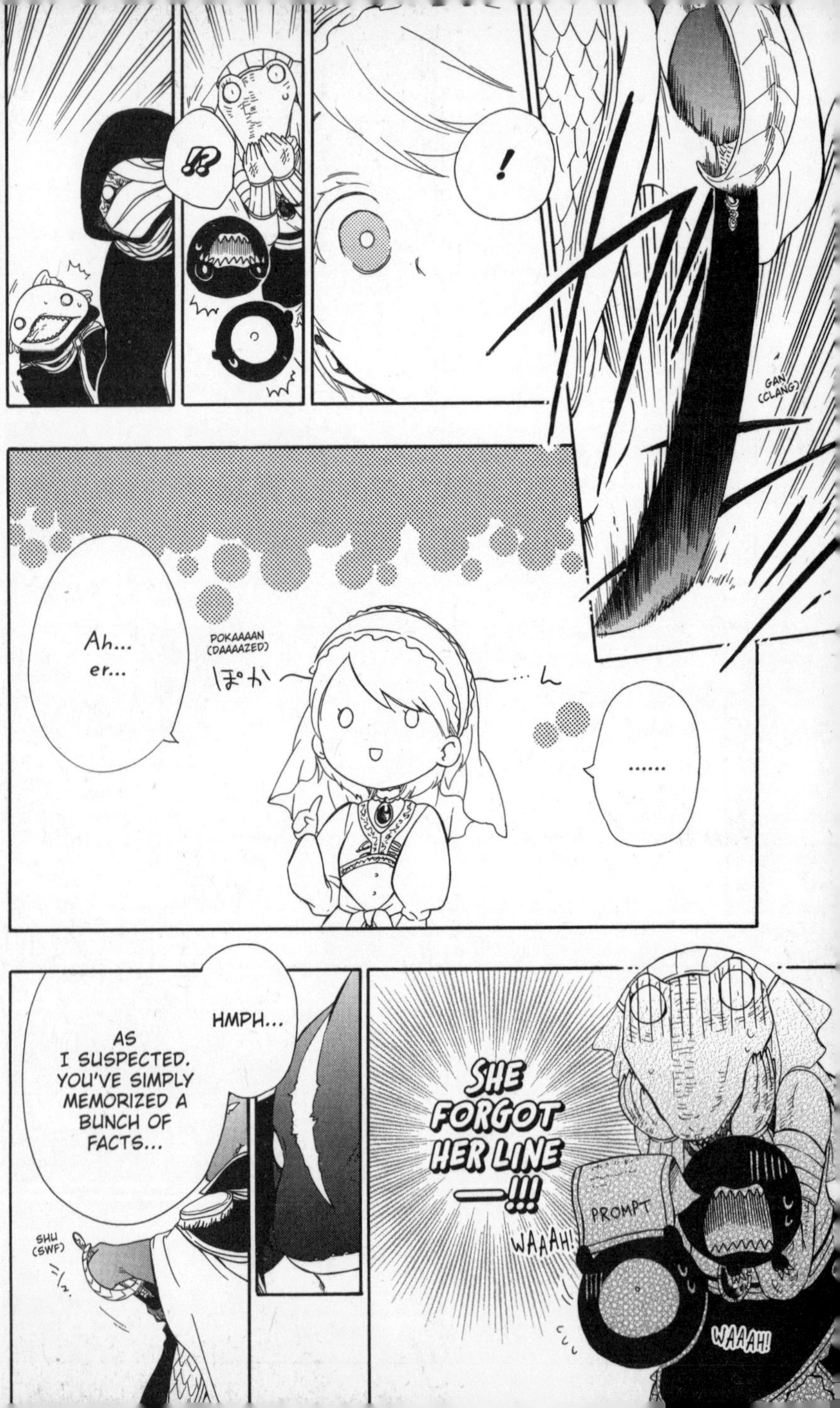
GAN (CLANG)
!
!?
......
POKAAAAN (DAAAAZED)
ぽか……ん
Ah... er...
SHE FORGOT HER LINE—!!!
PROMPT
WAAAH!
WAAAH!
HMPH...
AS I SUSPECTED. YOU'VE SIMPLY MEMORIZED A BUNCH OF FACTS...
SHU (SWF)

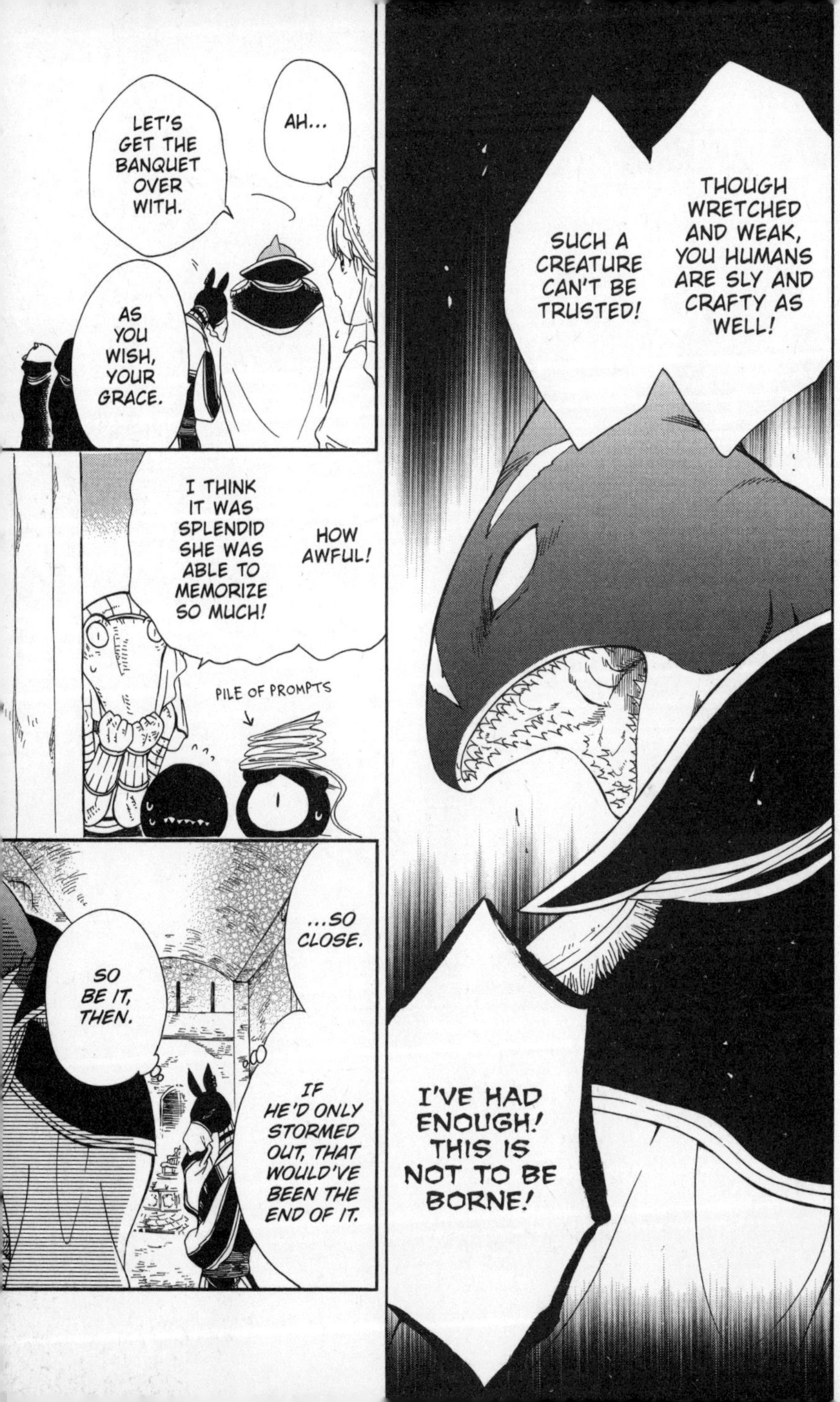
THOUGH WRETCHED AND WEAK, YOU HUMANS ARE SLY AND CRAFTY AS WELL!
SUCH A CREATURE CAN'T BE TRUSTED!
I'VE HAD ENOUGH! THIS IS NOT TO BE BORNE!
AH...
LET'S GET THE BANQUET OVER WITH.
AS YOU WISH, YOUR GRACE.
HOW AWFUL!
I THINK IT WAS SPLENDID SHE WAS ABLE TO MEMORIZE SO MUCH!
PILE OF PROMPTS
...SO CLOSE.
SO BE IT, THEN.
IF HE'D ONLY STORMED OUT, THAT WOULD'VE BEEN THE END OF IT.

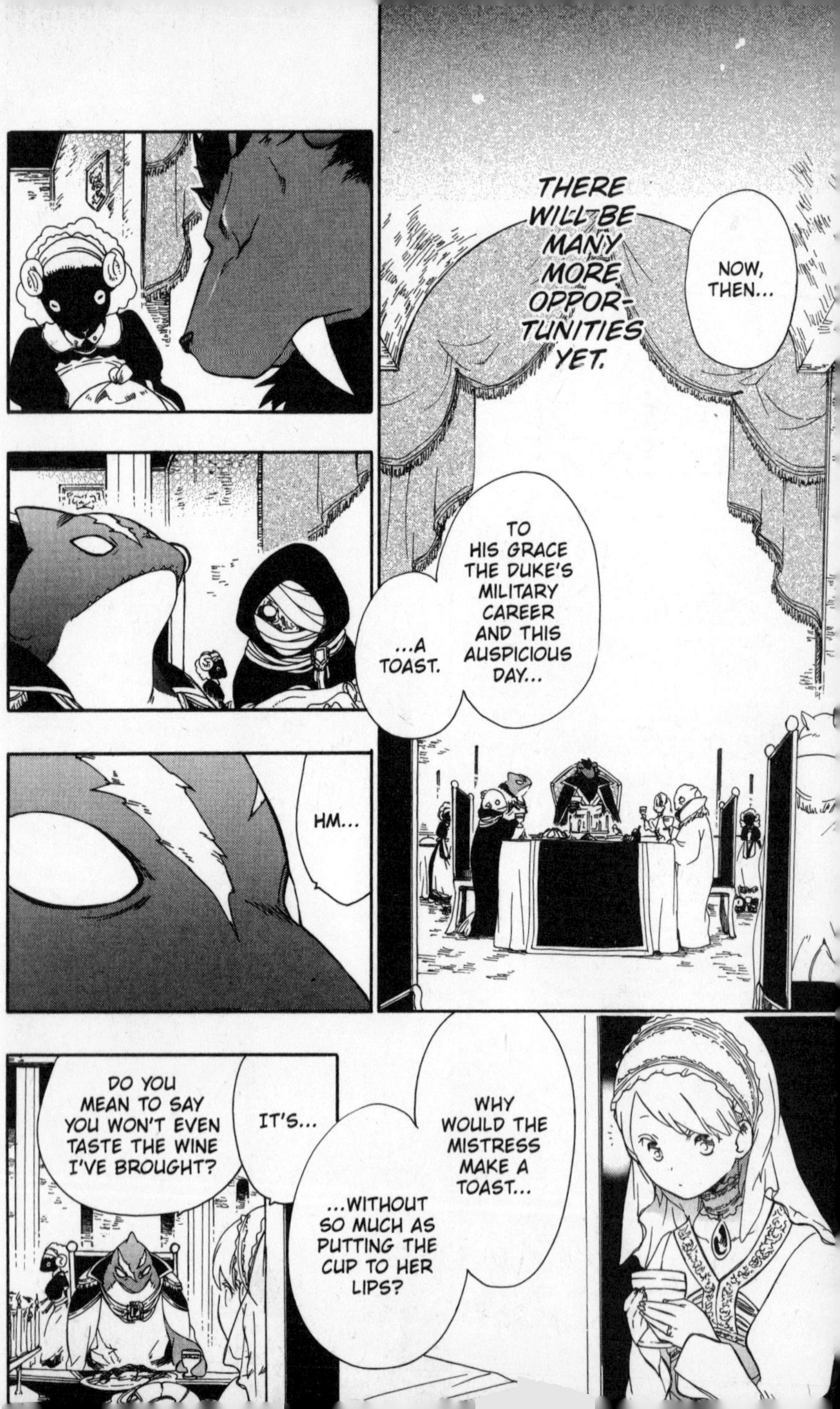
THERE WILL BE MANY MORE OPPORTUNITIES YET.
NOW, THEN...
TO HIS GRACE THE DUKE'S MILITARY CAREER AND THIS AUSPICIOUS DAY...
...A TOAST.
HM...
WHY WOULD THE MISTRESS MAKE A TOAST...
...WITHOUT SO MUCH AS PUTTING THE CUP TO HER LIPS?
IT'S...
DO YOU MEAN TO SAY YOU WON'T EVEN TASTE THE WINE I'VE BROUGHT?

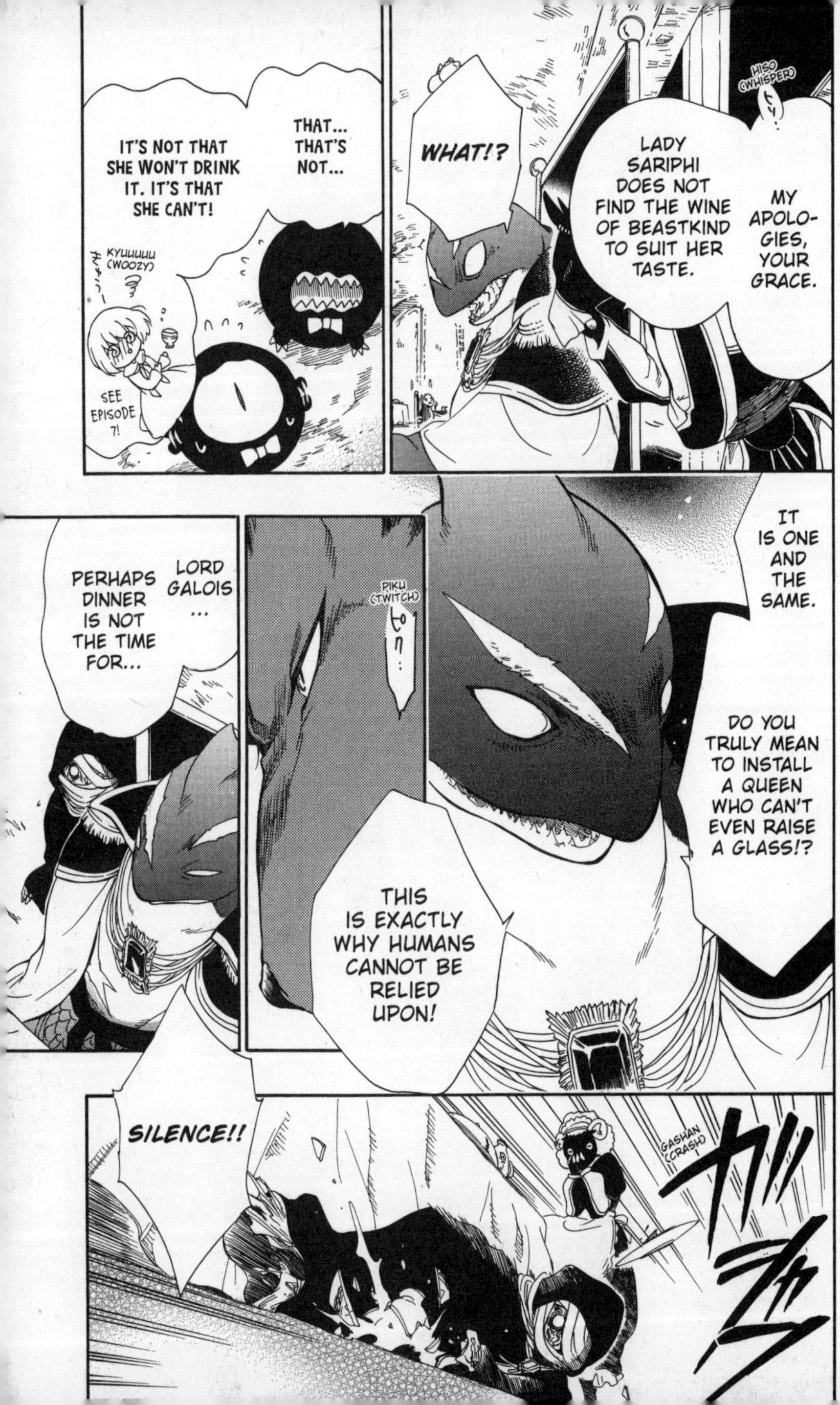
HISO (WHISPER)
MY APOLOGIES, YOUR GRACE.
LADY SARIPHI DOES NOT FIND THE WINE OF BEASTKIND TO SUIT HER TASTE.
WHAT!?
THAT... THAT'S NOT...
IT'S NOT THAT SHE WON'T DRINK IT. IT'S THAT SHE CAN'T!
KYUUUUU (WOOZY)
SEE EPISODE 7!
IT IS ONE AND THE SAME.
DO YOU TRULY MEAN TO INSTALL A QUEEN WHO CAN'T EVEN RAISE A GLASS!?
PIKU (TWITCH)
THIS IS EXACTLY WHY HUMANS CANNOT BE RELIED UPON!
LORD GALOIS...
PERHAPS DINNER IS NOT THE TIME FOR...
GASHAN (CRASH)
SILENCE!!

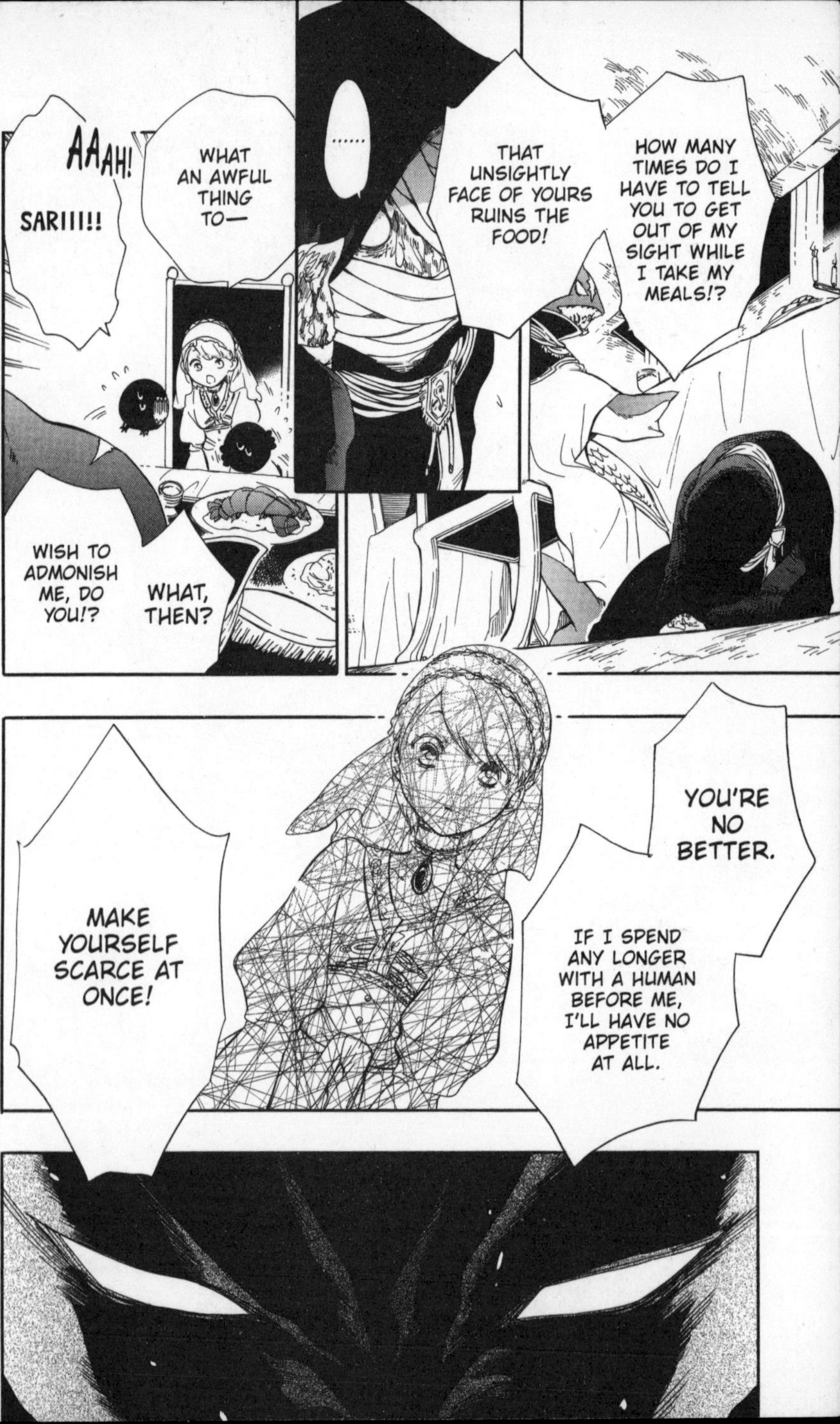
HOW MANY TIMES DO I HAVE TO TELL YOU TO GET OUT OF MY SIGHT WHILE I TAKE MY MEALS!?
THAT UNSIGHTLY FACE OF YOURS RUINS THE FOOD!
......
WHAT AN AWFUL THING TO—
AAAH! SARIIII!!
WHAT, THEN?
WISH TO ADMONISH ME, DO YOU!?
YOU'RE NO BETTER.
IF I SPEND ANY LONGER WITH A HUMAN BEFORE ME, I'LL HAVE NO APPETITE AT ALL.
MAKE YOURSELF SCARCE AT ONCE!

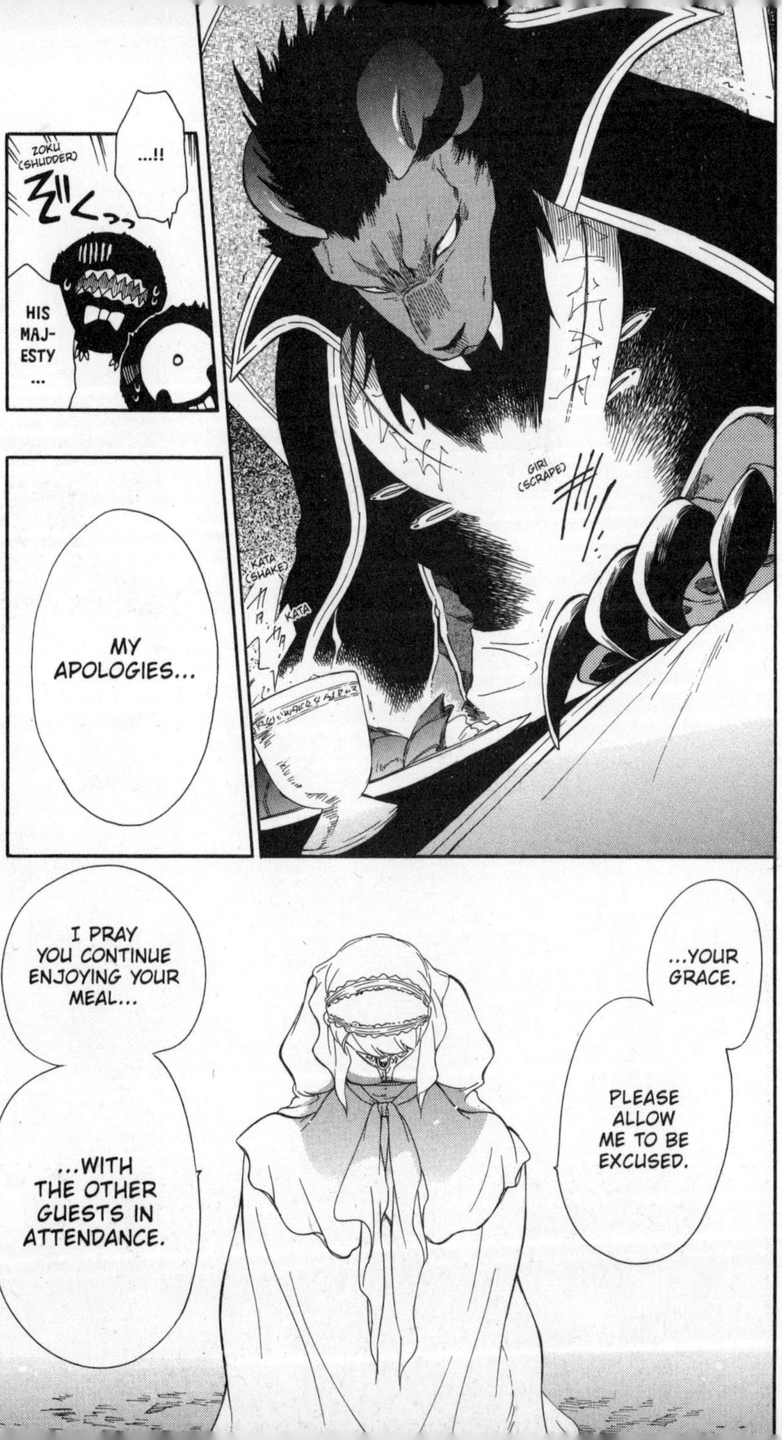

GIRI (SCRAPE)
KATA (SHAKE)
KATA
ZOKU (SHUDDER)
...!!
HIS MAJ-ESTY ...
MY APOLOGIES...
...YOUR GRACE.
PLEASE ALLOW ME TO BE EXCUSED.
I PRAY YOU CONTINUE ENJOYING YOUR MEAL...
...WITH THE OTHER GUESTS IN ATTENDANCE.

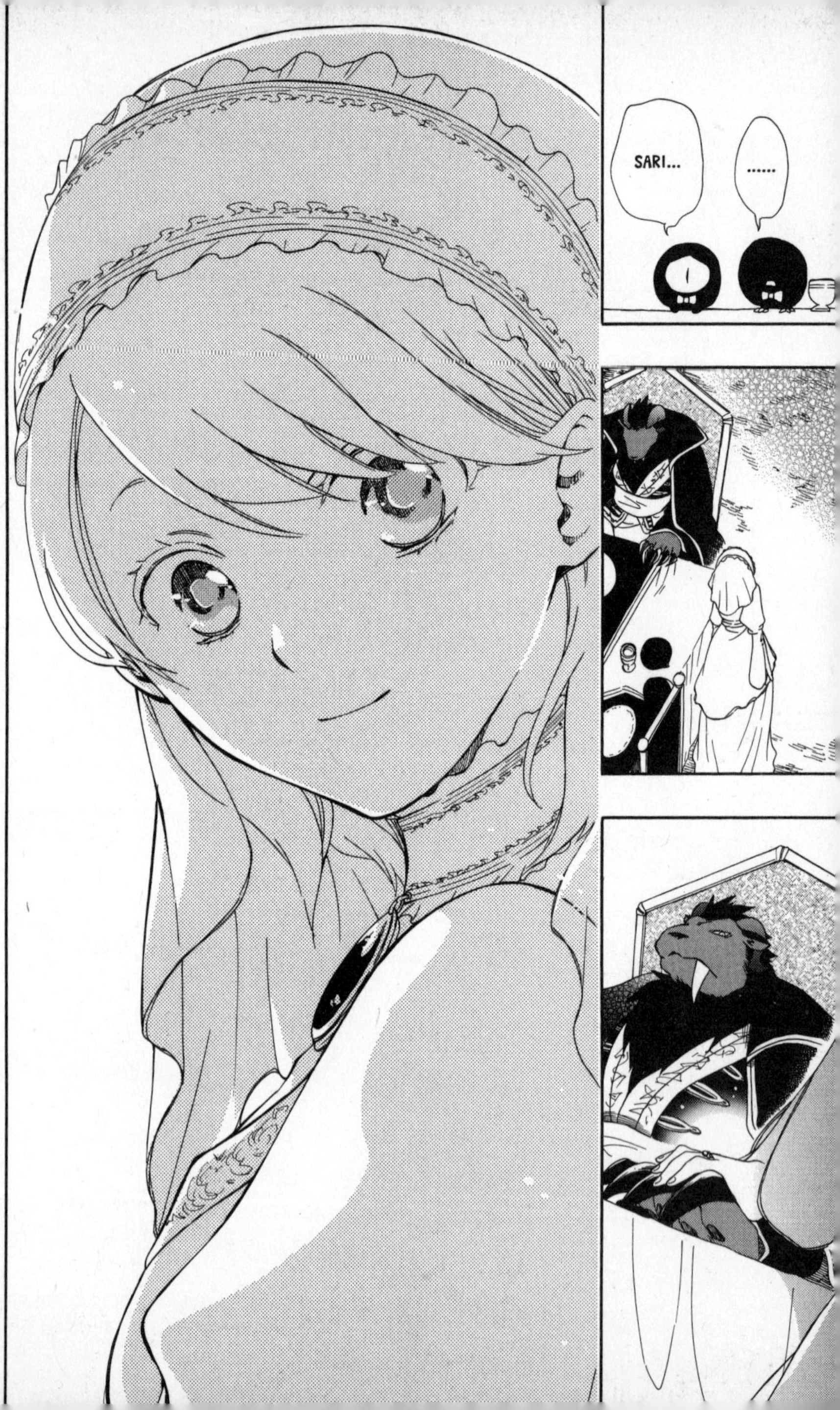
......
SARI...

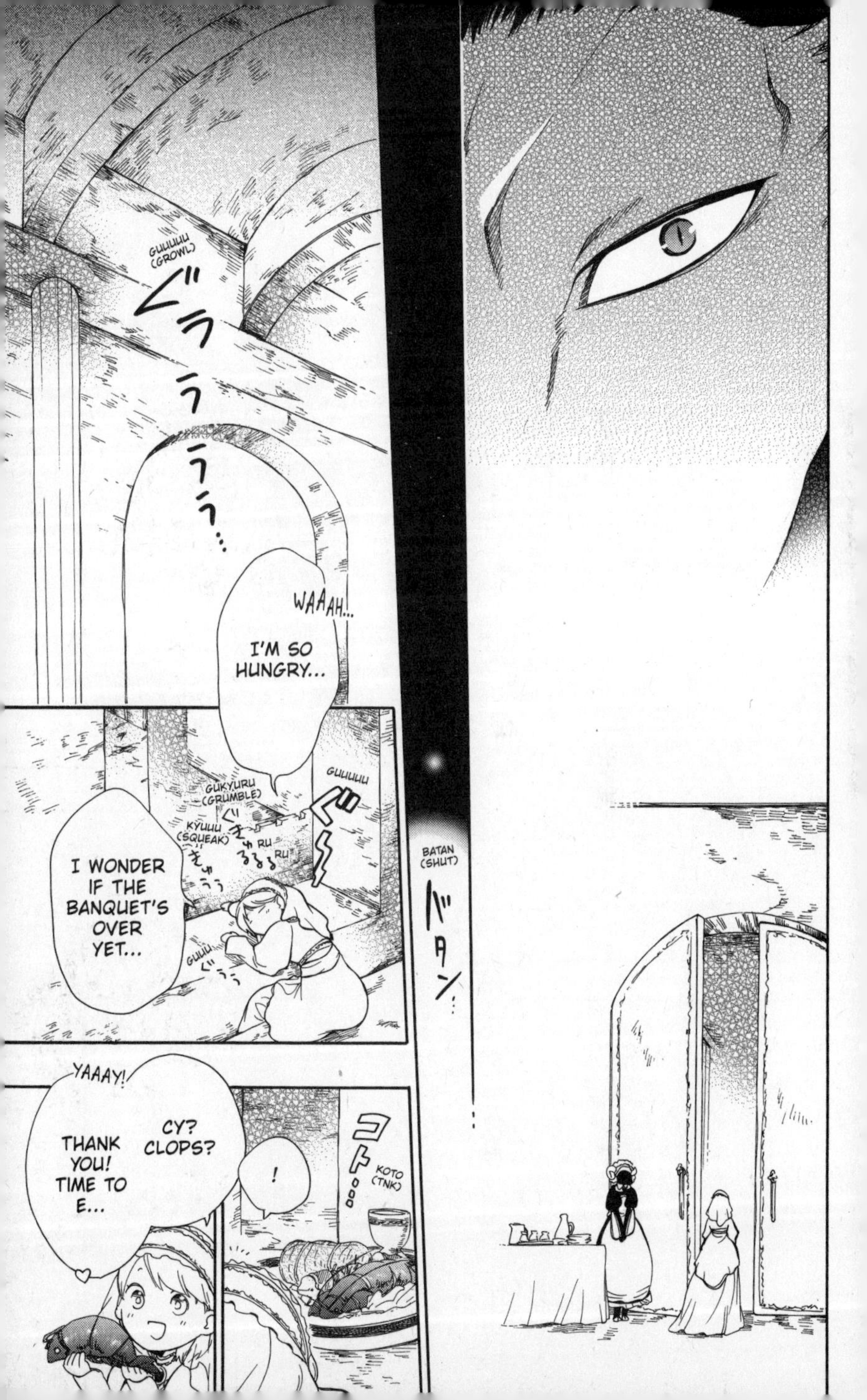
BATAN (SHUT)
GUUUUUU (GROWL)
WAAAH...
I'M SO HUNGRY...
GUUUUUU
GUKYURU (GRUMBLE) RU RU
KYUUU (SQUEAK)
I WONDER IF THE BANQUET'S OVER YET...
GUUU
KOTO (TNK)
!
CY? CLOPS?
YAAAY!
THANK YOU! TIME TO E...

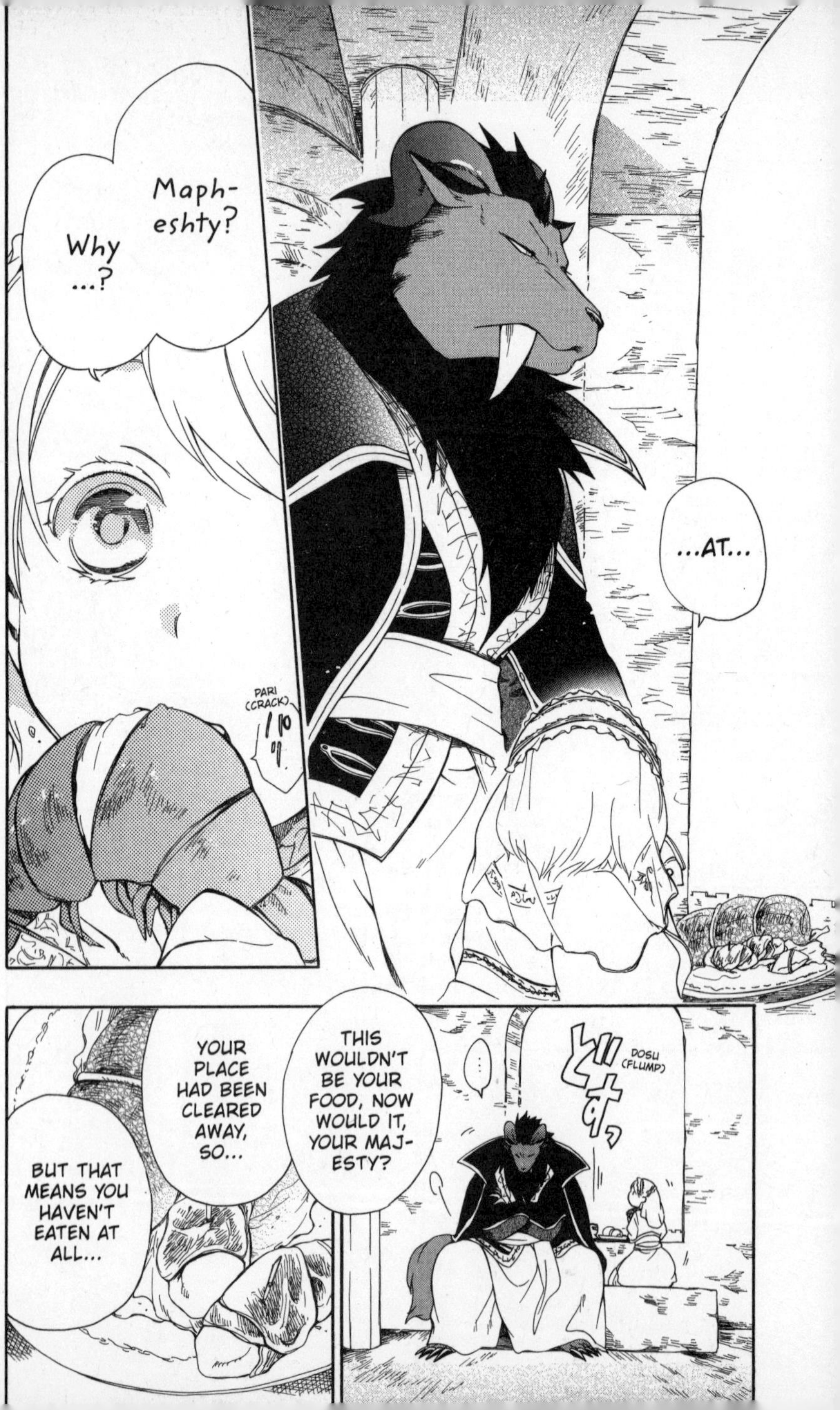
...AT...
Maph-eshty? Why ...?
PARI (CRACK)
DOSU (FLUMP)
...
THIS WOULDN'T BE YOUR FOOD, NOW WOULD IT, YOUR MAJ-ESTY?
YOUR PLACE HAD BEEN CLEARED AWAY, SO...
BUT THAT MEANS YOU HAVEN'T EATEN AT ALL...

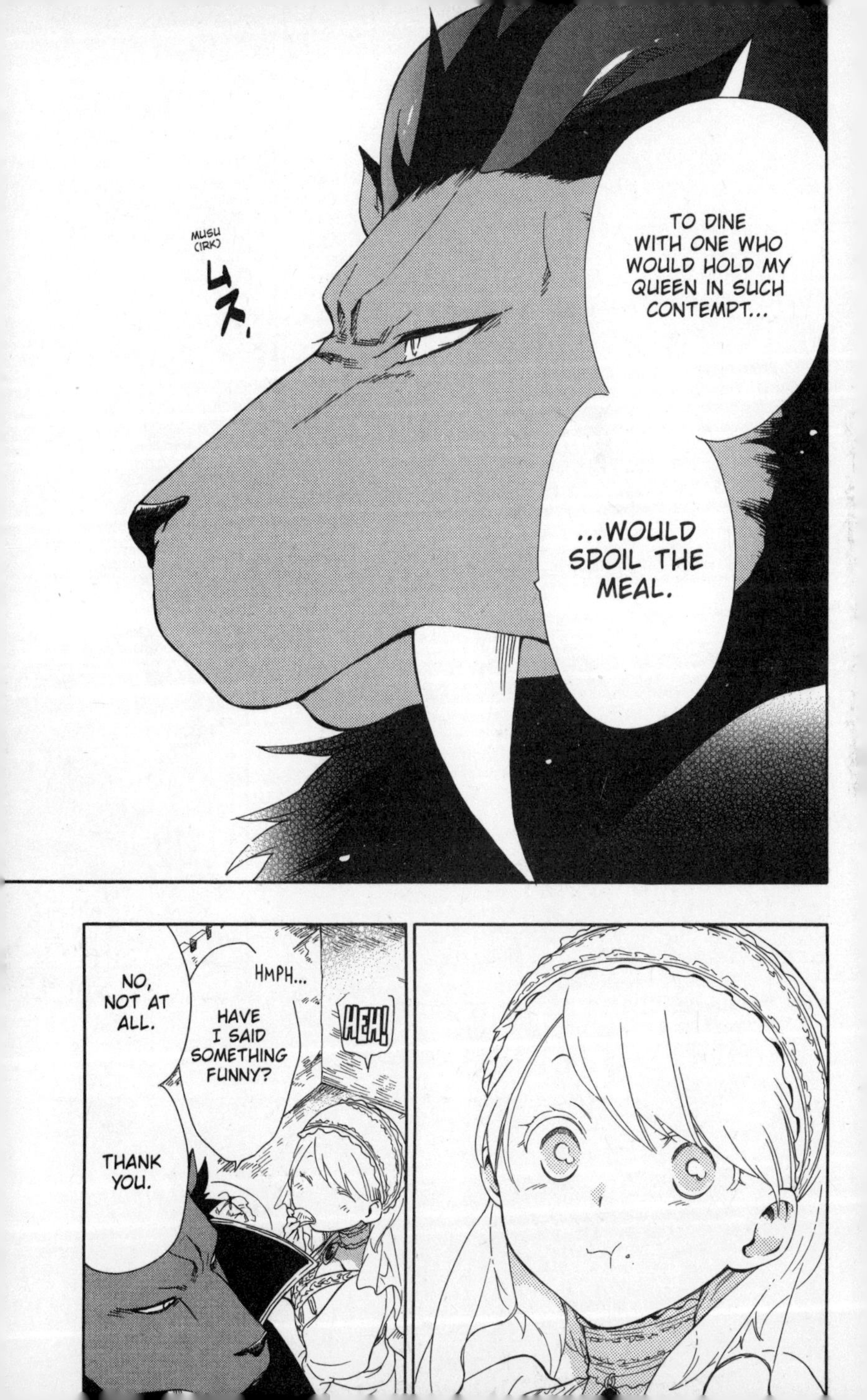
TO DINE WITH ONE WHO WOULD HOLD MY QUEEN IN SUCH CONTEMPT...
...WOULD SPOIL THE MEAL.
MUSU (IRK)
ムス、
HEH!
HMPH...
HAVE I SAID SOMETHING FUNNY?
NO, NOT AT ALL.
THANK YOU.

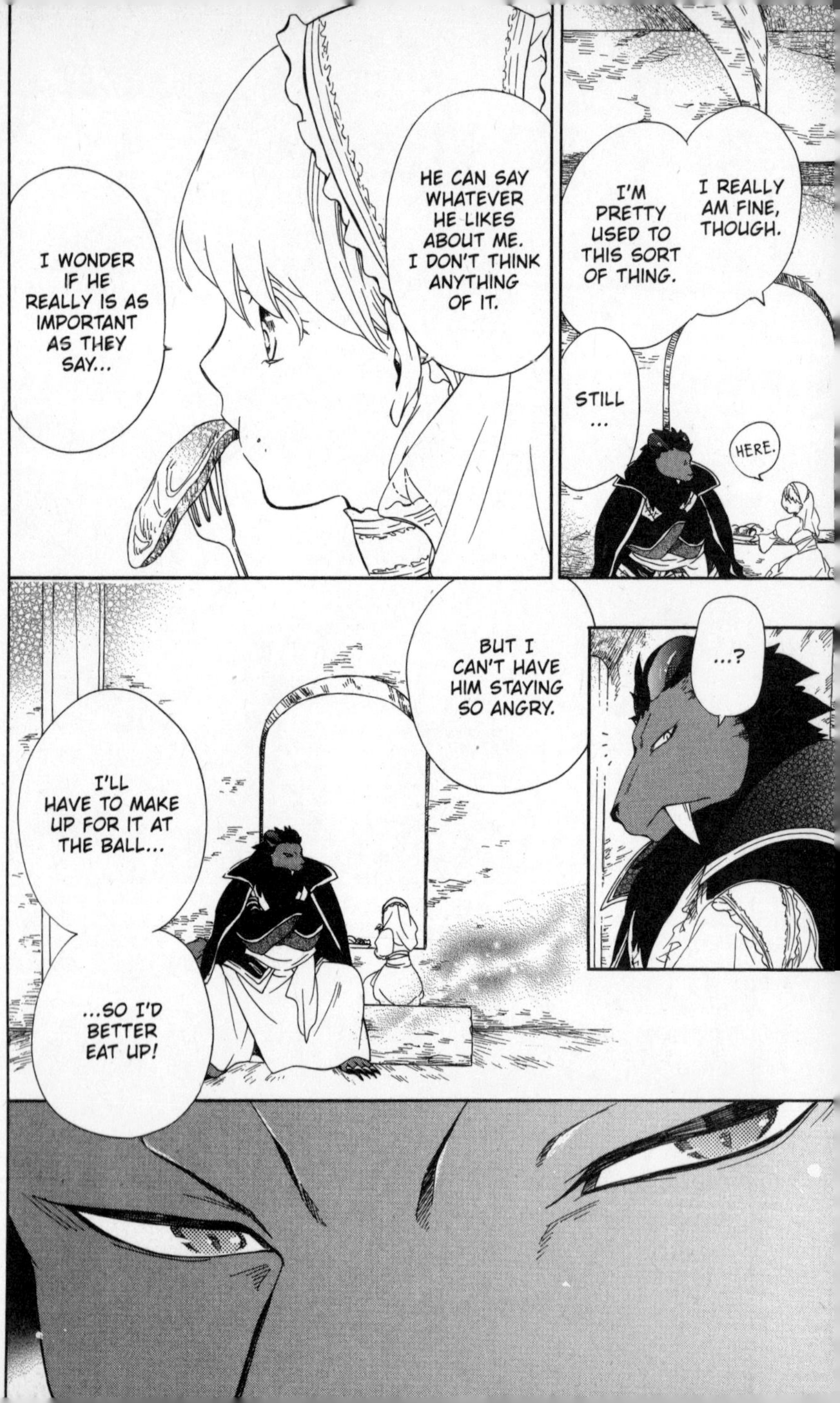
I REALLY AM FINE, THOUGH.
I'M PRETTY USED TO THIS SORT OF THING.
STILL...
HERE.
HE CAN SAY WHATEVER HE LIKES ABOUT ME. I DON'T THINK ANYTHING OF IT.
I WONDER IF HE REALLY IS AS IMPORTANT AS THEY SAY...
...?
BUT I CAN'T HAVE HIM STAYING SO ANGRY.
I'LL HAVE TO MAKE UP FOR IT AT THE BALL...
...SO I'D BETTER EAT UP!

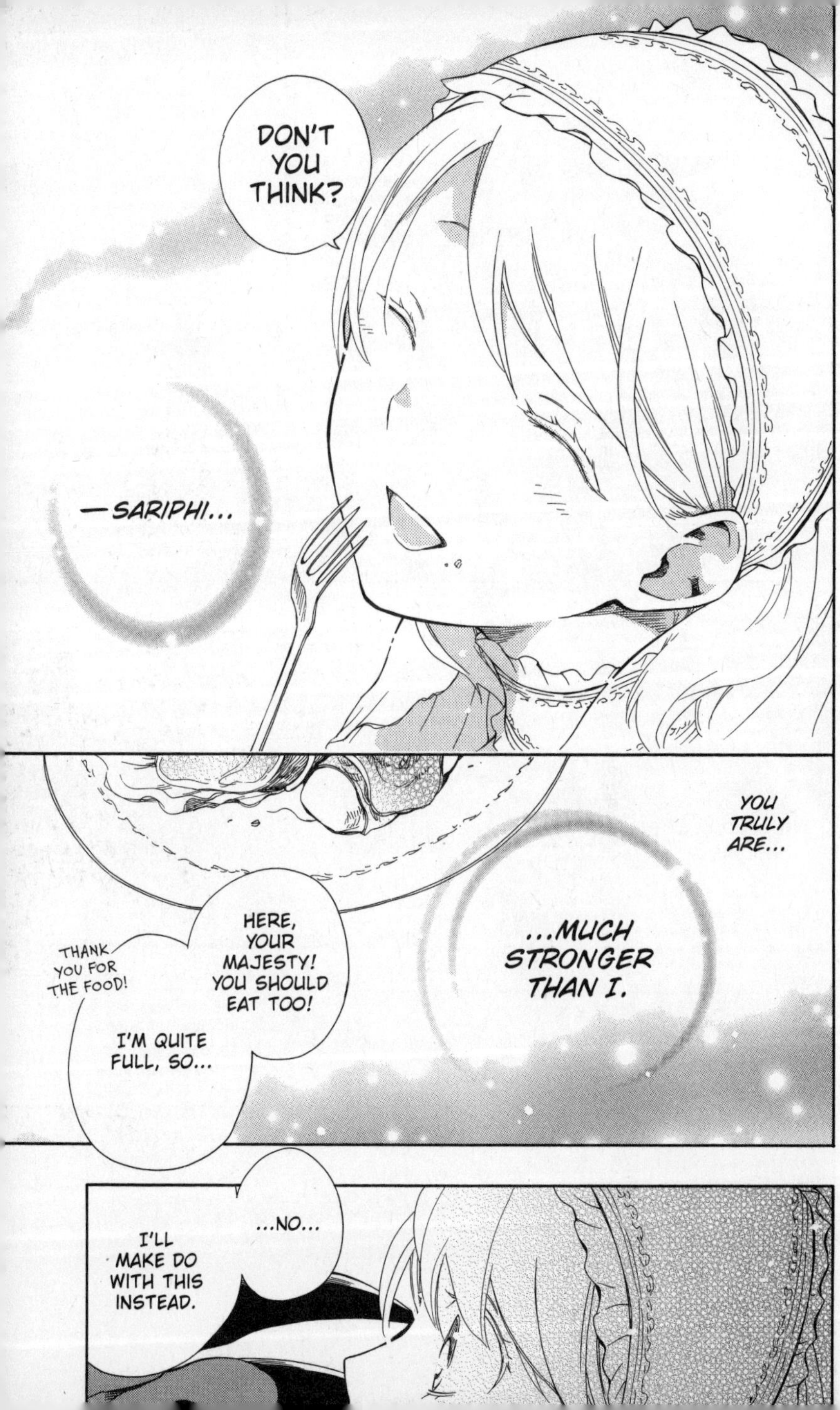
DON'T YOU THINK?
—SARIPHI...
YOU TRULY ARE...
...MUCH STRONGER THAN I.
HERE, YOUR MAJESTY! YOU SHOULD EAT TOO!
THANK YOU FOR THE FOOD!
I'M QUITE FULL, SO...
...NO...
I'LL MAKE DO WITH THIS INSTEAD.

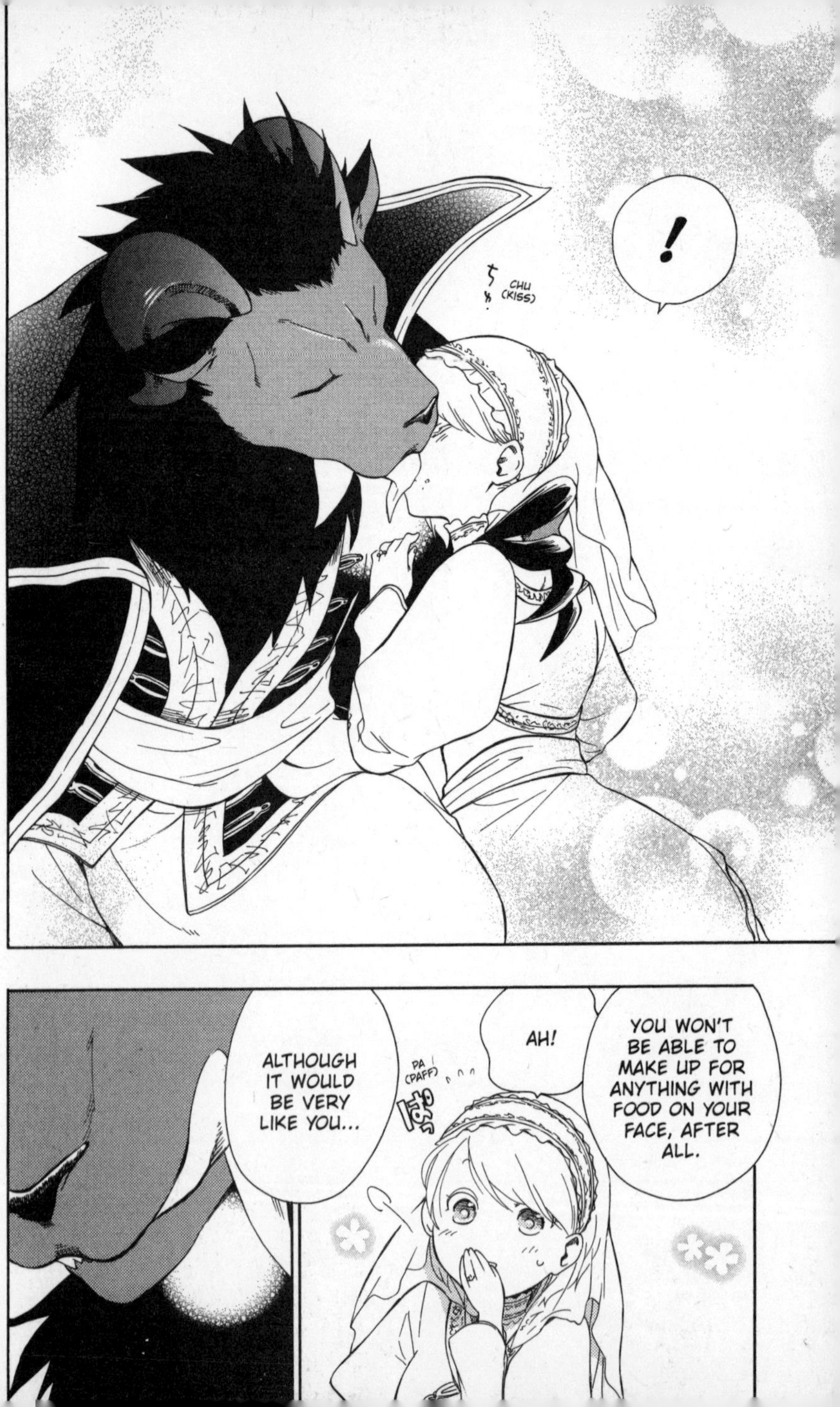

CHU (KISS)
!
YOU WON'T BE ABLE TO MAKE UP FOR ANYTHING WITH FOOD ON YOUR FACE, AFTER ALL.
AH!
PA! (PAFF)
ALTHOUGH IT WOULD BE VERY LIKE YOU...

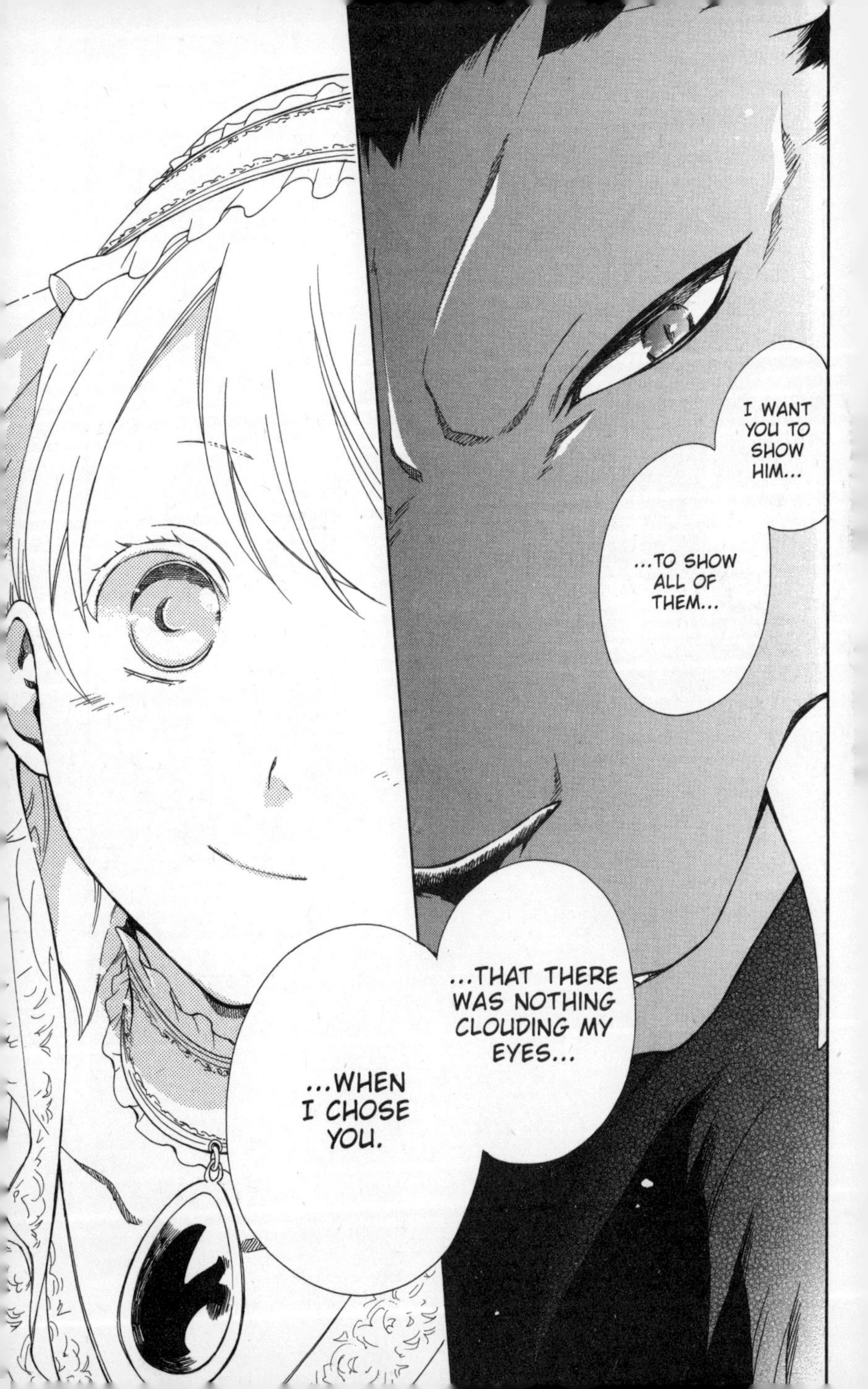
I WANT YOU TO SHOW HIM...
...TO SHOW ALL OF THEM...
...THAT THERE WAS NOTHING CLOUDING MY EYES...
...WHEN I CHOSE YOU.

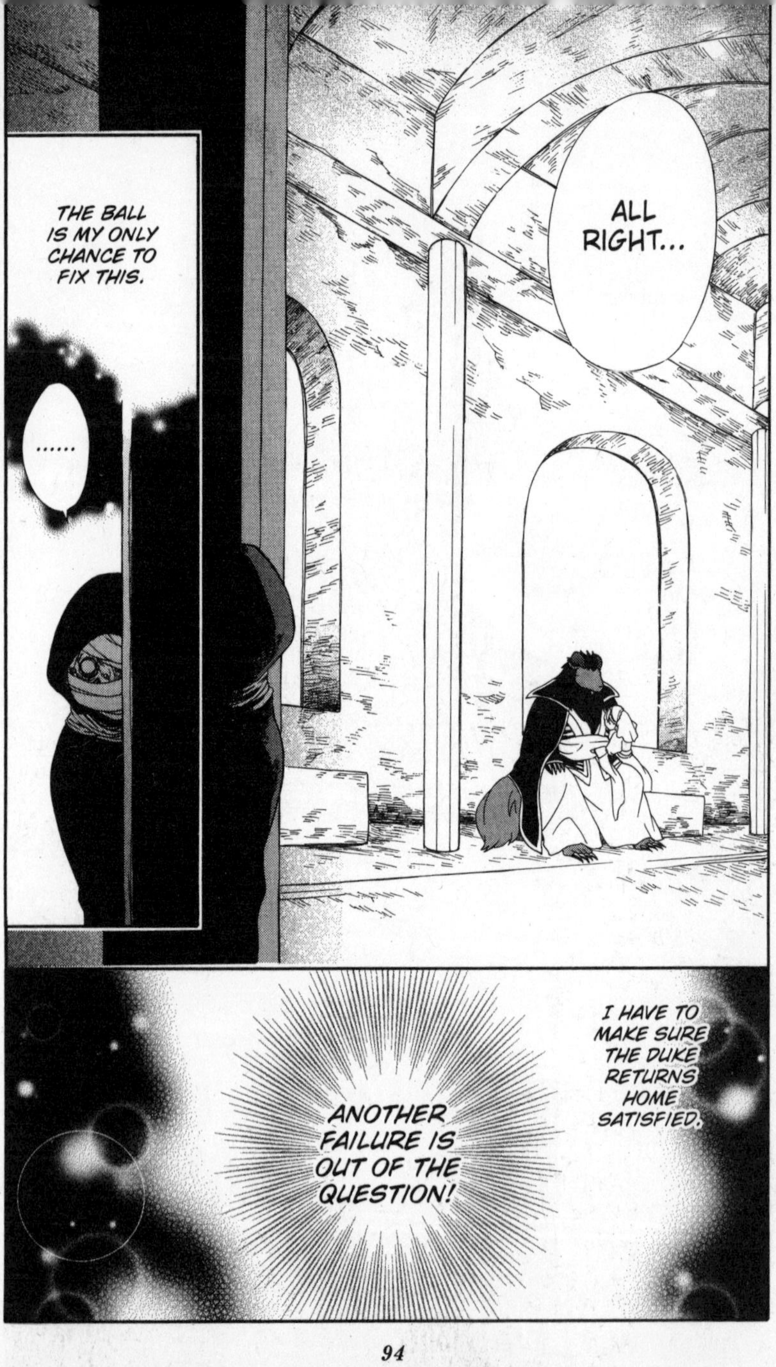
ALL RIGHT...
THE BALL IS MY ONLY CHANCE TO FIX THIS.
......
I HAVE TO MAKE SURE THE DUKE RETURNS HOME SATISFIED.
ANOTHER FAILURE IS OUT OF THE QUESTION!

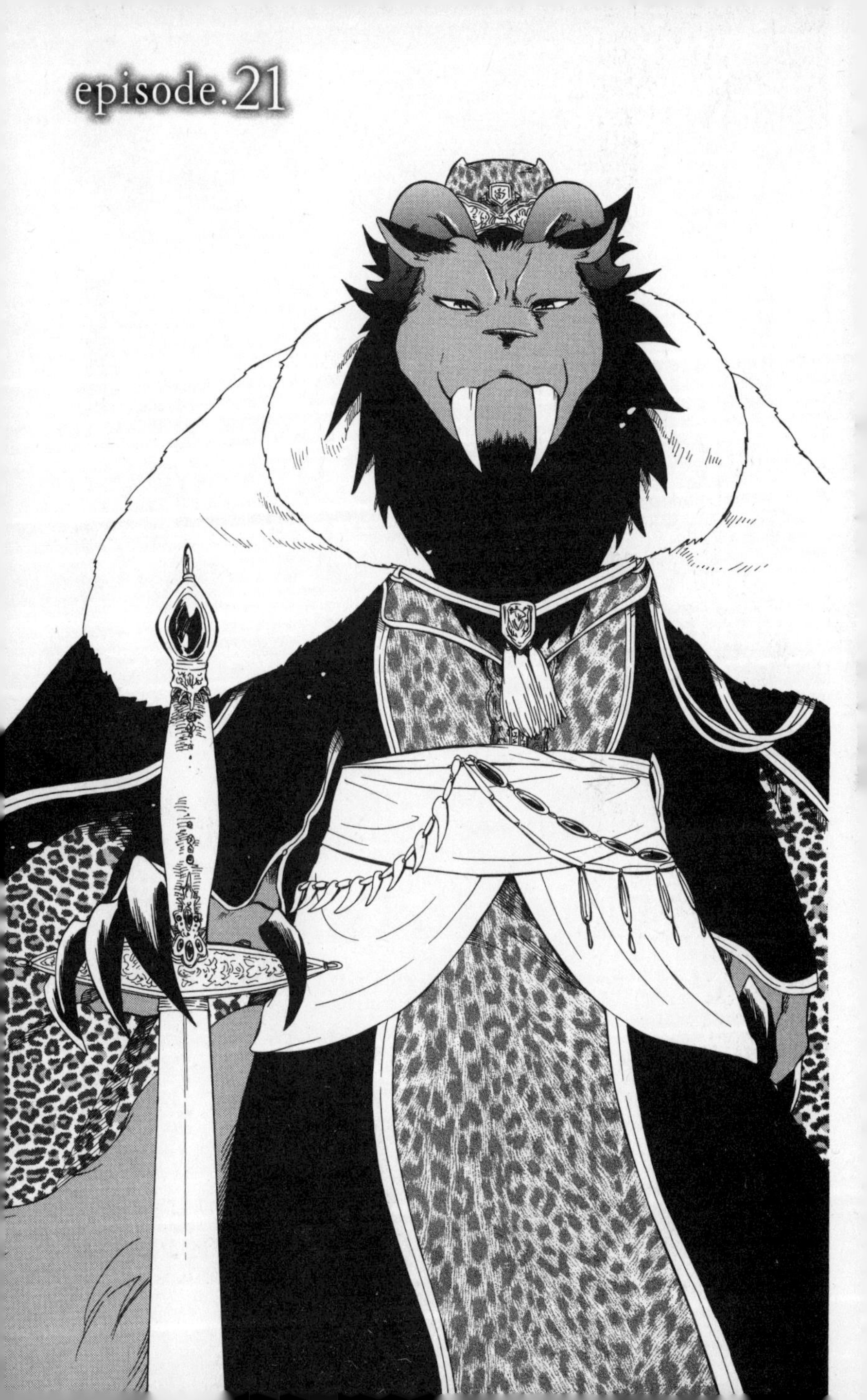
episode.21

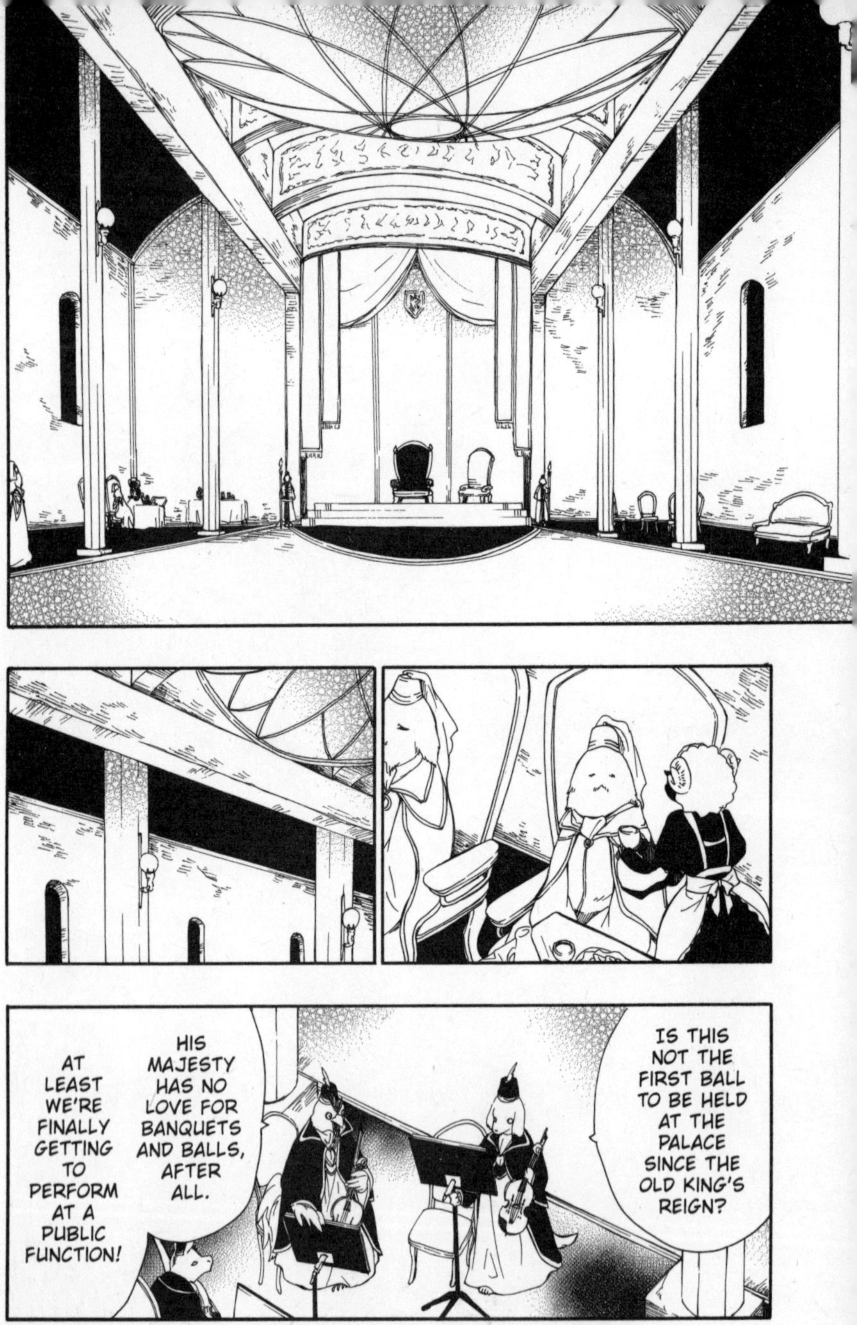
IS THIS NOT THE FIRST BALL TO BE HELD AT THE PALACE SINCE THE OLD KING'S REIGN?
HIS MAJESTY HAS NO LOVE FOR BANQUETS AND BALLS, AFTER ALL.
AT LEAST WE'RE FINALLY GETTING TO PERFORM AT A PUBLIC FUNCTION!

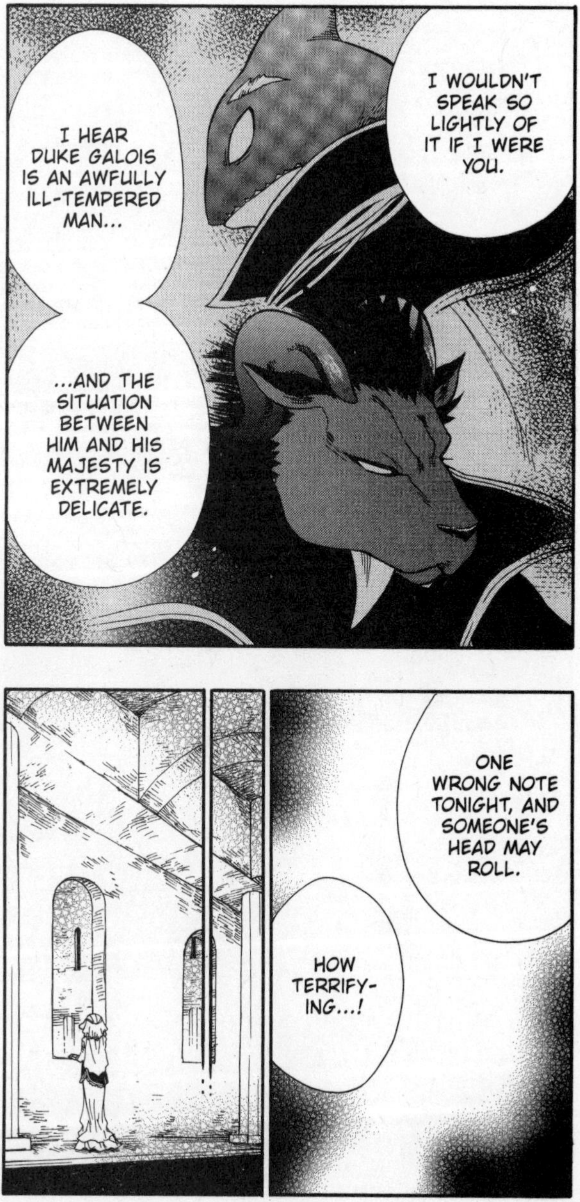
I HEAR DUKE GALOIS IS AN AWFULLY ILL-TEMPERED MAN...
...AND THE SITUATION BETWEEN HIM AND HIS MAJESTY IS EXTREMELY DELICATE.
I WOULDN'T SPEAK SO LIGHTLY OF IT IF I WERE YOU.
ONE WRONG NOTE TONIGHT, AND SOMEONE'S HEAD MAY ROLL.
HOW TERRIFY-ING...!

QUICK & DIRTY DETAILS

ANUBIS

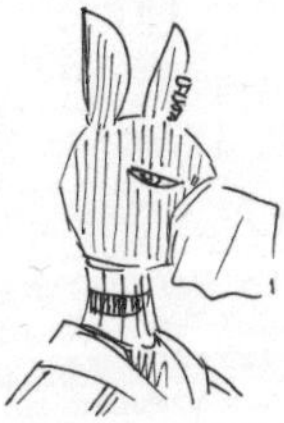

- AGE: MID-TWENTIES (IN HUMAN YEARS)
- 185cm (6'1") TALL
- DISLIKES: ANYONE WHO WOULD HARM THE KING
- LIKES: WINNING ARGUMENTS

JORMUNGAND

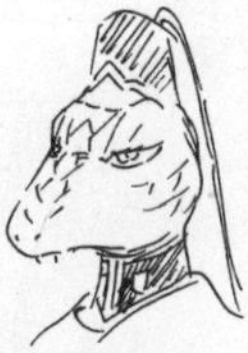

- AGE: MID-TWENTIES (IN HUMAN YEARS)
- ABOUT TWO METERS (6'6") TALL
- DISLIKES: SLOPPY, HALF-DONE THINGS
- LIKES: APPLES

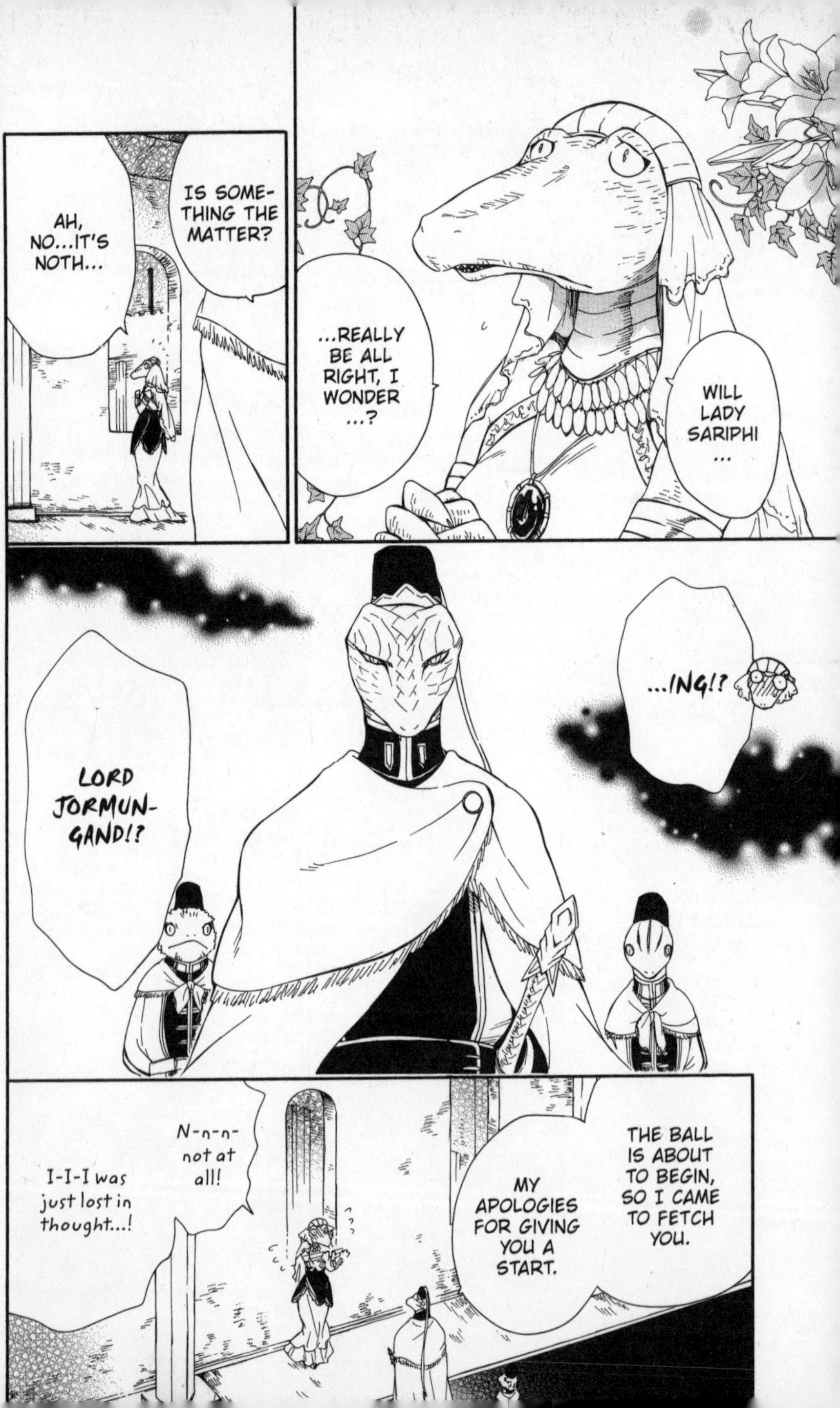
WILL LADY SARIPHI ...
...REALLY BE ALL RIGHT, I WONDER ...?
IS SOME-THING THE MATTER?
AH, NO...IT'S NOTH...
...ING!?
LORD JORMUN-GAND!?
THE BALL IS ABOUT TO BEGIN, SO I CAME TO FETCH YOU.
MY APOLOGIES FOR GIVING YOU A START.
N-n-n-not at all!
I-I-I was just lost in thought...!

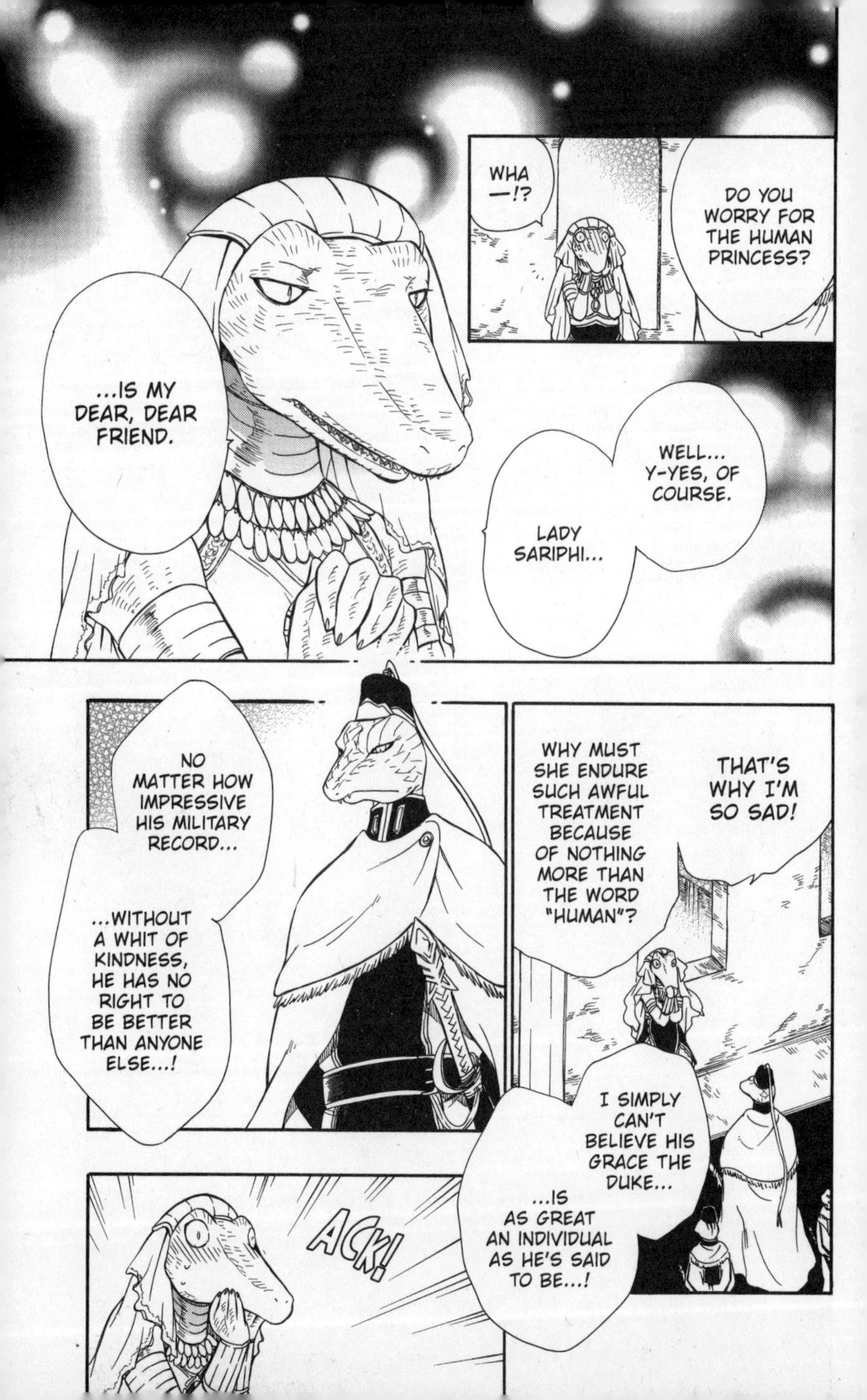
DO YOU WORRY FOR THE HUMAN PRINCESS?
WHA—!?
WELL... Y-YES, OF COURSE.
LADY SARIPHI...
...IS MY DEAR, DEAR FRIEND.
THAT'S WHY I'M SO SAD!
WHY MUST SHE ENDURE SUCH AWFUL TREATMENT BECAUSE OF NOTHING MORE THAN THE WORD "HUMAN"?
I SIMPLY CAN'T BELIEVE HIS GRACE THE DUKE...
...IS AS GREAT AN INDIVIDUAL AS HE'S SAID TO BE...!
NO MATTER HOW IMPRESSIVE HIS MILITARY RECORD...
...WITHOUT A WHIT OF KINDNESS, HE HAS NO RIGHT TO BE BETTER THAN ANYONE ELSE...!
ACK!

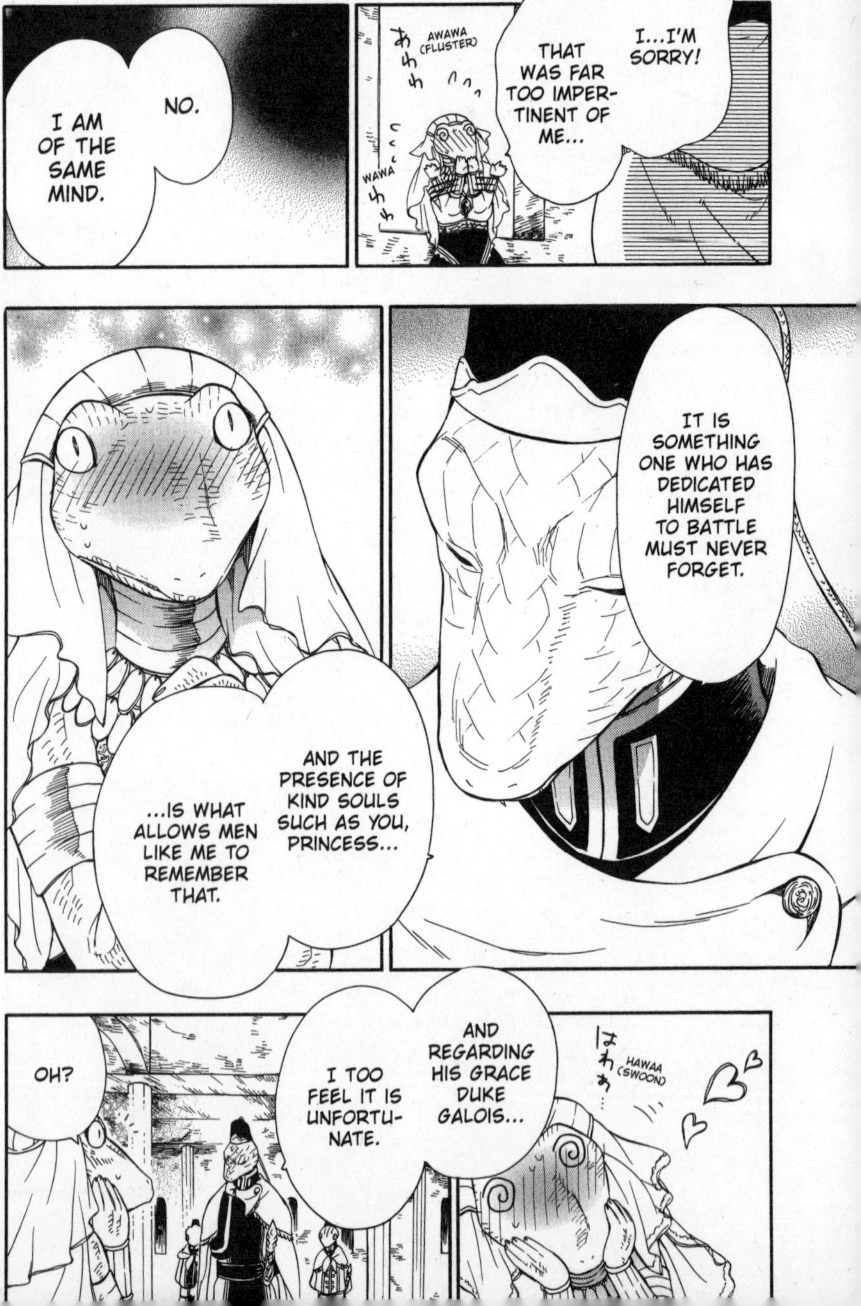
AWAWA (FLUSTER)
WAWA
I...I'M SORRY!
THAT WAS FAR TOO IMPER-TINENT OF ME...
NO.
I AM OF THE SAME MIND.
IT IS SOMETHING ONE WHO HAS DEDICATED HIMSELF TO BATTLE MUST NEVER FORGET.
AND THE PRESENCE OF KIND SOULS SUCH AS YOU, PRINCESS...
...IS WHAT ALLOWS MEN LIKE ME TO REMEMBER THAT.
HAWAA (SWOON)
AND REGARDING HIS GRACE DUKE GALOIS...
I TOO FEEL IT IS UNFORTU-NATE.
OH?

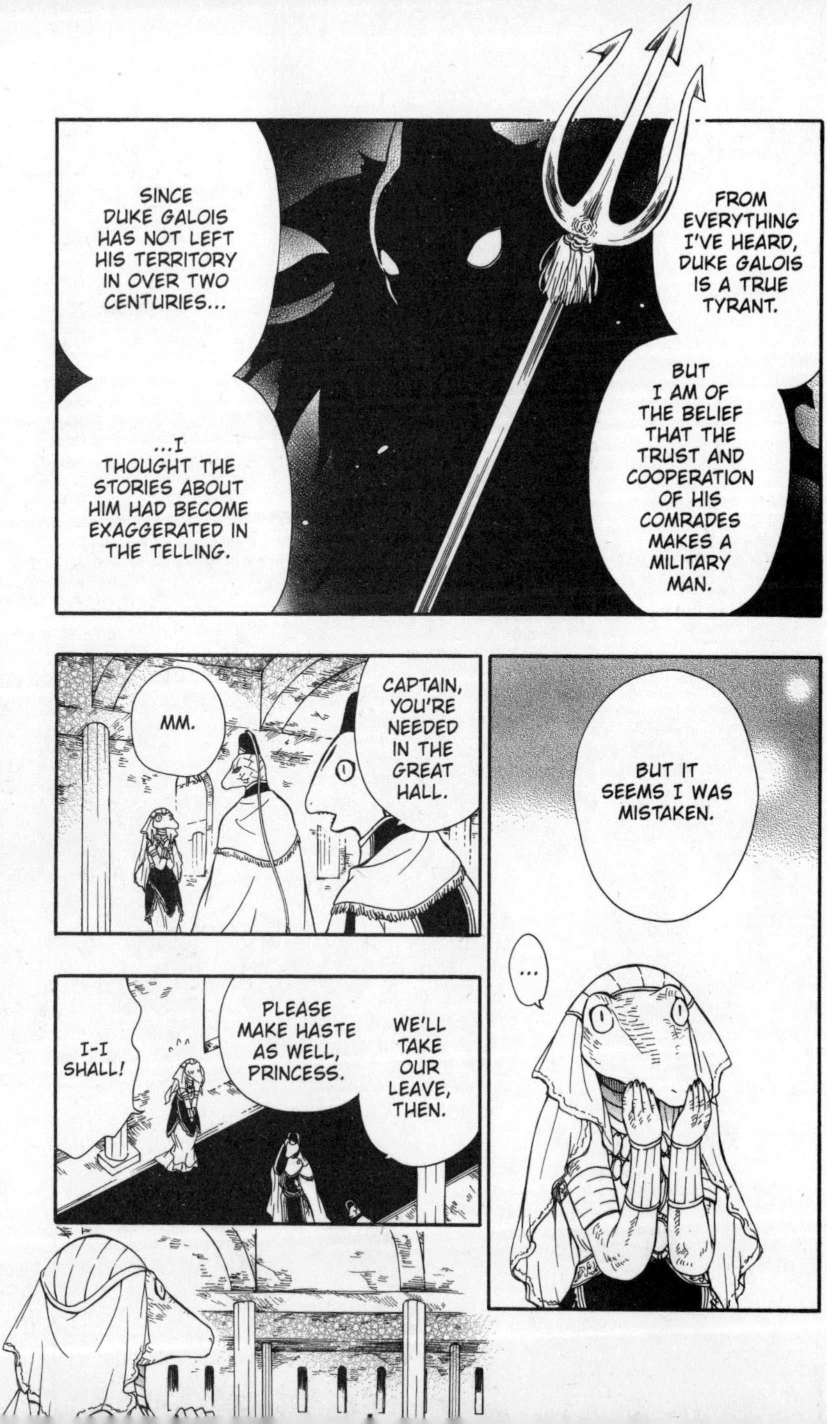
FROM EVERYTHING I'VE HEARD, DUKE GALOIS IS A TRUE TYRANT.
BUT I AM OF THE BELIEF THAT THE TRUST AND COOPERATION OF HIS COMRADES MAKES A MILITARY MAN.
SINCE DUKE GALOIS HAS NOT LEFT HIS TERRITORY IN OVER TWO CENTURIES...
...I THOUGHT THE STORIES ABOUT HIM HAD BECOME EXAGGERATED IN THE TELLING.
BUT IT SEEMS I WAS MISTAKEN.
...
CAPTAIN, YOU'RE NEEDED IN THE GREAT HALL.
MM.
WE'LL TAKE OUR LEAVE, THEN.
PLEASE MAKE HASTE AS WELL, PRINCESS.
I-I SHALL!

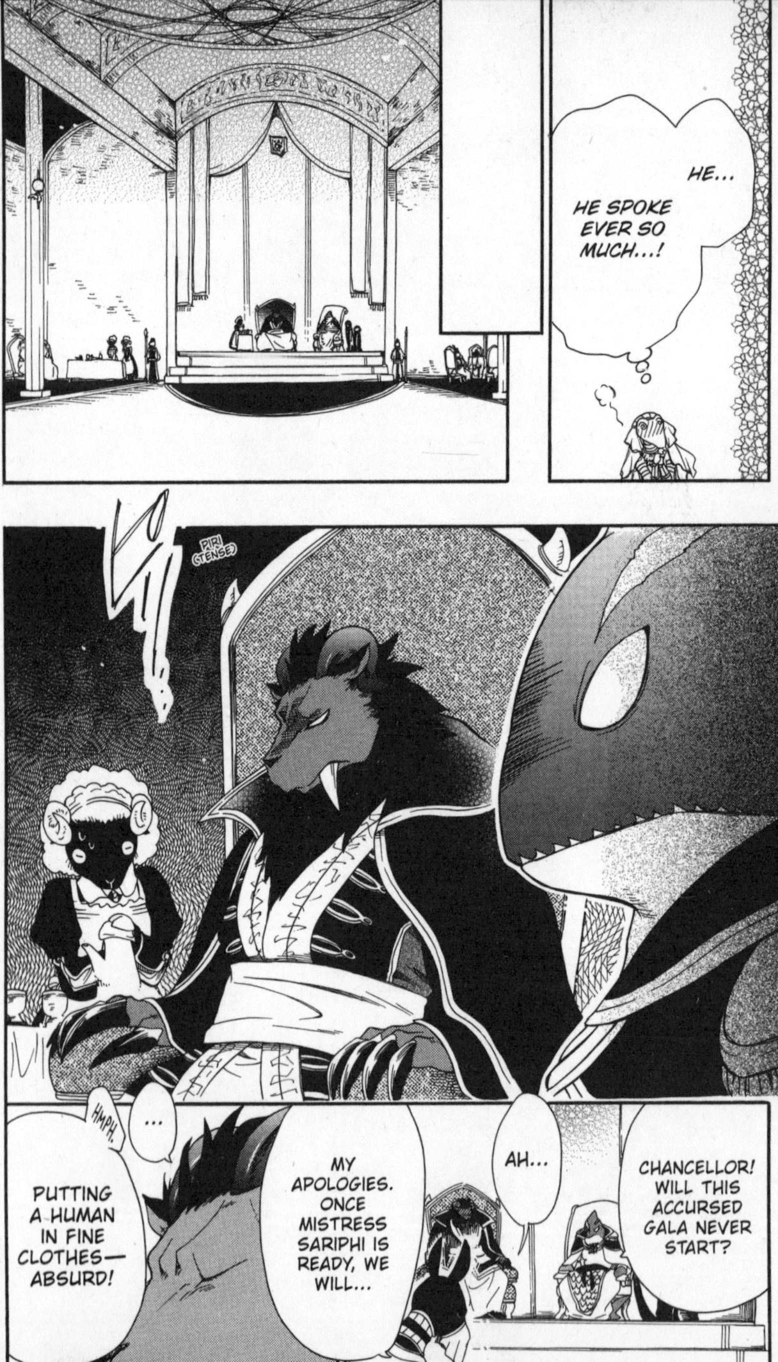
HE...
HE SPOKE EVER SO MUCH...!
PIRI (TENSE)
CHANCELLOR! WILL THIS ACCURSED GALA NEVER START?
AH...
MY APOLOGIES. ONCE MISTRESS SARIPHI IS READY, WE WILL...
...
HMPH.
PUTTING A HUMAN IN FINE CLOTHES— ABSURD!

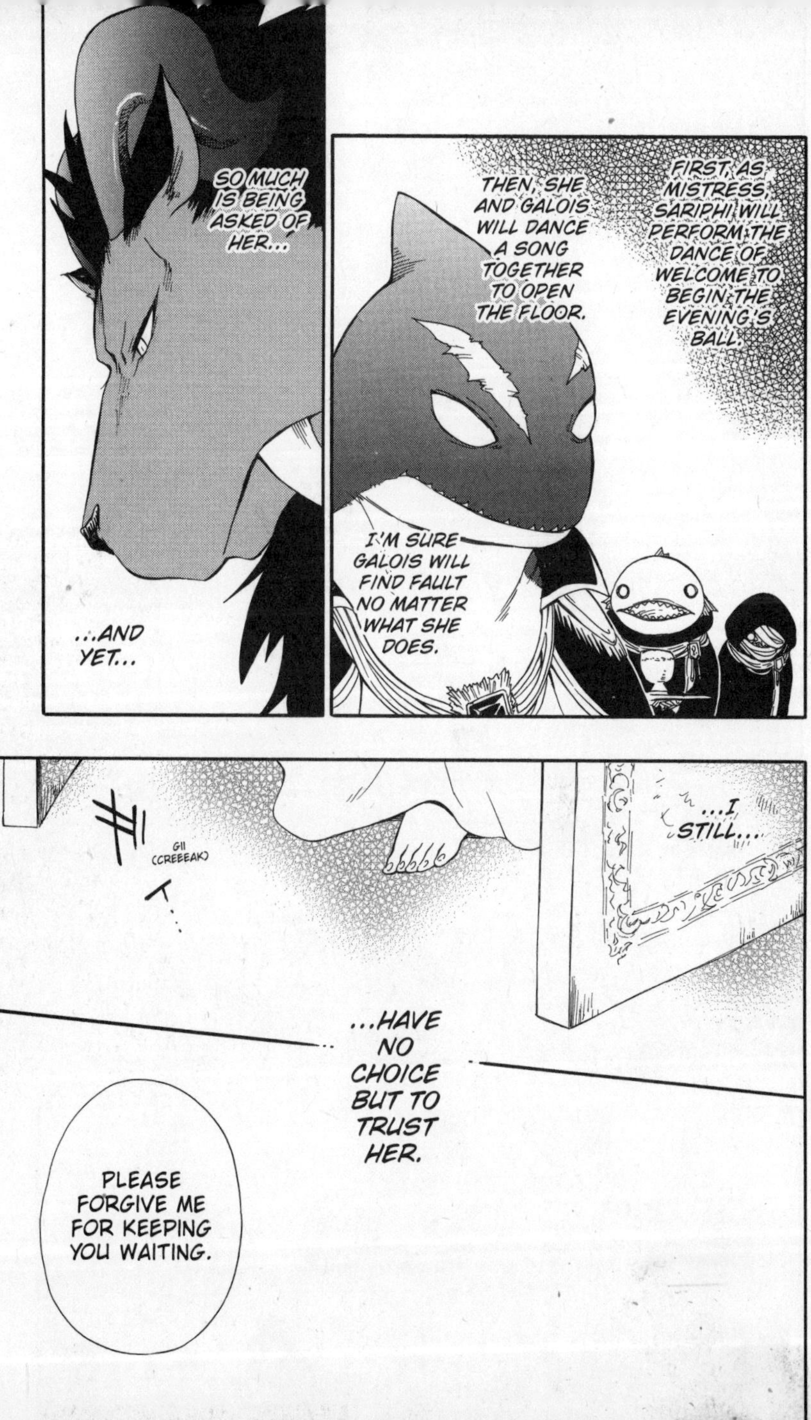
FIRST, AS MISTRESS, SARIPHI WILL PERFORM THE DANCE OF WELCOME TO BEGIN THE EVENING'S BALL.
THEN, SHE AND GALOIS WILL DANCE A SONG TOGETHER TO OPEN THE FLOOR.
I'M SURE GALOIS WILL FIND FAULT NO MATTER WHAT SHE DOES.
SO MUCH IS BEING ASKED OF HER...
...AND YET...
...I STILL...
GII (CREEEAK)
...HAVE NO CHOICE BUT TO TRUST HER.
PLEASE FORGIVE ME FOR KEEPING YOU WAITING.

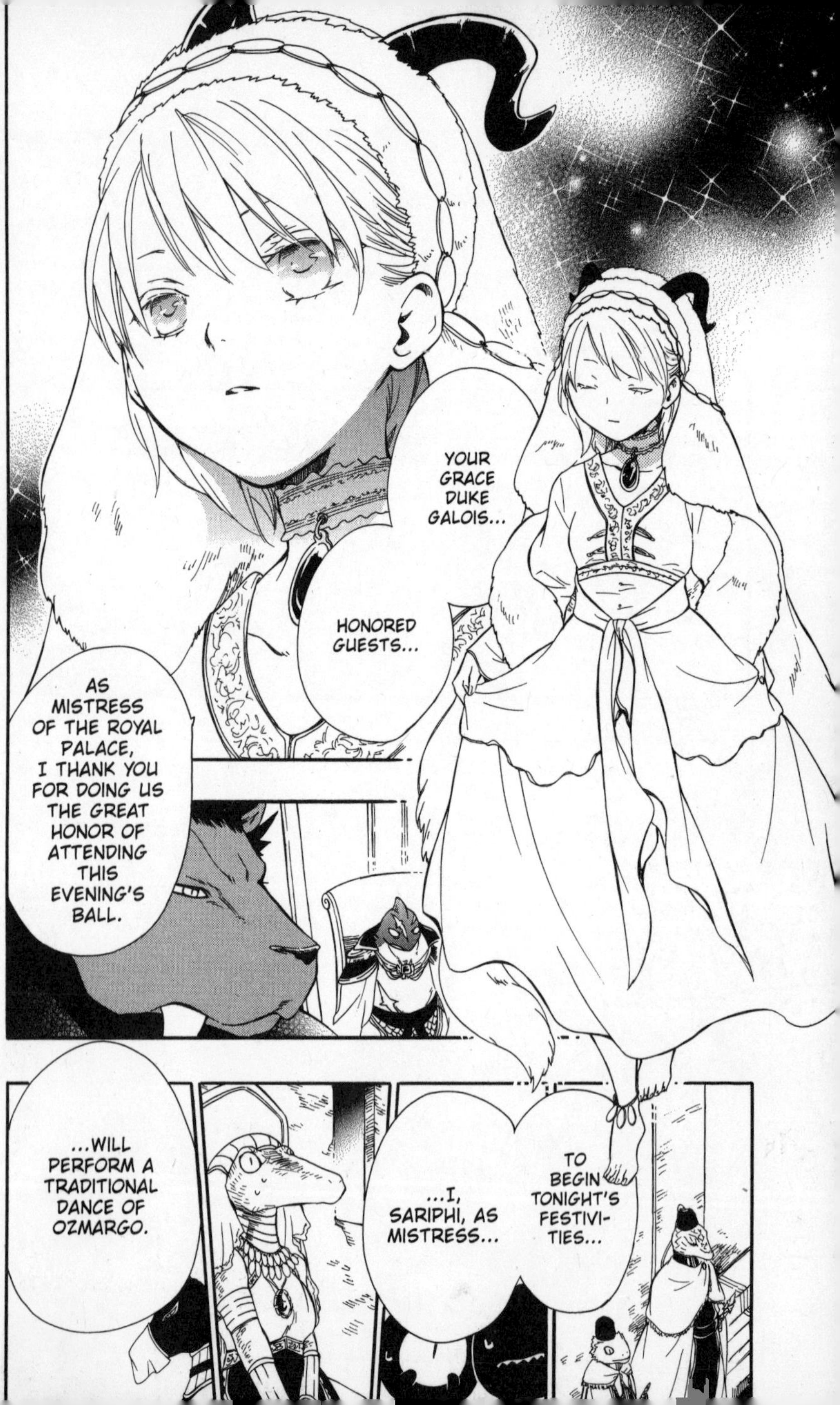
YOUR GRACE DUKE GALOIS...
HONORED GUESTS...
AS MISTRESS OF THE ROYAL PALACE, I THANK YOU FOR DOING US THE GREAT HONOR OF ATTENDING THIS EVENING'S BALL.
TO BEGIN TONIGHT'S FESTIVI-TIES...
...I, SARIPHI, AS MISTRESS...
...WILL PERFORM A TRADITIONAL DANCE OF OZMARGO.

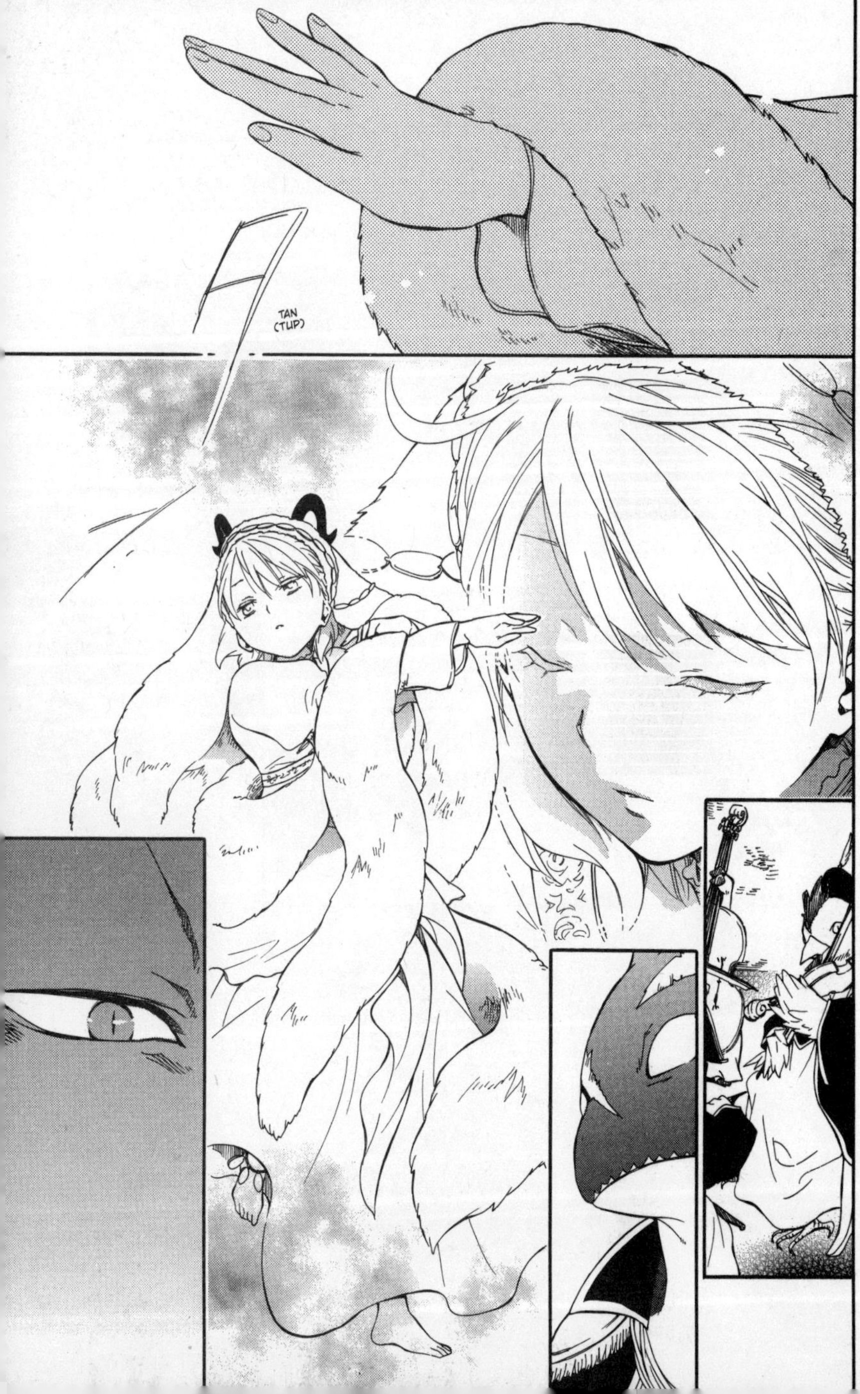
TAN
(TUP)

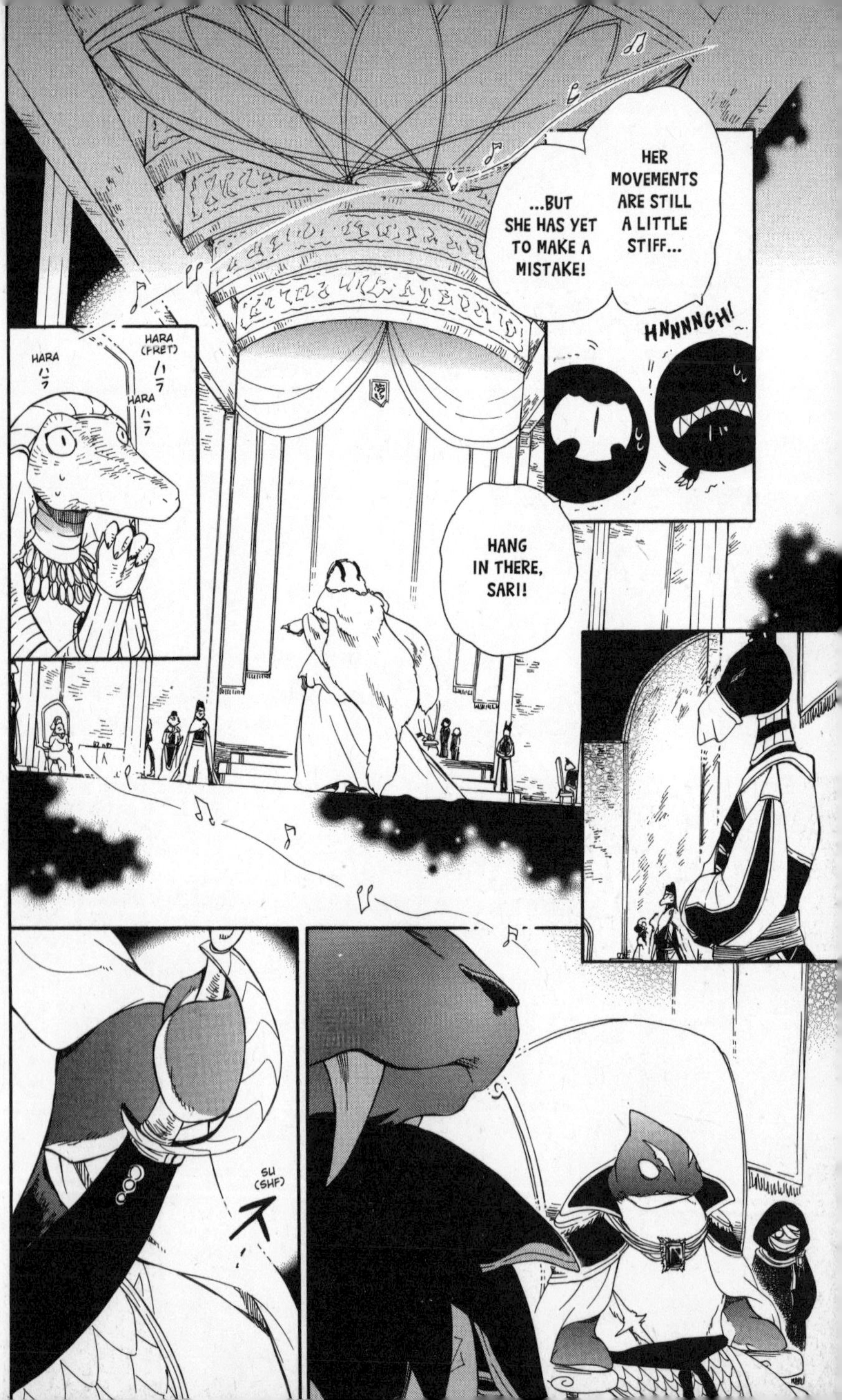
HER MOVEMENTS ARE STILL A LITTLE STIFF...
...BUT SHE HAS YET TO MAKE A MISTAKE!
HNNNNGH!
HARA (FRET)
HARA
HARA
HANG IN THERE, SARI!
SU (SHF)

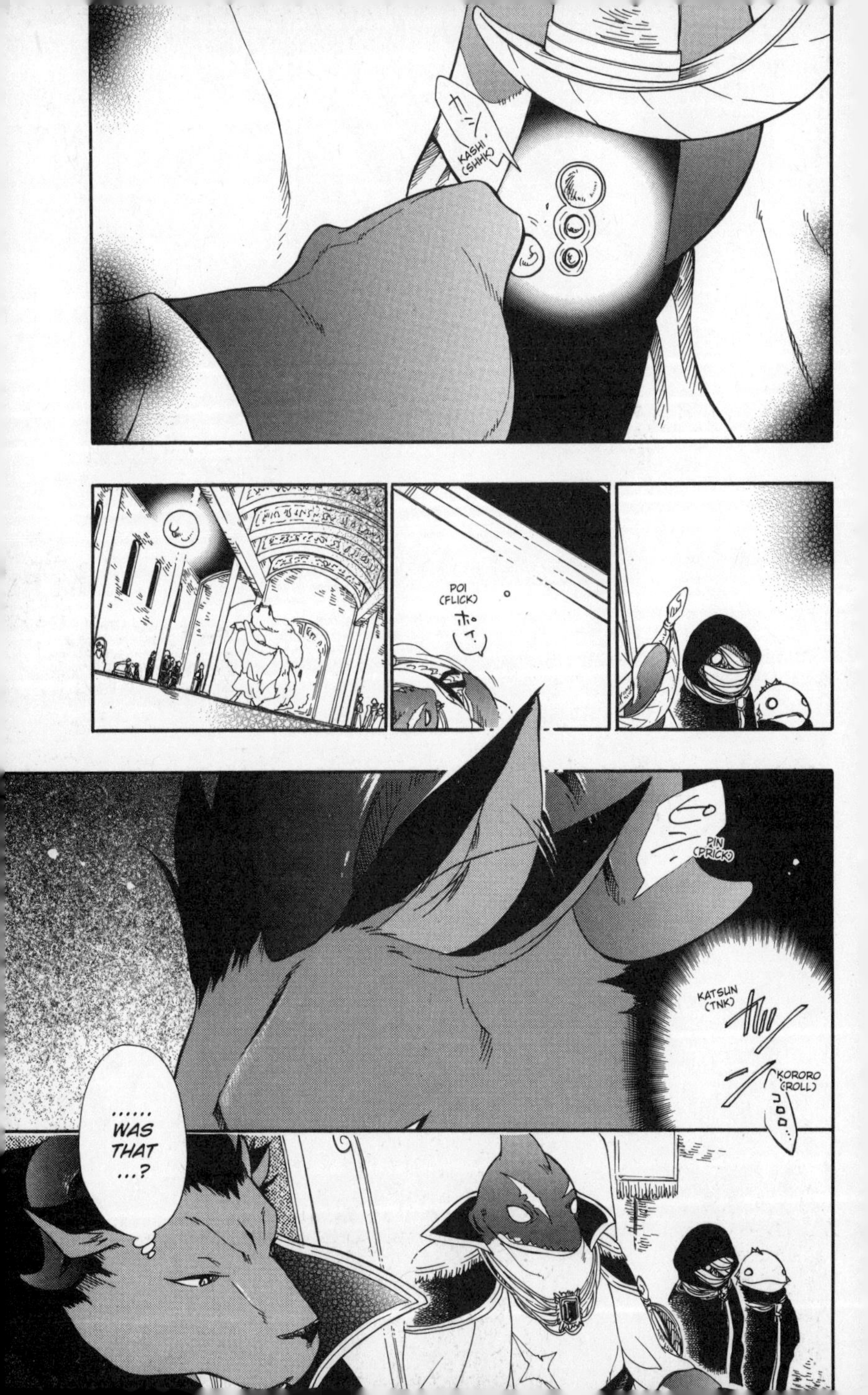
カシ
KASHI (SHHK)
ポイ
POI (FLICK)
ピン
PIN (PRICK)
KATSUN (TNK)
カツン
コロロ…
KORORO (ROLL)
......WAS THAT ...?

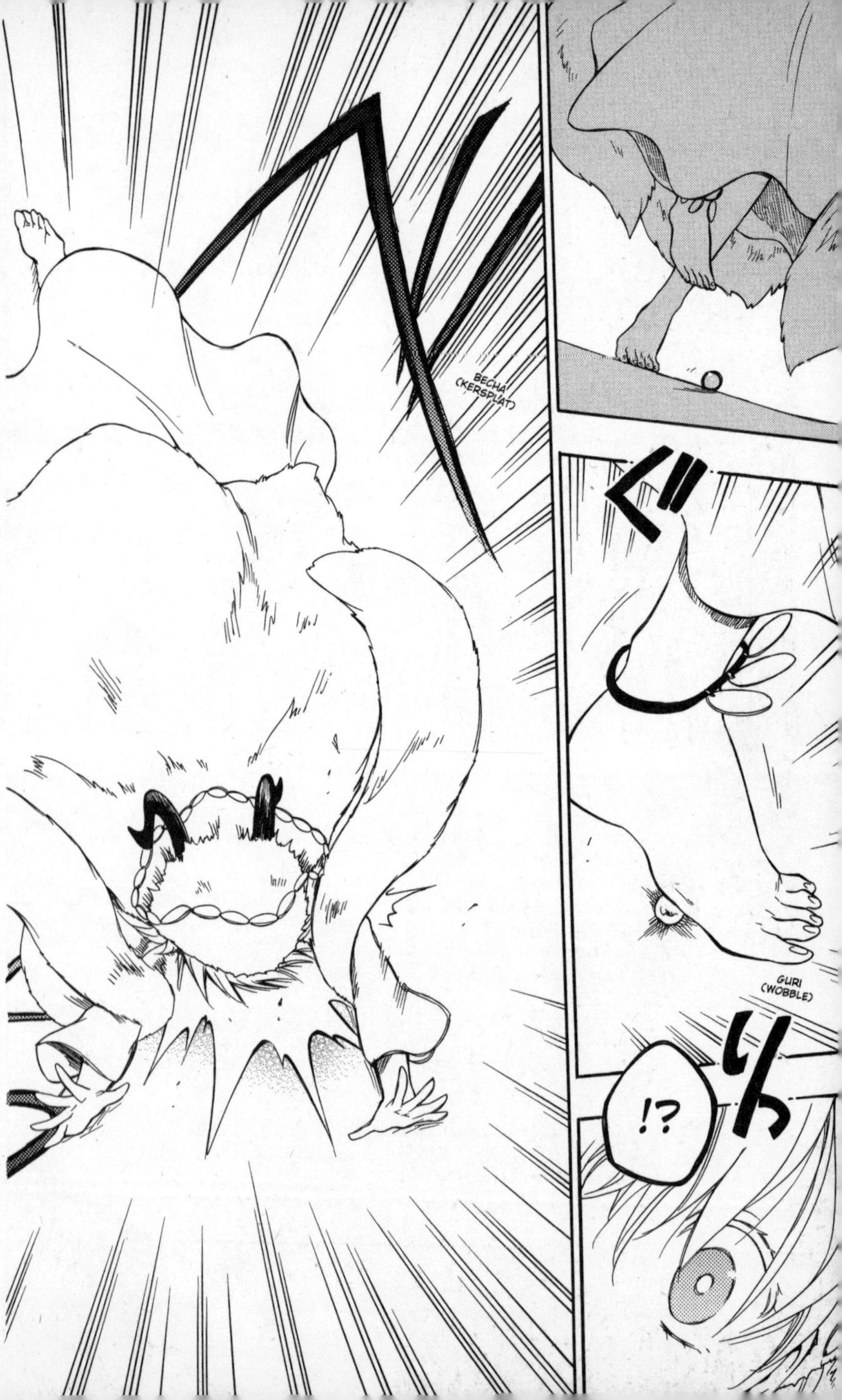
GURI
(WOBBLE)
!?
BECHA
(KERSPLAT)

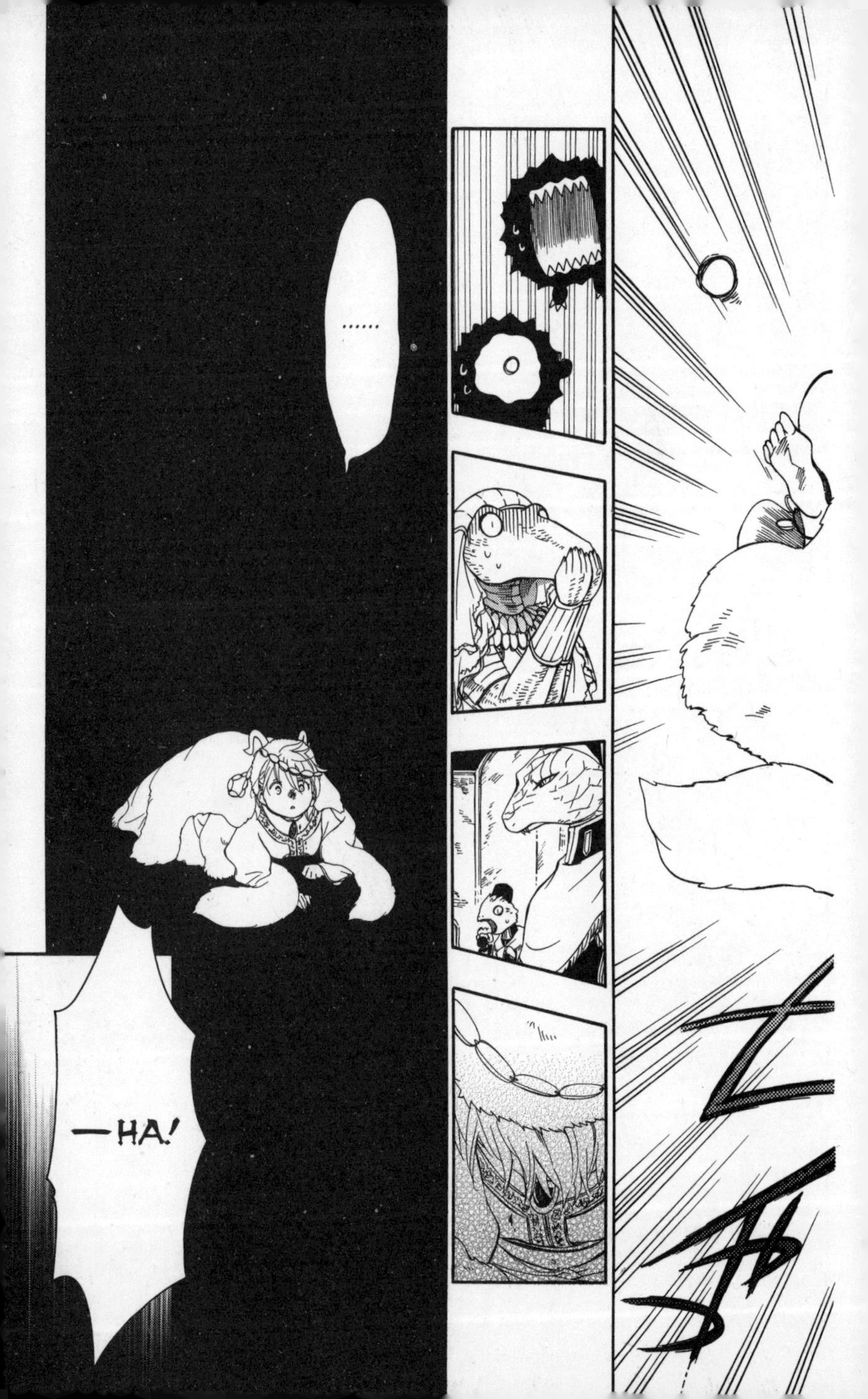
......
—HA!

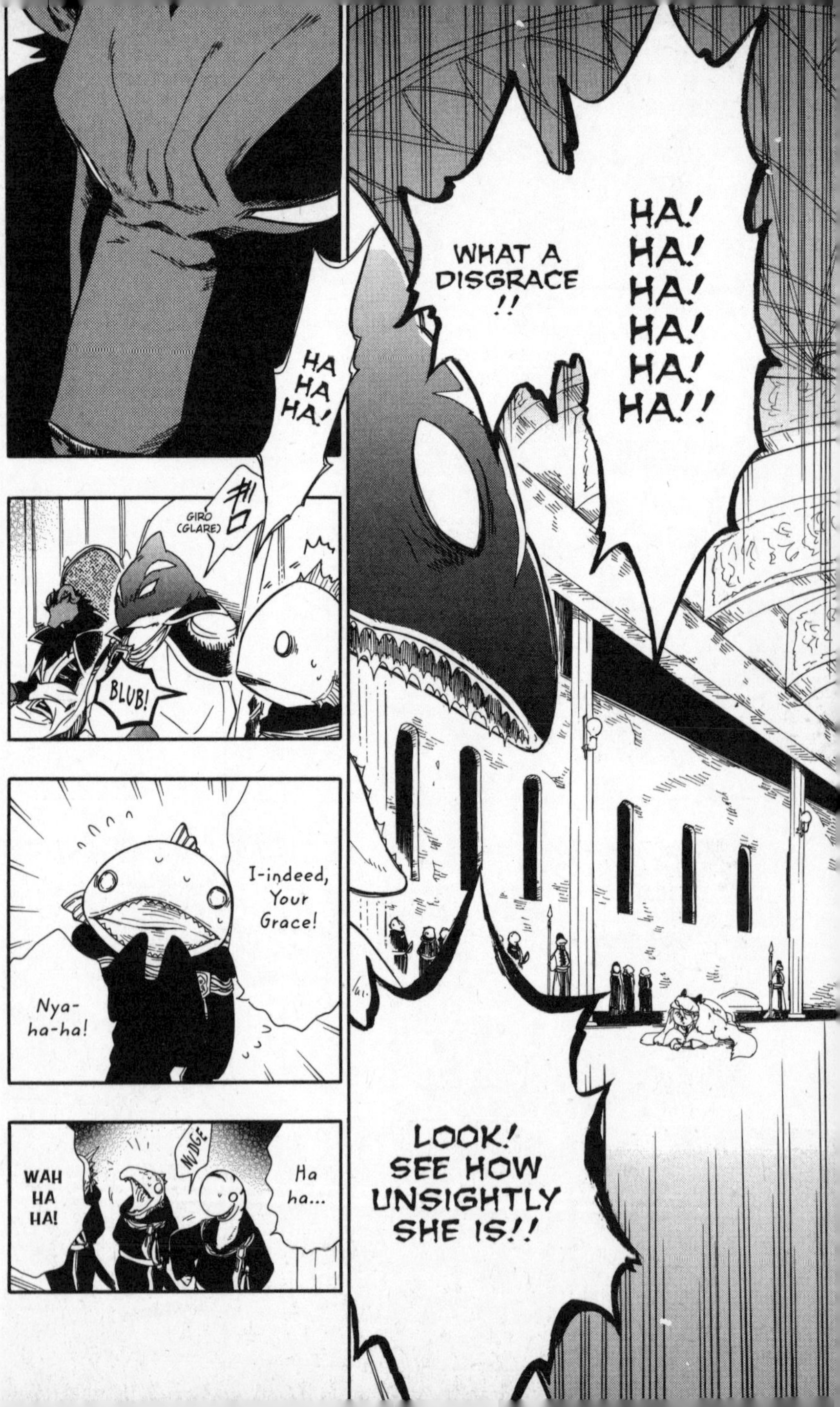
HA! HA! HA! HA! HA! HA!!
WHAT A DISGRACE!!
LOOK! SEE HOW UNSIGHTLY SHE IS!!
HA HA HA!
GIRO (GLARE)
BLUB!
I-indeed, Your Grace!
Nya-ha-ha!
Ha ha...
NUDGE
WAH HA HA!

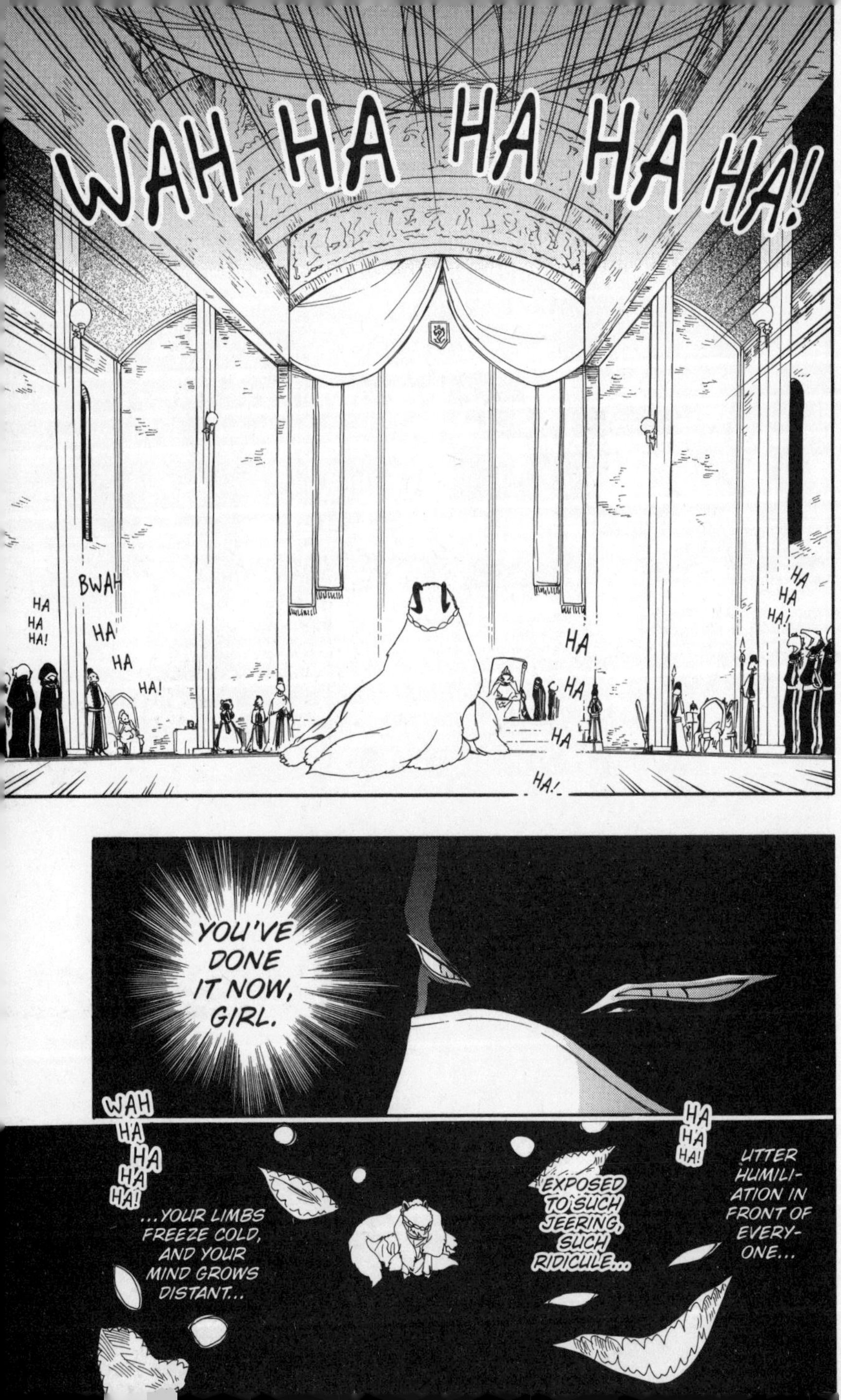
WAH HA HA HA HA HA!
HA HA HA!
HA HA HA HA!
BWAH HA HA HA!
HA HA HA!
YOU'VE DONE IT NOW, GIRL.
HA HA HA!
UTTER HUMILIATION IN FRONT OF EVERYONE...
EXPOSED TO SUCH JEERING, SUCH RIDICULE...
WAH HA HA HA HA!
...YOUR LIMBS FREEZE COLD, AND YOUR MIND GROWS DISTANT...

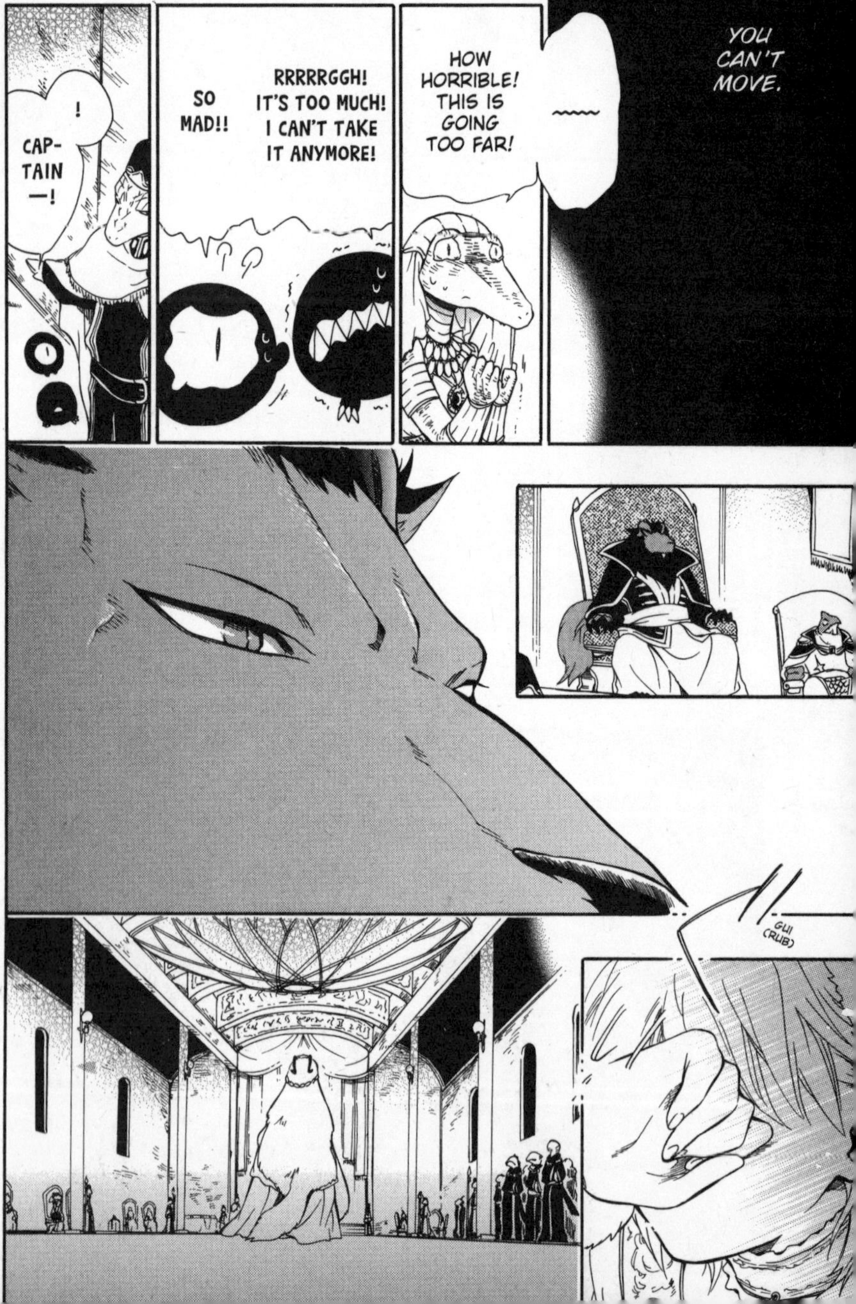
YOU CAN'T MOVE.
~~~~
HOW HORRIBLE! THIS IS GOING TOO FAR!
RRRRRGGH! IT'S TOO MUCH! I CAN'T TAKE IT ANYMORE!
SO MAD!!
!
CAP-TAIN—!
GUI (RUB)
~~~~

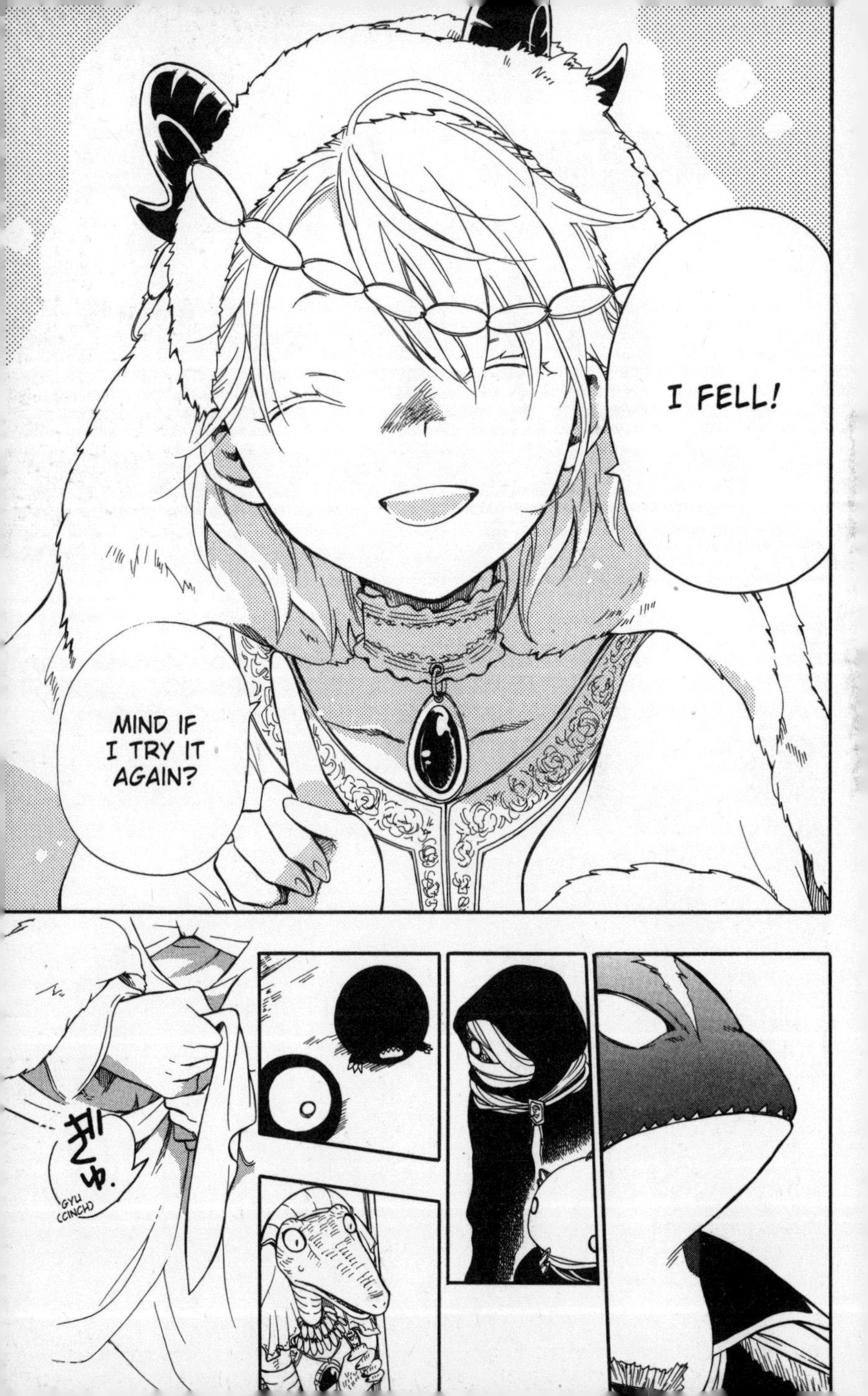
I FELL!
MIND IF I TRY IT AGAIN?
ぎゅ.
GYU (CINCH)

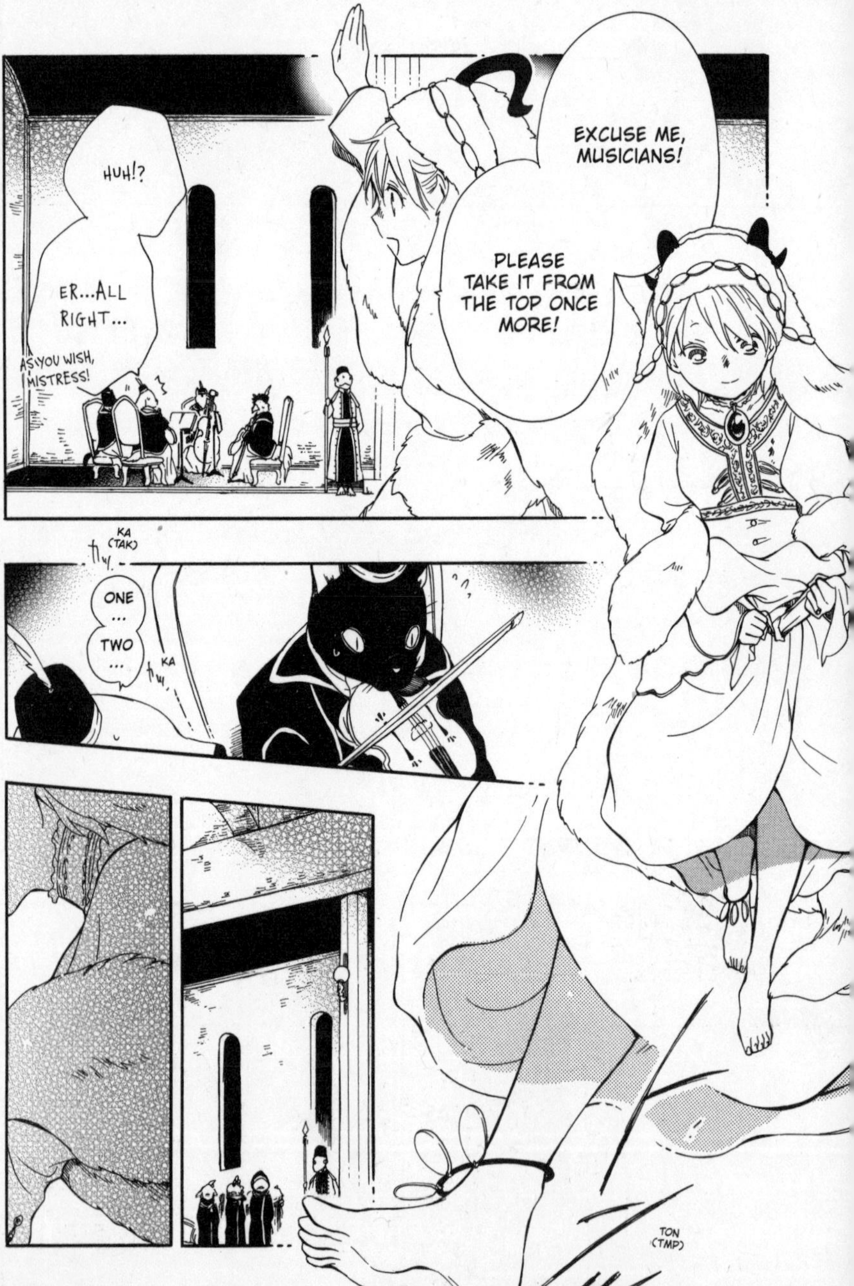
EXCUSE ME, MUSICIANS!
PLEASE TAKE IT FROM THE TOP ONCE MORE!
HUH!?
ER...ALL RIGHT...
AS YOU WISH, MISTRESS!
KA (TAK)
ONE ... TWO ...
KA
TON (TMP)

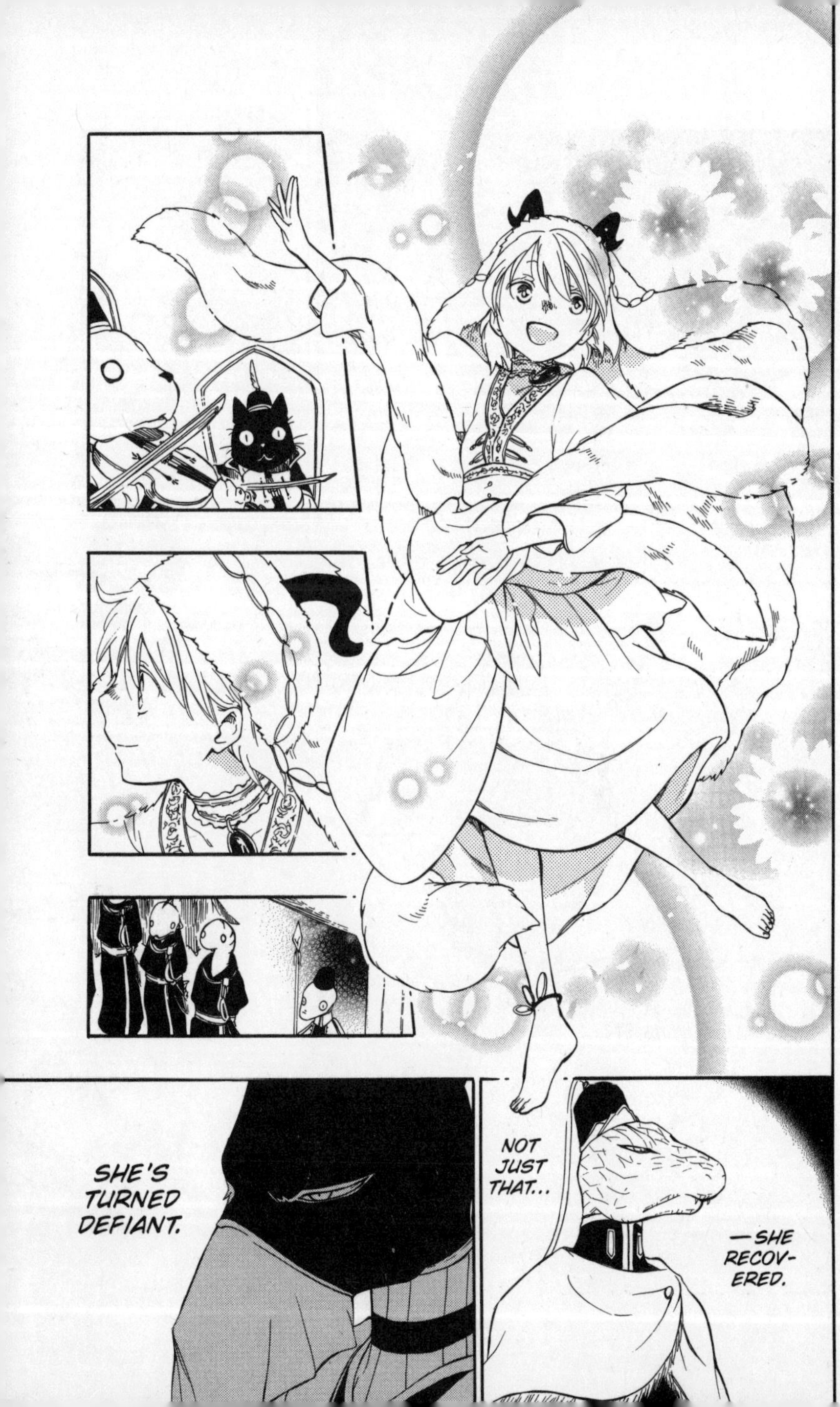
NOT JUST THAT...
—SHE RECOVERED.
SHE'S TURNED DEFIANT.

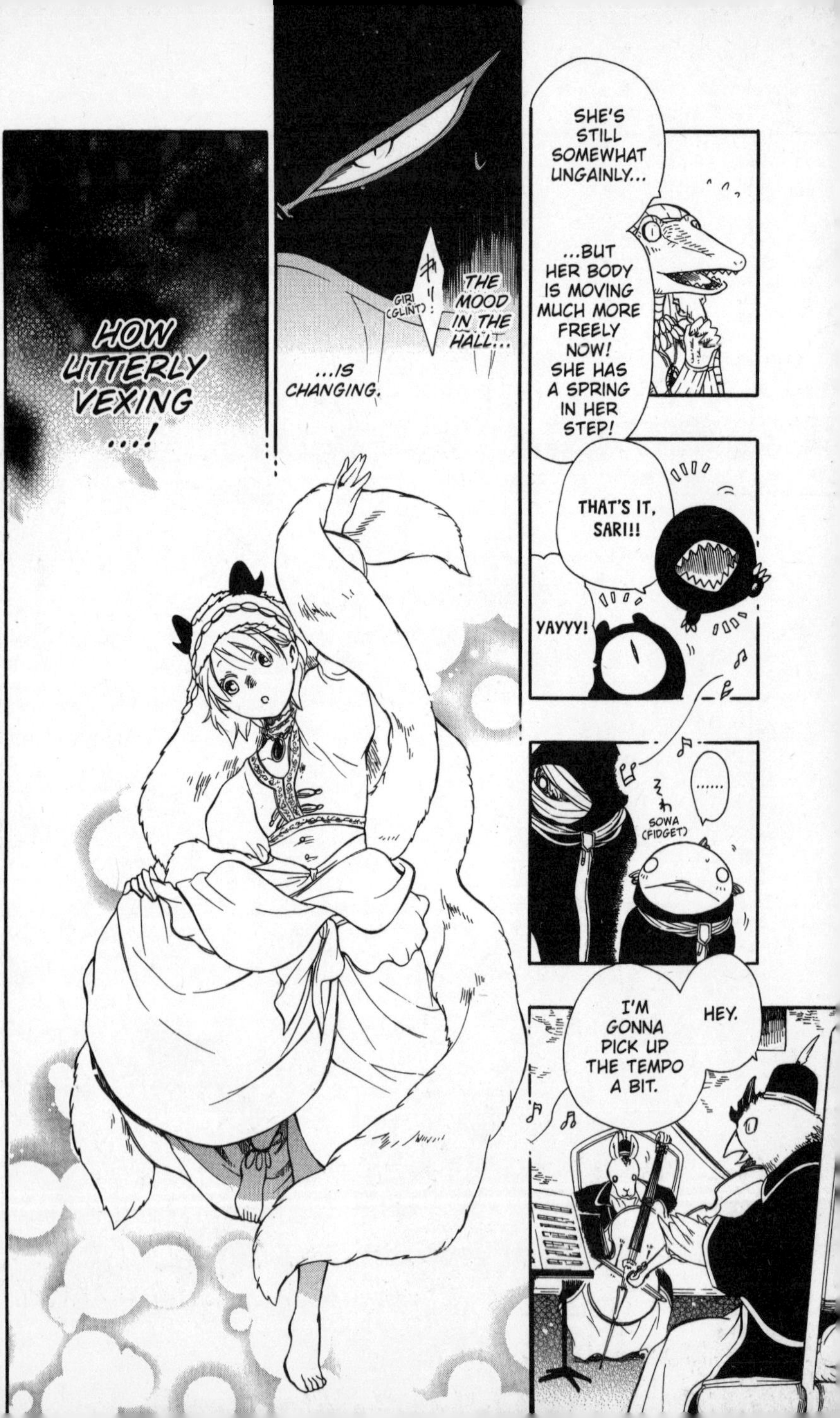
SHE'S STILL SOMEWHAT UNGAINLY...
...BUT HER BODY IS MOVING MUCH MORE FREELY NOW! SHE HAS A SPRING IN HER STEP!
THAT'S IT, SARI!!
YAYYY!
......
SOWA (FIDGET)
HEY.
I'M GONNA PICK UP THE TEMPO A BIT.
GIRI (GLINT)
THE MOOD IN THE HALL...
...IS CHANGING.
HOW UTTERLY VEXING ...!

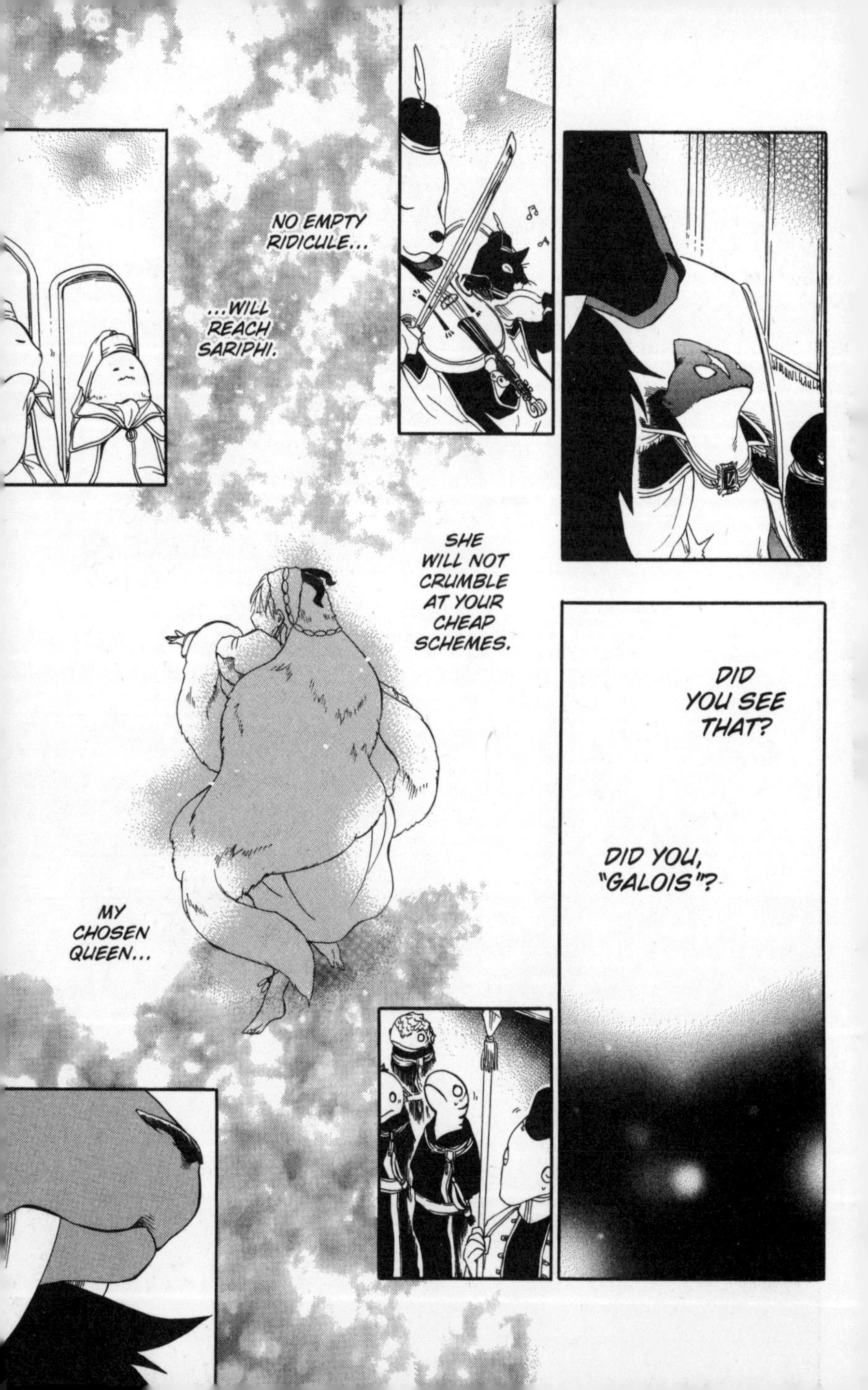
NO EMPTY RIDICULE...
...WILL REACH SARIPHI.
SHE WILL NOT CRUMBLE AT YOUR CHEAP SCHEMES.
MY CHOSEN QUEEN...
DID YOU SEE THAT?
DID YOU, "GALOIS"?

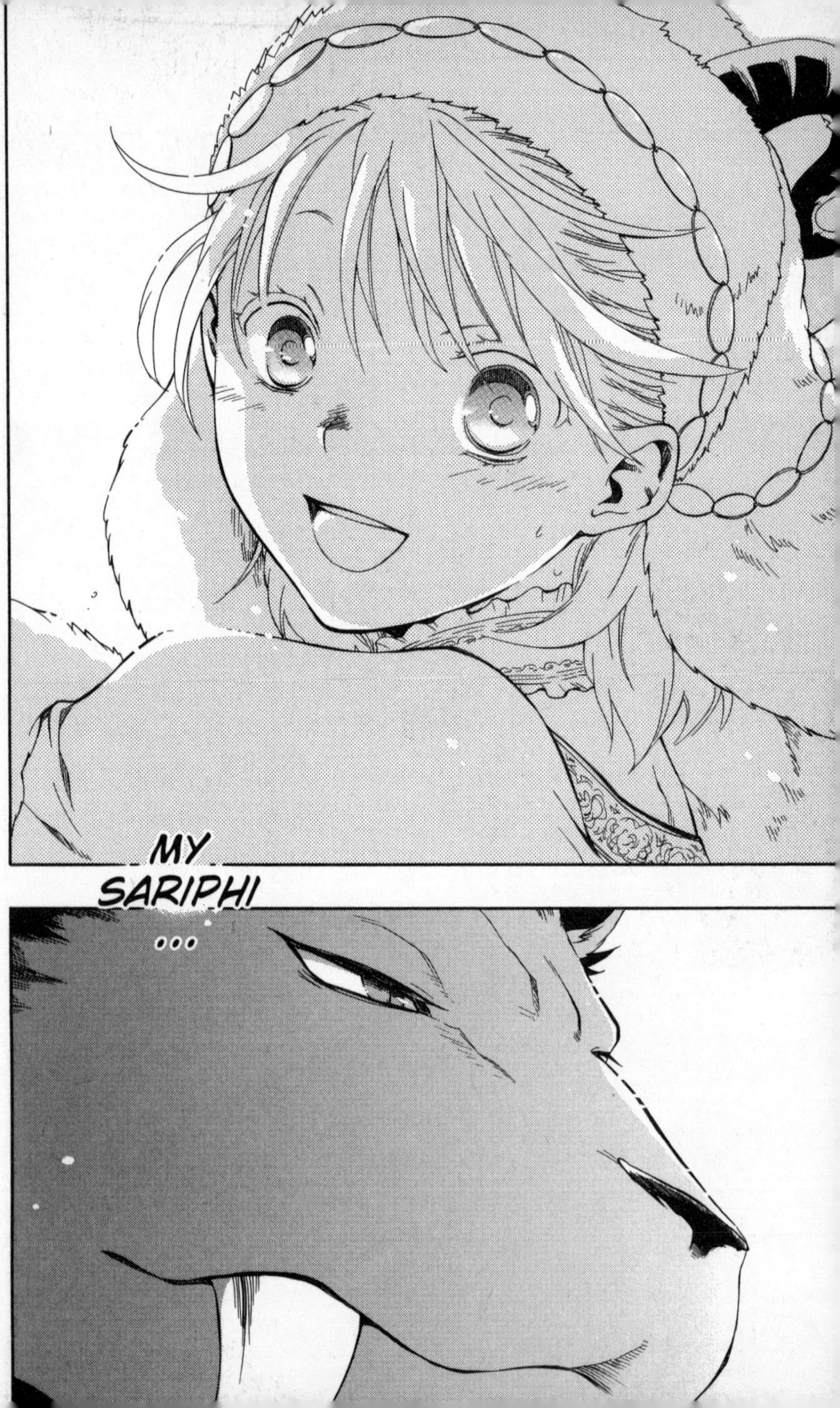
MY SARIPHI
...

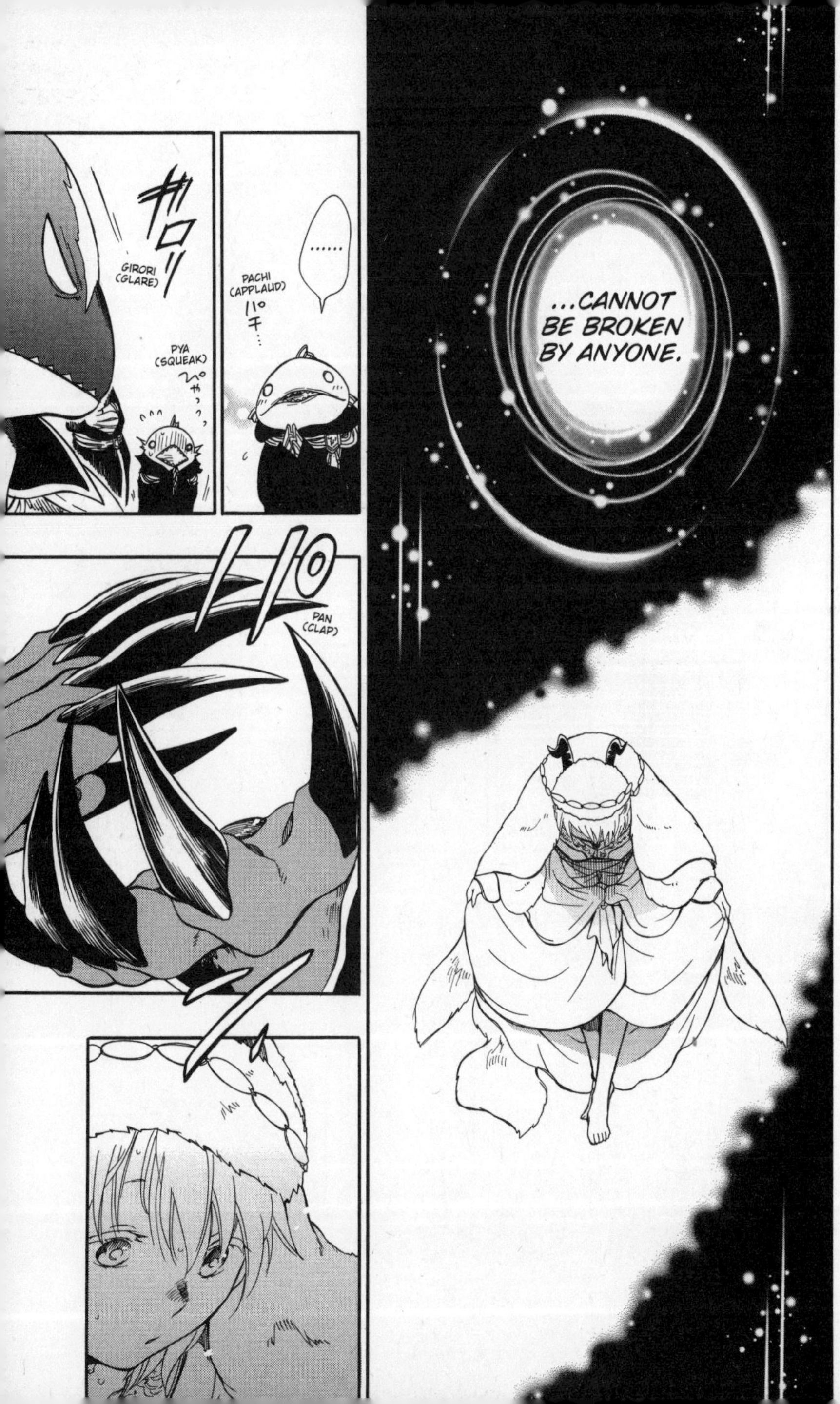
...CANNOT BE BROKEN BY ANYONE.
......
PACHI (APPLAUD)
GIRORI (GLARE)
PYA (SQUEAK)
PAN (CLAP)

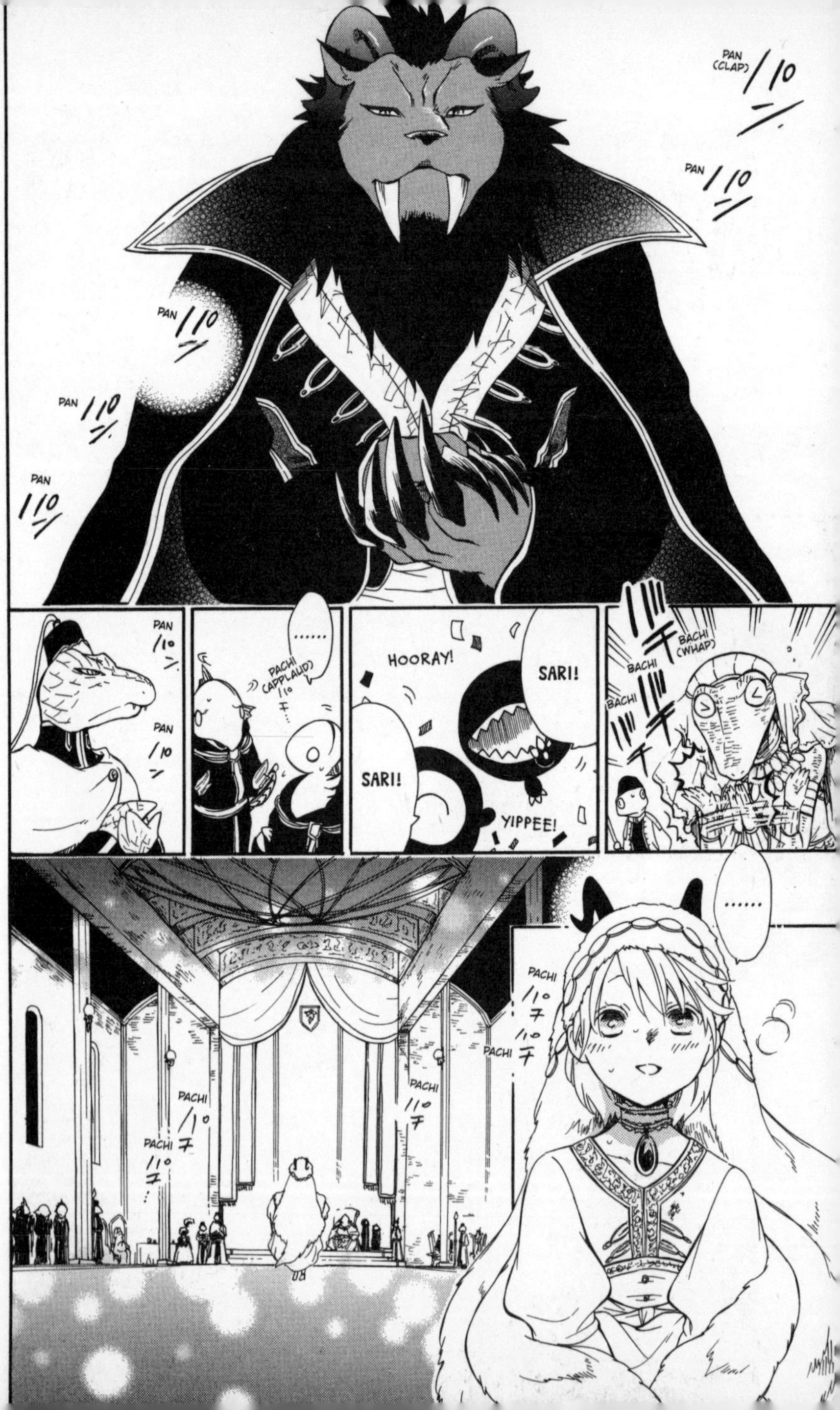
PAN (CLAP)
PAN
PAN
PAN
PAN
BACHI (WHAP)
BACHI
BACHI
SARI!
HOORAY!
SARI!
YIPPEE!
......
PACHI (APPLAUD)
PAN
PAN
......
PACHI
PACHI
PACHI
PACHI
PACHI

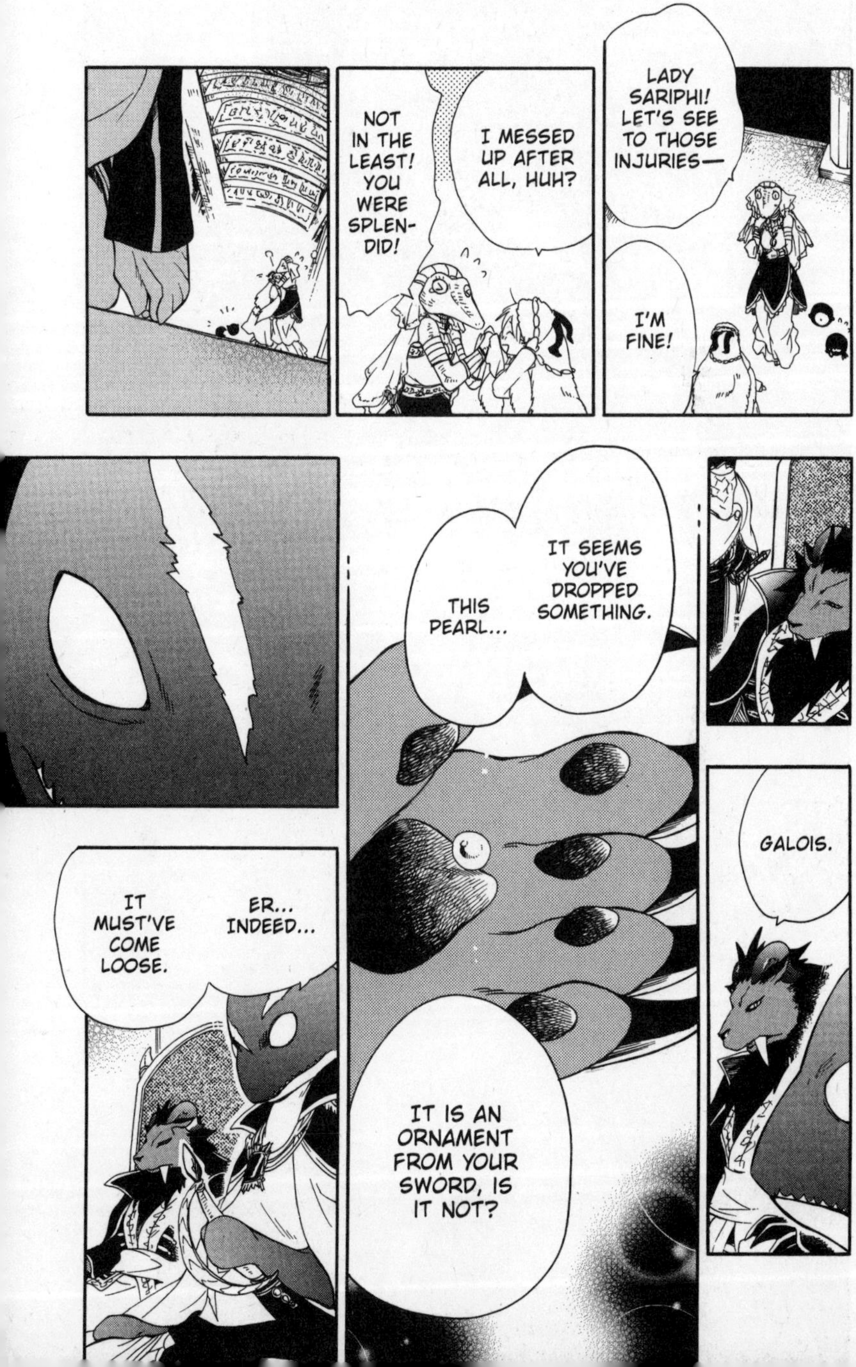
LADY SARIPHI! LET'S SEE TO THOSE INJURIES—
I'M FINE!
I MESSED UP AFTER ALL, HUH?
NOT IN THE LEAST! YOU WERE SPLEN-DID!
GALOIS.
IT SEEMS YOU'VE DROPPED SOMETHING.
THIS PEARL...
IT IS AN ORNAMENT FROM YOUR SWORD, IS IT NOT?
ER... INDEED...
IT MUST'VE COME LOOSE.

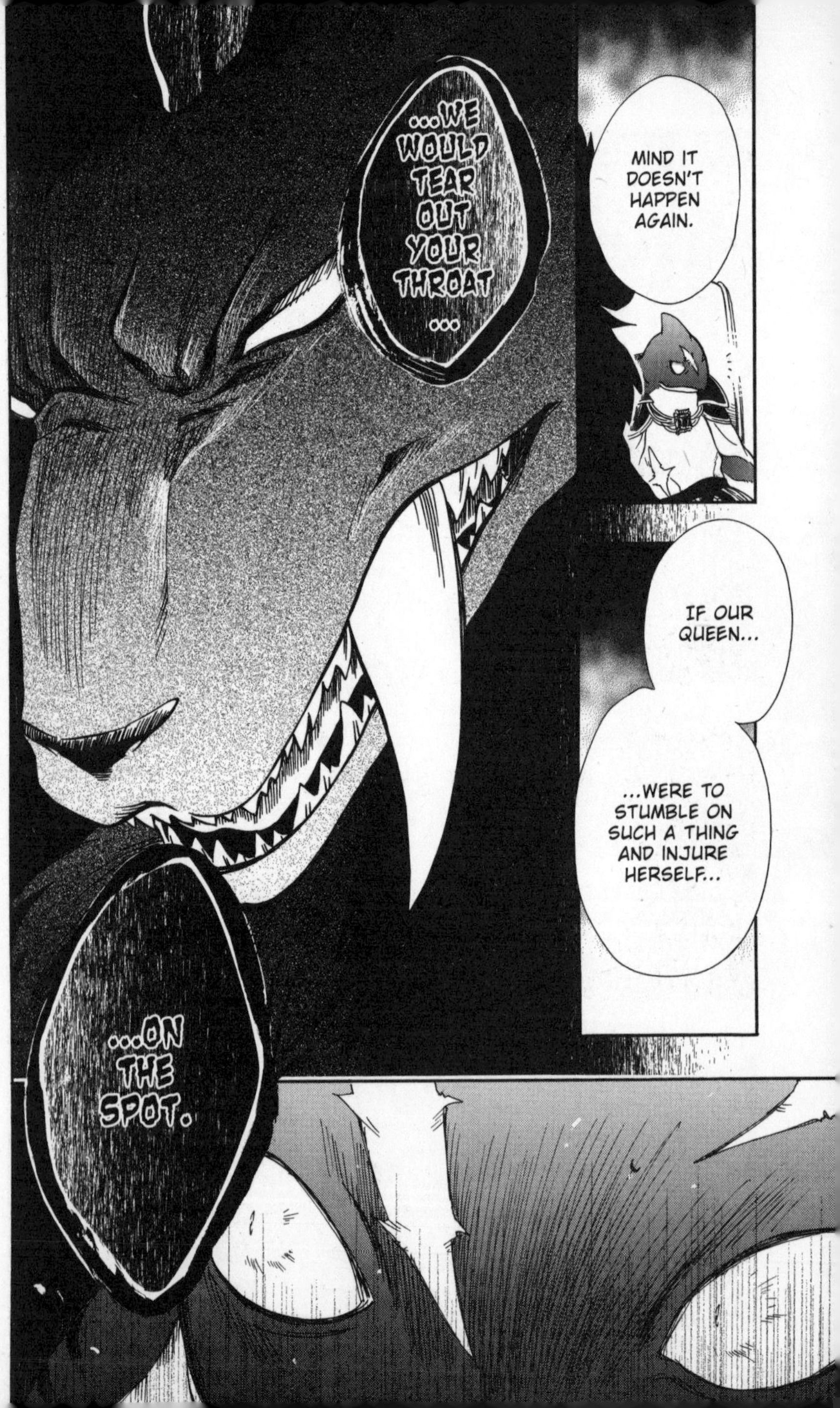
MIND IT DOESN'T HAPPEN AGAIN.
IF OUR QUEEN...
...WERE TO STUMBLE ON SUCH A THING AND INJURE HERSELF...
...WE WOULD TEAR OUT YOUR THROAT...
...ON THE SPOT.

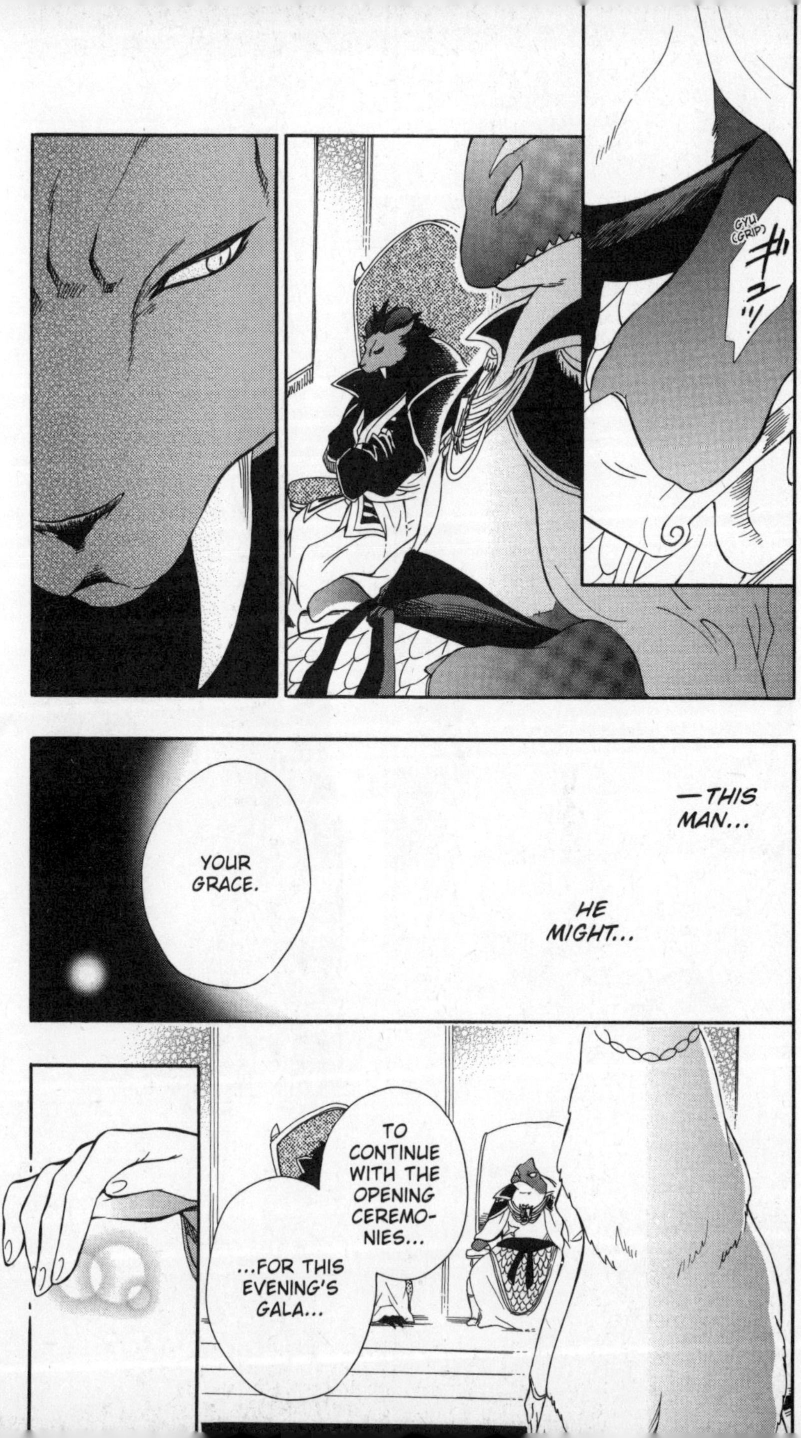
GYU (GRIP)
ギュッ
—THIS MAN...
HE MIGHT...
YOUR GRACE.
TO CONTINUE WITH THE OPENING CEREMO-NIES...
...FOR THIS EVENING'S GALA...

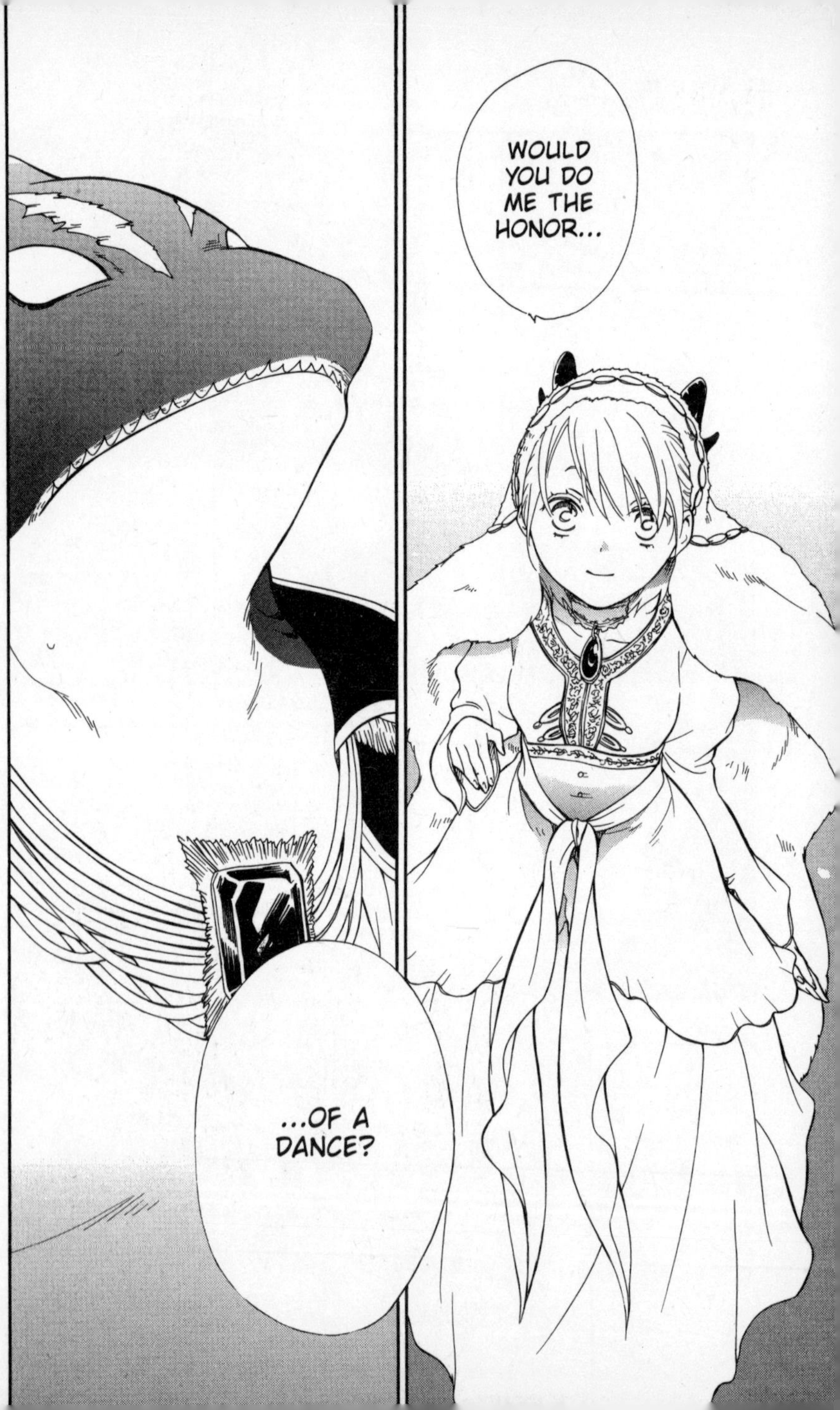
WOULD YOU DO ME THE HONOR...
...OF A DANCE?

episode.22

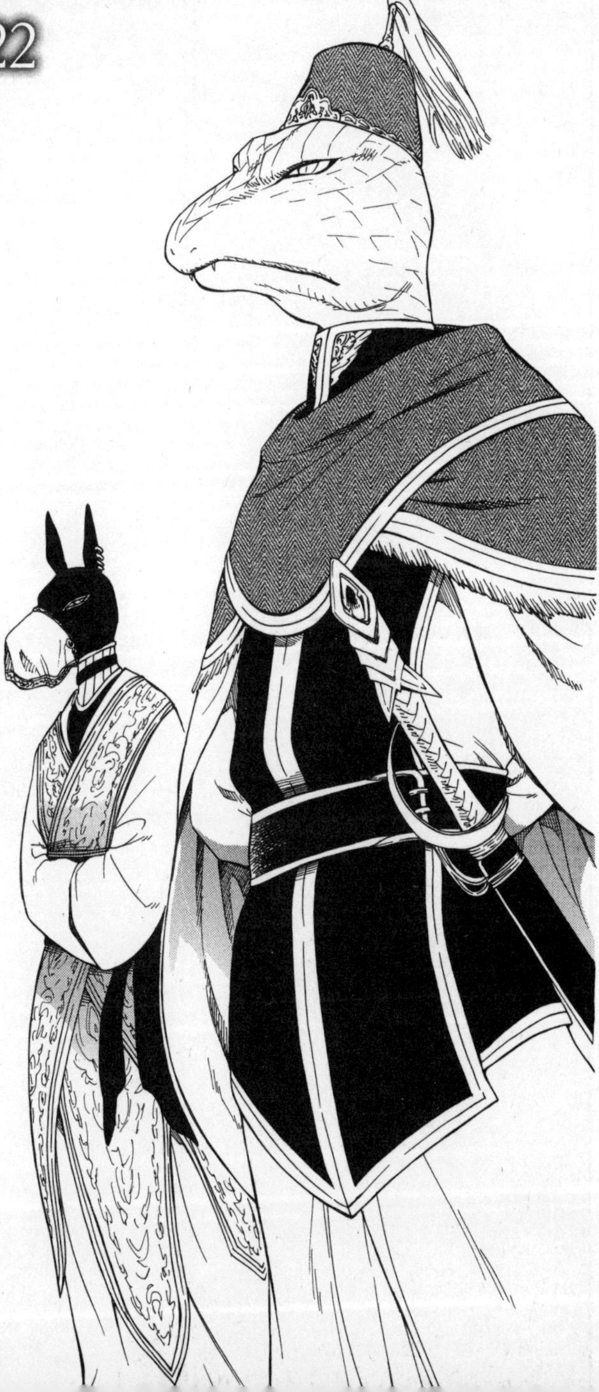

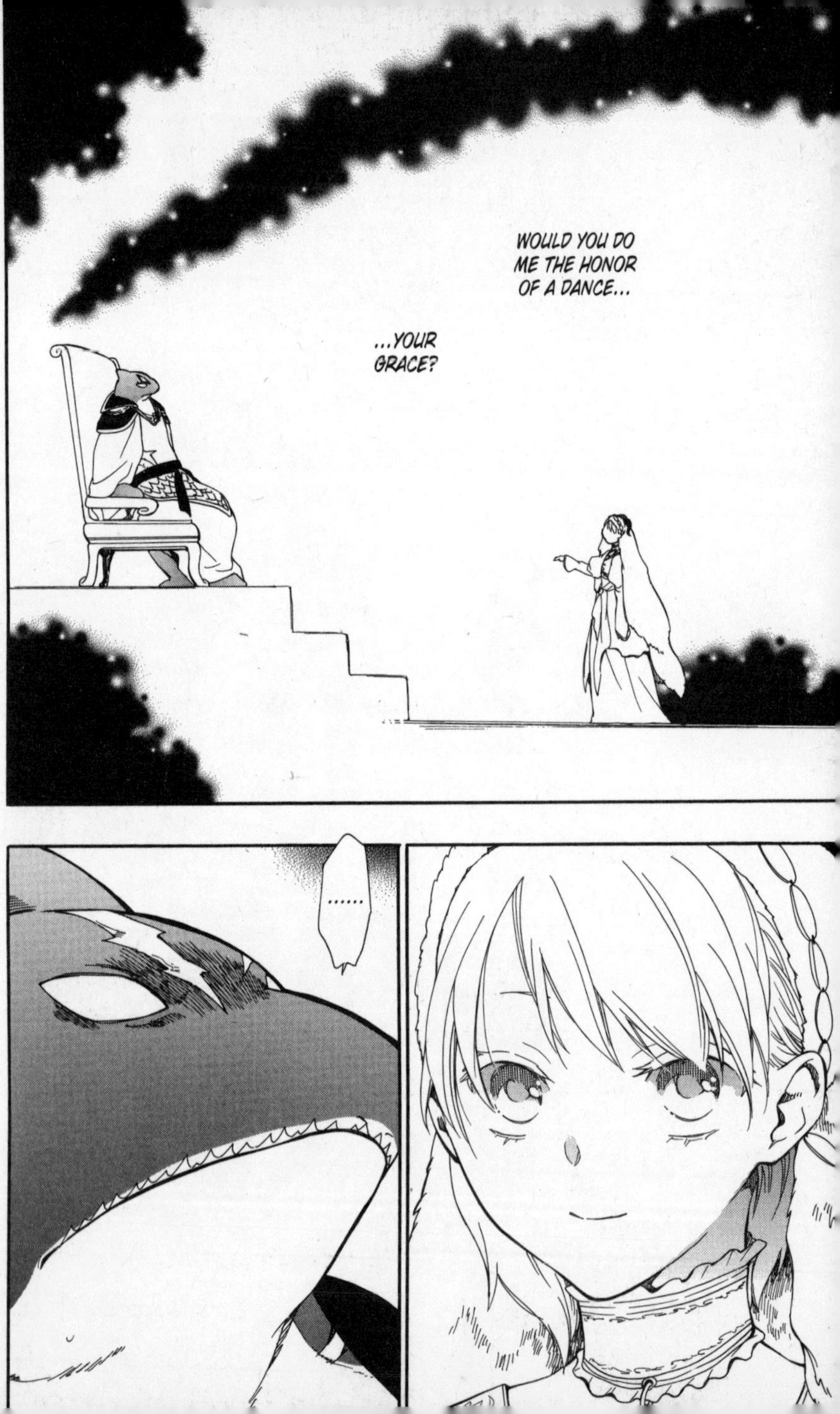
WOULD YOU DO ME THE HONOR OF A DANCE...
...YOUR GRACE?
......

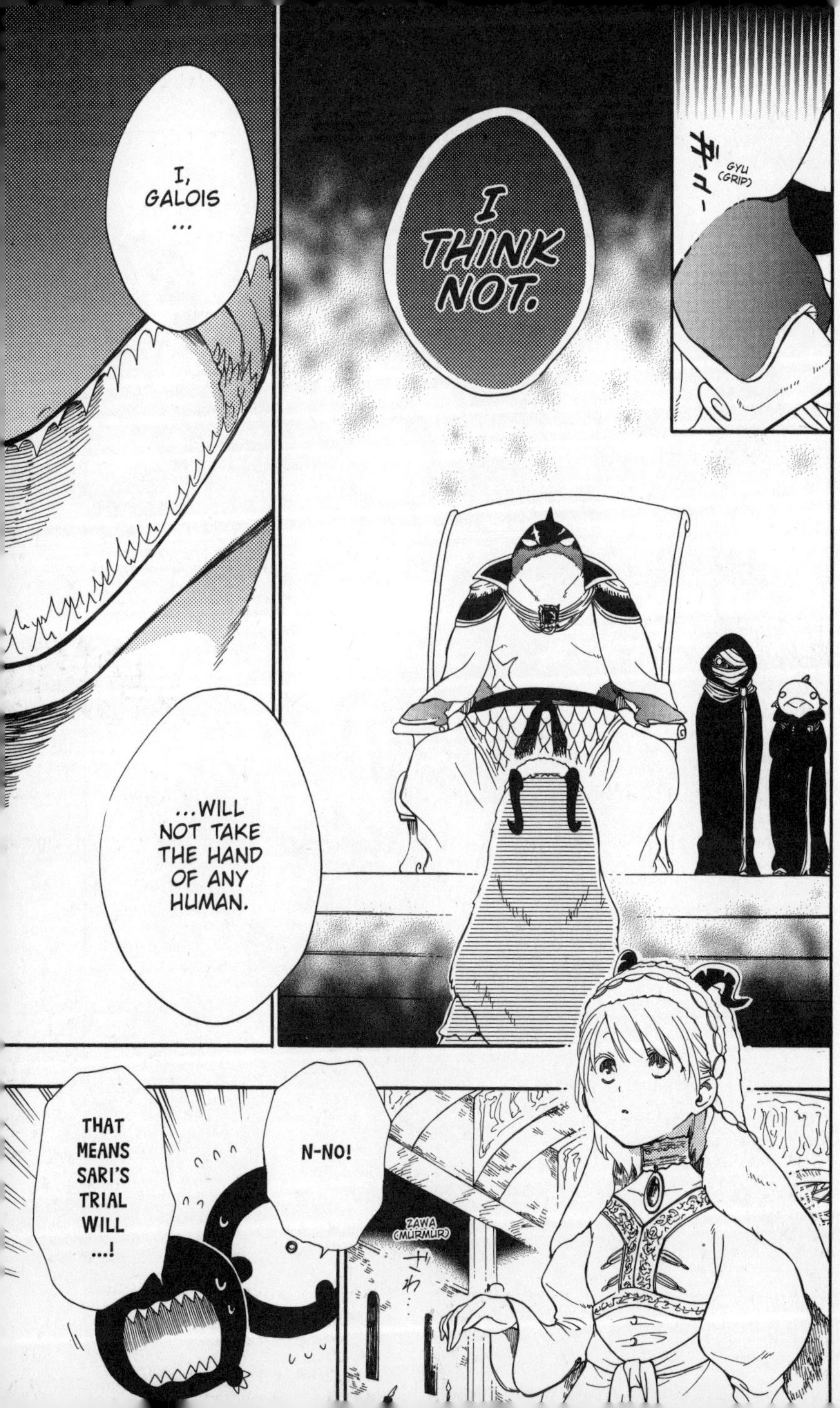
ギュー
GYU (GRIP)
I THINK NOT.
I, GALOIS ...
...WILL NOT TAKE THE HAND OF ANY HUMAN.
ざわ…
ZAWA (MURMUR)
N-NO!
THAT MEANS SARI'S TRIAL WILL ...!

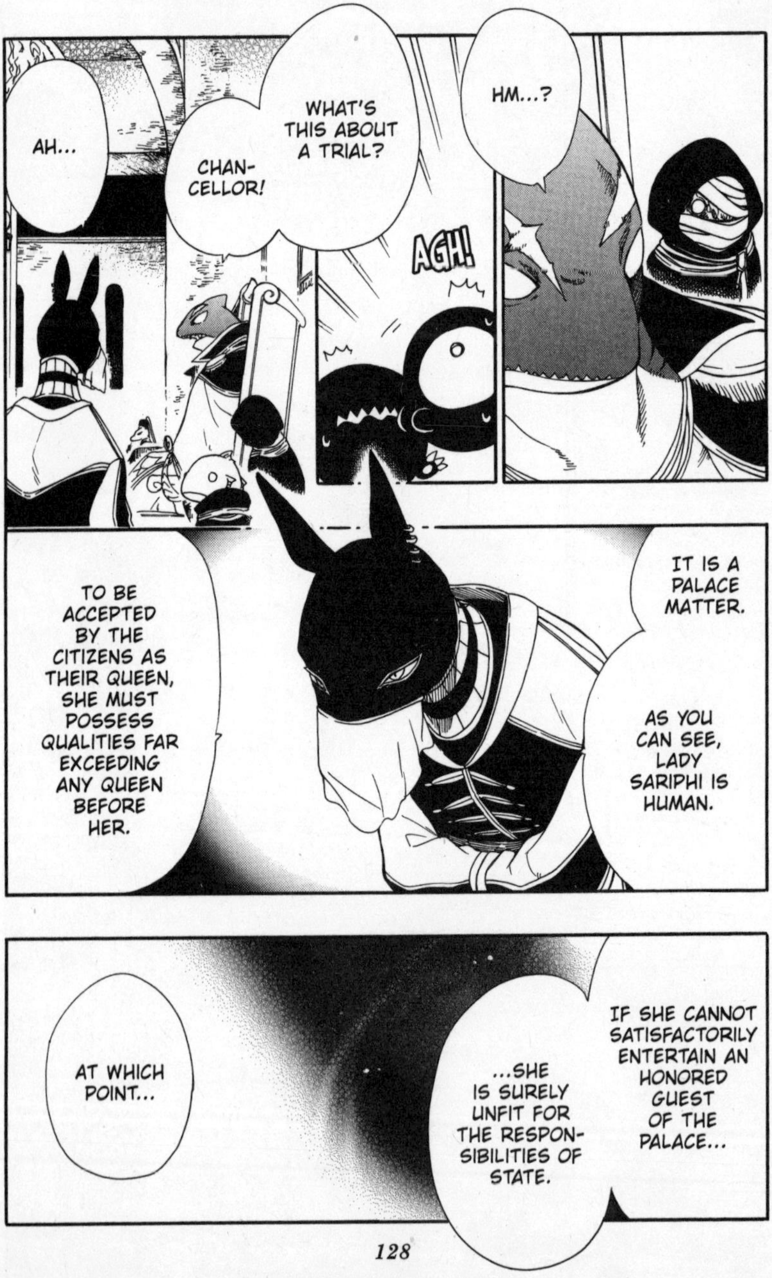
HM...?
AGH!
WHAT'S THIS ABOUT A TRIAL?
CHAN-CELLOR!
AH...
IT IS A PALACE MATTER.
AS YOU CAN SEE, LADY SARIPHI IS HUMAN.
TO BE ACCEPTED BY THE CITIZENS AS THEIR QUEEN, SHE MUST POSSESS QUALITIES FAR EXCEEDING ANY QUEEN BEFORE HER.
IF SHE CANNOT SATISFACTORILY ENTERTAIN AN HONORED GUEST OF THE PALACE...
...SHE IS SURELY UNFIT FOR THE RESPON-SIBILITIES OF STATE.
AT WHICH POINT...

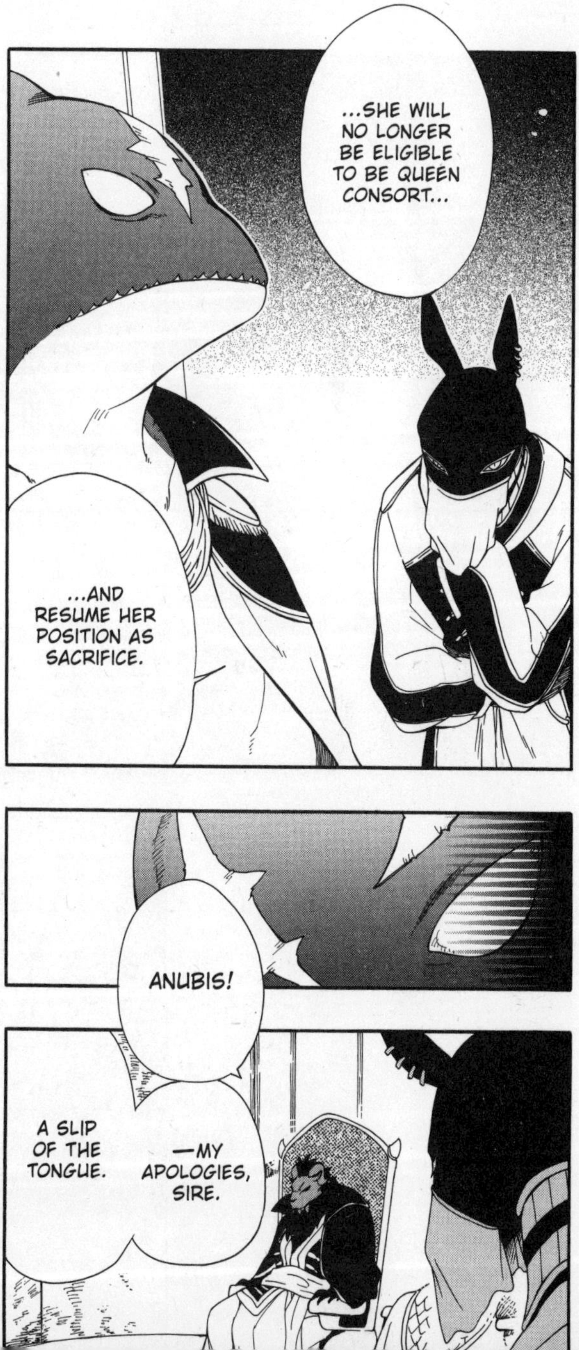
...SHE WILL NO LONGER BE ELIGIBLE TO BE QUEEN CONSORT...
...AND RESUME HER POSITION AS SACRIFICE.
ANUBIS!
—MY APOLOGIES, SIRE.
A SLIP OF THE TONGUE.

QUICK & DIRTY DETAILS

PRINCESS AMIT
- ABOUT EIGHTEEN IN HUMAN YEARS
- 190cm (6'2") TALL

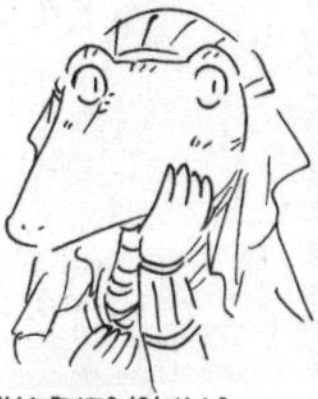

- HOBBIES/SKILLS: COOKING, SEWING
- LIKES: ANYTHING CUTE
- DISLIKES: ANYTHING SCARY

BENNU
- APPARENTLY AROUND 10,000 YEARS OLD
- ABOUT 8cm (4") TALL

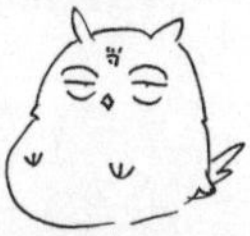

- DISLIKES: BEING ORDERED AROUND
- LIKES: PEANUTS

ILYA
- 18 YEARS OLD
- 175cm (5'8") TALL

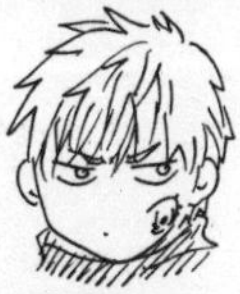

- DISLIKES: BEASTKIND
- LIKES: CHEESE RISOTTO

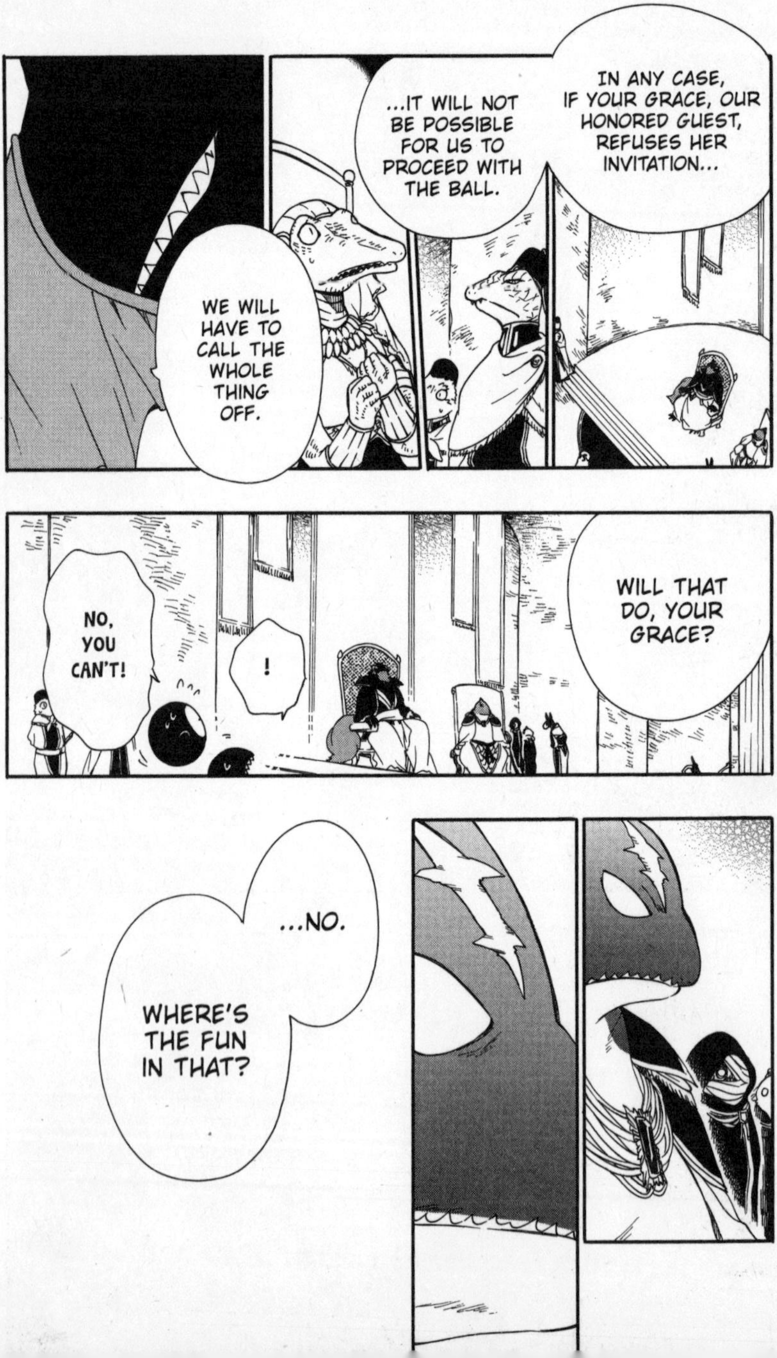
IN ANY CASE, IF YOUR GRACE, OUR HONORED GUEST, REFUSES HER INVITATION...
...IT WILL NOT BE POSSIBLE FOR US TO PROCEED WITH THE BALL.
WE WILL HAVE TO CALL THE WHOLE THING OFF.
WILL THAT DO, YOUR GRACE?
!
NO, YOU CAN'T!
...NO.
WHERE'S THE FUN IN THAT?

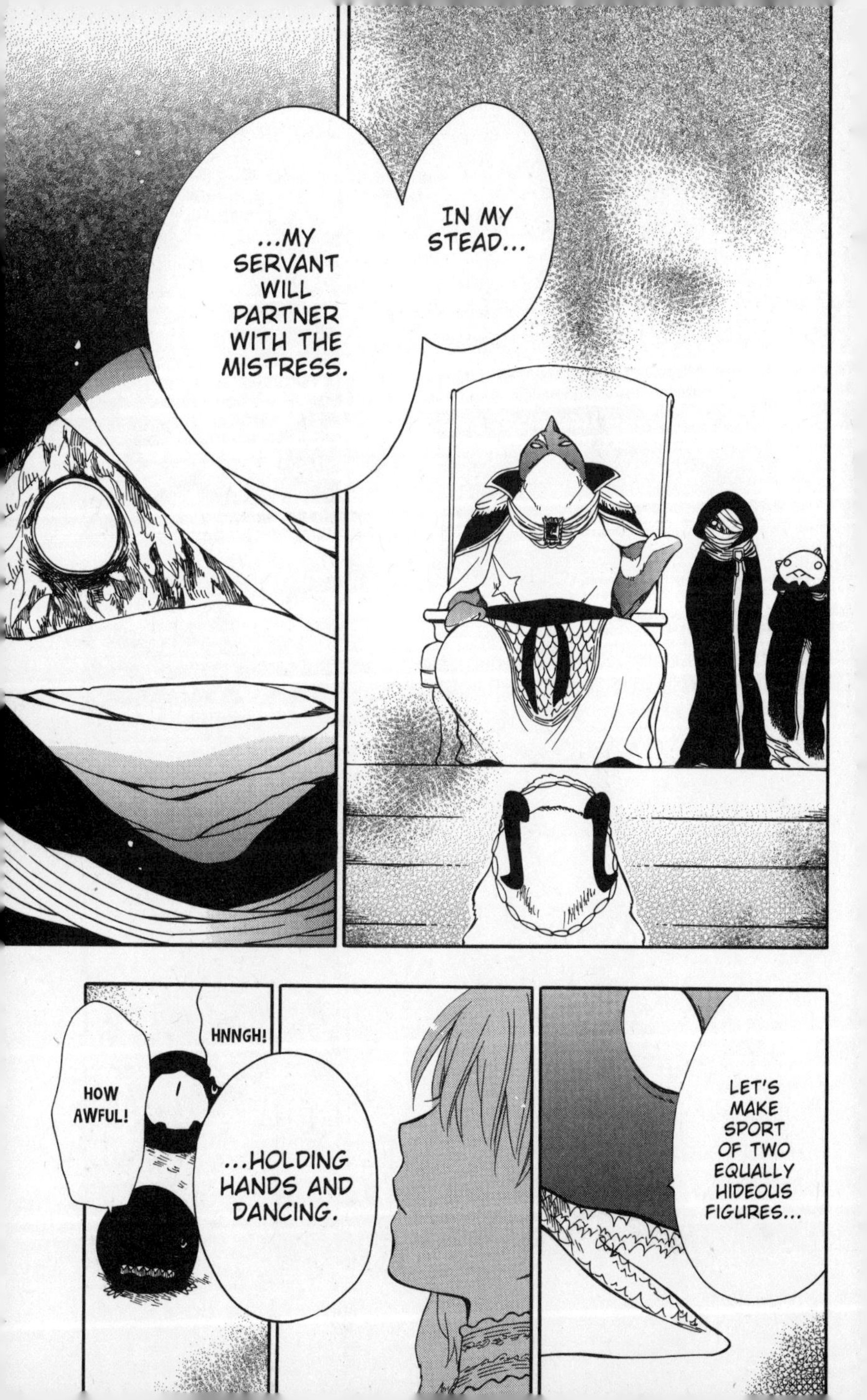
IN MY STEAD...
...MY SERVANT WILL PARTNER WITH THE MISTRESS.
LET'S MAKE SPORT OF TWO EQUALLY HIDEOUS FIGURES...
...HOLDING HANDS AND DANCING.
HNNGH!
HOW AWFUL!

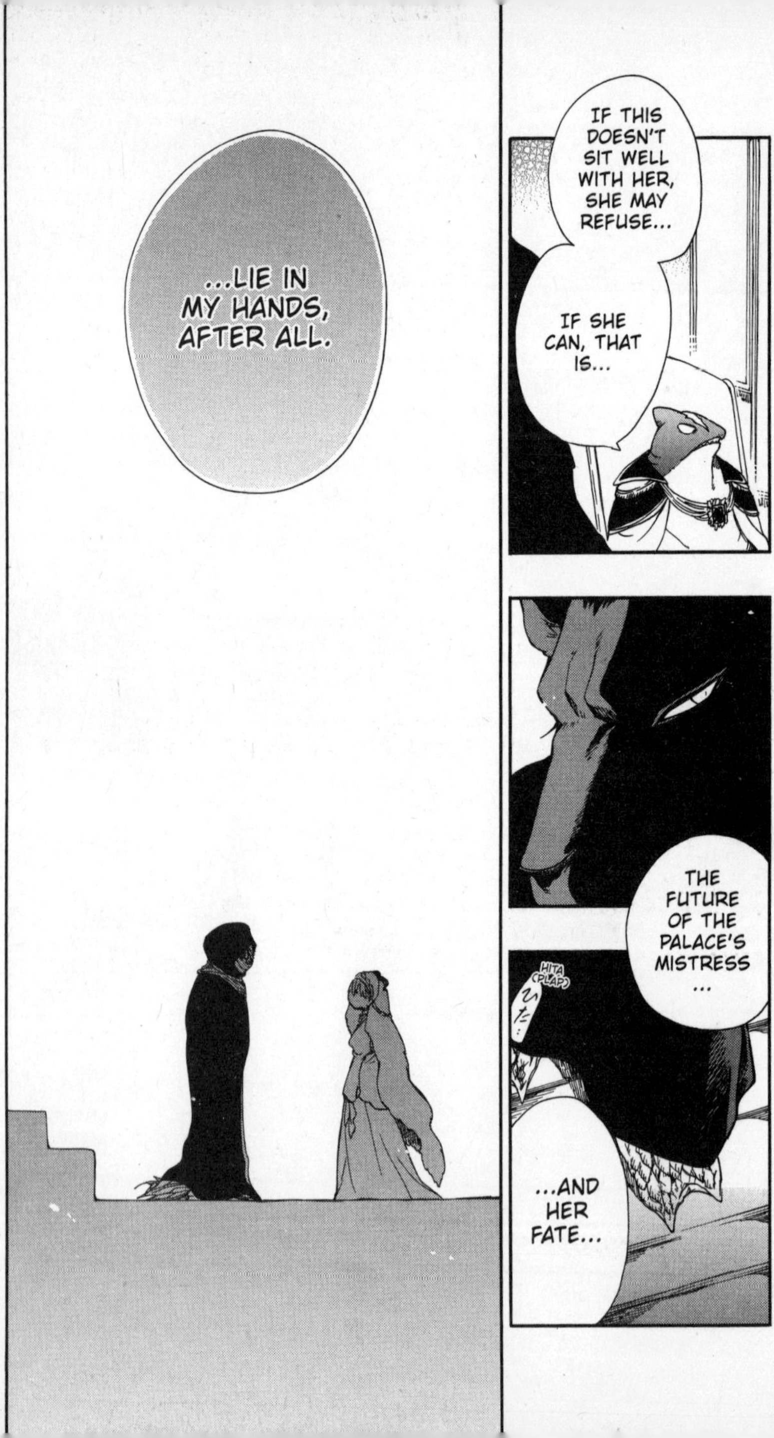
IF THIS DOESN'T SIT WELL WITH HER, SHE MAY REFUSE...
IF SHE CAN, THAT IS...
THE FUTURE OF THE PALACE'S MISTRESS ...
HITA (PLAP)
ひた…
...AND HER FATE...
...LIE IN MY HANDS, AFTER ALL.

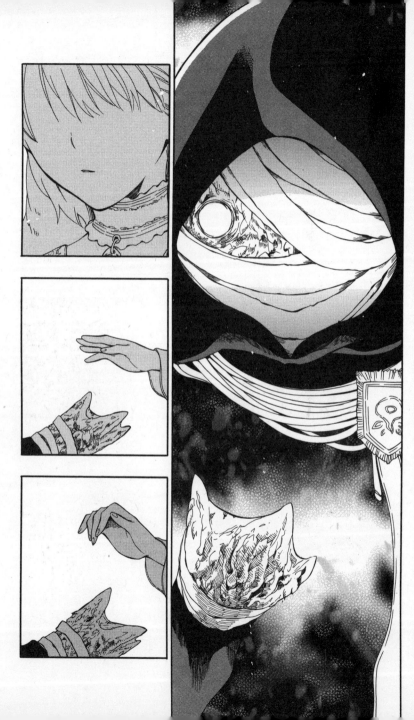

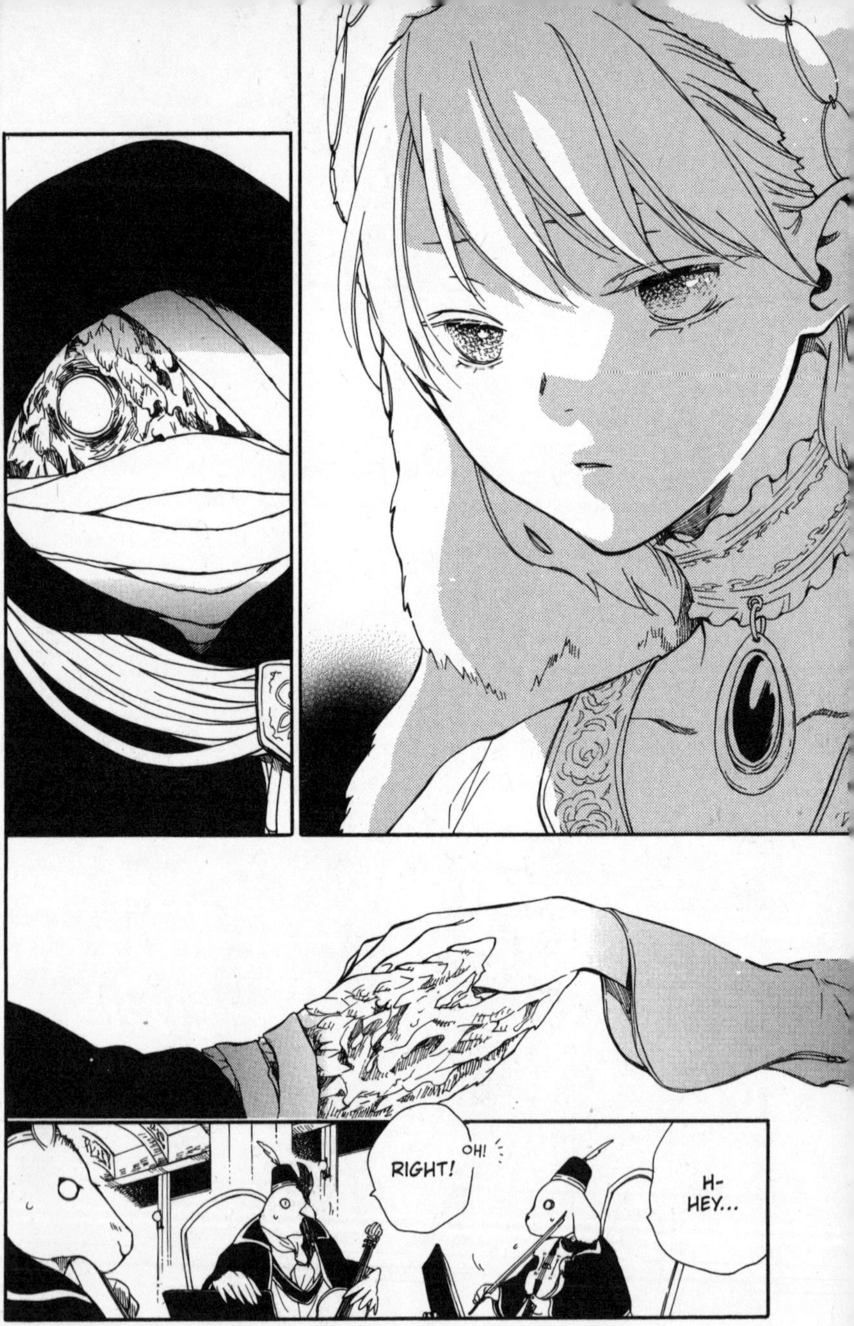
H- HEY...
OH!
RIGHT!

IT'S JUST SO HORRIBLE ...

UGH ...

STILL...

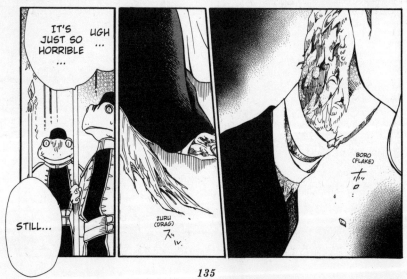

ZURU (DRAG)

BORO (FLAKE)

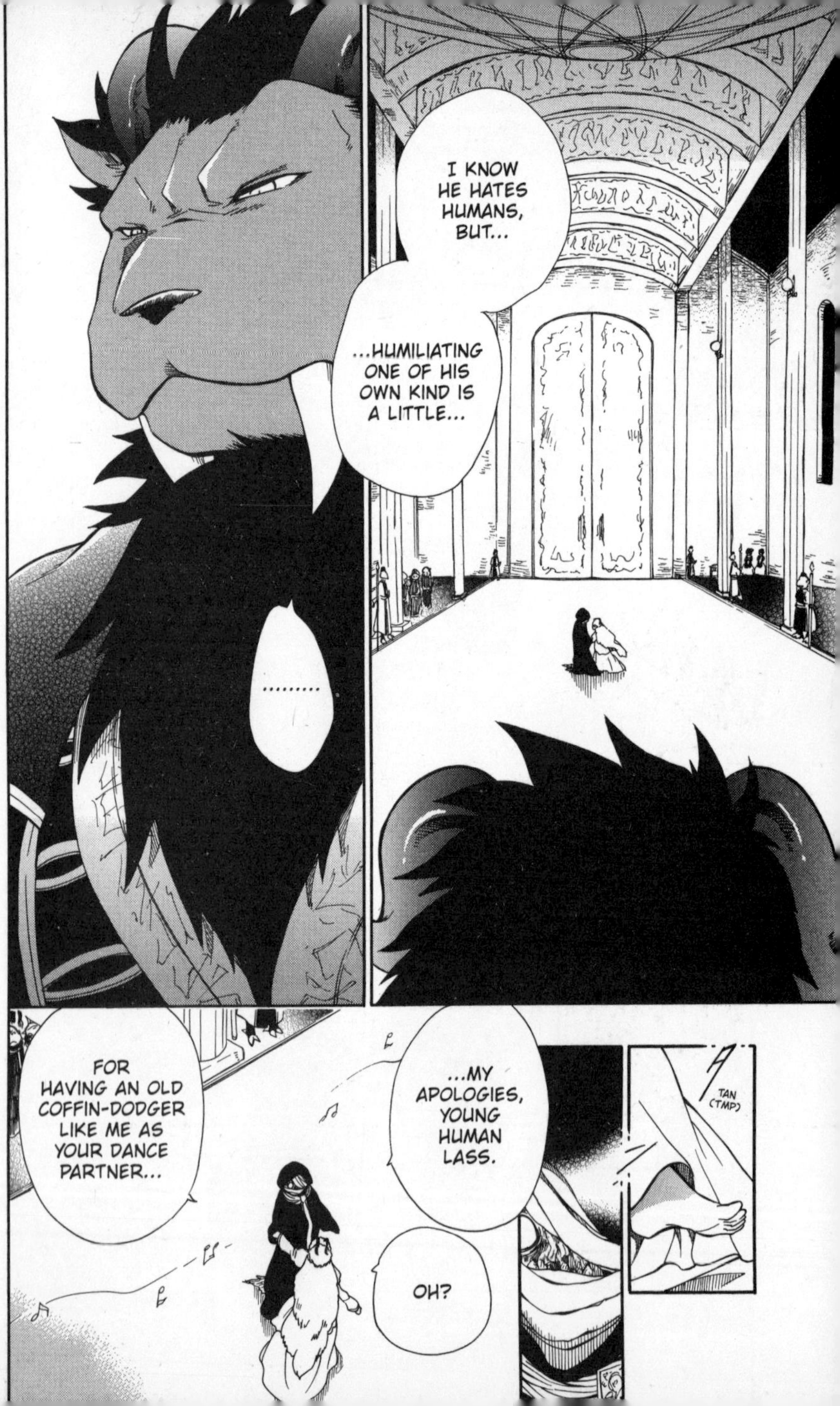

I KNOW HE HATES HUMANS, BUT...
...HUMILIATING ONE OF HIS OWN KIND IS A LITTLE...
....
TAN (TMP)
...MY APOLOGIES, YOUNG HUMAN LASS.
FOR HAVING AN OLD COFFIN-DODGER LIKE ME AS YOUR DANCE PARTNER...
OH?

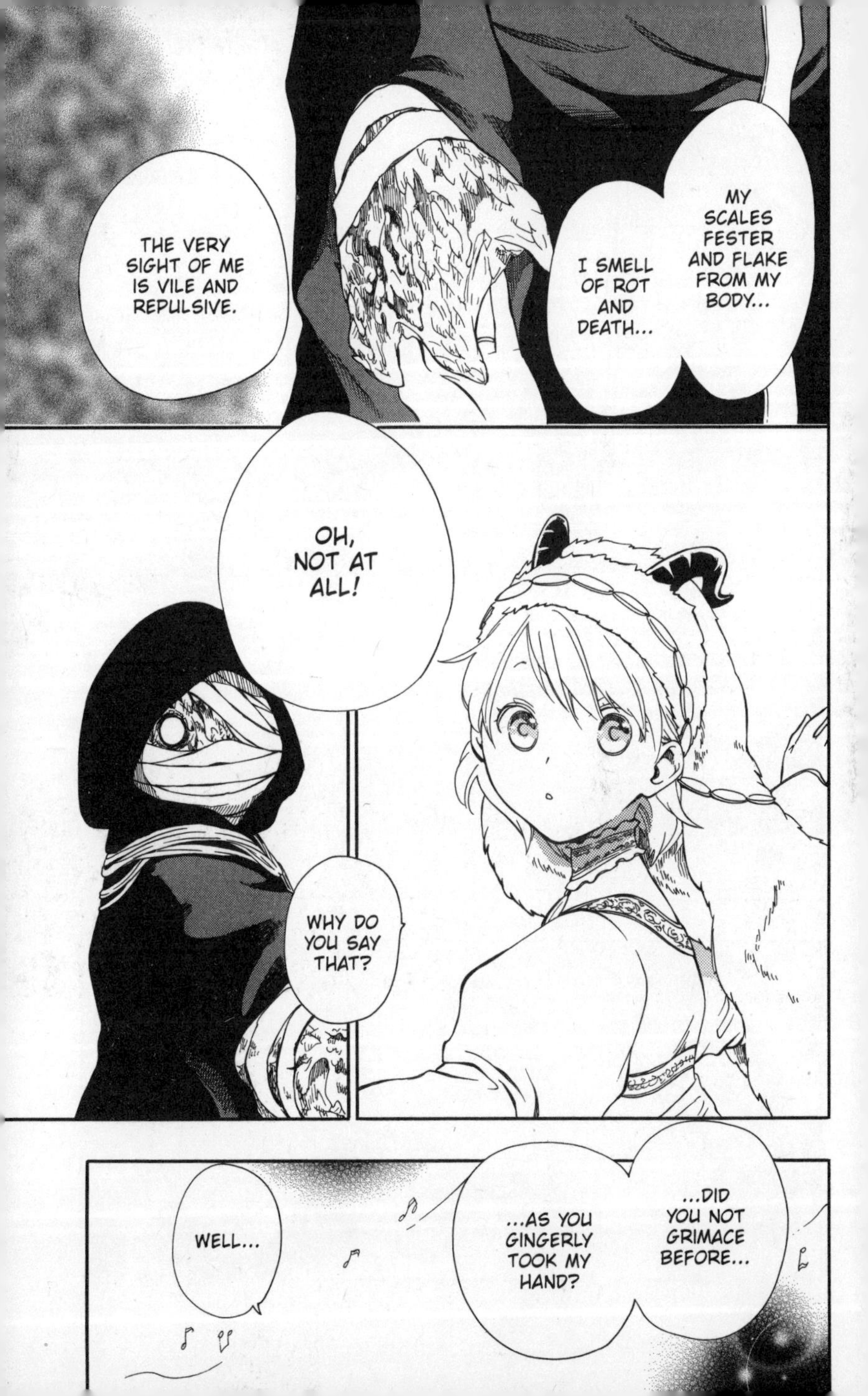
MY SCALES FESTER AND FLAKE FROM MY BODY...
I SMELL OF ROT AND DEATH...
THE VERY SIGHT OF ME IS VILE AND REPULSIVE.
OH, NOT AT ALL!
WHY DO YOU SAY THAT?
...DID YOU NOT GRIMACE BEFORE...
...AS YOU GINGERLY TOOK MY HAND?
WELL...

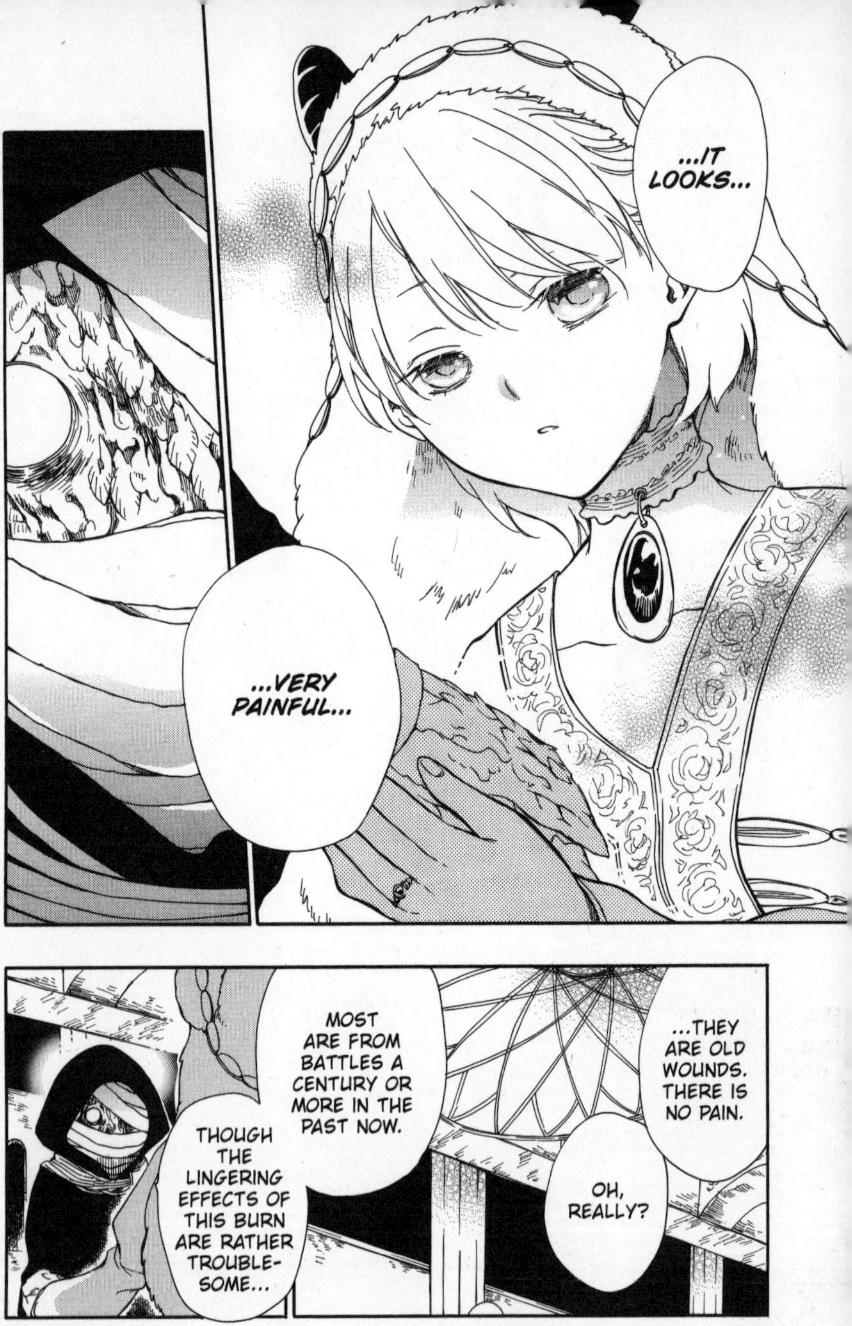
...IT LOOKS...
...VERY PAINFUL...
...THEY ARE OLD WOUNDS. THERE IS NO PAIN.
OH, REALLY?
MOST ARE FROM BATTLES A CENTURY OR MORE IN THE PAST NOW.
THOUGH THE LINGERING EFFECTS OF THIS BURN ARE RATHER TROUBLE-SOME...

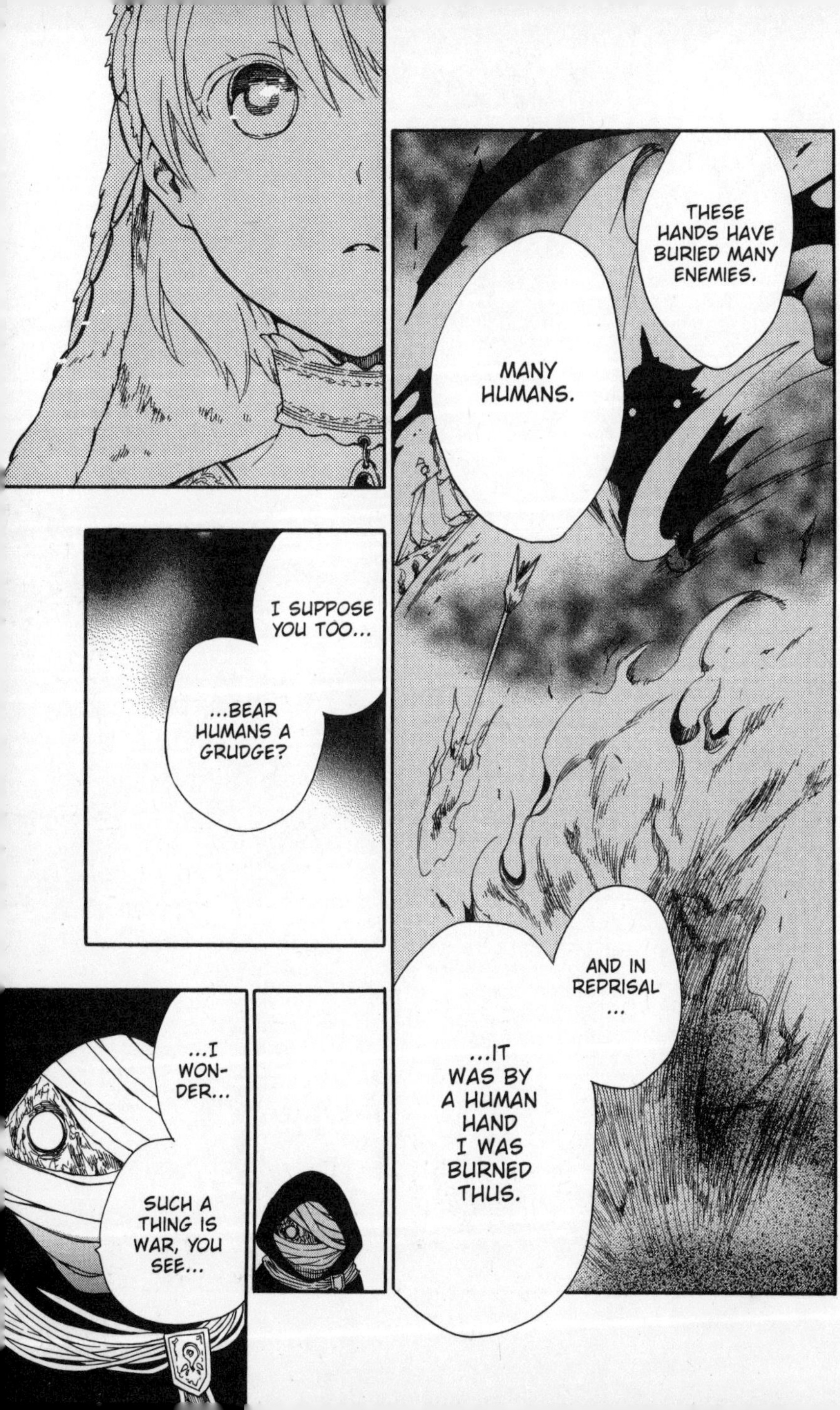
THESE HANDS HAVE BURIED MANY ENEMIES.
MANY HUMANS.
AND IN REPRISAL...
...IT WAS BY A HUMAN HAND I WAS BURNED THUS.
I SUPPOSE YOU TOO...
...BEAR HUMANS A GRUDGE?
...I WONDER...
SUCH A THING IS WAR, YOU SEE...

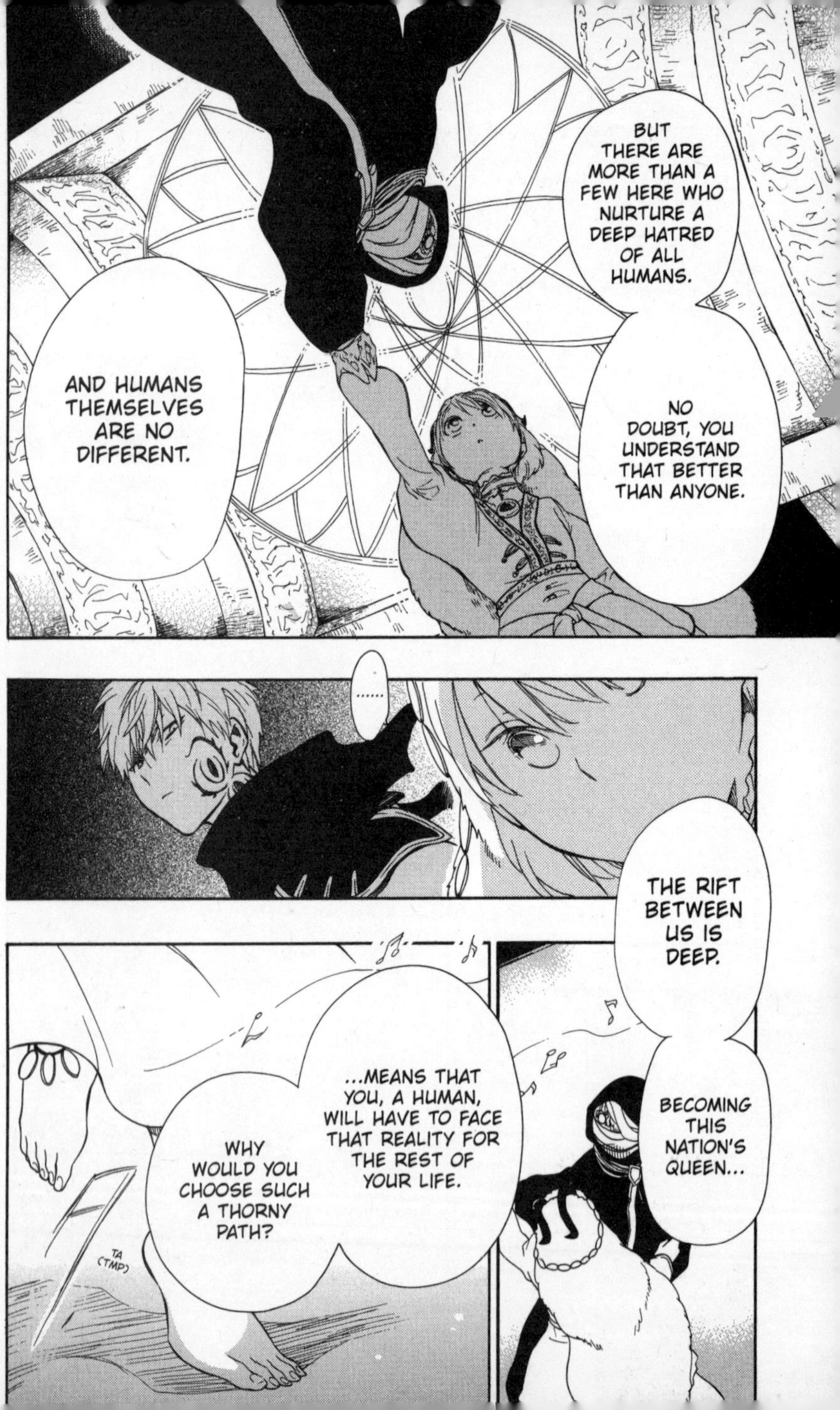
BUT THERE ARE MORE THAN A FEW HERE WHO NURTURE A DEEP HATRED OF ALL HUMANS.
NO DOUBT, YOU UNDERSTAND THAT BETTER THAN ANYONE.
AND HUMANS THEMSELVES ARE NO DIFFERENT.
THE RIFT BETWEEN US IS DEEP.
......
BECOMING THIS NATION'S QUEEN...
...MEANS THAT YOU, A HUMAN, WILL HAVE TO FACE THAT REALITY FOR THE REST OF YOUR LIFE.
WHY WOULD YOU CHOOSE SUCH A THORNY PATH?
TA (TMP)

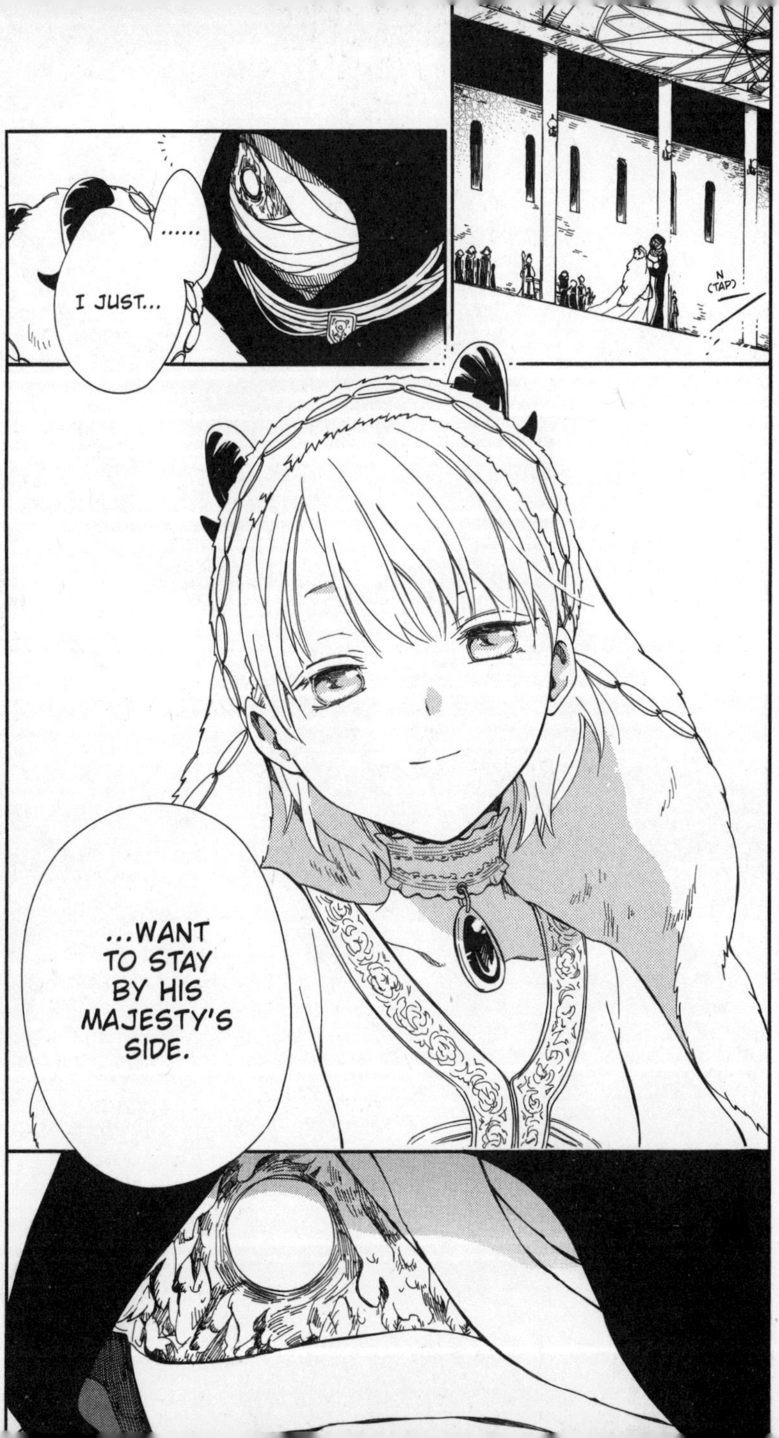
N
(TAP)
......
I JUST...
...WANT TO STAY BY HIS MAJESTY'S SIDE.

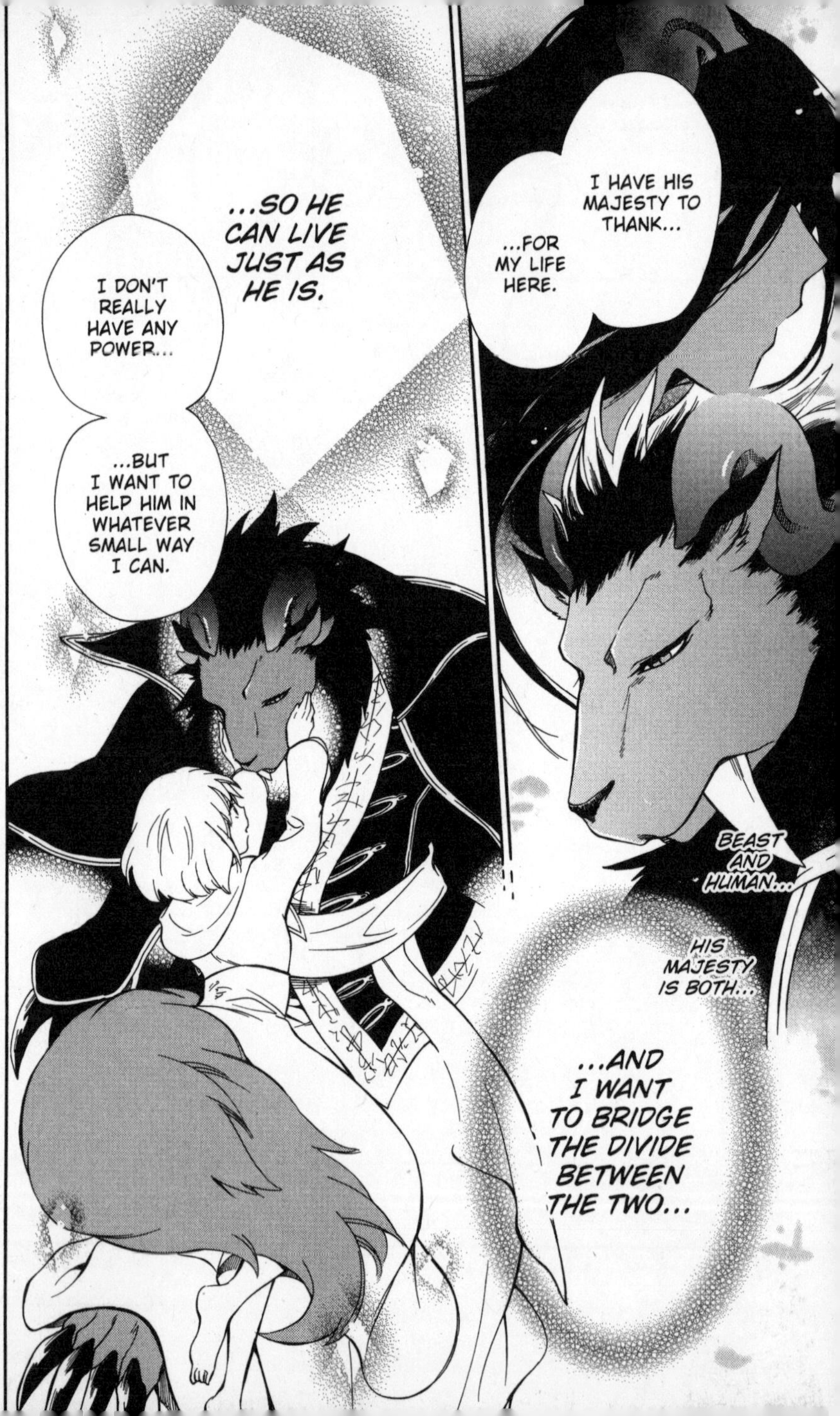
I HAVE HIS MAJESTY TO THANK...
...FOR MY LIFE HERE.
BEAST AND HUMAN...
HIS MAJESTY IS BOTH...
...AND I WANT TO BRIDGE THE DIVIDE BETWEEN THE TWO...
...SO HE CAN LIVE JUST AS HE IS.
I DON'T REALLY HAVE ANY POWER...
...BUT I WANT TO HELP HIM IN WHATEVER SMALL WAY I CAN.

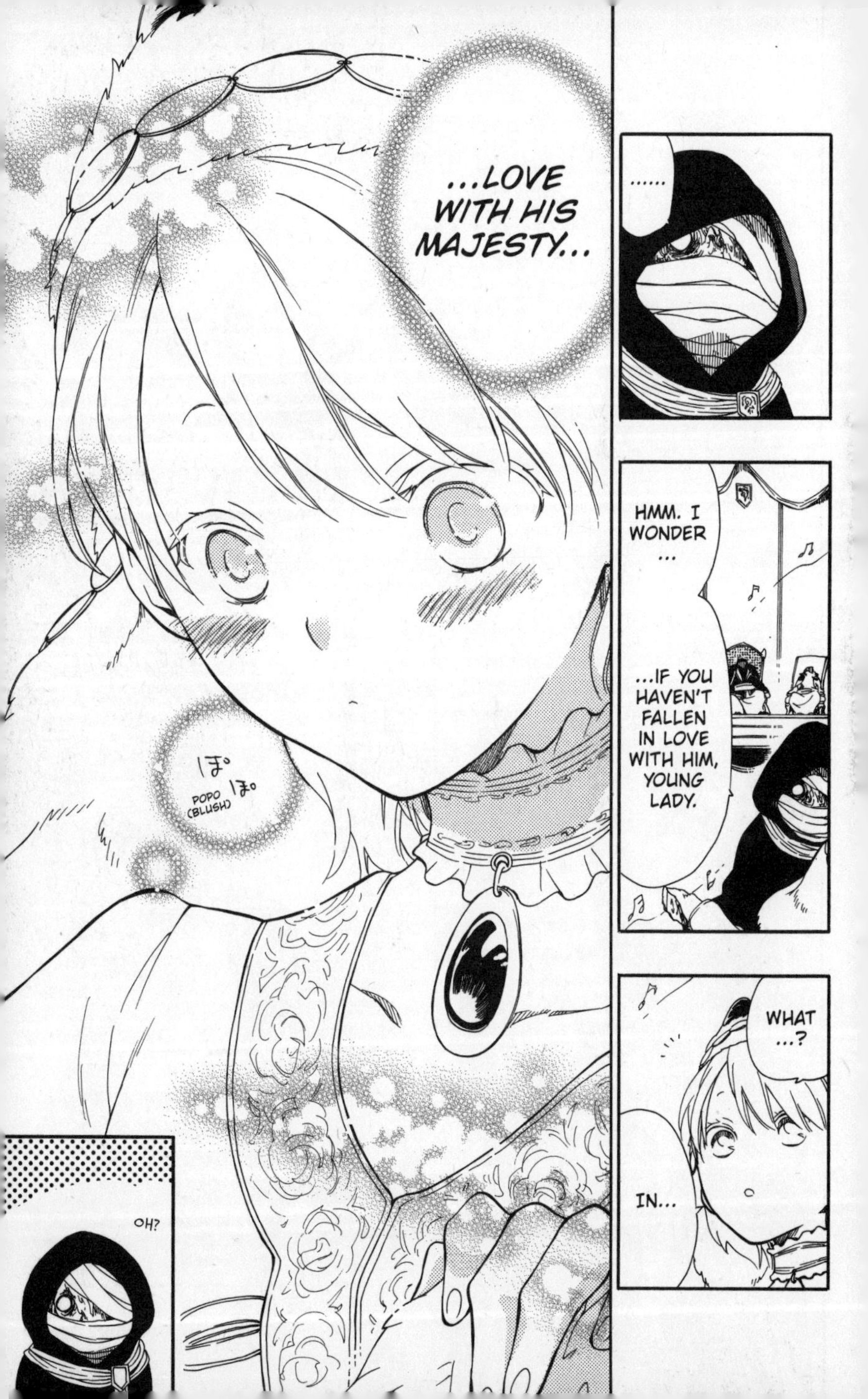
......
HMM. I WONDER ...
...IF YOU HAVEN'T FALLEN IN LOVE WITH HIM, YOUNG LADY.
WHAT ...?
IN...
...LOVE WITH HIS MAJESTY...
ぽぽ
POPO (BLUSH)
OH?

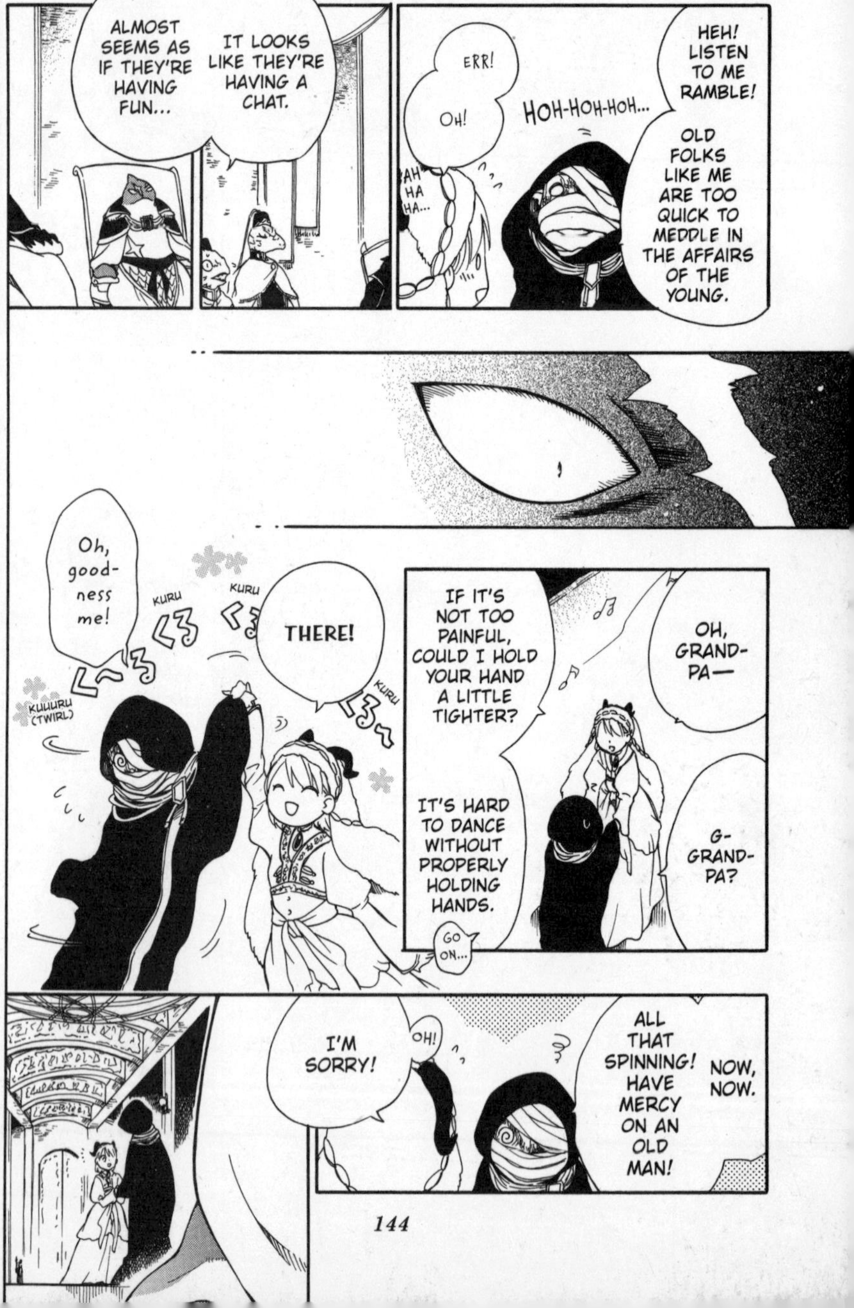
HEH! LISTEN TO ME RAMBLE!
OLD FOLKS LIKE ME ARE TOO QUICK TO MEDDLE IN THE AFFAIRS OF THE YOUNG.
HOH-HOH-HOH...
ERR!
OH!
AH HA HA...
IT LOOKS LIKE THEY'RE HAVING A CHAT.
ALMOST SEEMS AS IF THEY'RE HAVING FUN...
OH, GRANDPA—
IF IT'S NOT TOO PAINFUL, COULD I HOLD YOUR HAND A LITTLE TIGHTER?
G-GRANDPA?
IT'S HARD TO DANCE WITHOUT PROPERLY HOLDING HANDS.
GO ON...
KURU
THERE!
KURU
KURU
Oh, goodness me!
KUUURU (TWIRL)
NOW, NOW.
ALL THAT SPINNING! HAVE MERCY ON AN OLD MAN!
OH!
I'M SORRY!

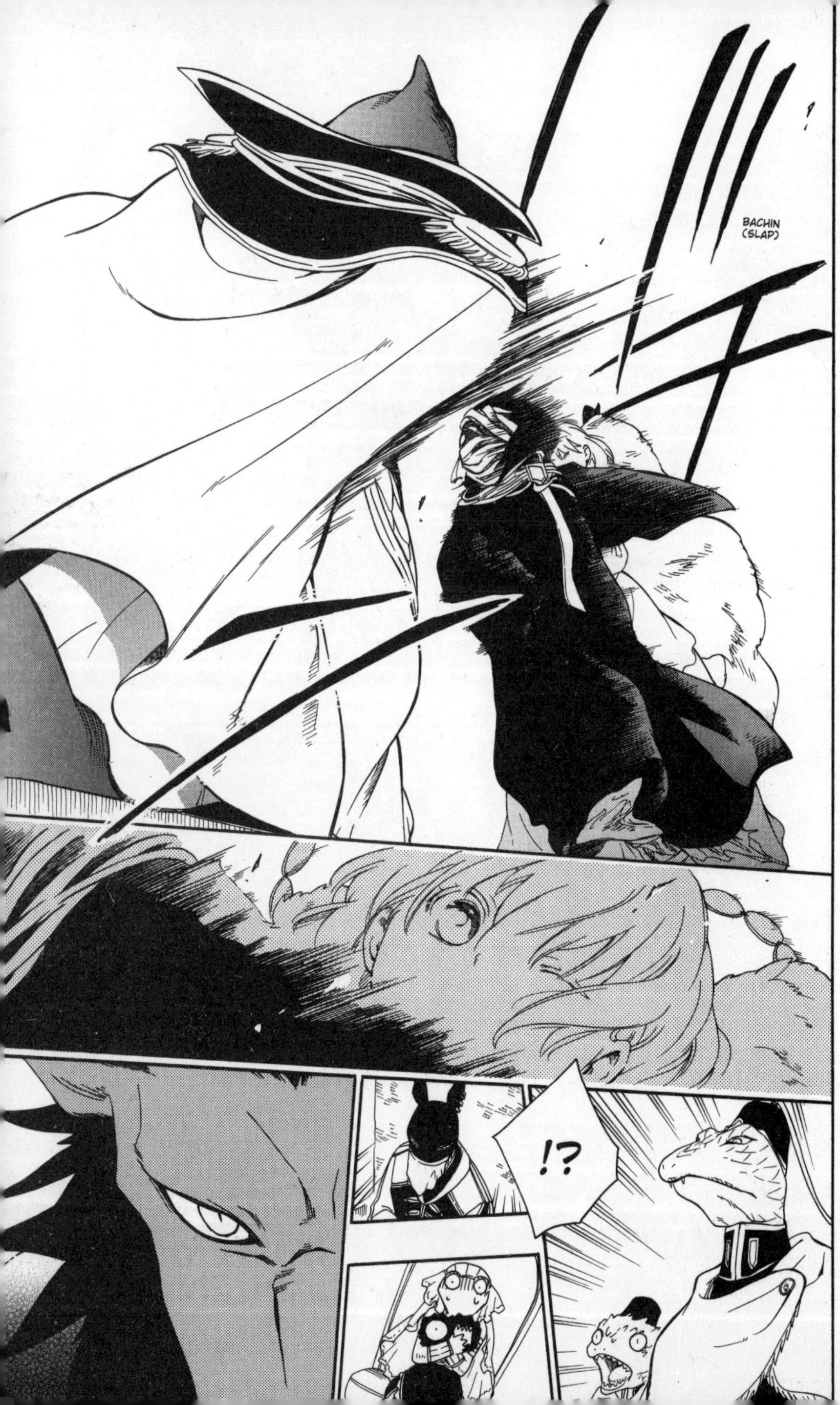
BACHIN
(SLAP)
!?

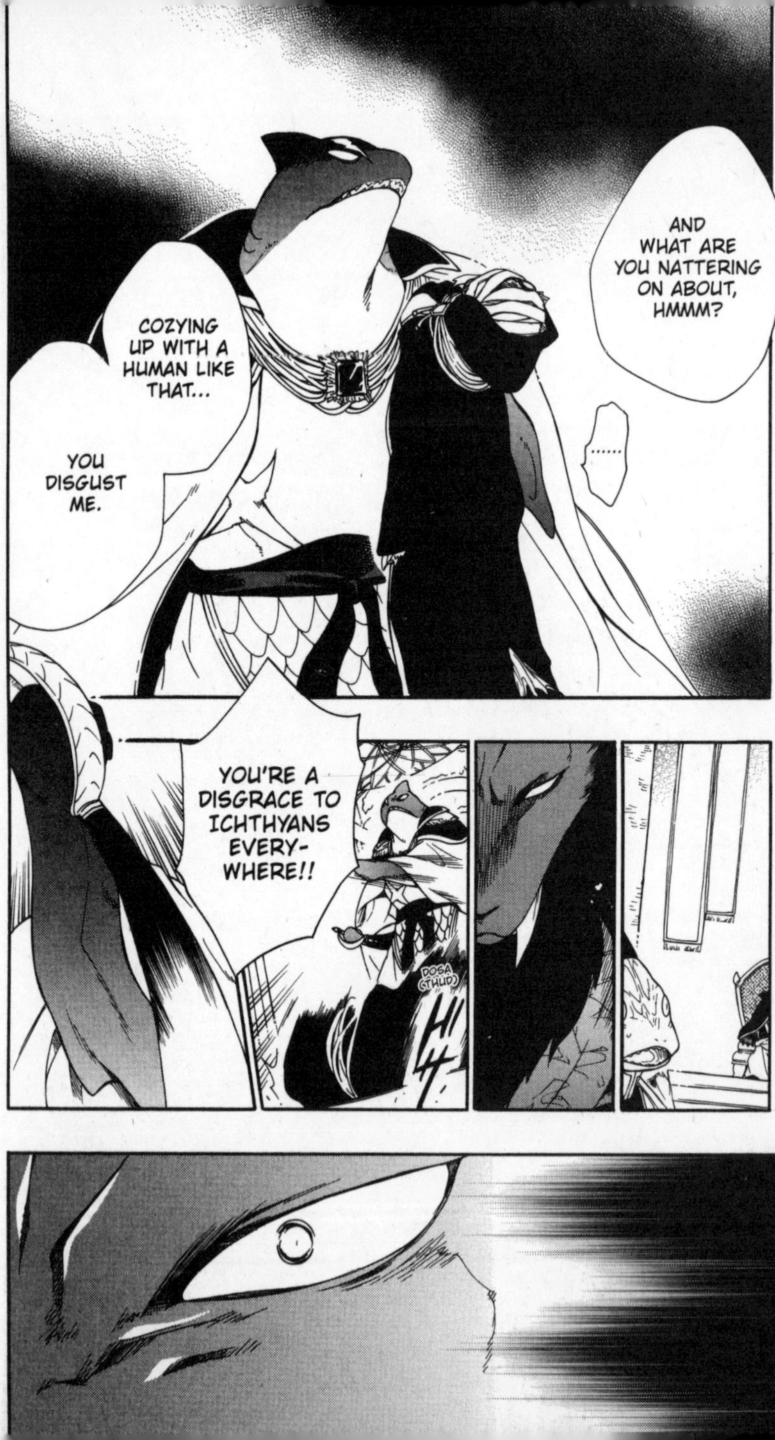
AND WHAT ARE YOU NATTERING ON ABOUT, HMMM?
......
COZYING UP WITH A HUMAN LIKE THAT...
YOU DISGUST ME.
DOSA (THUD)
YOU'RE A DISGRACE TO ICHTHYANS EVERY-WHERE!!

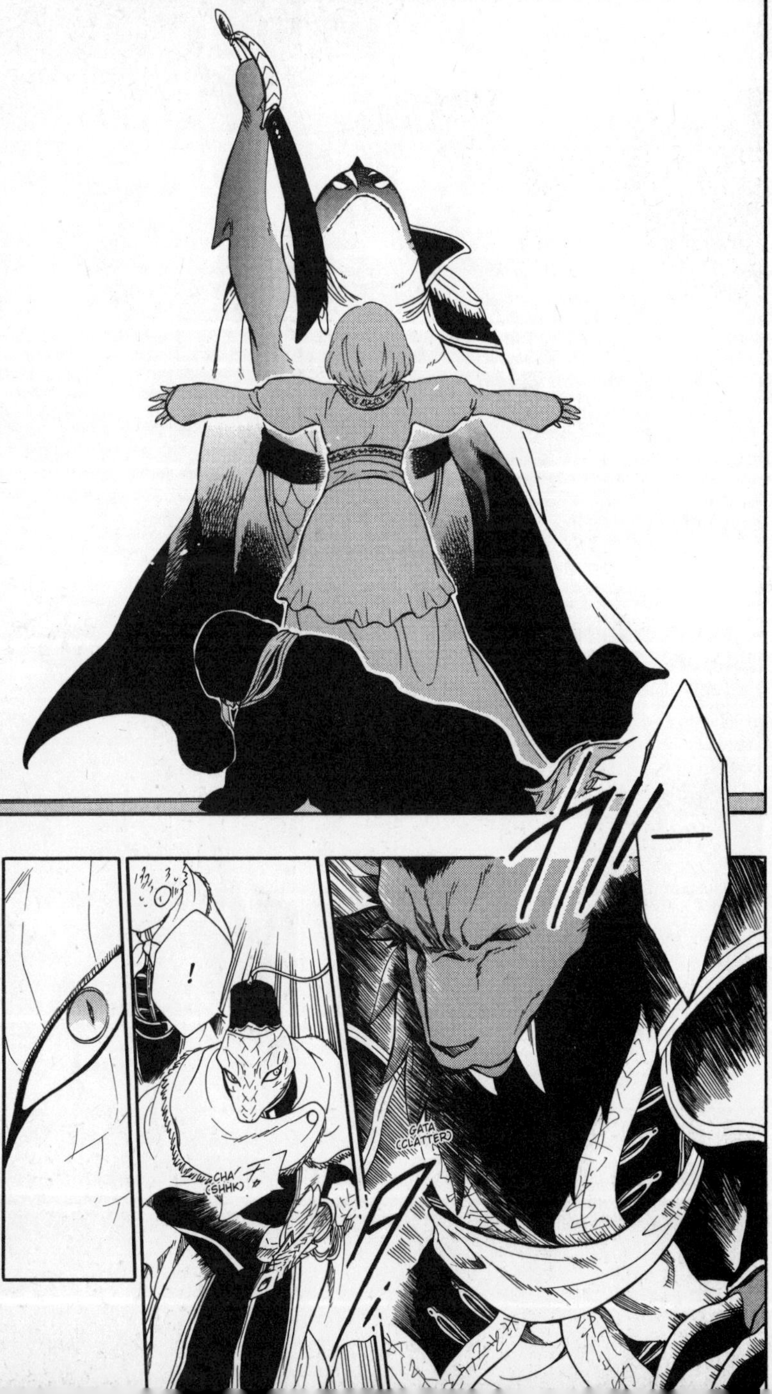
GATA
(CLATTER)
!
CHA
(SHHK)

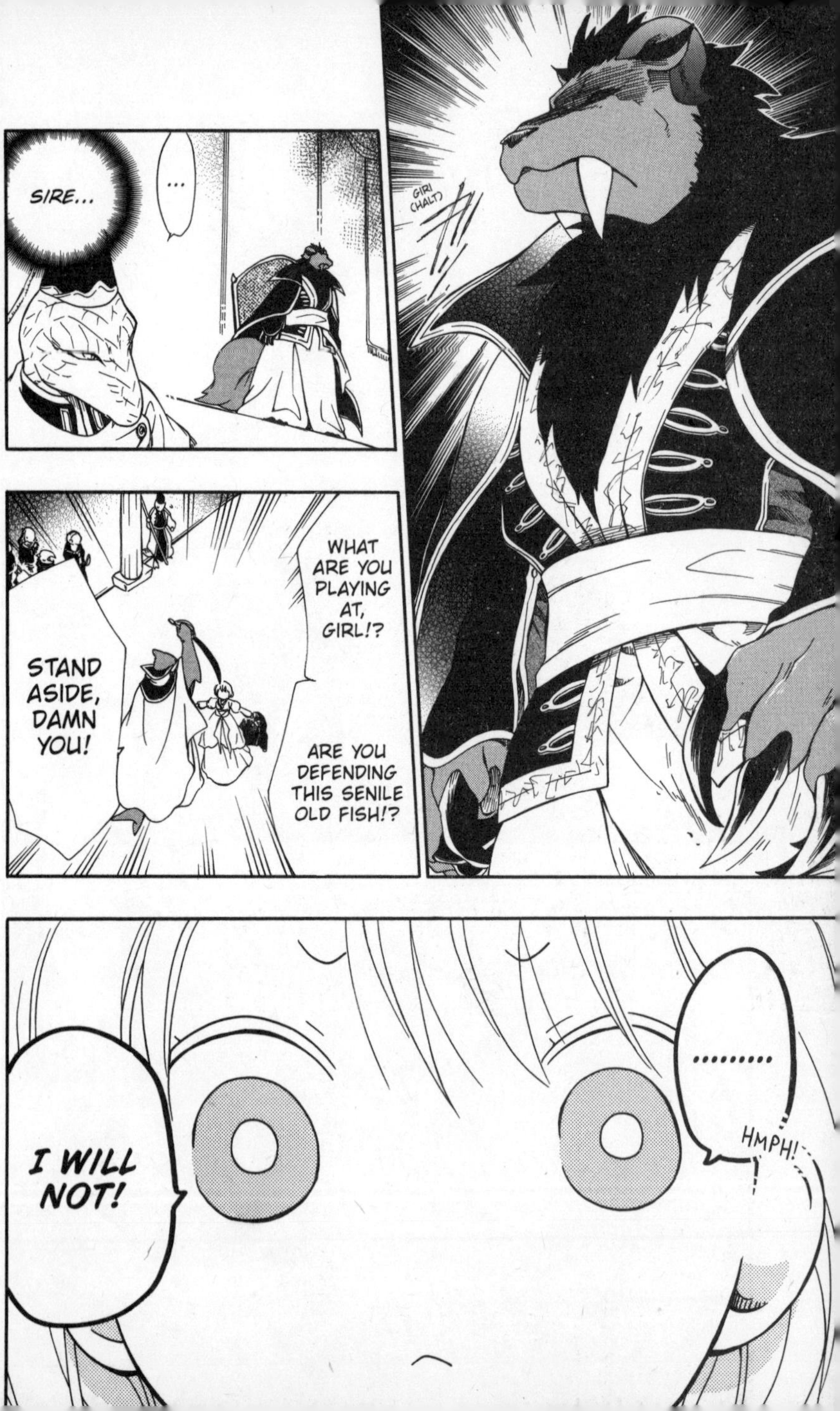
GIRI (HALT)
...
SIRE...
WHAT ARE YOU PLAYING AT, GIRL!?
ARE YOU DEFENDING THIS SENILE OLD FISH!?
STAND ASIDE, DAMN YOU!
....
HMPH!
I WILL NOT!

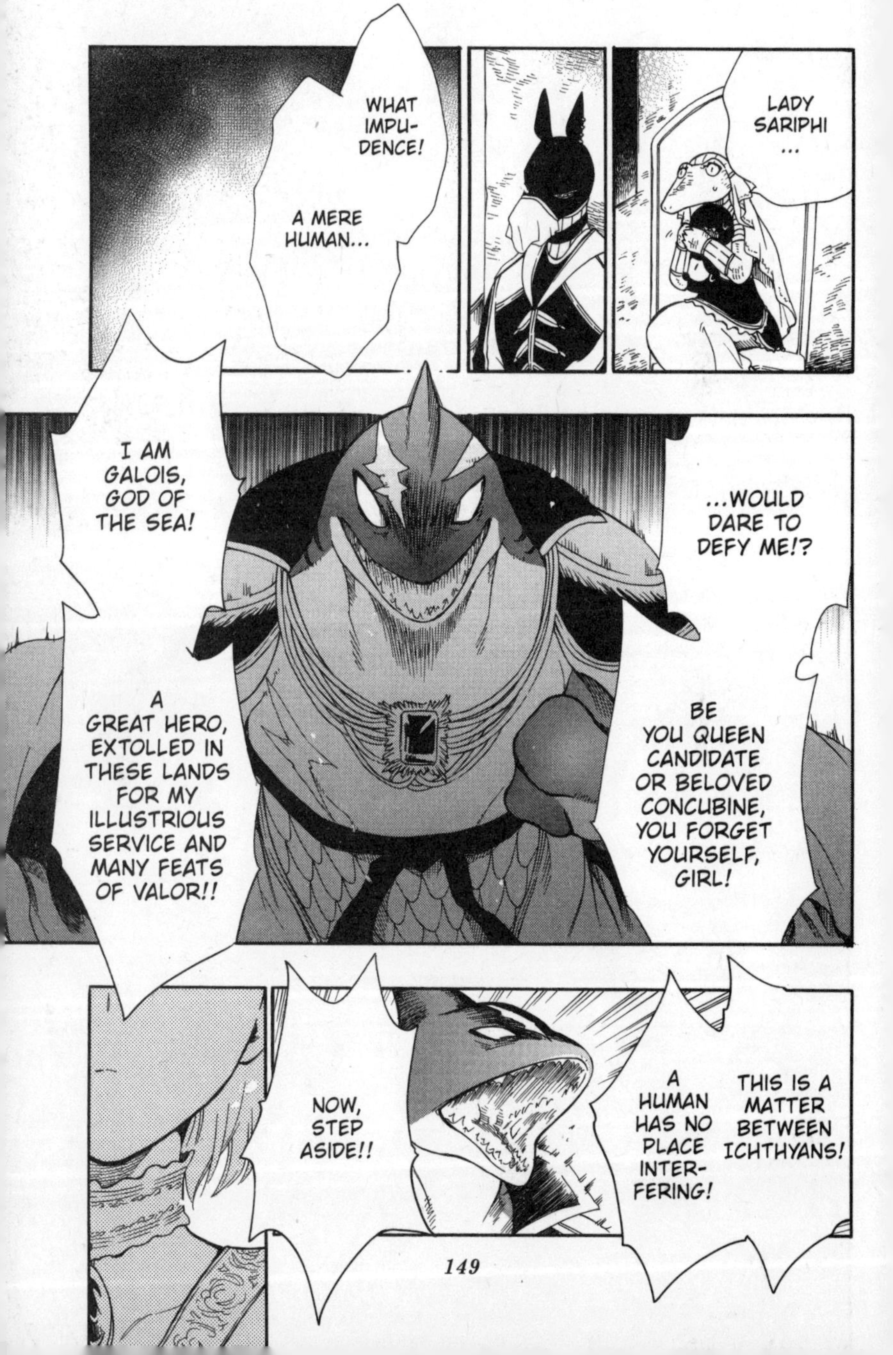
LADY SARIPHI ...
WHAT IMPU-DENCE!
A MERE HUMAN...
...WOULD DARE TO DEFY ME!?
I AM GALOIS, GOD OF THE SEA!
BE YOU QUEEN CANDIDATE OR BELOVED CONCUBINE, YOU FORGET YOURSELF, GIRL!
A GREAT HERO, EXTOLLED IN THESE LANDS FOR MY ILLUSTRIOUS SERVICE AND MANY FEATS OF VALOR!!
THIS IS A MATTER BETWEEN ICHTHYANS!
A HUMAN HAS NO PLACE INTER-FERING!
NOW, STEP ASIDE!!

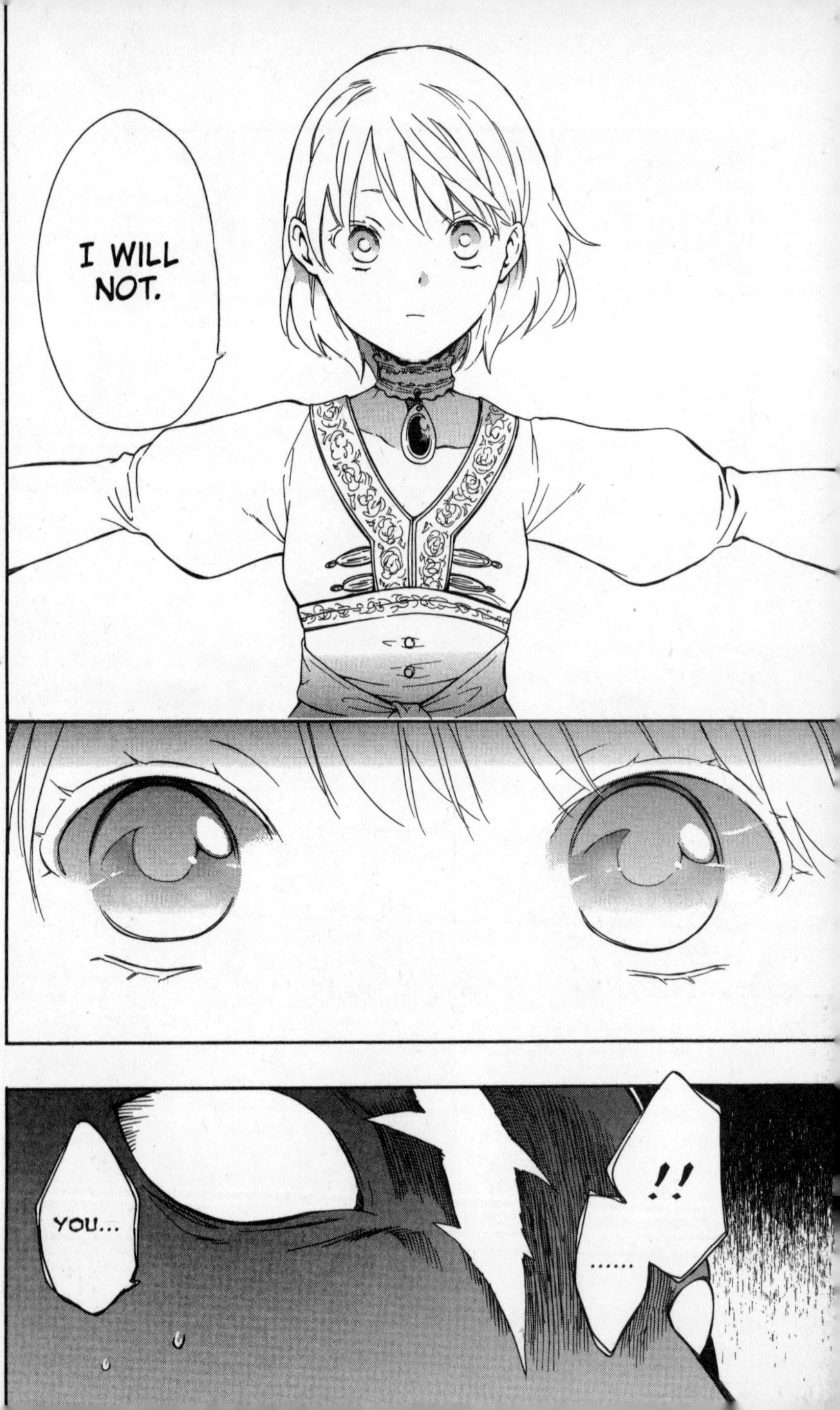
I WILL NOT.
!!
......
YOU...

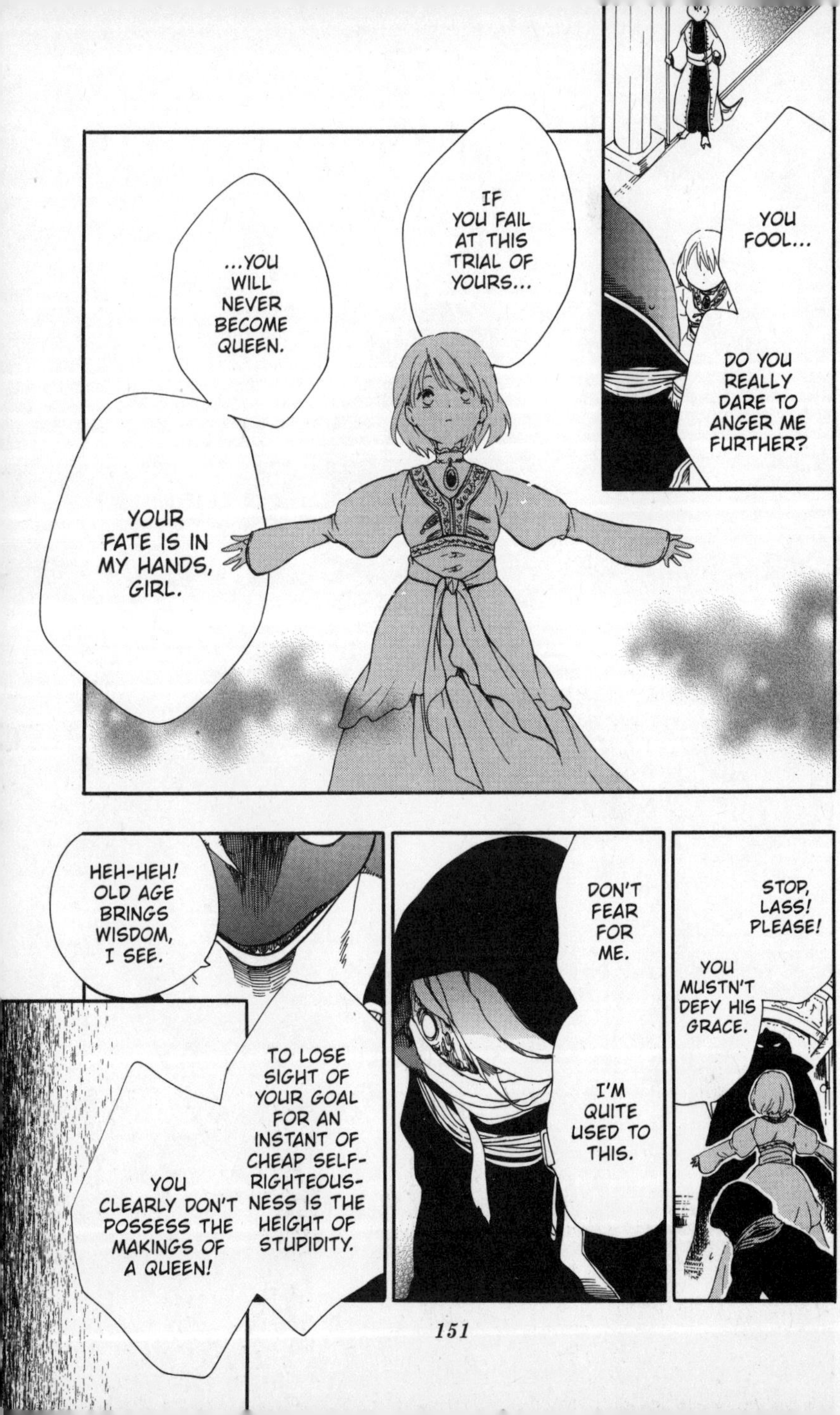
YOU FOOL...
DO YOU REALLY DARE TO ANGER ME FURTHER?
IF YOU FAIL AT THIS TRIAL OF YOURS...
...YOU WILL NEVER BECOME QUEEN.
YOUR FATE IS IN MY HANDS, GIRL.
STOP, LASS! PLEASE!
YOU MUSTN'T DEFY HIS GRACE.
DON'T FEAR FOR ME.
I'M QUITE USED TO THIS.
HEH-HEH! OLD AGE BRINGS WISDOM, I SEE.
TO LOSE SIGHT OF YOUR GOAL FOR AN INSTANT OF CHEAP SELF-RIGHTEOUSNESS IS THE HEIGHT OF STUPIDITY.
YOU CLEARLY DON'T POSSESS THE MAKINGS OF A QUEEN!

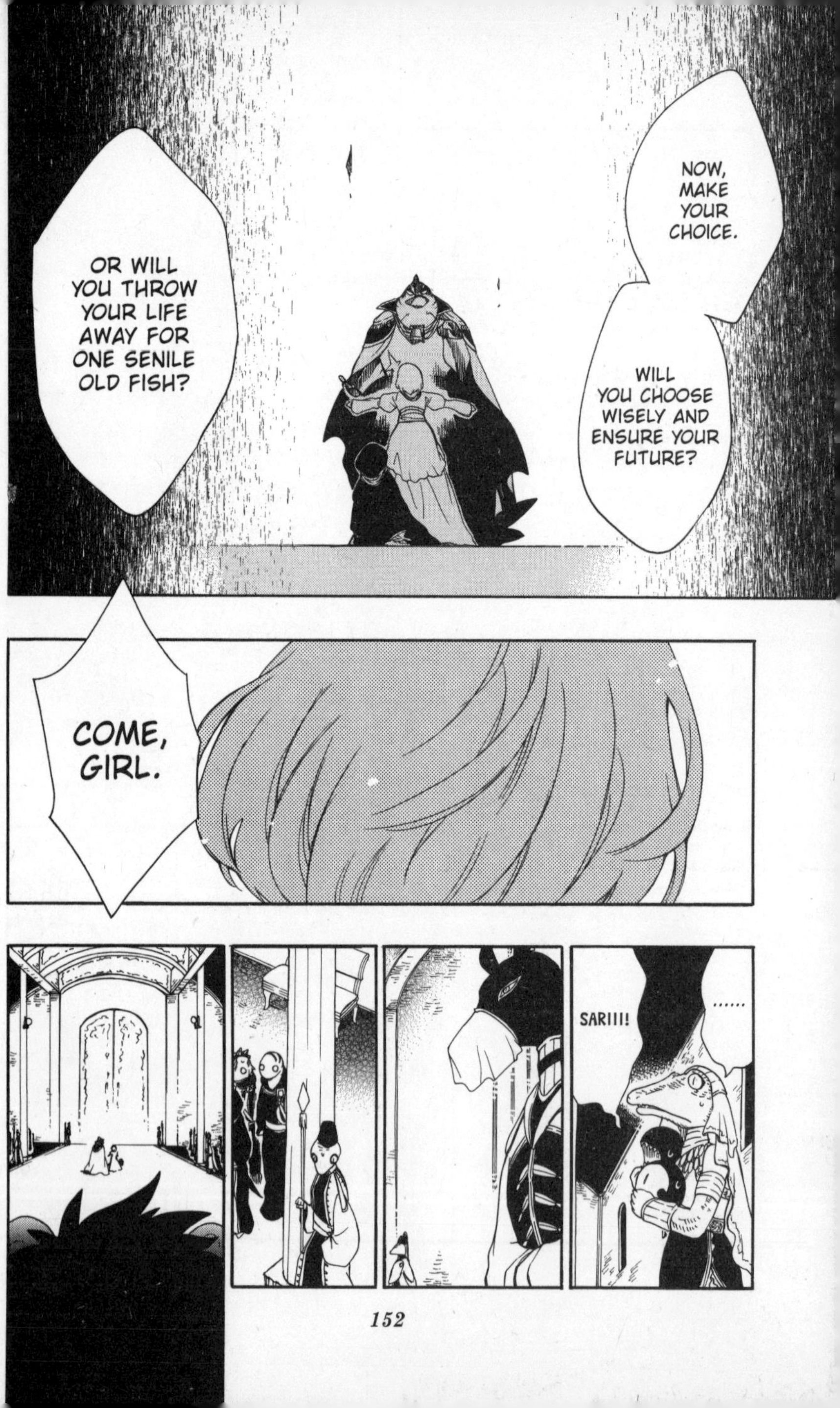
NOW, MAKE YOUR CHOICE.
WILL YOU CHOOSE WISELY AND ENSURE YOUR FUTURE?
OR WILL YOU THROW YOUR LIFE AWAY FOR ONE SENILE OLD FISH?
COME, GIRL.
......
SARIIII!

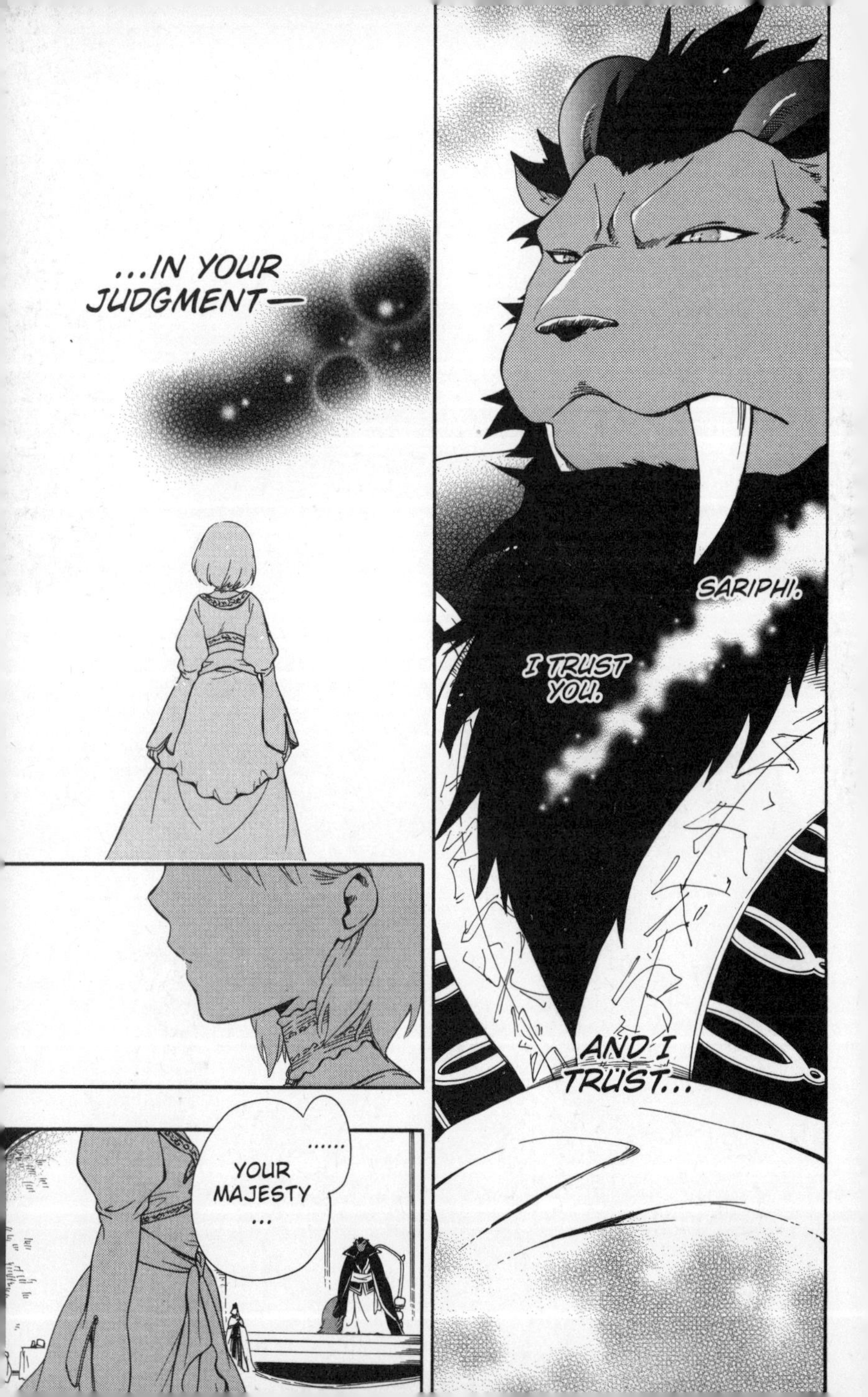
SARIPHI.
I TRUST YOU.
AND I TRUST...
...IN YOUR JUDGMENT—
......
YOUR MAJESTY ...

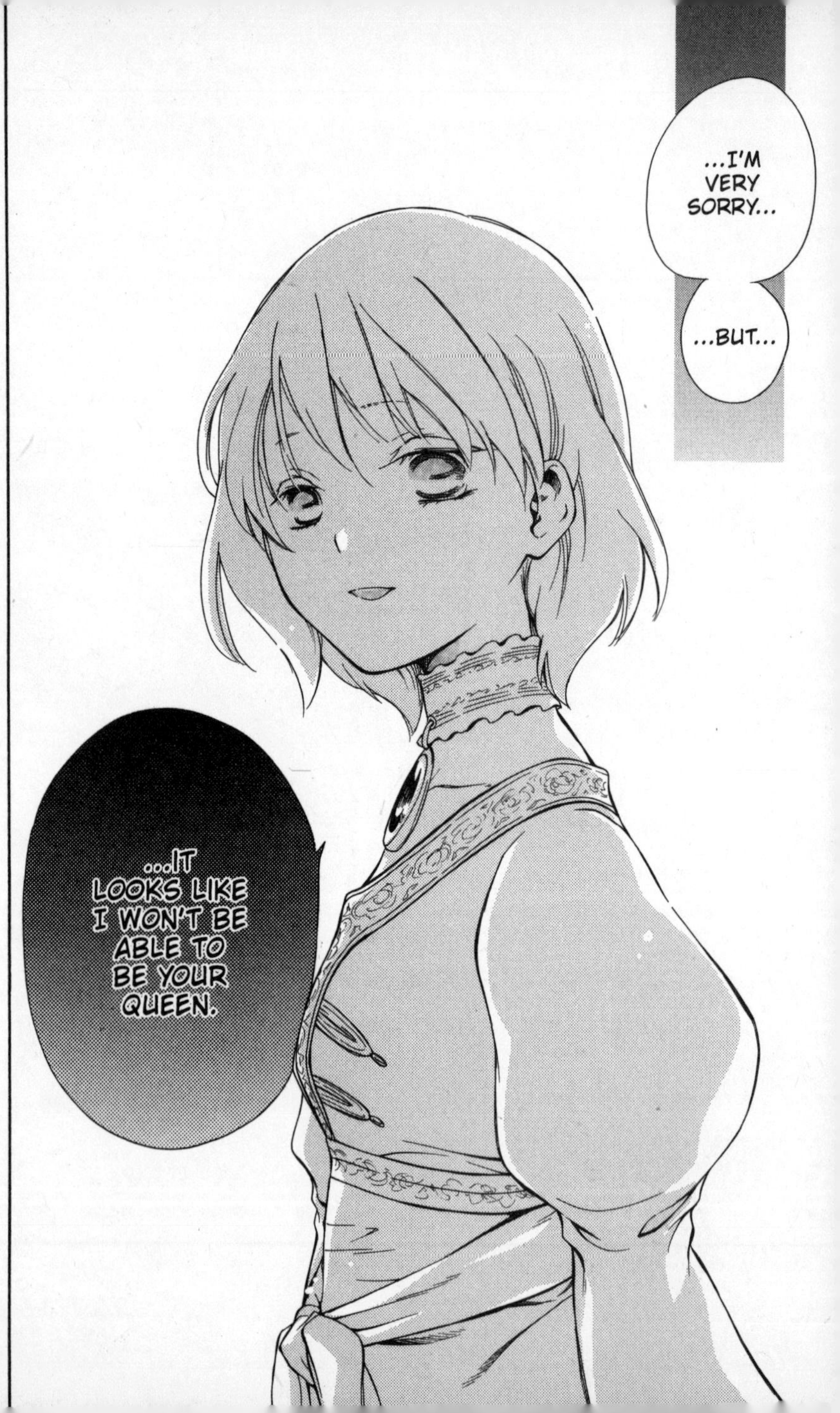
...I'M VERY SORRY...
...BUT...
...IT LOOKS LIKE I WON'T BE ABLE TO BE YOUR QUEEN.

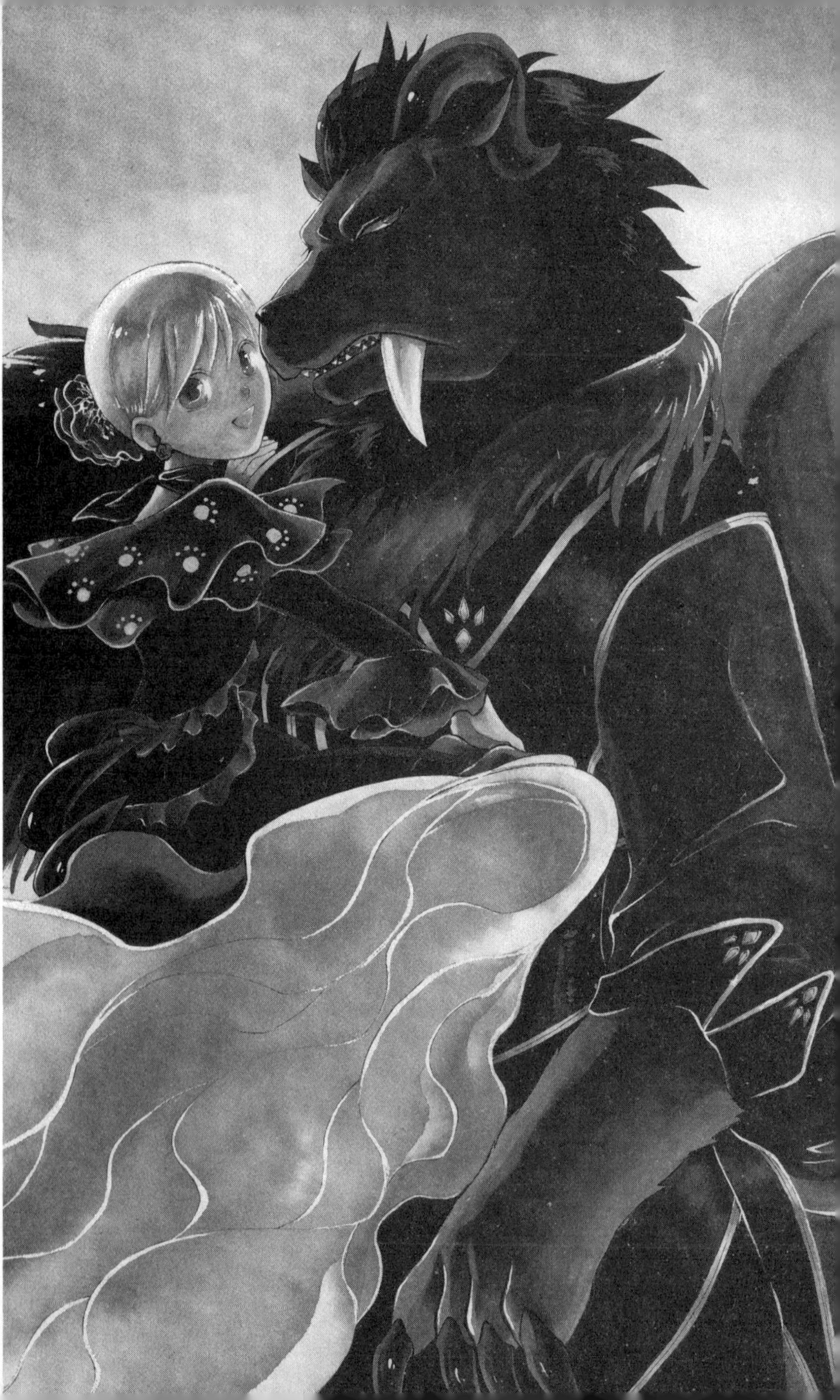

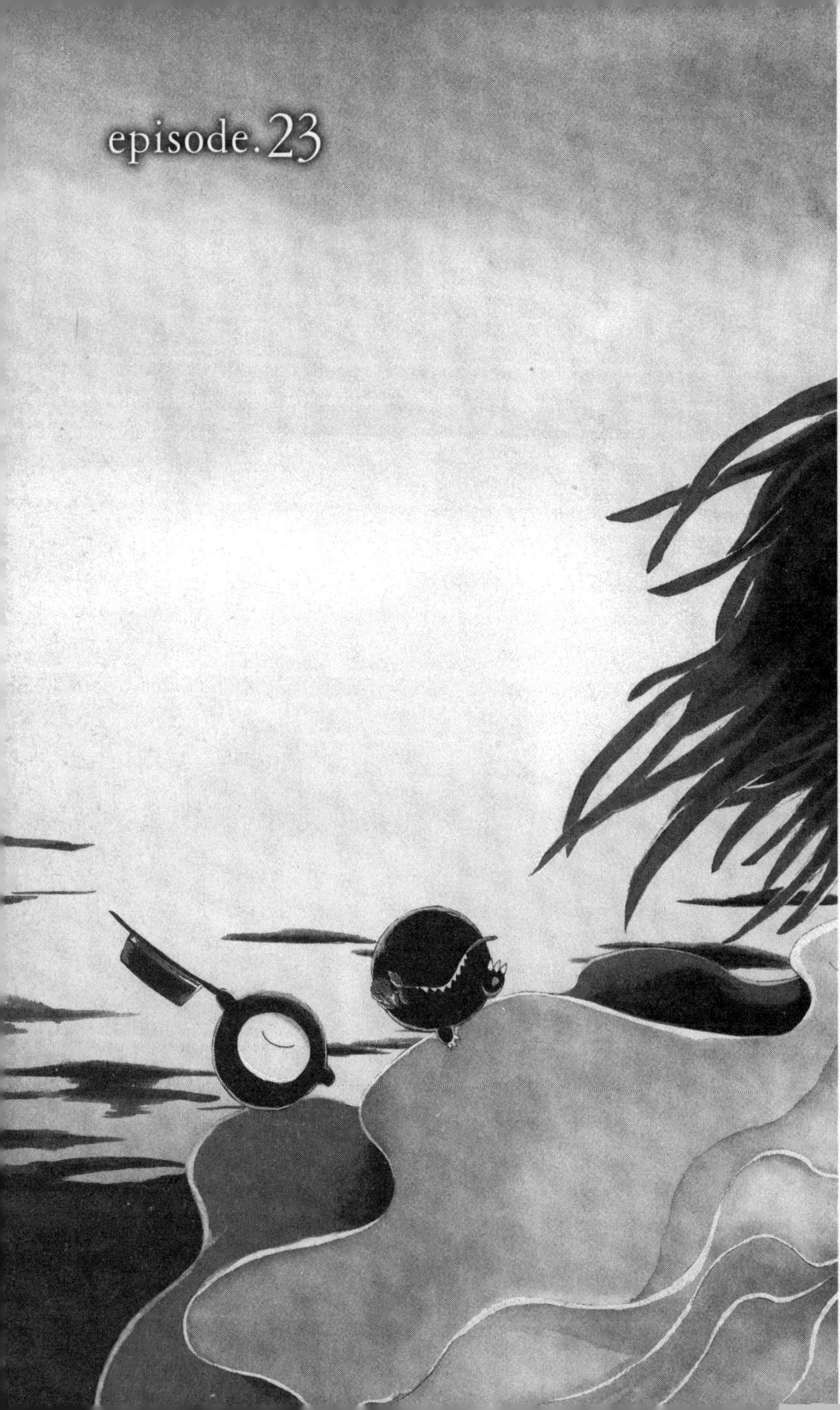
episode.23

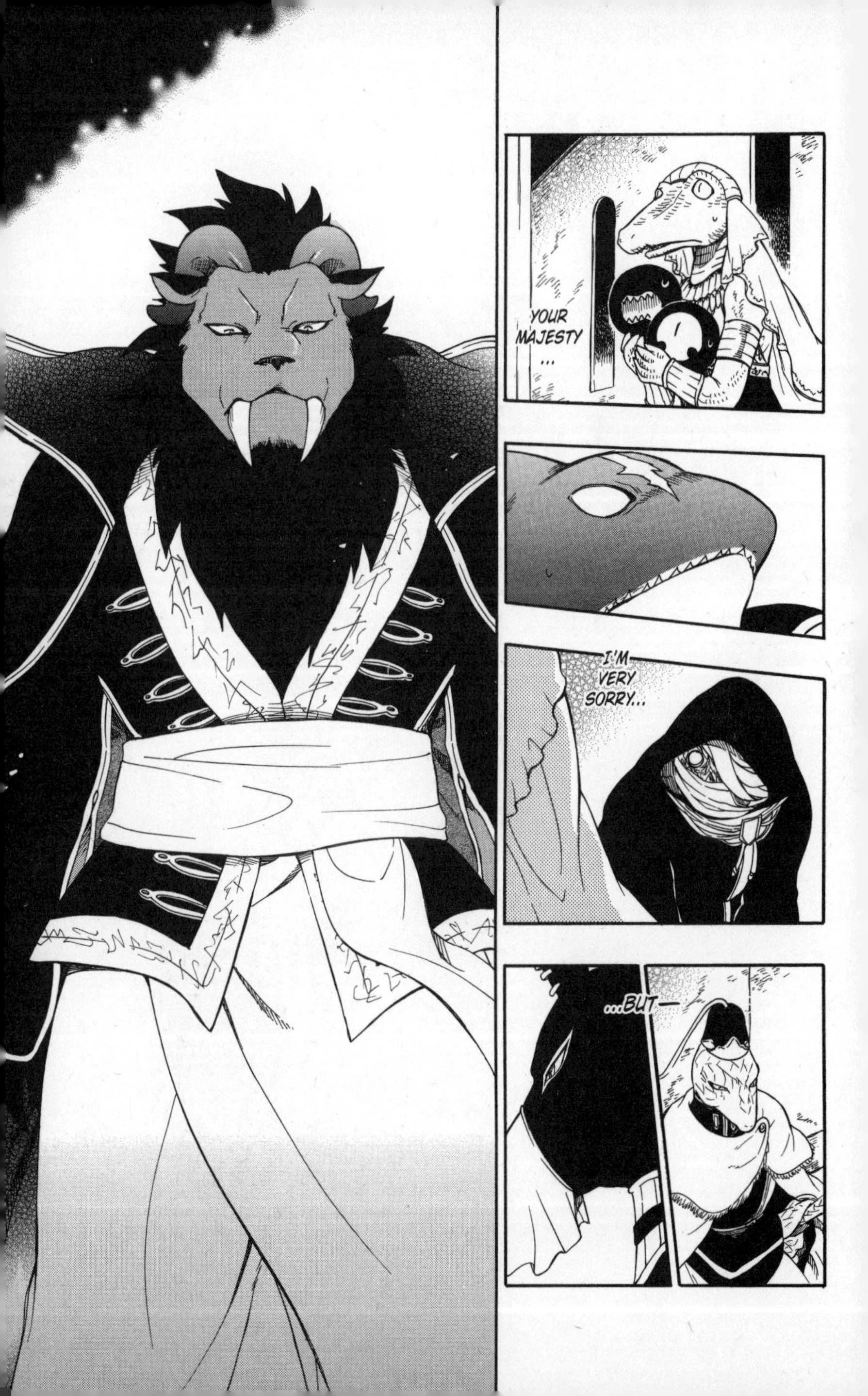
YOUR MAJESTY ...
I'M VERY SORRY...
...BUT—

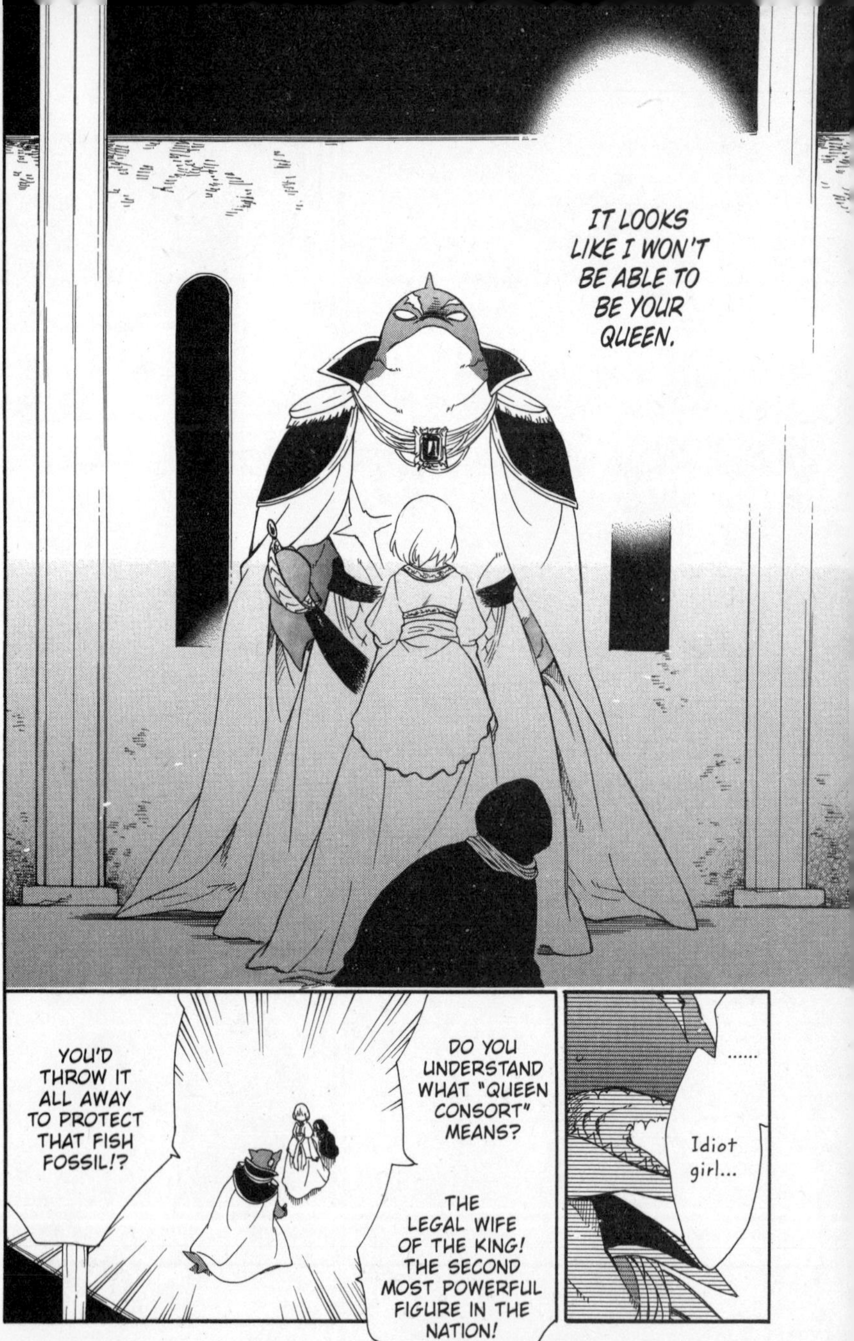
IT LOOKS LIKE I WON'T BE ABLE TO BE YOUR QUEEN.
......
Idiot girl...
DO YOU UNDERSTAND WHAT "QUEEN CONSORT" MEANS?
THE LEGAL WIFE OF THE KING! THE SECOND MOST POWERFUL FIGURE IN THE NATION!
YOU'D THROW IT ALL AWAY TO PROTECT THAT FISH FOSSIL!?

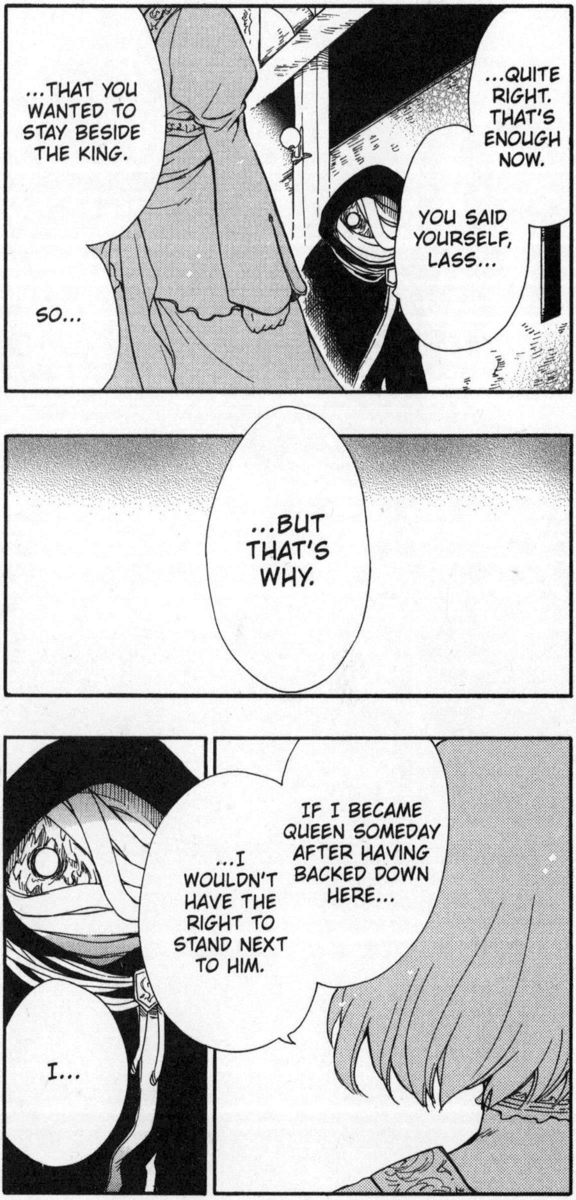
...QUITE RIGHT. THAT'S ENOUGH NOW.
YOU SAID YOURSELF, LASS...
...THAT YOU WANTED TO STAY BESIDE THE KING.
SO...
...BUT THAT'S WHY.
IF I BECAME QUEEN SOMEDAY AFTER HAVING BACKED DOWN HERE...
...I WOULDN'T HAVE THE RIGHT TO STAND NEXT TO HIM.
I...

AND SO THE FOURTH VOLUME OF *SACRIFICIAL PRINCESS* COMES TO AN END. FOUR VOLUMES... IT FEELS LIKE I'M GOING TO RUN OUT OF THINGS TO WRITE IN THIS SPACE RATHER SOON. SINCE BOTH MY HANDWRITING AND MY COMPOSITION ARE RATHER BAD, I'M GRATEFUL IF YOU UNDERSTAND EVEN HALF OF WHAT I'M SAYING. IT'S HARD TO FEEL LIKE IT'S REAL, BUT ASSUMING NOTHING HAPPENS, THERE'S GOING TO BE A FIFTH VOLUME, SO I HOPE TO SEE YOU THERE! UNTIL THEN, FAREWELL, AND THANK YOU!

TOMOFUJI

AS ALWAYS, THANKS TO MY ASSISTANTS, S-SAN AND O-SAN!

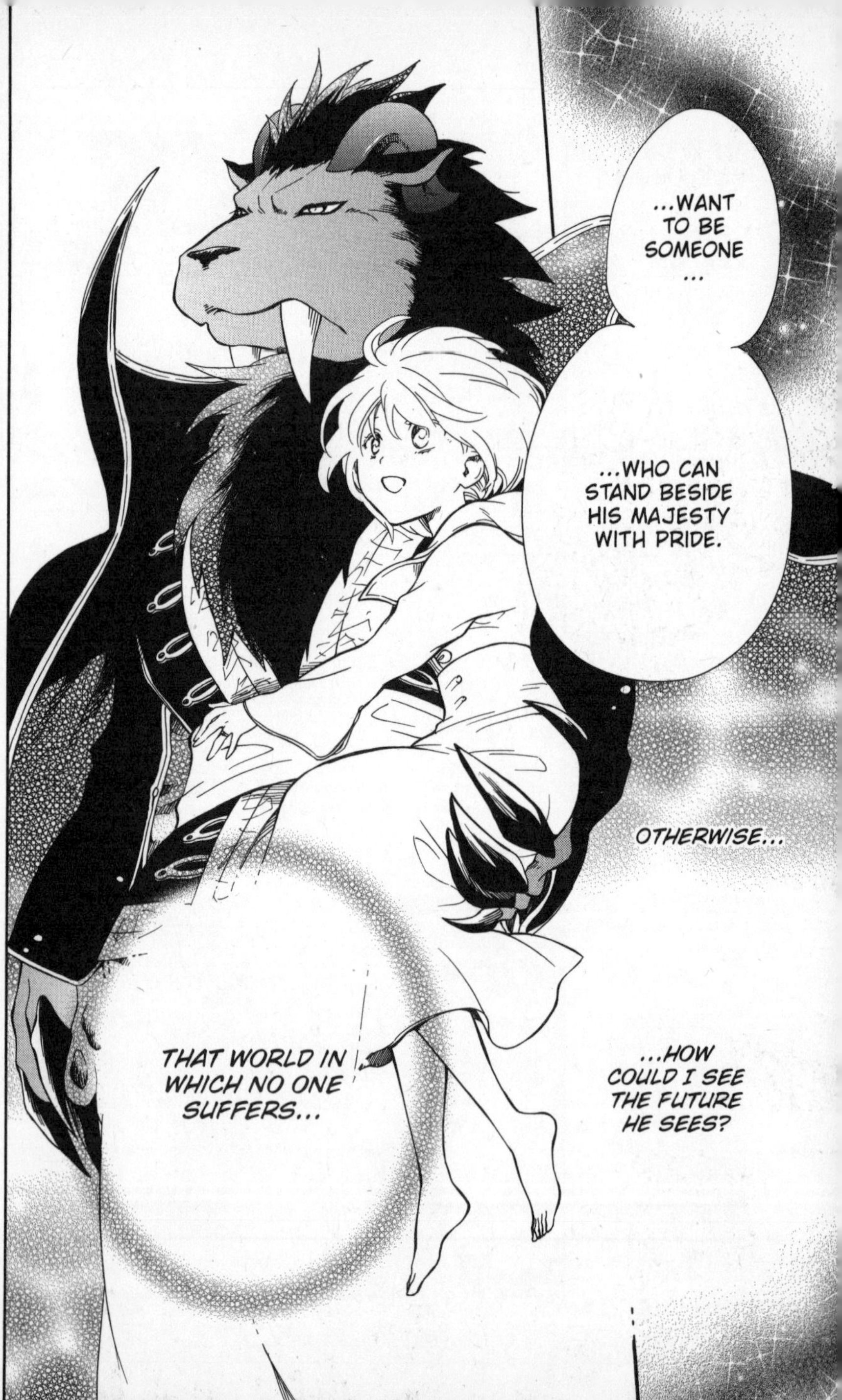
...WANT TO BE SOMEONE ...
...WHO CAN STAND BESIDE HIS MAJESTY WITH PRIDE.
OTHERWISE...
...HOW COULD I SEE THE FUTURE HE SEES?
THAT WORLD IN WHICH NO ONE SUFFERS...

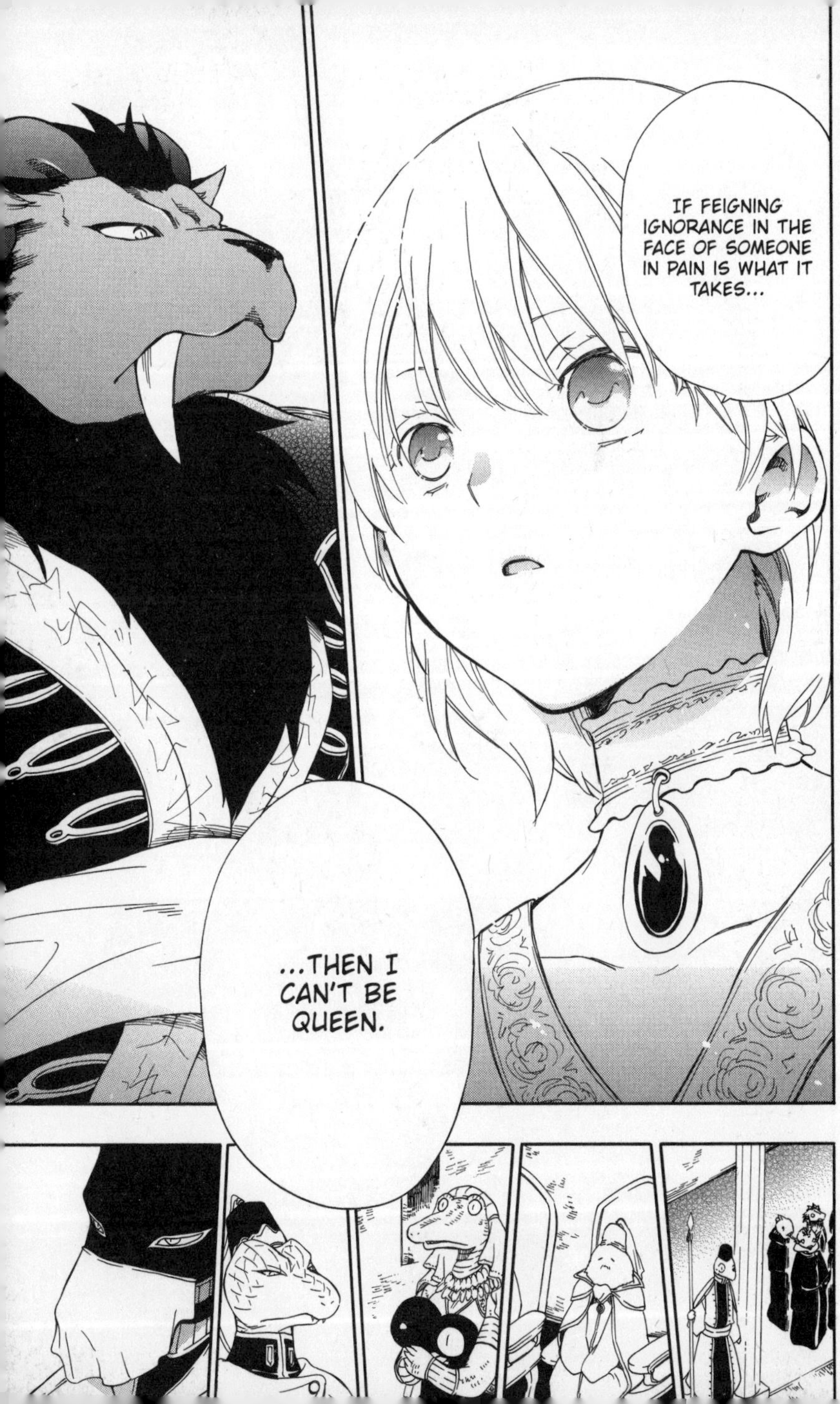
IF FEIGNING IGNORANCE IN THE FACE OF SOMEONE IN PAIN IS WHAT IT TAKES...
...THEN I CAN'T BE QUEEN.

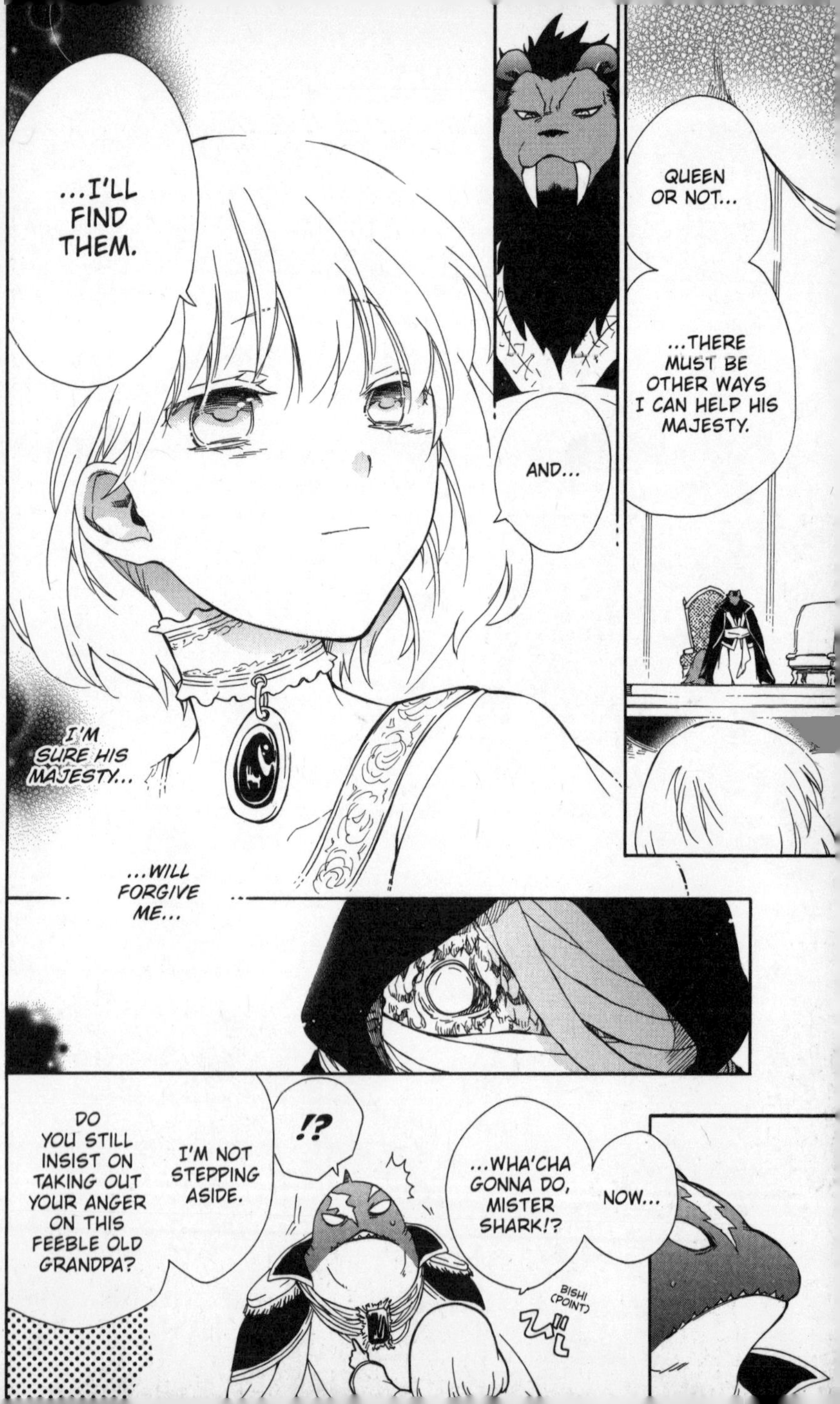
QUEEN OR NOT...
...THERE MUST BE OTHER WAYS I CAN HELP HIS MAJESTY.
AND...
...I'LL FIND THEM.
I'M SURE HIS MAJESTY...
...WILL FORGIVE ME...
NOW...
...WHA'CHA GONNA DO, MISTER SHARK!?
BISHI (POINT)
!?
I'M NOT STEPPING ASIDE.
DO YOU STILL INSIST ON TAKING OUT YOUR ANGER ON THIS FEEBLE OLD GRANDPA?

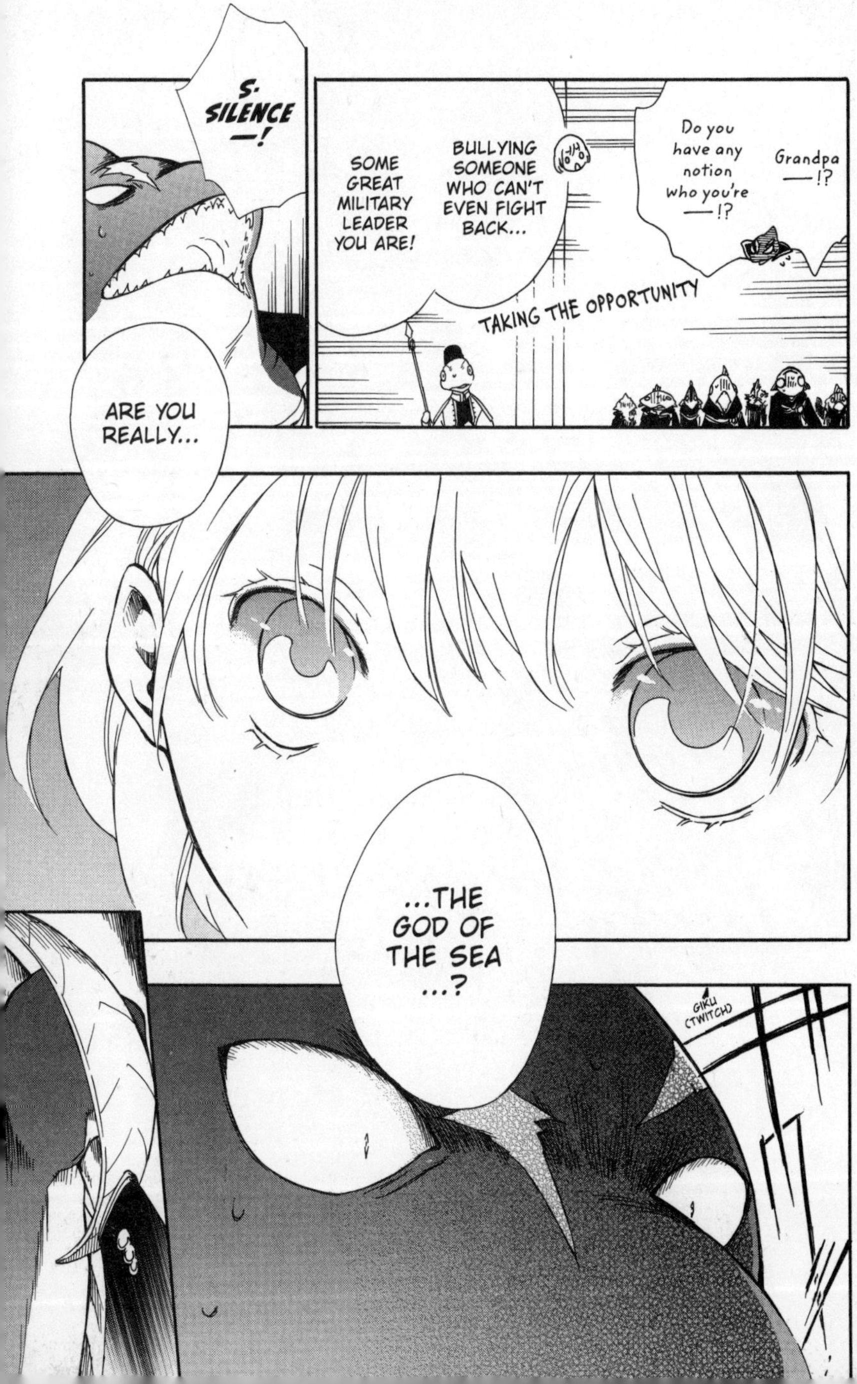
Grandpa —!?
Do you have any notion who you're —!?
BULLYING SOMEONE WHO CAN'T EVEN FIGHT BACK...
SOME GREAT MILITARY LEADER YOU ARE!
TAKING THE OPPORTUNITY
S-SILENCE —!
ARE YOU REALLY...
...THE GOD OF THE SEA ...?
GIKU (TWITCH)

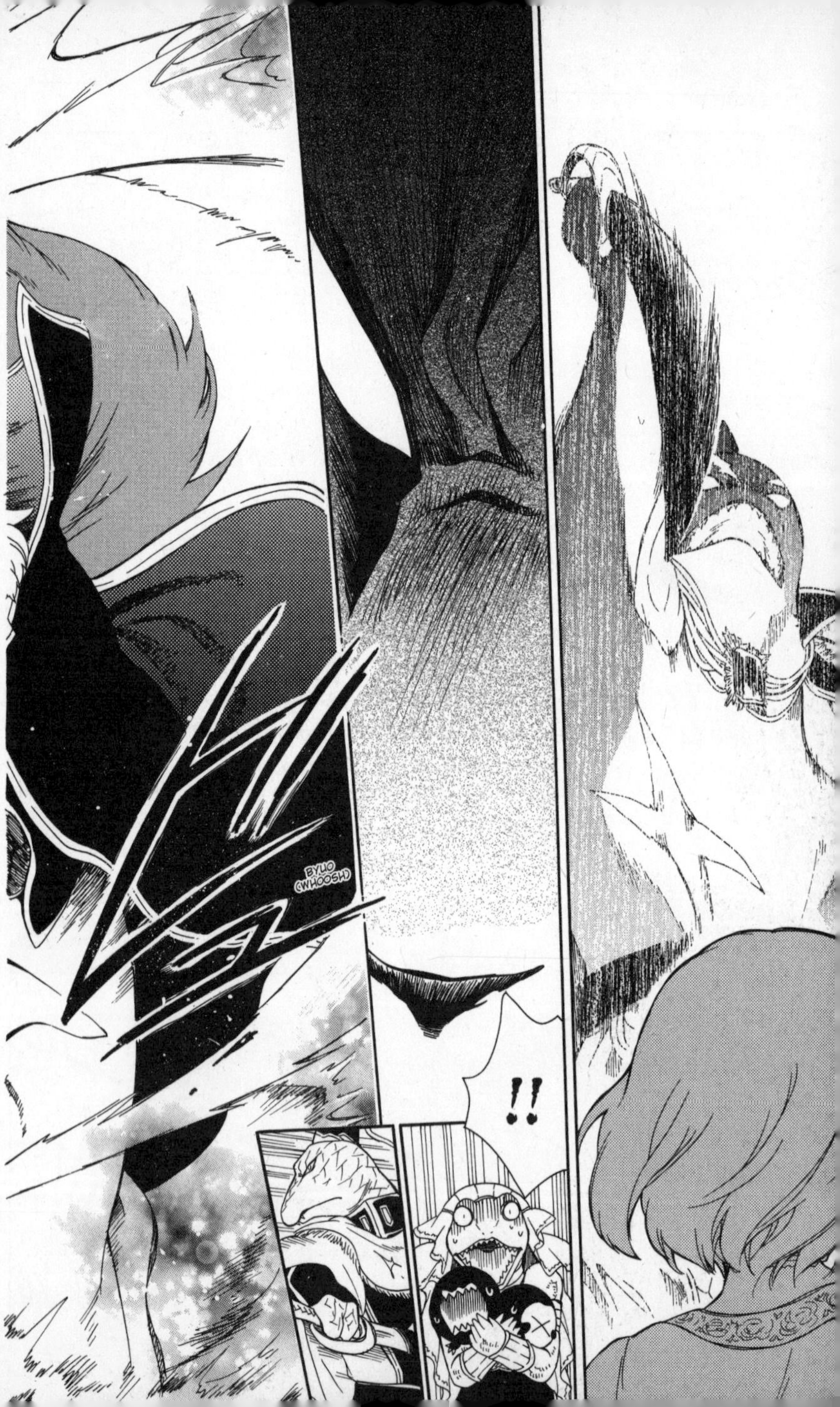
BYUO (WHOOSH)
!!

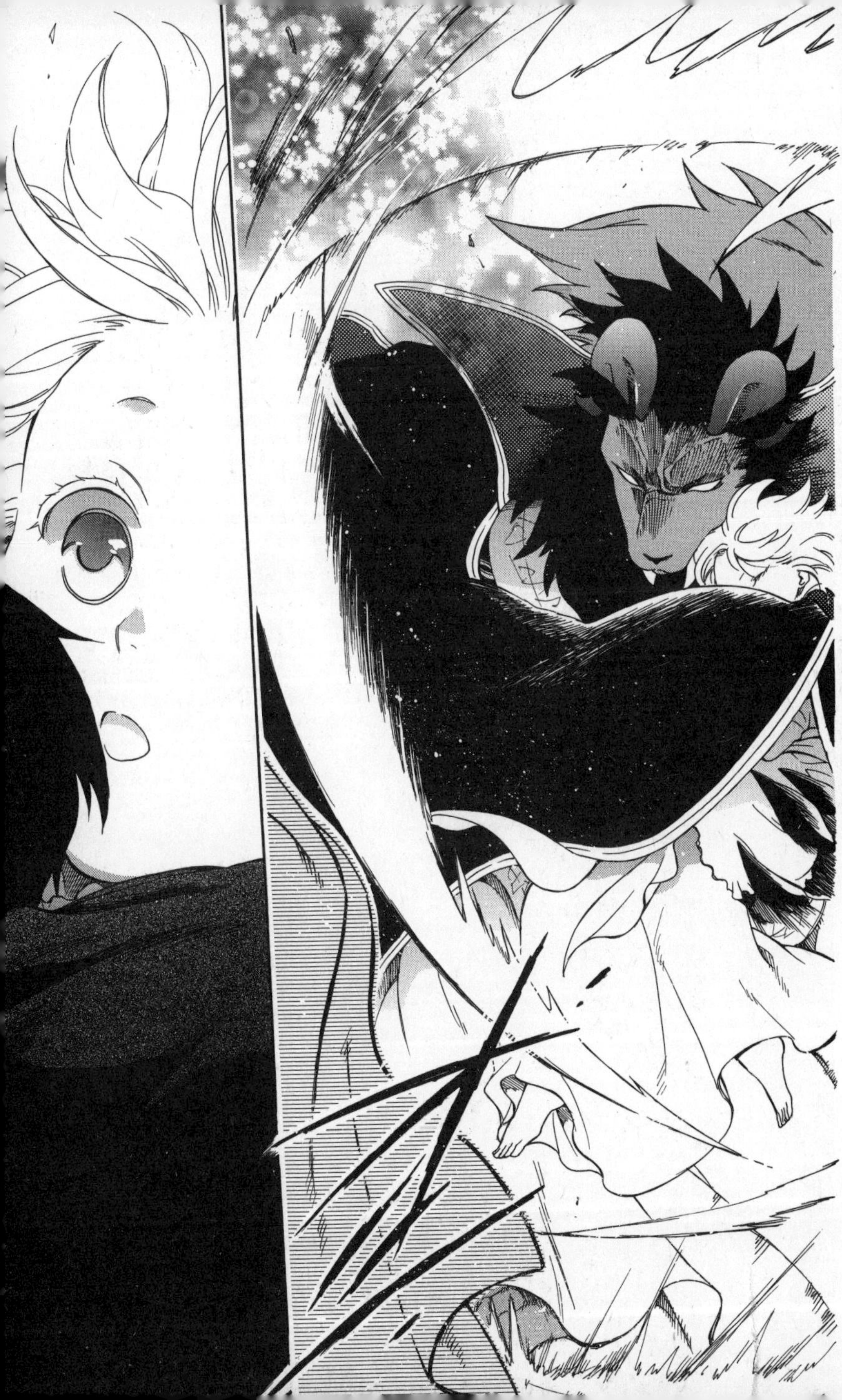

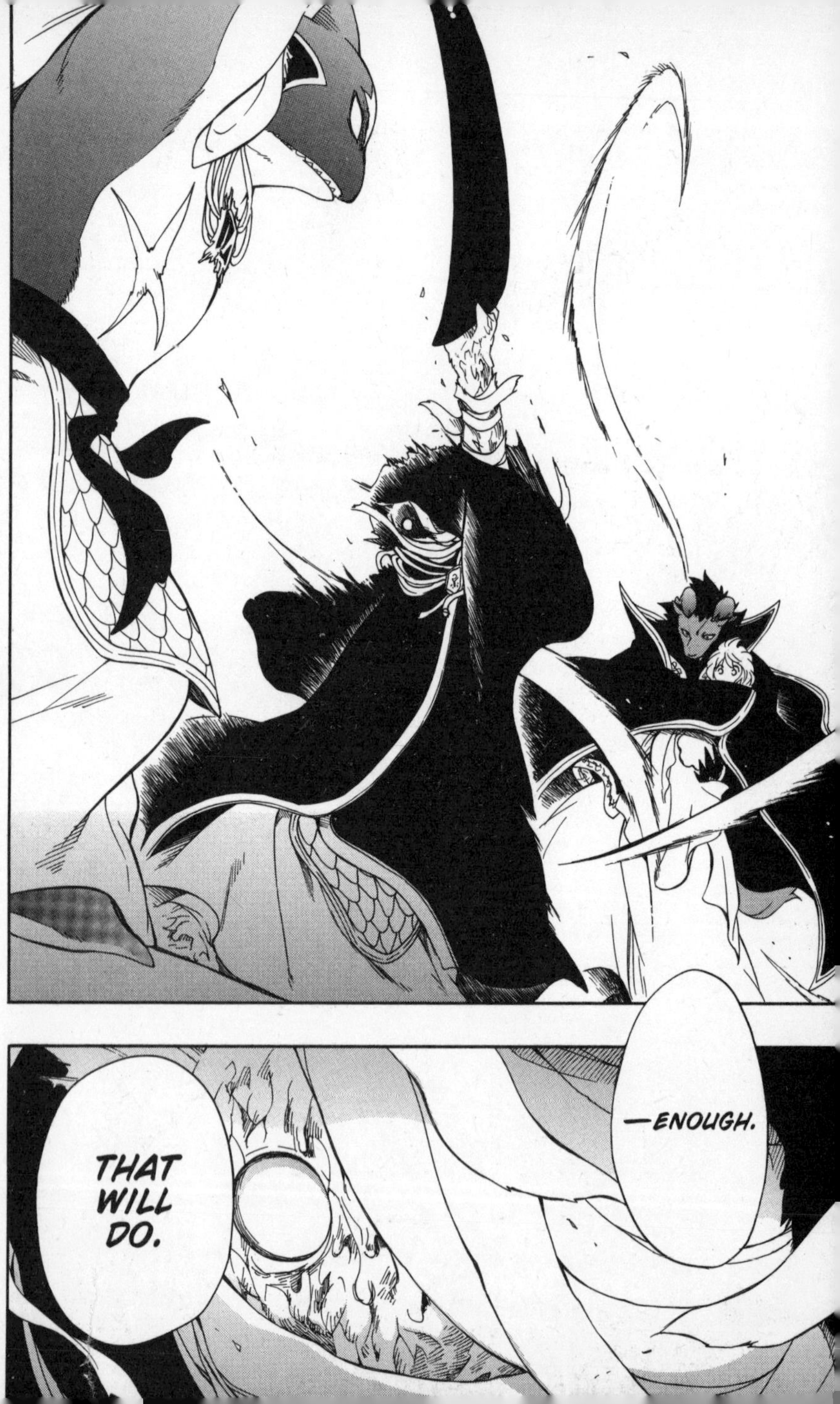
—ENOUGH.
THAT WILL DO.

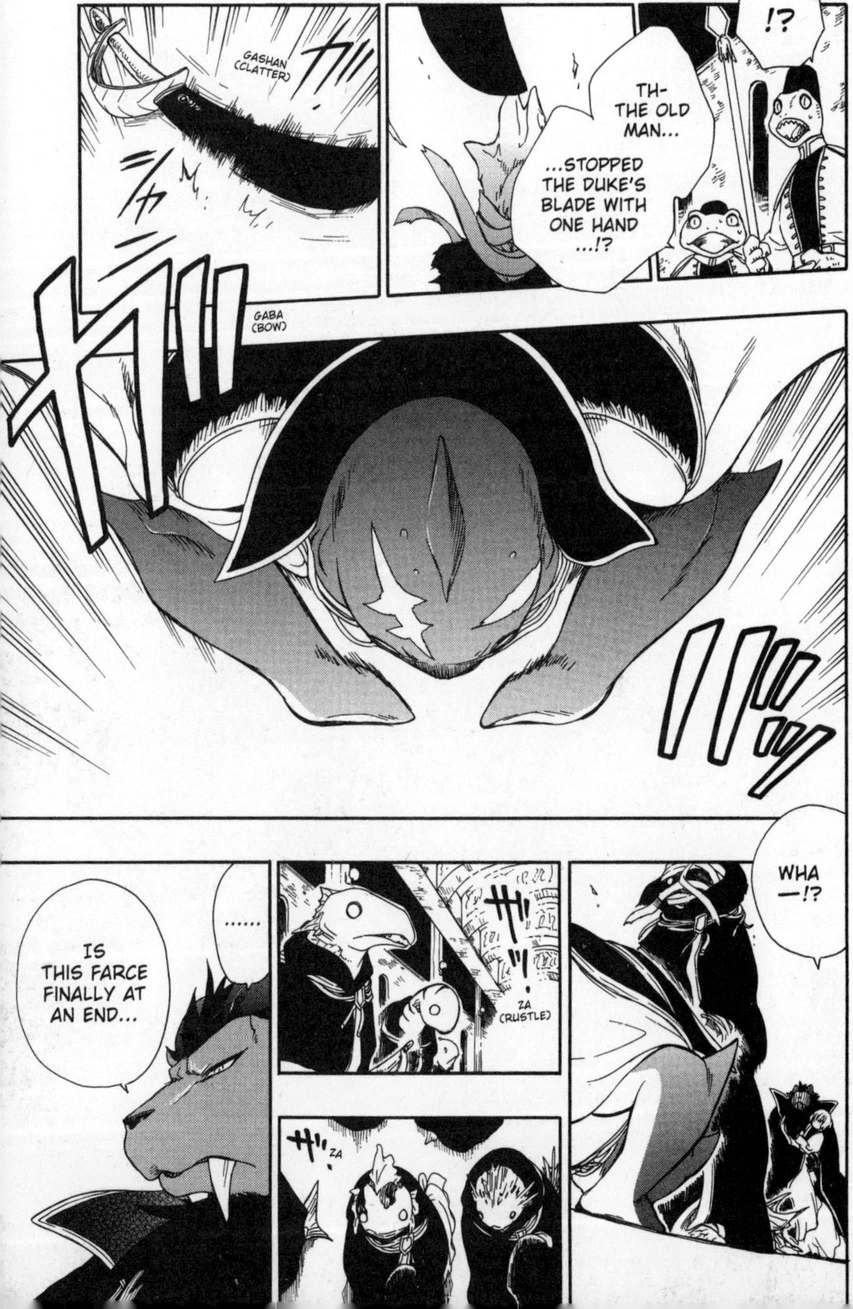
!?
TH- THE OLD MAN...
...STOPPED THE DUKE'S BLADE WITH ONE HAND ...!?
GASHAN (CLATTER)
GABA (BOW)
WHA—!?
ZA (RUSTLE)
ZA
......
IS THIS FARCE FINALLY AT AN END...

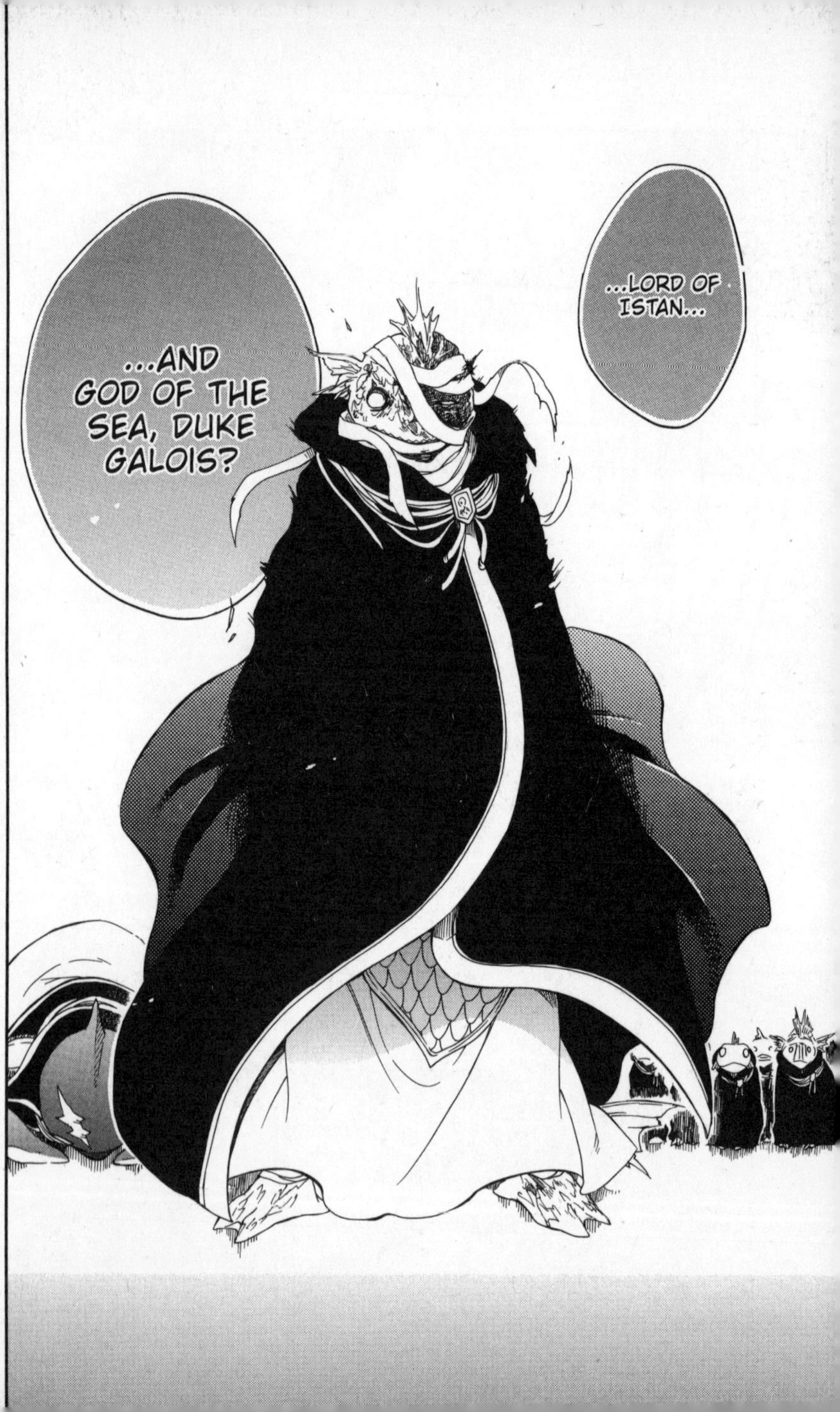
...LORD OF ISTAN...
...AND GOD OF THE SEA, DUKE GALOIS?

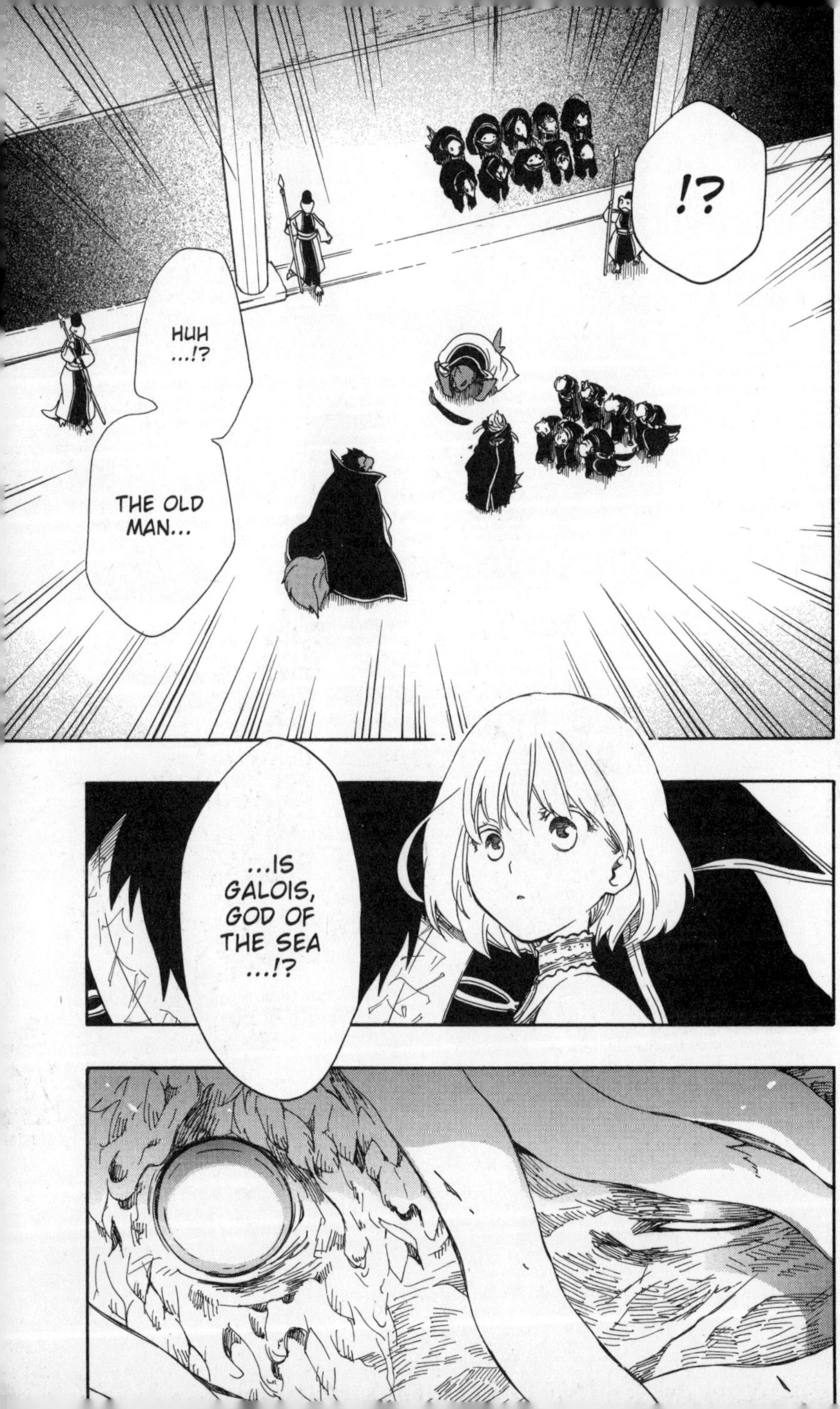
!?
HUH ...!?
THE OLD MAN...
...IS GALOIS, GOD OF THE SEA ...!?

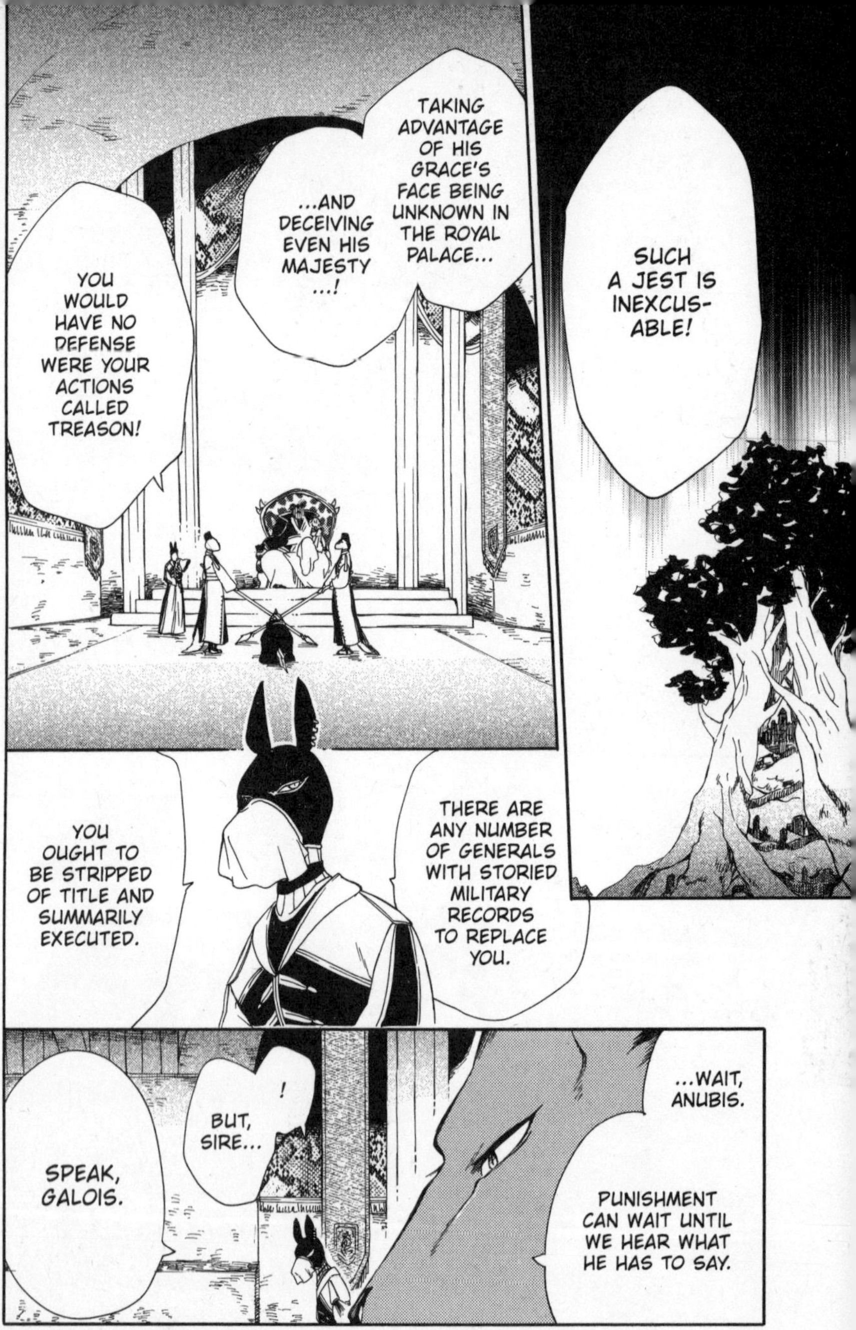
SUCH A JEST IS INEXCUS-ABLE!
TAKING ADVANTAGE OF HIS GRACE'S FACE BEING UNKNOWN IN THE ROYAL PALACE...
...AND DECEIVING EVEN HIS MAJESTY ...!
YOU WOULD HAVE NO DEFENSE WERE YOUR ACTIONS CALLED TREASON!
THERE ARE ANY NUMBER OF GENERALS WITH STORIED MILITARY RECORDS TO REPLACE YOU.
YOU OUGHT TO BE STRIPPED OF TITLE AND SUMMARILY EXECUTED.
...WAIT, ANUBIS.
PUNISHMENT CAN WAIT UNTIL WE HEAR WHAT HE HAS TO SAY.
!
BUT, SIRE...
SPEAK, GALOIS.

WHY WOULD YOU EMPLOY SUCH DECEPTION?

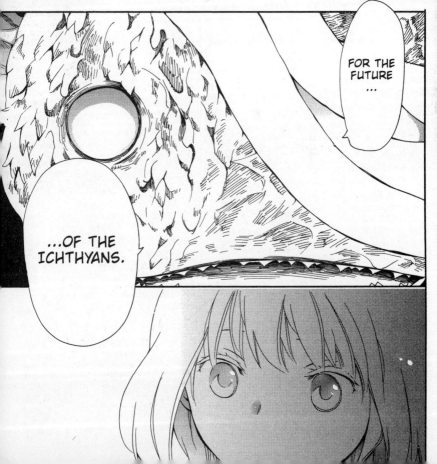

FOR THE FUTURE...

...OF THE ICHTHYANS.

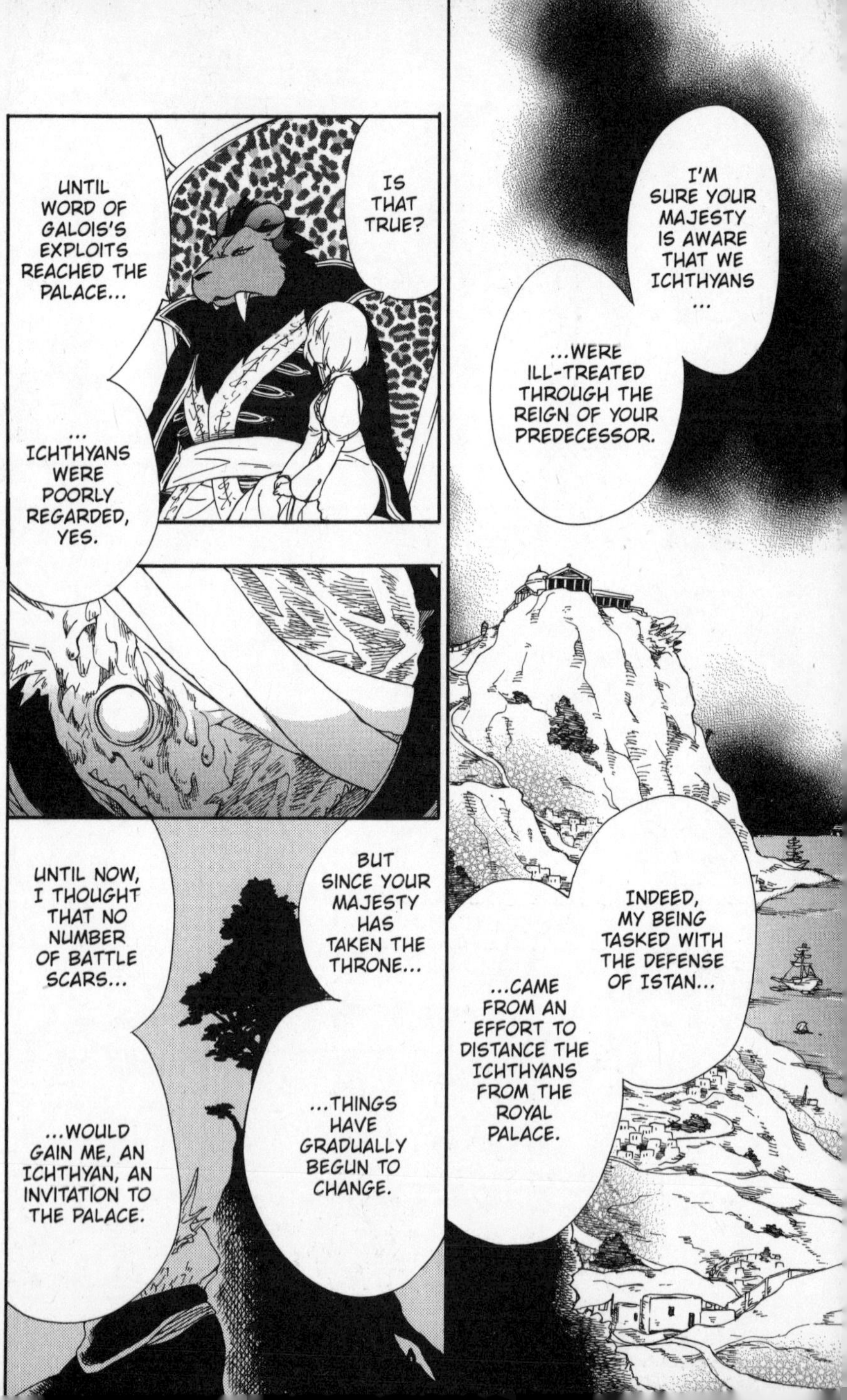
I'M SURE YOUR MAJESTY IS AWARE THAT WE ICHTHYANS ...
...WERE ILL-TREATED THROUGH THE REIGN OF YOUR PREDECESSOR.
INDEED, MY BEING TASKED WITH THE DEFENSE OF ISTAN...
...CAME FROM AN EFFORT TO DISTANCE THE ICHTHYANS FROM THE ROYAL PALACE.
IS THAT TRUE?
UNTIL WORD OF GALOIS'S EXPLOITS REACHED THE PALACE...
... ICHTHYANS WERE POORLY REGARDED, YES.
BUT SINCE YOUR MAJESTY HAS TAKEN THE THRONE...
...THINGS HAVE GRADUALLY BEGUN TO CHANGE.
UNTIL NOW, I THOUGHT THAT NO NUMBER OF BATTLE SCARS...
...WOULD GAIN ME, AN ICHTHYAN, AN INVITATION TO THE PALACE.

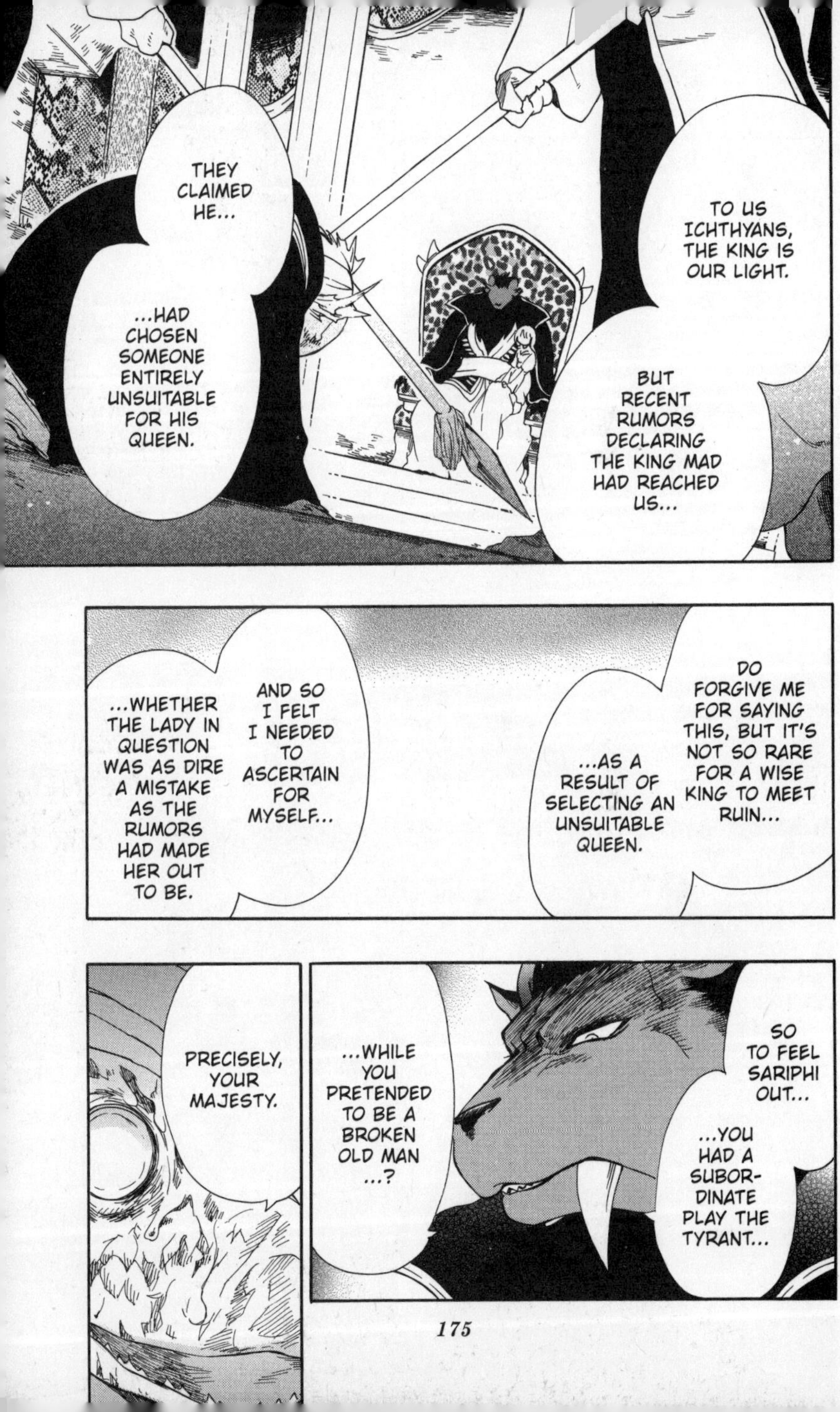
TO US ICHTHYANS, THE KING IS OUR LIGHT.
BUT RECENT RUMORS DECLARING THE KING MAD HAD REACHED US...
THEY CLAIMED HE...
...HAD CHOSEN SOMEONE ENTIRELY UNSUITABLE FOR HIS QUEEN.
DO FORGIVE ME FOR SAYING THIS, BUT IT'S NOT SO RARE FOR A WISE KING TO MEET RUIN...
...AS A RESULT OF SELECTING AN UNSUITABLE QUEEN.
AND SO I FELT I NEEDED TO ASCERTAIN FOR MYSELF...
...WHETHER THE LADY IN QUESTION WAS AS DIRE A MISTAKE AS THE RUMORS HAD MADE HER OUT TO BE.
SO TO FEEL SARIPHI OUT...
...YOU HAD A SUBOR-DINATE PLAY THE TYRANT...
...WHILE YOU PRETENDED TO BE A BROKEN OLD MAN ...?
PRECISELY, YOUR MAJESTY.

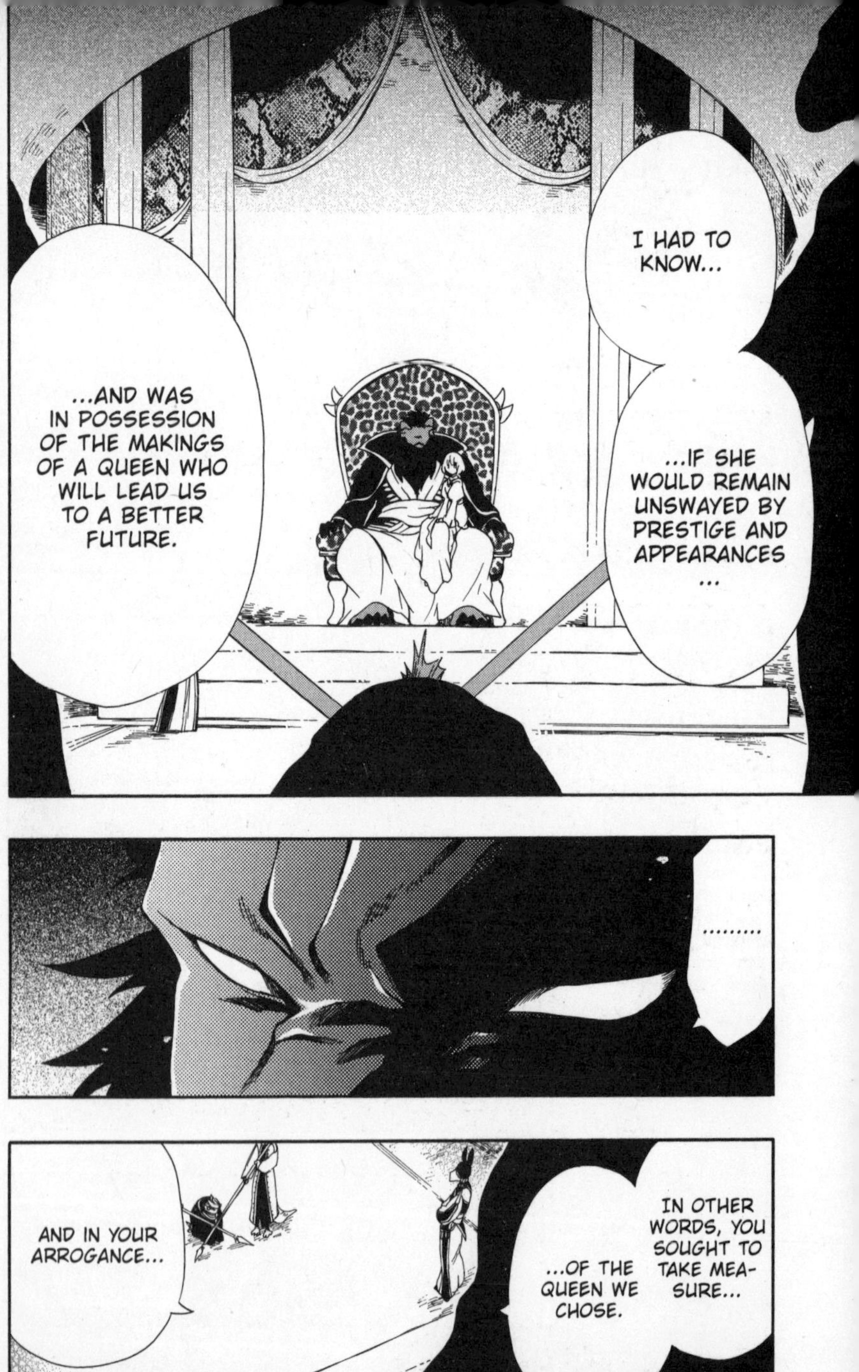
I HAD TO KNOW...
...IF SHE WOULD REMAIN UNSWAYED BY PRESTIGE AND APPEARANCES...
...AND WAS IN POSSESSION OF THE MAKINGS OF A QUEEN WHO WILL LEAD US TO A BETTER FUTURE.
....
IN OTHER WORDS, YOU SOUGHT TO TAKE MEA-SURE...
...OF THE QUEEN WE CHOSE.
AND IN YOUR ARROGANCE...

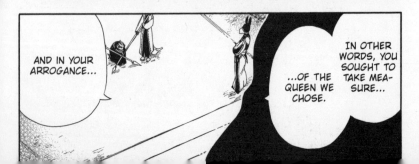

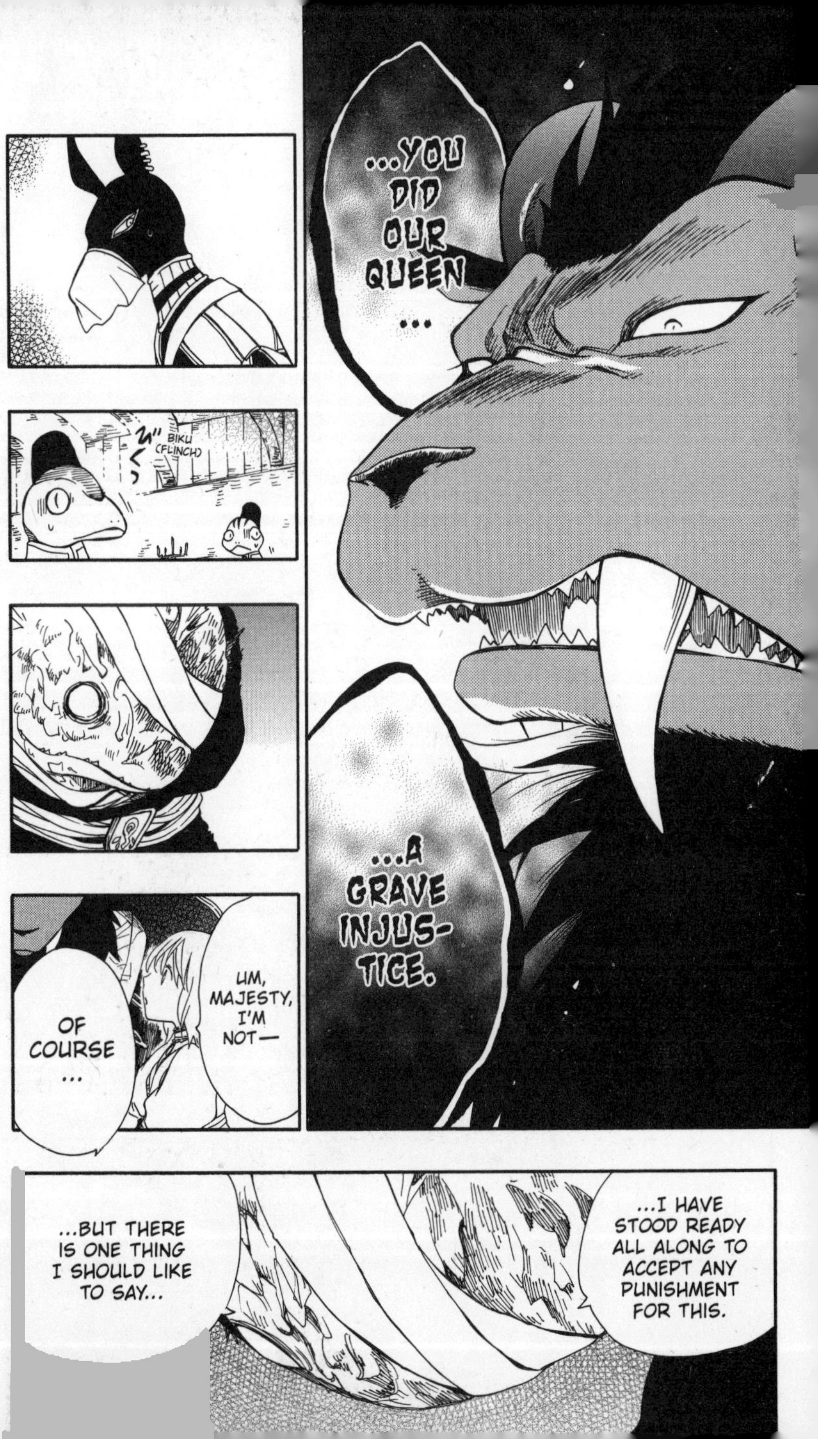
...YOU DID OUR QUEEN...
...A GRAVE INJUSTICE.
BIKU (FLINCH)
UM, MAJESTY, I'M NOT—
OF COURSE...
...I HAVE STOOD READY ALL ALONG TO ACCEPT ANY PUNISHMENT FOR THIS.
...BUT THERE IS ONE THING I SHOULD LIKE TO SAY...

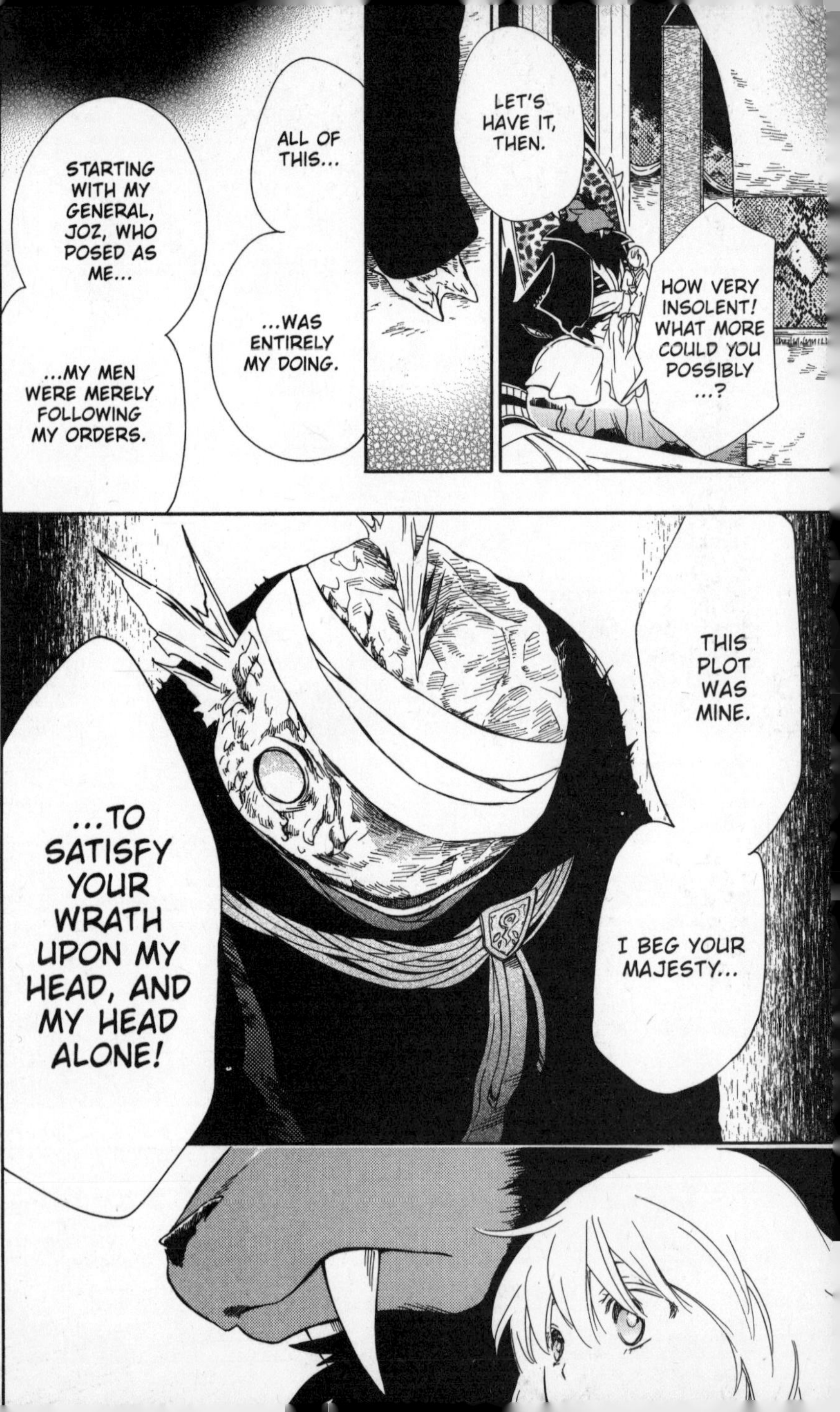
HOW VERY INSOLENT! WHAT MORE COULD YOU POSSIBLY ...?
LET'S HAVE IT, THEN.
ALL OF THIS...
...WAS ENTIRELY MY DOING.
STARTING WITH MY GENERAL, JOZ, WHO POSED AS ME...
...MY MEN WERE MERELY FOLLOWING MY ORDERS.
THIS PLOT WAS MINE.
I BEG YOUR MAJESTY...
...TO SATISFY YOUR WRATH UPON MY HEAD, AND MY HEAD ALONE!

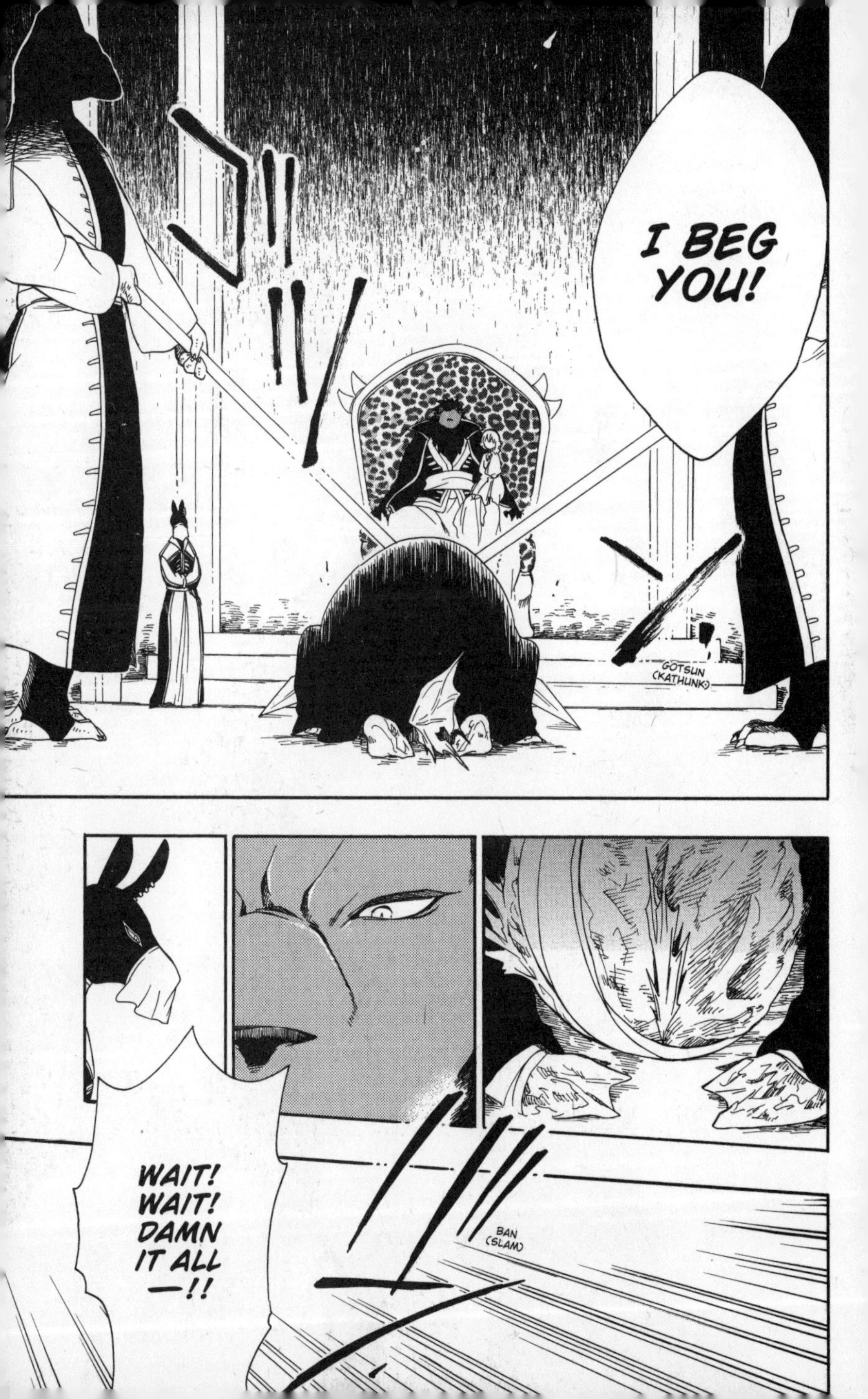
I BEG YOU!
GOTSUN (KATHUNK)
BAN (SLAM)
WAIT! WAIT! DAMN IT ALL —!!

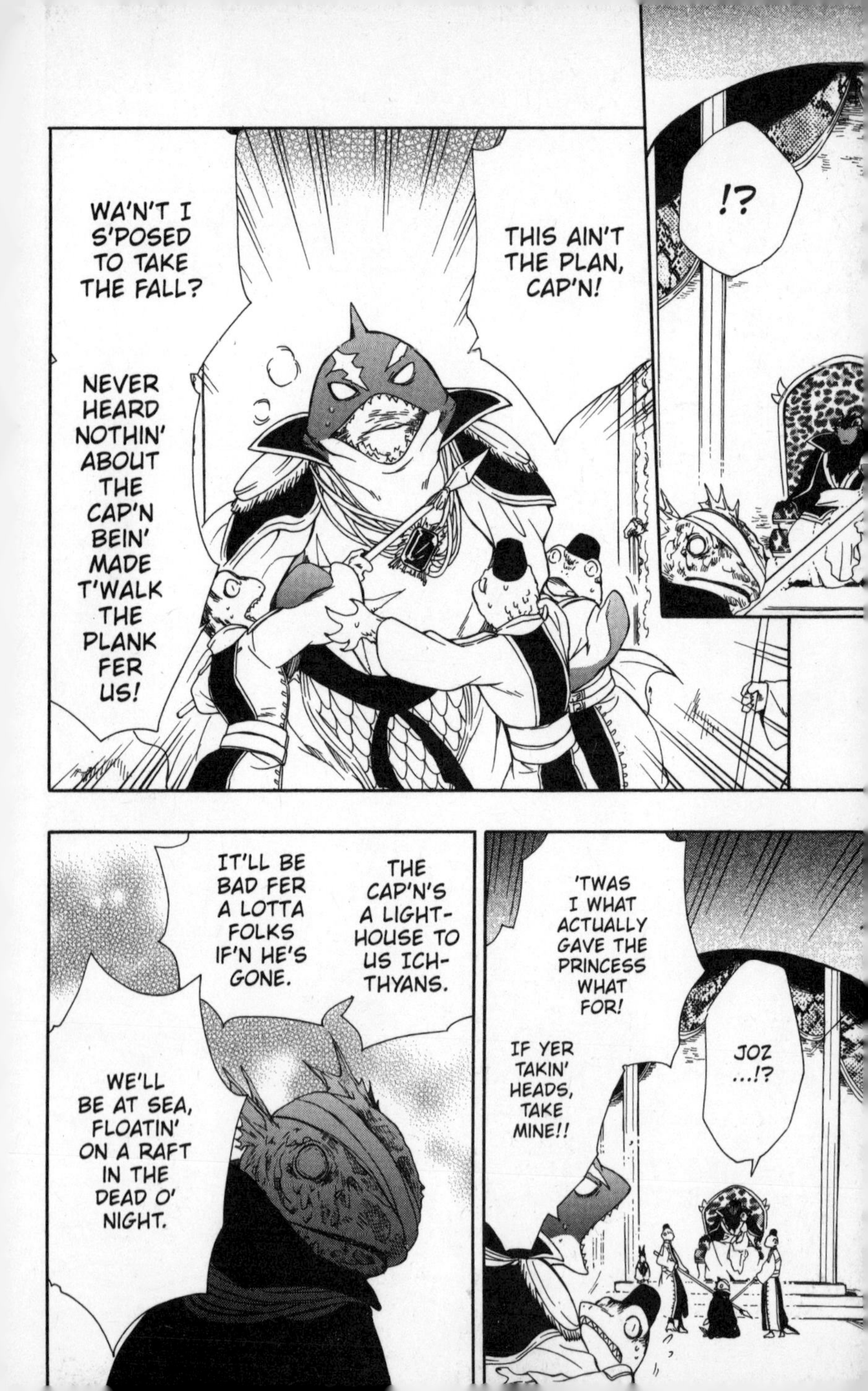
!?
THIS AIN'T THE PLAN, CAP'N!
WA'N'T I S'POSED TO TAKE THE FALL?
NEVER HEARD NOTHIN' ABOUT THE CAP'N BEIN' MADE T'WALK THE PLANK FER US!
'TWAS I WHAT ACTUALLY GAVE THE PRINCESS WHAT FOR!
IF YER TAKIN' HEADS, TAKE MINE!!
JOZ ...!?
THE CAP'N'S A LIGHT-HOUSE TO US ICH-THYANS.
IT'LL BE BAD FER A LOTTA FOLKS IF'N HE'S GONE.
WE'LL BE AT SEA, FLOATIN' ON A RAFT IN THE DEAD O' NIGHT.

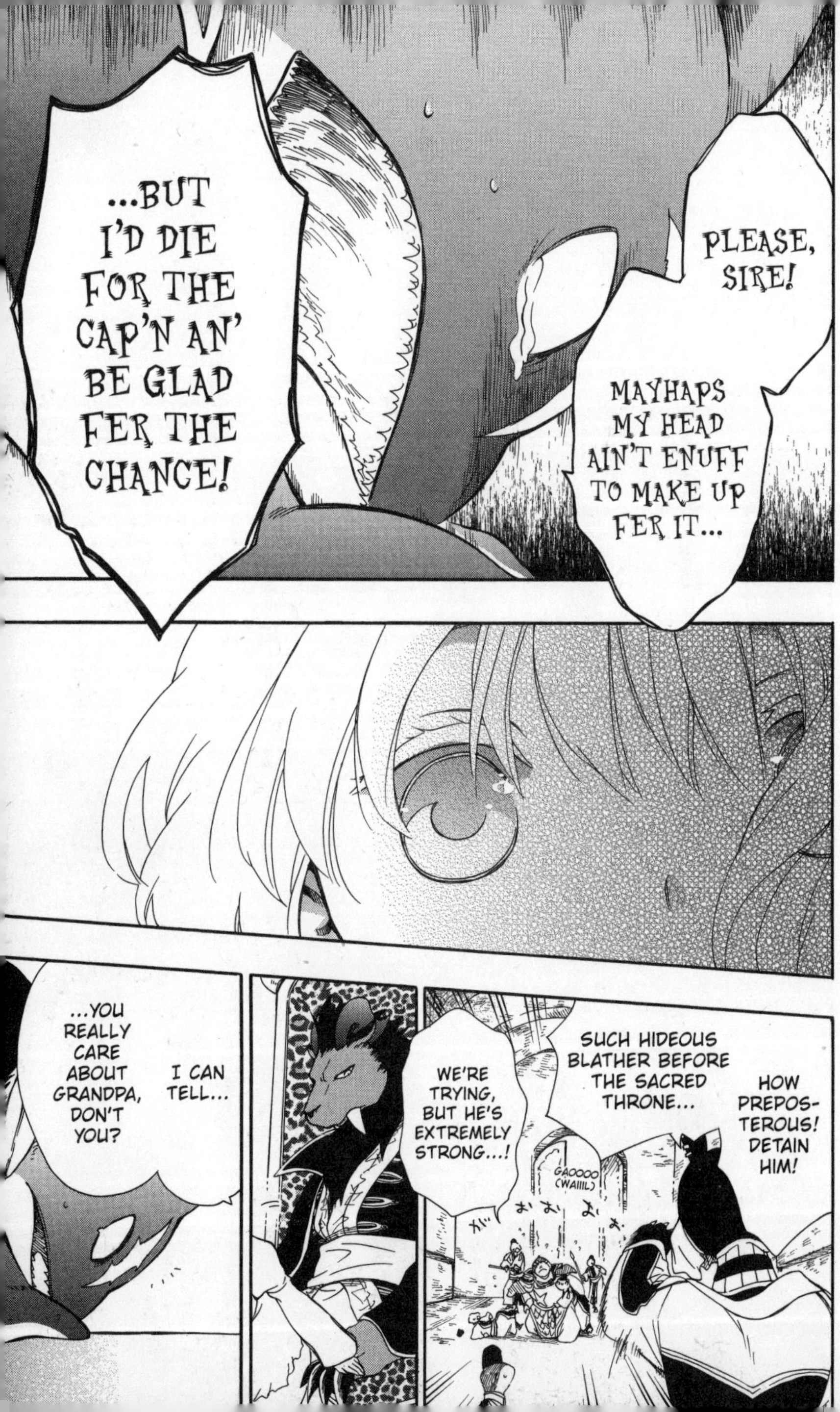
PLEASE, SIRE!
MAYHAPS MY HEAD AIN'T ENUFF TO MAKE UP FER IT...
...BUT I'D DIE FOR THE CAP'N AN' BE GLAD FER THE CHANCE!
SUCH HIDEOUS BLATHER BEFORE THE SACRED THRONE...
HOW PREPOSTEROUS! DETAIN HIM!
GAOOOO (WAIIIL)
WE'RE TRYING, BUT HE'S EXTREMELY STRONG...!
I CAN TELL...
...YOU REALLY CARE ABOUT GRANDPA, DON'T YOU?

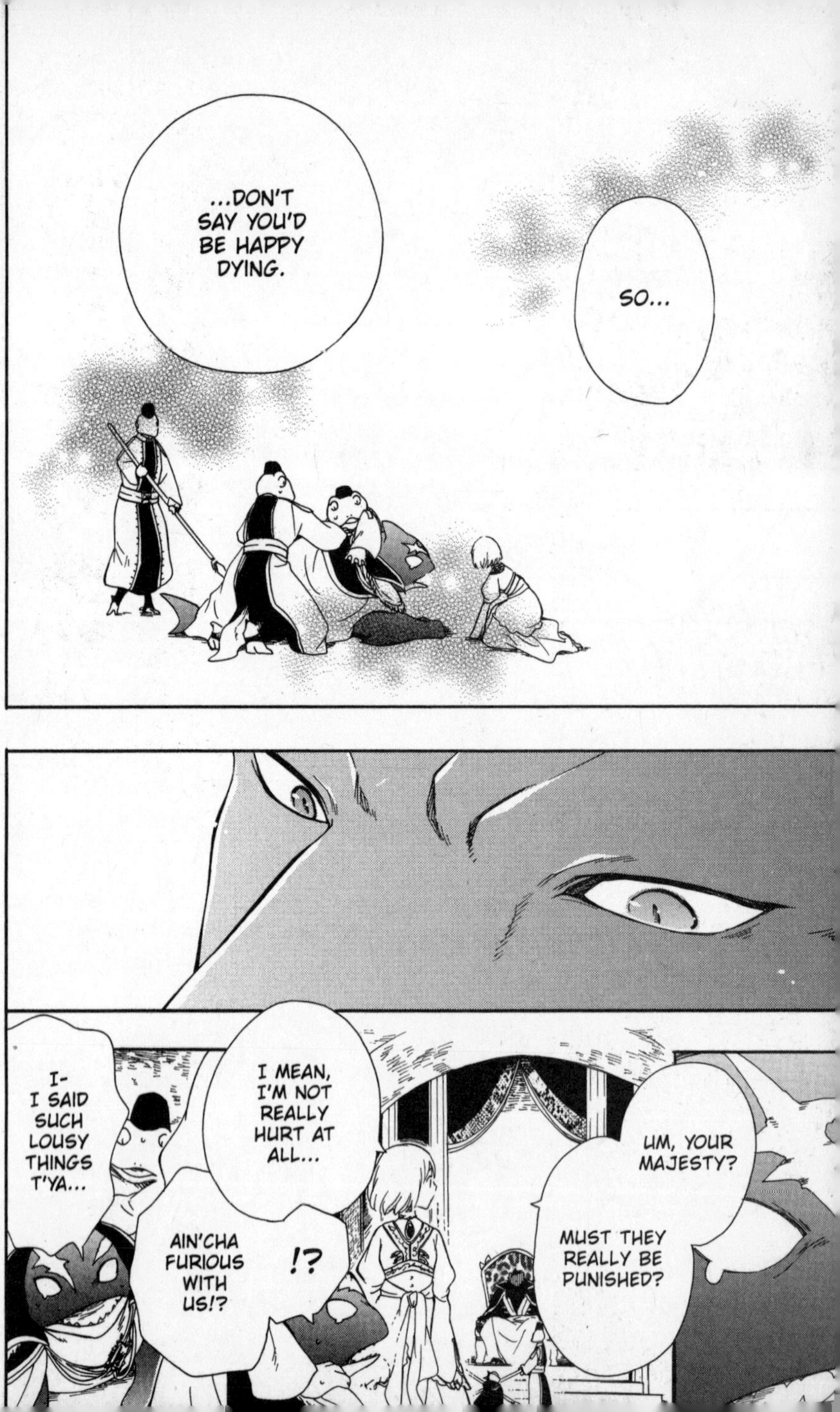
SO...
...DON'T SAY YOU'D BE HAPPY DYING.
UM, YOUR MAJESTY?
MUST THEY REALLY BE PUNISHED?
I MEAN, I'M NOT REALLY HURT AT ALL...
!?
I- I SAID SUCH LOUSY THINGS T'YA...
AIN'CHA FURIOUS WITH US!?

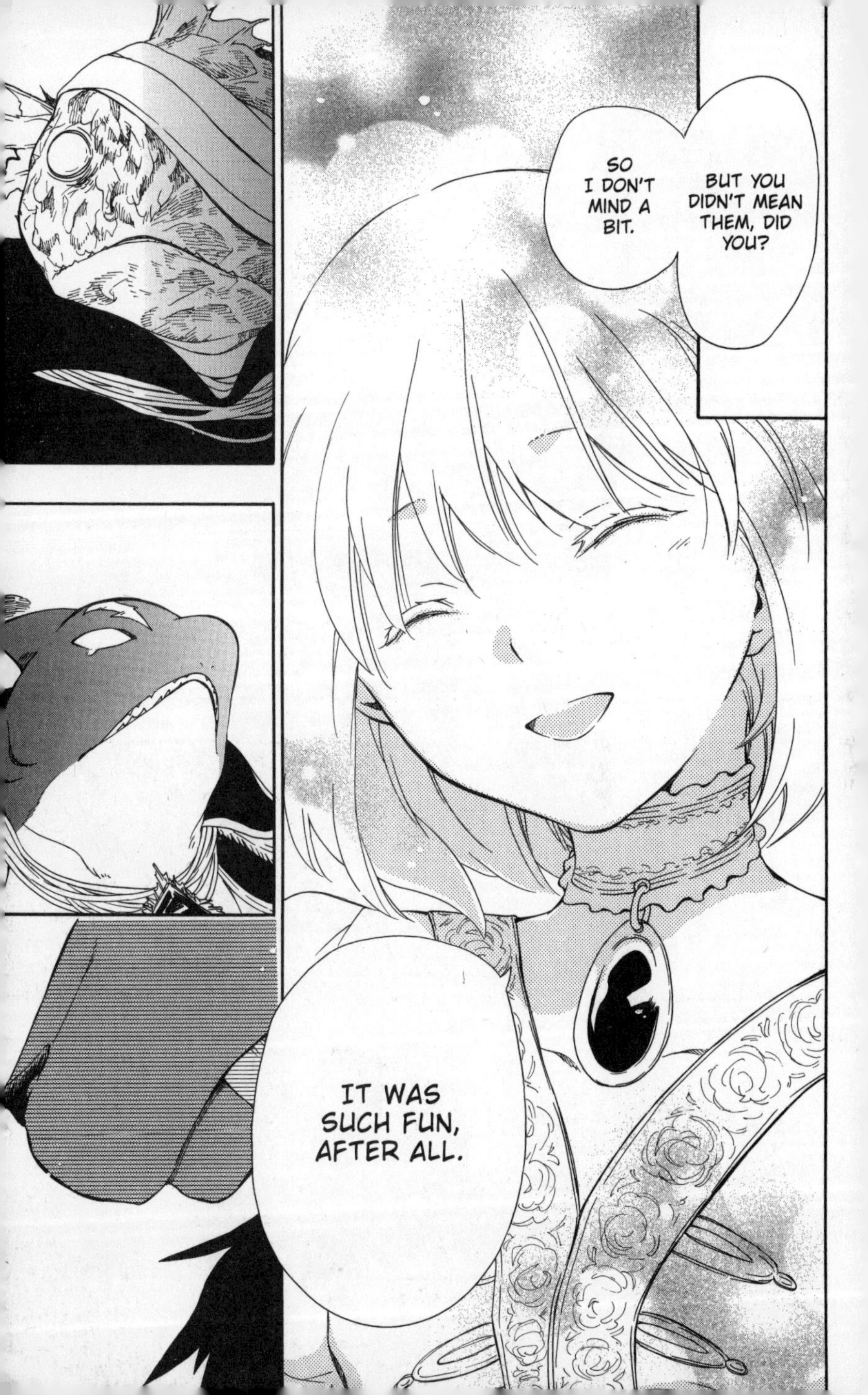
BUT YOU DIDN'T MEAN THEM, DID YOU?
SO I DON'T MIND A BIT.
IT WAS SUCH FUN, AFTER ALL.

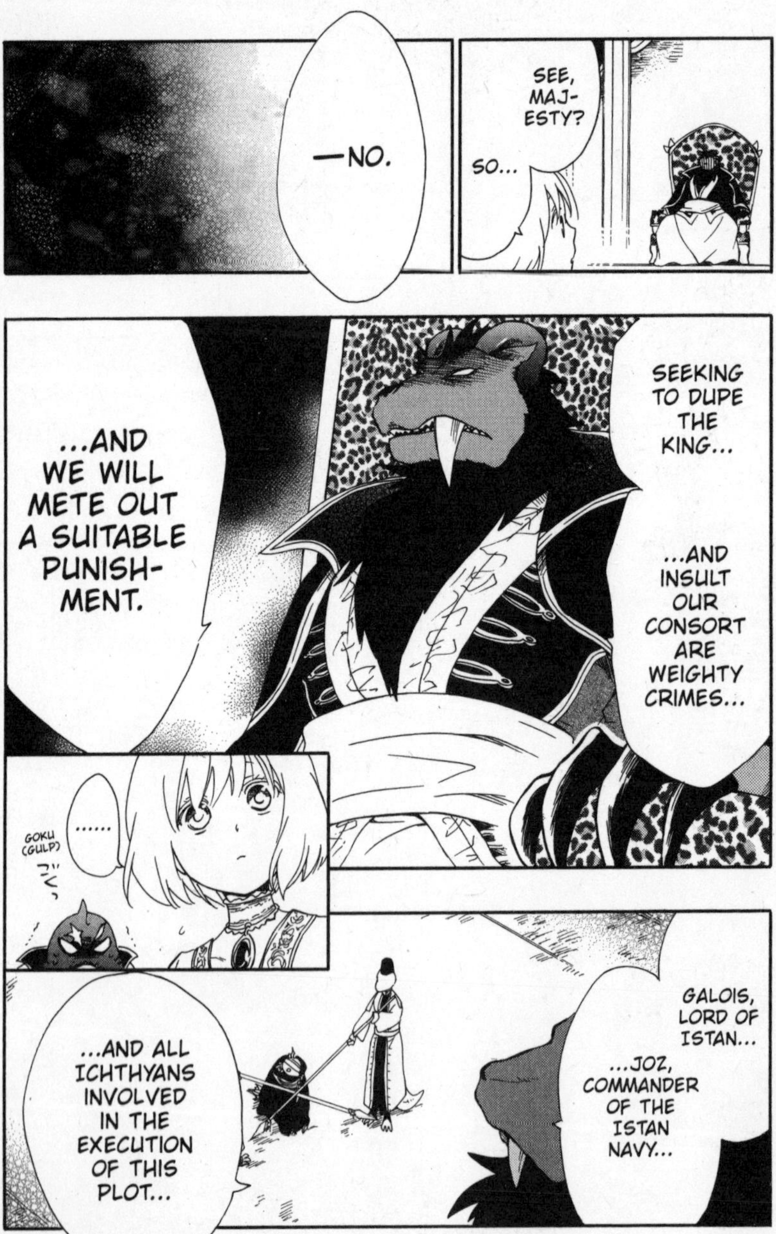
SEE, MAJ-ESTY?
SO...
—NO.
SEEKING TO DUPE THE KING...
...AND INSULT OUR CONSORT ARE WEIGHTY CRIMES...
...AND WE WILL METE OUT A SUITABLE PUNISH-MENT.
......
GOKU (GULP)
GALOIS, LORD OF ISTAN...
...JOZ, COMMANDER OF THE ISTAN NAVY...
...AND ALL ICHTHYANS INVOLVED IN THE EXECUTION OF THIS PLOT...

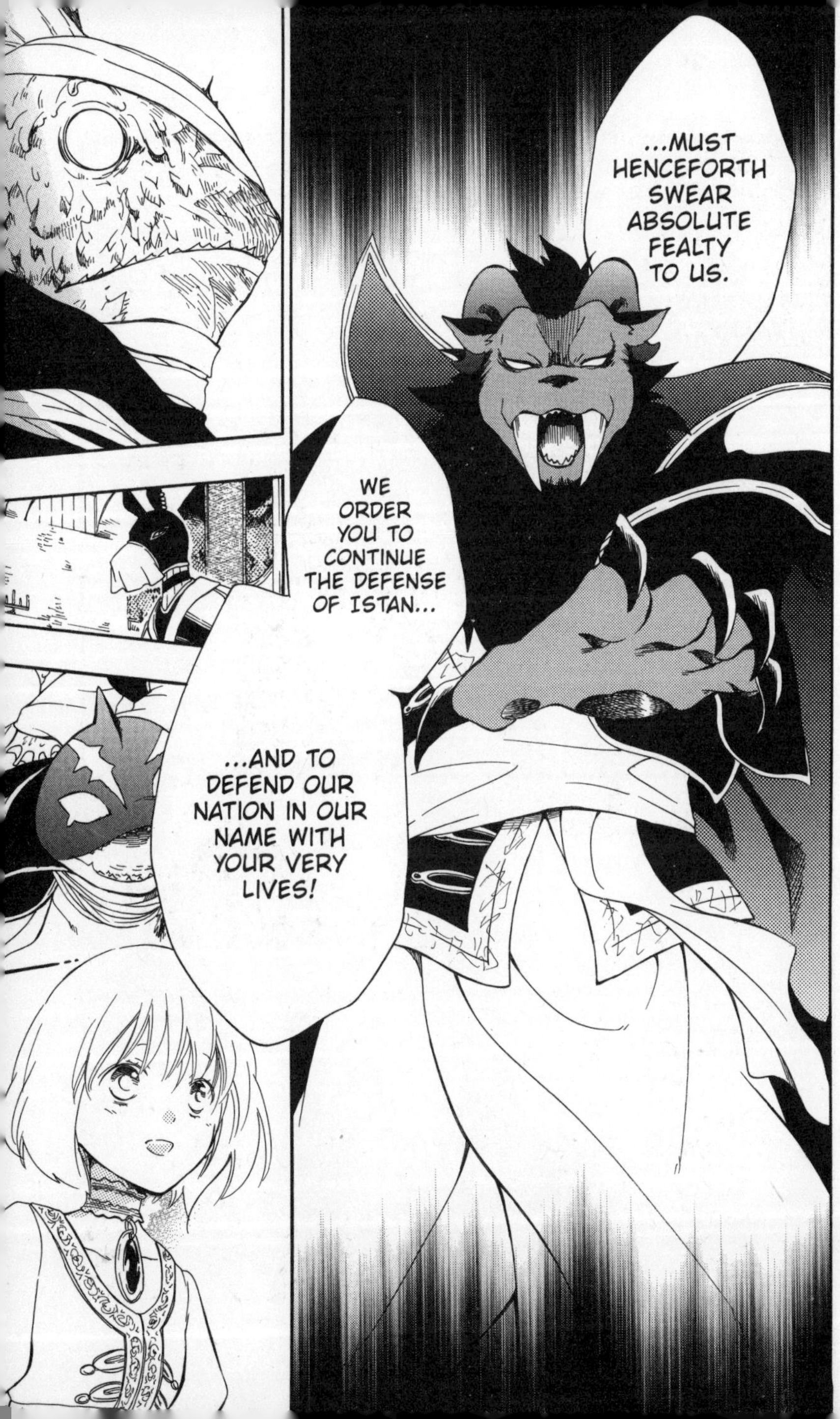
...MUST HENCEFORTH SWEAR ABSOLUTE FEALTY TO US.
WE ORDER YOU TO CONTINUE THE DEFENSE OF ISTAN...
...AND TO DEFEND OUR NATION IN OUR NAME WITH YOUR VERY LIVES!

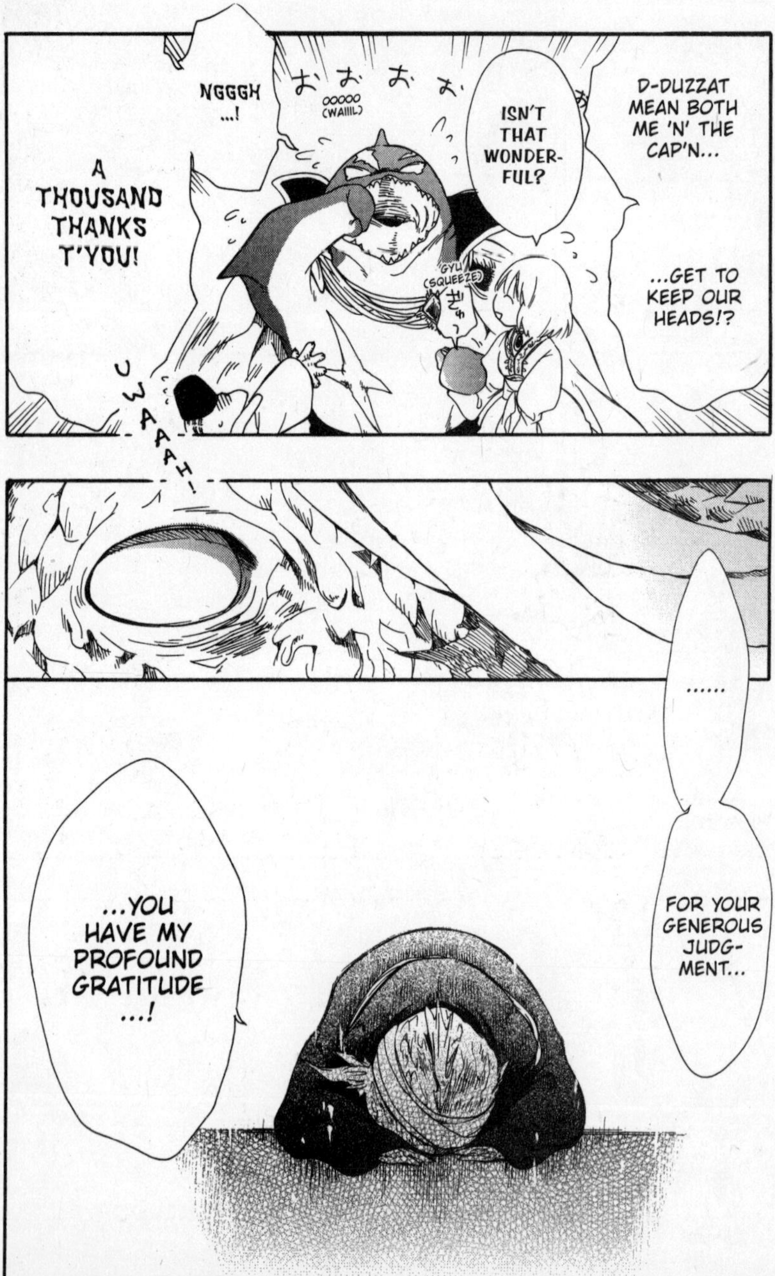
D-DUZZAT MEAN BOTH ME 'N' THE CAP'N...
...GET TO KEEP OUR HEADS!?
ISN'T THAT WONDERFUL?
GYU (SQUEEZE)
ぎゅ
おおおおあ
OOOOO (WAIIIL)
NGGGH ...!
A THOUSAND THANKS T'YOU!
UWAAAAH!
......
FOR YOUR GENEROUS JUDGMENT...
...YOU HAVE MY PROFOUND GRATITUDE ...!

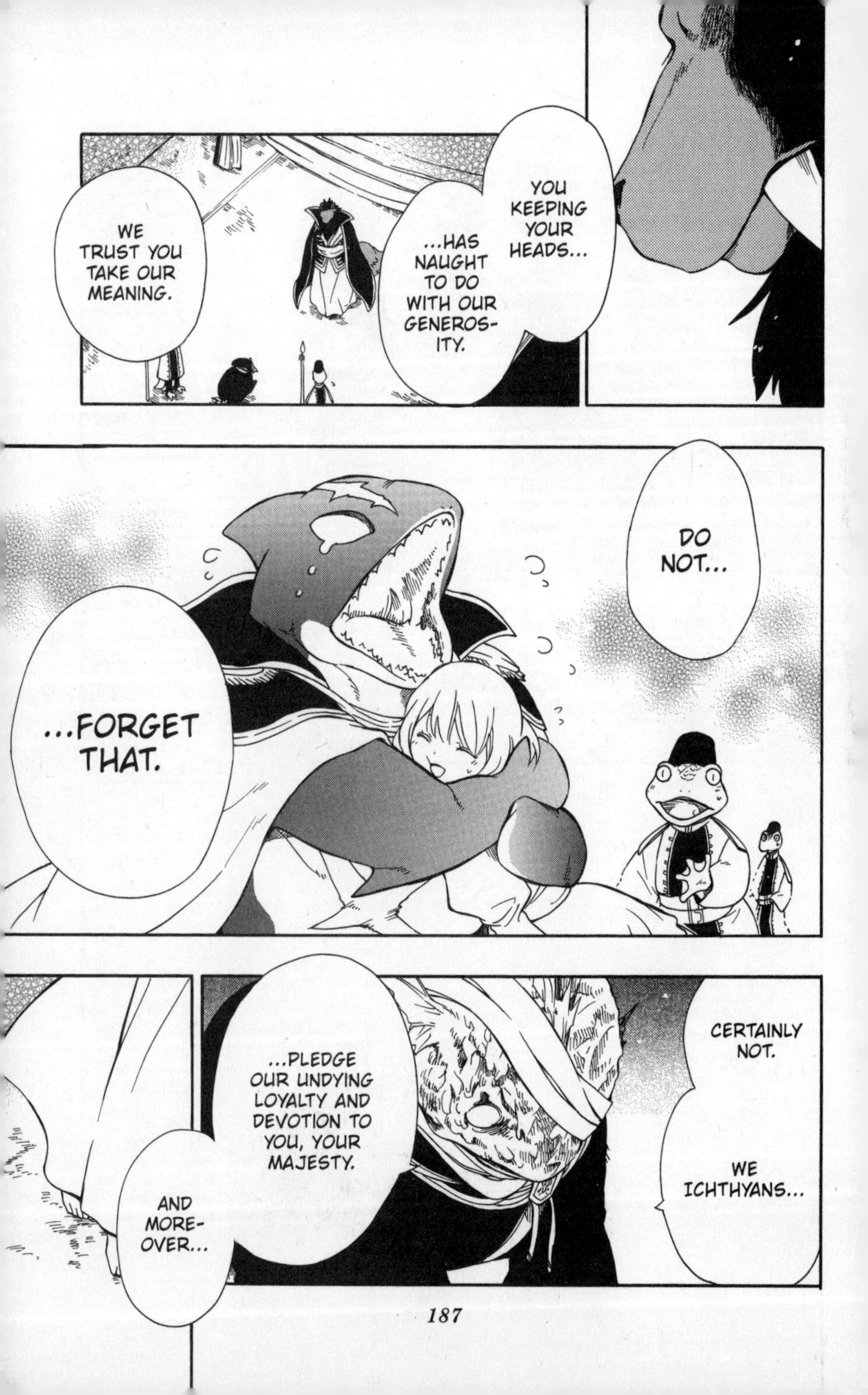
YOU KEEPING YOUR HEADS...
...HAS NAUGHT TO DO WITH OUR GENEROS-ITY.
WE TRUST YOU TAKE OUR MEANING.
DO NOT...
...FORGET THAT.
CERTAINLY NOT.
WE ICHTHYANS...
...PLEDGE OUR UNDYING LOYALTY AND DEVOTION TO YOU, YOUR MAJESTY.
AND MORE-OVER...

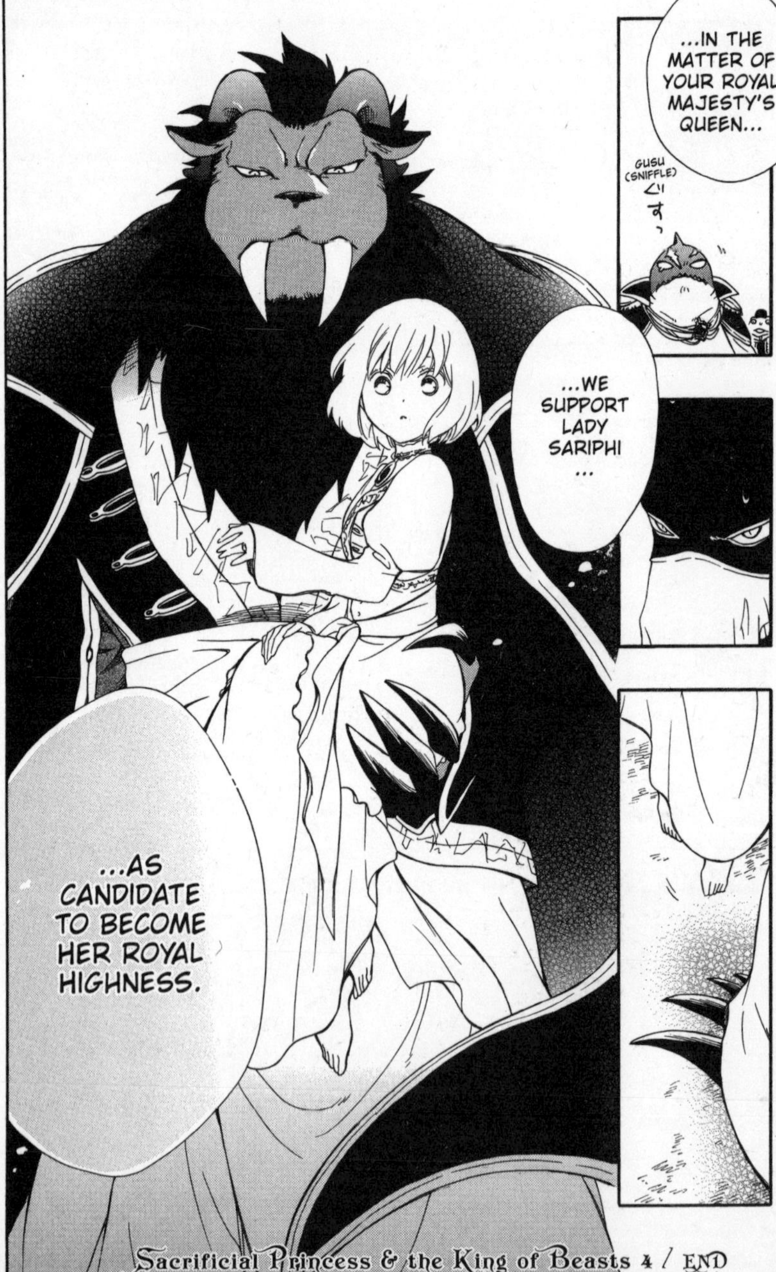
...IN THE MATTER OF YOUR ROYAL MAJESTY'S QUEEN...
GUSU (SNIFFLE)
ぐすっ
...WE SUPPORT LADY SARIPHI ...
...AS CANDIDATE TO BECOME HER ROYAL HIGHNESS.
Sacrificial Princess & the King of Beasts 4 / END

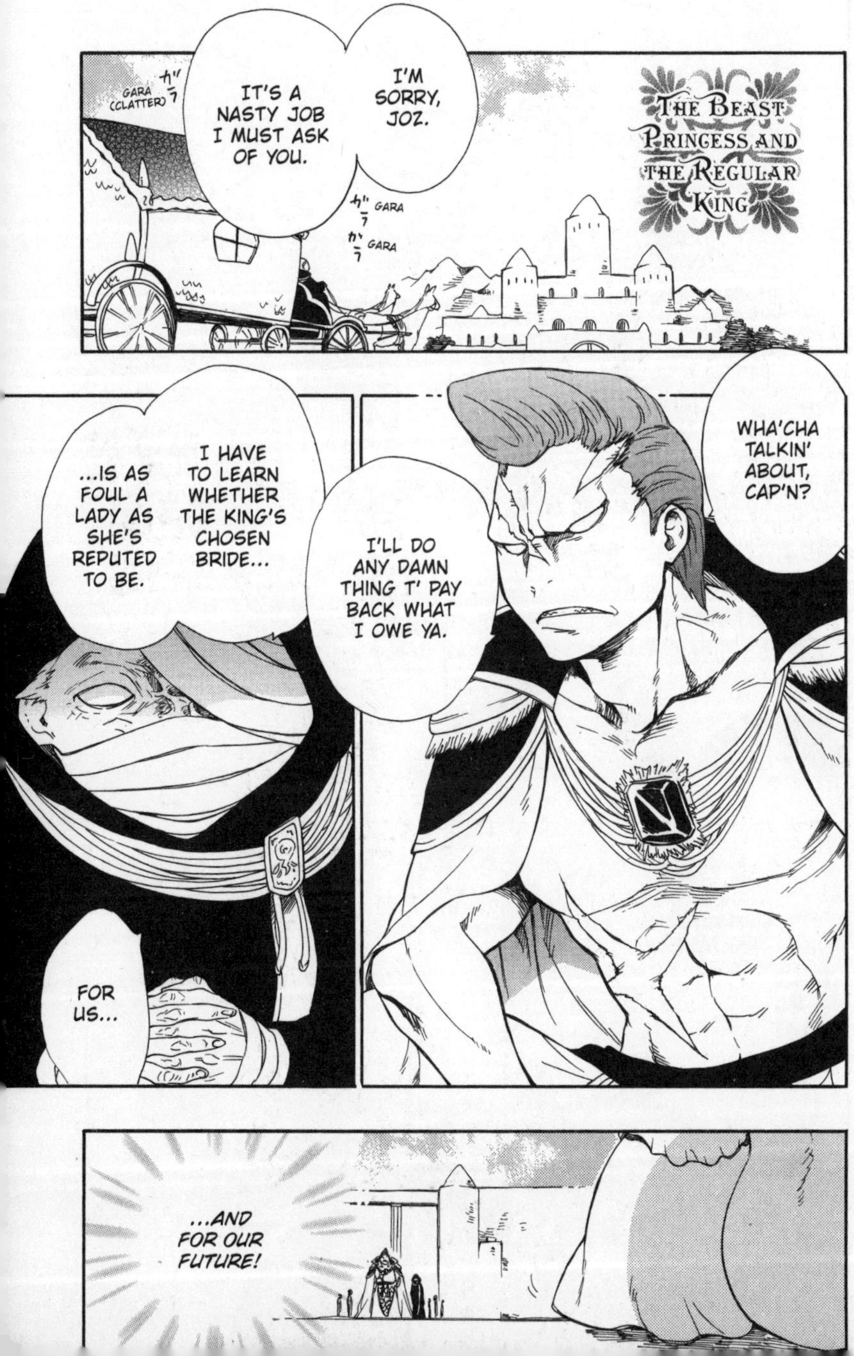
THE BEAST PRINCESS AND THE REGULAR KING
I'M SORRY, JOZ.
IT'S A NASTY JOB I MUST ASK OF YOU.
GARA
GARA
GARA (CLATTER)
WHA'CHA TALKIN' ABOUT, CAP'N?
I'LL DO ANY DAMN THING T' PAY BACK WHAT I OWE YA.
I HAVE TO LEARN WHETHER THE KING'S CHOSEN BRIDE...
...IS AS FOUL A LADY AS SHE'S REPUTED TO BE.
FOR US...
...AND FOR OUR FUTURE!

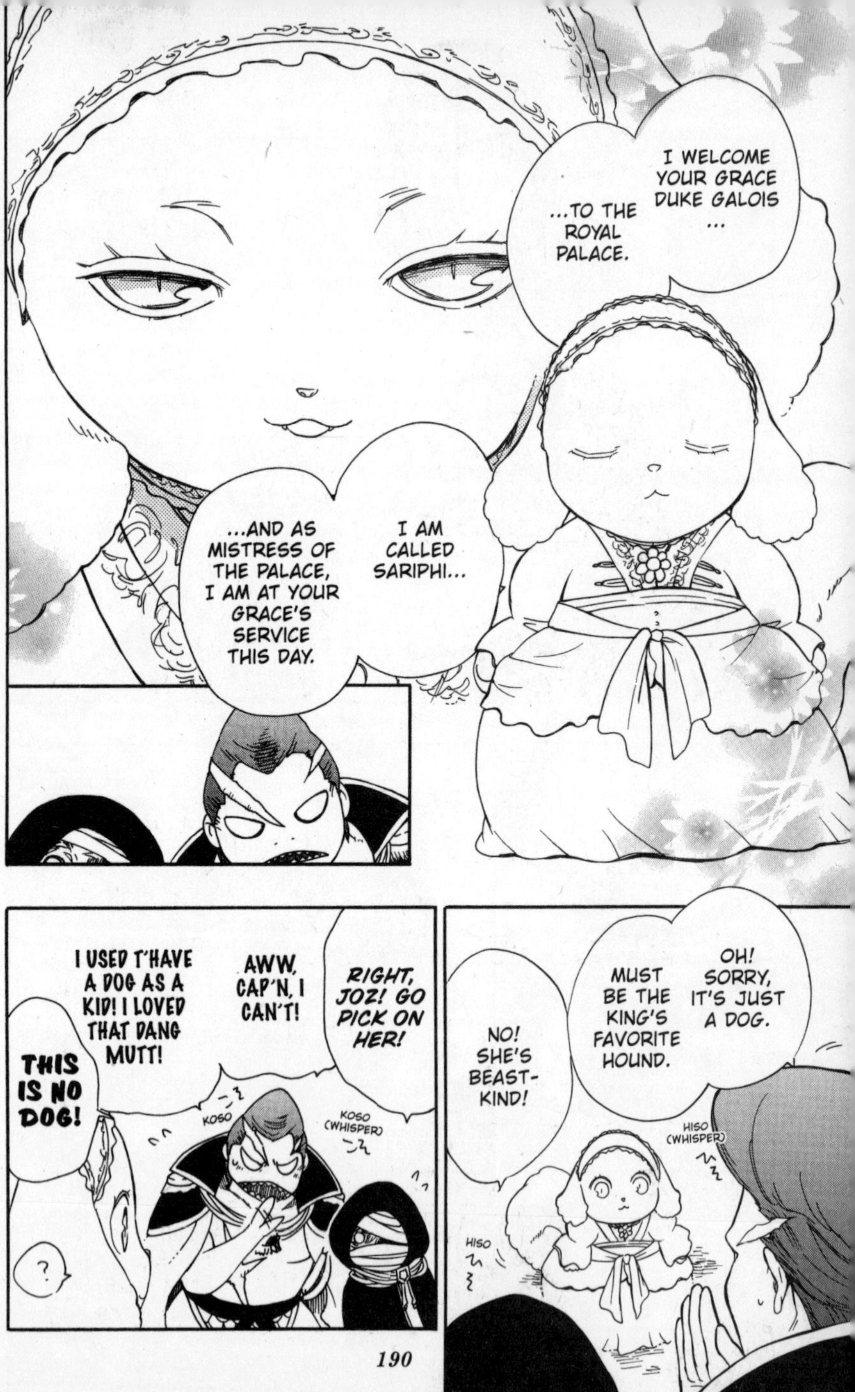
I WELCOME YOUR GRACE DUKE GALOIS ...
...TO THE ROYAL PALACE.
I AM CALLED SARIPHI...
...AND AS MISTRESS OF THE PALACE, I AM AT YOUR GRACE'S SERVICE THIS DAY.
OH! SORRY, IT'S JUST A DOG.
MUST BE THE KING'S FAVORITE HOUND.
NO! SHE'S BEAST-KIND!
HISO (WHISPER)
HISO
RIGHT, JOZ! GO PICK ON HER!
KOSO (WHISPER)
AWW, CAP'N, I CAN'T!
KOSO
I USED T'HAVE A DOG AS A KID! I LOVED THAT DANG MUTT!
THIS IS NO DOG!
?

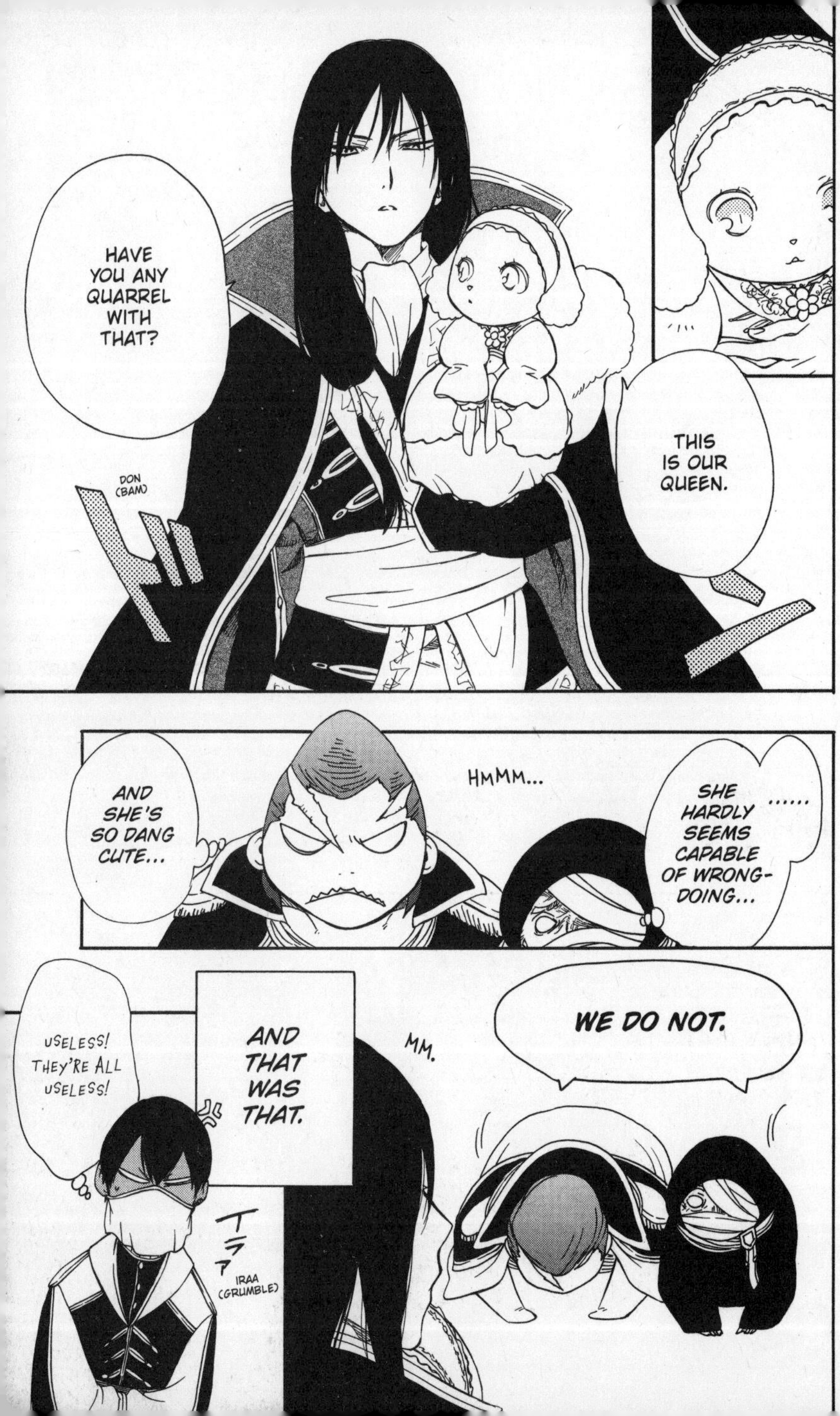
THIS IS OUR QUEEN.
HAVE YOU ANY QUARREL WITH THAT?
DON (BAM)
......
SHE HARDLY SEEMS CAPABLE OF WRONG-DOING...
HMMM...
AND SHE'S SO DANG CUTE...
WE DO NOT.
MM.
AND THAT WAS THAT.
USELESS! THEY'RE ALL USELESS!
IRAA (GRUMBLE)

SACRIFICIAL PRINCESS AND THE King of Beasts

4

Yu Tomofuji

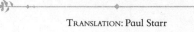

TRANSLATION: Paul Starr

LETTERING: Lys Blakeslee

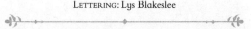

This book is a work of fiction. Names, characters, places, and incidents are the product of the author's imagination or are used fictitiously. Any resemblance to actual events, locales, or persons, living or dead, is coincidental.

NIEHIME TO KEMONO NO OH by Yu Tomofuji
© Yu Tomofuji 2017
All rights reserved.
First published in Japan in 2017 by HAKUSENSHA, Inc., Tokyo.
English language translation rights in U.S.A., Canada and U.K. arranged with
HAKUSENSHA, Inc., Tokyo through Tuttle-Mori Agency, Inc., Tokyo.

English translation © 2019 by Yen Press, LLC

Yen Press
1290 Avenue of the Americas
New York, NY 10104

Visit us at yenpress.com ✦ facebook.com/yenpress ✦ twitter.com/yenpress
yenpress.tumblr.com ✦ instagram.com/yenpress

First Yen Press Edition: January 2019

Yen Press is an imprint of Yen Press, LLC.
The Yen Press name and logo are trademarks of Yen Press, LLC.

The publisher is not responsible for websites (or their
content) that are not owned by the publisher.

Library of Congress Control Number: 2018930817

ISBNs: 978-0-316-48108-3 (paperback)
978-0-316-48109-0 (ebook)

10 9 8 7 6 5 4 3 2 1

WOR

Printed in the United States of America